MW00911717

A Most Civil War

By

Greg Parkes

ALL THE BEST

GREG PARKES

Buffalo Creek Books
Alden NY

For Marcy, to whom I shall be
forever indebted

Front Cover:

A drawing room at St. James's Palace in London: This engraving was published as Plate 76 of *Microcosm of London* (1810) Thomas Rowlandson (1756–1827) and Augustus Charles Pugin (1762–1832) (after) John Bluck (fl. 1791–1819), Joseph Constantine Stadler (fl. 1780–1812), Thomas Sutherland (1785–1838), J. Hill, and Harraden (aquatint engravers) New York Public Library

Back Cover:

MARGARET SCHOOLCRAFT (1733?-1805) John Singleton Copley, about 1775.
Courtesy of the Fort Ticonderoga Museum

Book I

Boston, November 1777

The poor boy just stood, dumbfounded, mouth hanging open, staring at her. After a long pause, he stammered,

"Wh-wh-where is Mr. B-B-Brush?"

"I," she said, pausing for emphasis, "am not Mr. Brush's keeper."

She watched the color drain from his face. He stood for a second longer before bolting out of the cell.

She stepped to the single window of the cell in the old stone warehouse the rebels had turned into a jail. In the early November dawn she looked across the wharves toward Boston harbor. The sun was just an expectant bump in the horizon. The new day allowed her to survey the sparse room, the heavy wooden partitions, a couple of mattresses on the floor, a poor chair and a worse table. A necessary pot stood alone in one corner. It had been planned for two occupants but Crean Brush's rank and notoriety had given privacy. Had he been a private soldier, ten or twelve might have been expected in the space. Iron bars for the window would have been too great an expense; they had simply bricked up so much of the window that no man could squeeze out. Now it could no longer be opened for ventilation and the place stank of old urine and feces and of unwashed prisoners.

She had come to Boston under a flag of truce; the ship had carried rebel prisoners for exchange. In the nine months since then she had been coming to this fetid place daily. She was used to it, she knew the guards, she knew the prisoners, soldiers all, and she knew the routine.

*****

The sergeant of the guard burst through the door. Full of bluster, he railed at her, cursing, demanding to know where her husband had gone. The verbal torrent washed over her. She walked to the chair and sat. She knew they were embarrassed by the escape, fearful that they might be found complicit in it. She would not offer them any relief.

"I do not know where Mr. Brush may be."

That was actually true. She did know exactly where he should be by now, but was he there? She sat still, feeding the anger and delaying the search. That they were here in such a rage meant that Brush had not been caught or even missed until now. While they yelled at her, they were not in pursuit. It had been now ten minutes since the jailer had realized the prisoner had fled. Brush was almost a half mile further ahead of the hue and cry, a cry that could travel no faster than a horse could run. She had provided him with a good horse. She smiled, and enraged the sergeant yet more.

Keep swearing, you bumbling rebel oaf, she thought, and smiled again.

At last, seeing his words break uselessly upon her like the winter waves upon a rocky shore, he recollected his duty and ordered the alarm.

She sat, playing at solitaire for a full half hour before an officer, a captain, finally came to her cell. He had a pronounced limp, probably invalided out of active service after some battlefield injury. He looked around in disbelief.

"Madam, what have you done?"

She looked at him steadily. "My duty."

"Where has Brush gone?"

"*Mr.* Brush gone to our home in Westminster," she lied. "He is a man of consequence there you know, twice elected to the provincial assembly. He

2

plans to raise a company of loyal men to annoy and make himself obnoxious to your cause. It will take you a regiment to run him to ground, if you can."

"Am I to believe that you arranged all this?"

"Captain -- Carson, isn't it?--You may believe as you wish, but it is so. As you know, last night was what you Bostonais call 'Pope Night.' The town celebrates its disdain for the Papacy by dressing in the most outlandish costumes and parading about the streets. No one would remark a man in woman's clothes among the revelers. Half the population was too drunk to notice him if he wore a tiara and played the bagpipes. I brought Mr. Brush a dress yesterday. I wore two, one above the other. He walked out as a woman, took the horse I had left for him and was away. Quite simple, really."

"Perhaps simple, but the consequences will not be, not for you. You have exchanged yourself for him, a hostage against his return when we catch him. Your rooms will probably be searched and anything of value will be seized toward reparation of his looting."

After a breath, and with some heat, "Mr. Brush did not, as you say, 'loot'. He was an officer obeying orders of Generals Gage and Howe to sequester material which might be of use to an armed enemy. That you rebels choose to call it looting shows how little you regard the customs of war."

"Nonetheless, Captain, I do expect to be treated as an officer's lady should be, as you would hope your own wife might be treated in altered circumstances. I expect my right to purchase necessaries will not be abridged."

"Those are high words, given that you might be considered a spy!"

"How can I be a spy? I came to this place in full view of your people, identified myself and am known to them to be who I say—there was no deception in my coming. That I might wish my husband free should have been anticipated. It was a *ruse de guerre*—that your people chose to believe the word of an enemy speaks poorly of them, not me. Any man who trusts his enemy deserves to be fooled."

'Spy or no, you have demonstrated that you are a clever woman—perhaps a noble one but a devious one nonetheless. As you have so kindly pointed out,

3

I'm not at all sure I can believe what you have said, or may say in future. I don't suppose you might know how an empty whiskey jug came to be found under the guardhouse steps this morning?"

"Captain Carson, I give you my word of honor that I shall make no attempt to escape, nor communicate with General Clinton nor any member of his staff until such time as you see fit to release me. I shall be the very model prisoner. As to this whiskey jug, I choose not to drink whiskey, myself.

"If it offers you any solace, this was not an overnight plan—the germ of it came to me in August, and preparations had been underway ever since. A surreptitious enemy is harder to counter than a frontal assault."

He looked at her hard for a long time, considering. "Very well Madam, for now, you will remain here. You will be allowed to walk the yard for one hour each day. I must consult my superiors; they may well over-rule my conditions of your stay here. You perhaps do not understand the extent to which Mr. Brush is despised by the people of Boston. Let me say that I hope he appreciates your sacrifice. I can't think much of a man who would allow it."

"There was no choice—had Mr. Brush remained here it would have killed him—we both knew that, probably you did too. Perhaps that is what some were hoping for."

*****

The winter of 1777-78 was the coldest anyone could remember. At Valley Forge, Washington's army shivered in crude huts. General Howe was warm enough in Philadelphia while his troops shivered in shacks little better than those of the Americans. It was cold too in Boston. Margaret had hung a cloth over the window against the drafts. It was a poor comfort. Her jailors allowed the cell door to be open so that she might get some benefit from the guardroom fire. There was no other heat. Capt. Carson charged her ten shillings a week for firewood, more than she had paid for the little room she had occupied all summer. He charged five shillings more to allow a wizened street vender to bring her poor food. He probably charged the vendor too.

There had come word through her captors that Brush had reached safety in New York after an eleven-day flight across Connecticut. From him or her daughter there had come nothing, at least nothing that she had seen. The

4

isolation, the cold, her dwindling resources were beginning to wear on her. She had smuggled her valuables, the few she had brought to Boston, into the jail in the weeks before Brush's escape, but at this rate they would not last. It was a stark, hopeless existence.

Her allowed hour in the yard was the only exercise and she relished the warmth movement brought. As she returned one day in early December she found visitors in her cell.

The smaller woman turned to face her and threw back the hood of her cloak. "Good afternoon Mrs. Brush. My name is Mercy Warren. Perhaps you may have heard of me?"

Indeed Margaret had. The firebrand poetess of this rebellion, this friend of Sam Adams, and John Adams, and their Committees of Correspondence too, what could she possibly want? She had learned to expect little charity or even pity from rebels.

"You have some friends among us Ma'am, she continued. General Phillip Schuyler has asked me to look in upon you. I would ask if there was anything you needed, but I see that there is so much. Have you enough food?"

"Barely, Mrs. Warren. I buy what I can. It is poor stuff and seldom fresh. It is expensive here and I have little money left. All in all, it is not, as you may imagine, a pleasant life. I manage."

Mercy held out her hand, "The General has forwarded this to you. From your daughter. Please, read. I will wait outside"

Margaret snatched the letter from her extended hand. She read.

Dearest Mama,

Papa has come through safe. He spends much time at the headquarters, General Clinton has still not seen fit to employ him, but at least he has received his back pay. He chafes.

Such an unhappy year—First General Burgoyne is defeated at Saratoga, and you are a prisoner of war among our enemies.

I cannot believe what you have done, nor can any here. Had I known your design, I would not have let you go there alone. Your courage emboldens us all. Do be safe and well. Until we can re-unite.

Your loving daughter

F.

Margaret read it again, and again. She crossed her arms on the pitiful table, laid her head on them and wept. At the sound, Mercy re-entered the cell, put a comforting arm about her shoulder. "I can hardly appreciate your sacrifice, Mrs. Brush. But I do admire you for it, even as I wish you had not. Tell me, what can I do?"

Margaret's sorrow flashed to anger. "That sanctimonious, purse-mouthed Henry Clinton!—he is shunning my husband—who has lost so much for the Crown. Our lands, our fortunes, all gone! I cannot help him from here and now when he needs so much more than I. He is not a strong man, my husband. Imprisonment broke him. What am I to do?"

"It is possible to get a message to your daughter---just as that one reached here. This," she indicated the other woman, who stood in a corner holding a large basket, "is my girl Annie. Today is Friday; she will come to you again on Tuesday, and then twice a week thereafter. Communicate your needs to her, and I will do my best to supply them. Now, we have a custom here, well, really in Plymouth where I usually live, to remember the first comers to our shores with a large feast of thanksgiving at this time of year. I have brought you some leavings of ours, some books, paper and pencil. And a blanket."

"Oh thank you, it is too much, something to ease the time! I shall be forever in your debt."

"I think, Mrs. Brush, that you and I are much alike. Both our husbands are deeply engaged in this…conflict and our own behavior is governed by theirs. Yet we both have strong opinions. You do understand why I cannot come myself so often?"

"Yes, Mrs. Warren, I do. I am deeply grateful for your kindness. I hope you will not be injured by it. I shall do nothing to embarrass you, you have my word."

After her two visitors left, Margaret fell to the basket. She found a blanket, a loaf of bread, cheese, a bottle of sherry, the cold leg of game bird, and best of all, some potted meat! Two books, pencils and paper! She was giddy in her newfound wealth. Mercy Warren was truly a miracle worker.

Two books! Let's see, what have we? Tom Jones, *oh, good, that'll pass some time. What's this? John Locke,* Second Treatise on Government? *She may have misfired on that one. Is she attempting to subvert me?*

Margaret carefully picked the turkey bone bare, licking her fingers after. She selected the Fielding book, sat with her back to the guardroom wall-- the spot she knew to be the warmest-- pulled the blanket close around her throat and began to read, only her hands darting out periodically to turn a page.

Watervliet NY, June 1743

The road north from Albany was poor but better than many. Now four miles from the city, they had walked past the Van Renssalear mansion and were passing through the Schuyler farm. The broad Hudson lay off to her right, just beyond the fields, the slave quarters and the massive barns. To her left she saw the treed pasture where her father had camped as part of a northbound invasion army in 1711. There were more people living on this one farm than there were in her entire village in Schoharie.

The heavy door closed behind them with a soft click. This was the grandest entryway she had ever seen; the houses she knew had no entry hall at all. This was a narrow room, containing only an intricately carved chestnut settee and a small three-legged table. Portraits of the queerly dressed people of another generation hung along one wall.

She moved closer to her father. He gave her a reassuring smile and placed a protective hand on her shoulder. A girl, very blonde, but short, said, "Madam Schuyler is expecting you Mr. Schoolcraft. If you will just wait here, I will tell her you have arrived."

Her father nodded. She had heard of the Schuylers all her life; all of Albany County knew of them, one of the great families of the Hudson Valley. She even knew a little of this Madam Schuyler: a Schuyler herself, she had married her cousin, a childless marriage. They were fabulously rich. Margarite Schuyler was the arbitress of Albany society, of the whole Hudson valley. She and her husband lived here on this farm in Watervliet with sixty hands, slave and free. She had a house on State Street in Albany, the most desirable address in a town that had very few of them. It was usually occupied by one of her innumerable cousins. Unlike the southern planters who disdained all business activity and had the debts to prove it, in Albany, everyone, even Schuylers and Van Renssalears followed some trade. Phillip Schuyler had the reputation of being a very shrewd businessman who carried on an extensive, if barely legal, trade with the French in Montreal, but who derived most of his income from this farm, exporting the hides and lumber and grain it produced to the Caribbean islands.

That blonde girl had been so smooth and confident. How could she ever fit into such a house? Could she ever tell someone, even a poor schoolteacher as her father was, to wait while she informed her mistress? Could she ever be so meticulously polite to a farmer at the doorway of so grand a house? At home it would have been a different greeting indeed; "Hey Jacob, sit ye whilst I fetch the boss."

They were soon shown into a rather small room. A fireplace filled most of one wall between two windows. Through them she could see a formal garden and again the Hudson. Madam Schuyler sat facing them at a writing table centered upon a compass rose painted on the floor. There were bookcases as tall as Margaret herself on two walls. The early spring sun fell in two long bright strips across the painted floor. She scanned the books, looking for a friend among the titles.

"Good afternoon, Mr. Schoolcraft. Is this the child of whom I have heard so much?"

"Yes Madam, this is my daughter Margaret, she has just come on ten years, but she shows promise, she reads and understands far beyond her years, is a good student and a hard worker."

"So Margaret, do you think you could come to like living here, away from your home, your brothers and sisters?" Her English was precise, careful and studied.

"I am grateful that you would consider me for such an honor," she replied, just as her father had coached her.

"Well, I haven't, not just yet. I expect you know that the Lord has chosen not to bless my husband and I with children of our own, but a house needs young. Over the years, we have welcomed promising children from time to time. They stay with us for a period and then move on with their lives as useful citizens. Greitje, the girl who greeted you, has been with me ten years now and she will leave next month to wed an honest man who minds Patroon Van Renssalear's farm nearby. Others of my girls have wed good tradesmen, even officers of the army and Governor. Such may be your future if you are a willing study.

"Mr. Schoolcraft, I have found it helpful if I talk with Margaret alone. Greitje will show you to the kitchen. Greitje, please tell Mrs. Appelbaum that he may have what ever is convenient."

When they were alone, Margarite Schuyler surveyed the girl. Pale blue eyes, skin far too tanned from the country sun, of medium height with nice features, sandy hair tied back with a blue ribbon, in what was undoubtedly her best dress, worn but scrubbed clean, as was she herself. The ribbon matched the eyes so closely that Margarite wondered which berries the girl had crushed together to produce it.

"Being from Schoharie, I expect you know German?

"Yes—my mother was a Palatine German, just a child when she came in 1709. She spoke it at home. Her English was not good, even after thirty years here."

"Good. U kent de Nederlandse taal?"

"I'm sorry," afraid that she had already failed, "I think that is the Dutch; some talk it at the end of our valley, but I don't know it. But I can learn, really, I can!"

"I doubt it not, child. Have you the French?"

"Not a word, I fear."

"That you may learn as well in time. Travelers to Montreal pass by daily; Canadian gentlemen frequently stop, and of course, Dutch is the common language of this house, as well as much of Albany. Since you have two tongues, more should come."

"Madam," Margaret asked impulsively, "might I be allowed to read some of these books?"

"Certainly." That had never been the first question out of any child she had ever interviewed. This one might be a fascinating project. "Tell me, do you have books at home?"

10

"Yes, we have eleven," proudly. It was more than anyone else in her village. Even the pastor had only nine; she knew because she had read most of them. Looking about her at shelf after shelf, it felt like such a small thing.

"Which do you have?"

"Well, there is the Bible, of course, then we have <u>The Merchant of Venice</u> and <u>Hamlet</u> by Mr. Shakespeare, <u>Paradise Lost</u> by Mr. Milton…

"Have you *read* <u>Paradise Lost</u>, child?

"I have tried it a bit—there are wonderful words there, but the meaning of the thing seems just out of reach."

"As it is for most people," Madam Schuyler chuckled. "Have you a favorite?"

"Oh yes! I do so like <u>Gulliver's Travels</u> by Dean Swift—I have read it four times already, still I find funny new things there."

"Of Portia and Ophelia, which is your favorite?"

"Why Portia of course. 'The quality of mercy is not strained; It droppeth as the gentle rain from heaven' How I wish I could speak like that, though I wish she treated her suitors better—she seems mean to them. Poor Ophelia is such a broken soul—we have one in our village who could be her twin. Her parents are dead, brothers too. It's very sad, but all she does is weep and wail that she has no one but she won't help herself either."

"I understand your own mother has also died?"

The girl lowered her head and Margarite wondered if she had probed too deeply. "Yes," softly. Then she lifted her chin, eyes moist but voice firm, "It has been almost a year, my baby sister is strong and well. We must accept what we cannot change."

Watervliet, September 1753

"Very nice," said Margaret, as she surveyed the table the slave Maria was laying for dinner. "I should not have thought to use the yellow plates in that way. It does look so like the harvest time."

"Why Margaret" said Margarite Schuyler, emerging from her morning's reading. "Lovely table. What is Mrs. Applebaum sending out for us this day?"

"The table is Maria's invention, Aunt Schuyler. Our cook is sending out her pork fricasse in sauce. We have a fresh butchered hog, and the men do seem to enjoy it thoroughly."

"They do. I'm glad you chose your blue dress today, it shows you so marvelously!"

"Who will be joining us?" asked Margaret. "I know you and the Colonel, and Domine Frelinghuysen from the church, but we have a table laid for seven."

"Besides us, there will be two commercial gentlemen from Montreal, Messieurs Duplesis and Auger, and a Lieutenant of the Independent Company named Soumain."

"Oh" playfully, looking up from her work, "and for which of these am I to show 'marvelously'?"

"All of them," with equal playfulness, "and don't be impertinent. I do think you will find Lt. Soumain interesting. The Canadian gentlemen are married, and I don't see you as a minister's wife. Soumain was born and bred in Manhattan, the son of a silversmith there. I rather think you'll like him."

"Aunt Schuyler, you have been trying to get me married off for over a year now. I had no idea you were in such a hurry to be rid of me. What is so different about this one?"

"He's a good fellow and very pretty. You're getting little old to be single—do you aspire to spinsterhood? You know, dear, playing match-maker for you would be so much easier if you would only quit scaring these bachelors away."

"Easier, perhaps, but you wouldn't get nearly the enjoyment!"

"I seem to remember some little girl about ten years ago complaining of Portia's treatment of young men. Now, let me think, who could that have been?"

"It must have been someone who did not understand what a bother they can be! Can this one talk of else but himself?"

"That, my dear, is for you to discover. You know, it is disingenuous of you to pretend to not notice how much you bother these young men. If every one of them who wears his head on a swivel as you pass had the temerity to seek an introduction, I should be fully employed in shooing them away."

"I do see it some, and I'm as vulnerable to flattery as anyone—and I am ashamed for it. I make myself see it for what it is. I can't believe that it is any more than the watching of a bright colored bird, without significance."

*****

She watched from the portico as the officer turned from the road, the fine bay mare still full of energy after the trot from Albany. He rode effortlessly.

"Good Morning. Welcome to Colonel Schuyler's residence. Lientenant Soumain, I presume?"

"Yes. Simeon Soumain at your service. You seem to have the advantage of me, Miss."

"I am Margaret Schoolcraft, sir. The Colonel and Mrs. Schuyler regret they could not greet you. They are occupied with various business, but will join

13

us shortly. Would you care to freshen up after your ride? I'll have Apollo see to your horse."

She motioned to the gray headed groom waiting nearby.

"She's feeling her oats this morning, will he be able?

"Probably, Apollo has a real knack with horses." The slave appeared to be in deep conversation with the horse. He rubbed her nose and grinned up at Margaret, said something in Dutch.

"He believes they will manage," she translated.

* * * * *

They had gathered on the portico while the dinner preparations were finished. She had noticed that Mssrs. Duplesis and Auger, both in their thirties, had suddenly become a bit slimmer about the waist as she was introduced and greeted them in French, and then seen the light in their eyes dim as they caught sight of Soumain, brilliant in his red dress uniform. He was pretty, a fine figure of a man with a proper military bearing, a black ribbon in his blonde hair.

Dinner was a grand success. Lt. Soumain had proved to be an amiable dinner companion and Margaret was enjoying herself.

"Tell me, Lieutenant, what thinks the army of the French situation?" said Colonel Schuyler, casually, as he lobbed a social grenade down the table.

"Well Sir," temporizing, "I can hardly speak for the army, the generals seldom seem to seek my opinion. My colleagues have talked upon this at length and come to a sort of consensus. I would be happy to share that, if you wish?"

A nod from their host.

"Let me begin by saying that I believe that we colonists, New Yorkers as well as Canadians," nodding across the table, "could live in perfect amity. We face the same difficulties and have similar needs. It is the imperial directives that we all receive from London and Paris that cause the friction."

14

Oh, well played! thought Margaret.

"The French strategy is clear enough. They are intent on a chain of forts from the Great Lakes, along the Ohio to the Mississippi River. When these are in place, they will direct all Indian trade away from us. Our friends in Montreal will find that very advantageous whilr we here will suffer much by it.

"The real danger to us and especially to our settlers on the frontier, is not a few soldiers and a feeble stockadoe here and there. They could be removed by a trained company and a three-pounder gun. It comes instead from the trading post that is always attached. The savages have come to depend upon European goods, and will ally themselves with whoever can supply them. The French have their Hurons, we have our Iroquois. Each expends a great deal of effort and money to retain his own and lure away the other's. With the trade comes also the ability to incite savages to violence against frontier settlers."

"Yes" said Auger, thickly accented, "Our Hurons are quite tame, they really have no choice but to deal with us. Your Iroquois, however, are a different breed. They carry themselves so—how you say—*engloutir*?" He turned to his companion for help.

"Haughtily?' suggested Margaret.

"Oui! Merci Mademoiselle! These Iroquois carry themselves so haughtily, are so sure that they are the only Indians who matter. They have bullied and fought all of their neighbors into submission; they even receive tribute from the Illinois! They are fierce warriors, yet it is only their location which gives them the power, only Albany, which has made them the conduit for western trade. They have been playing against each of us in turn for a century, extracting as much as they can from one and then the other. If they ever truly commit to one of us, they will find their influence gone.

"All the barbarians find our relations more congenial than you English. We seek only to trade with them, their furs for our blankets and gunpowder. You are so full of people that you only want more farms for them. Your land hunger frightens and mystifies them. Sooner than not, they will come to realize that we French truly regard them more highly than you."

15

"And," interjected Domine Frelinghuysen, an intelligent man sometimes carried away by his own enthusiasm, "there is the issue of Popery. How do we reconcile to those who follow such a barbarous heresy?"

"I beg you sir," said Soumain, "do not speak to me of difficulties in reconciliation with Catholics; my own grandfather escaped St. Bartholomew's massacre by a hair, his two brothers did not. If my family can live with people of that faith, I suspect a whole colony can as well. Perhaps it is my upbringing in Manhattan which leads me to feel this way. We rub shoulders with almost every belief imaginable every day and find no trouble buying our meat from a Catholic or our bread from a Jew, so long as they are honest men. Not too long since there were reported to be Mohammadans living among us. They owned property and paid taxes just as anyone else."

"But, by treaty," said Duplesis, "France has right to all lands drained by the Great Lakes and St Lawrence. How do English justify claiming any of it?"

Soumain responded, "I'm not a legal scholar, sir, anymore than I rate as a theologian, but I have been told that we have fought two wars since that old treaty was writ—and none later hold any mention of such a claim.

"The real basis for our dispute is economic. We both want the western trade, and as well our larger population wants western lands. All else is rhetoric. Surely there is enough of each for both without either of us engrossing it all."

The conversation ran on into the afternoon, just as the Colonel had expected, just as discussions at this table were known to do. Soumain parried artfully, holding his ground without offending the three with whom he clearly disagreed. The Schuylers listened carefully, but did not contribute, absorbing information which might be of value in their business without disclosing any thoughts. Margaret did not participate. So many times she had been told— "keep your mouth closed and your ears open." Her own opinions of Soumain and the war everyone predicted were forming.

After the meal, the Colonel invited the Canadians to the garden, and Margarite Schuyler sought enlightenment on some point of theology, leaving Margaret alone to entertain Soumain.

They walked the path along the river, they laughed. They talked of the view, the birds, the dinner, and like everyone else, of the war. She found herself

16

telling her history: of her mother's passage from the Palatinate, the starvation, of the six who had left, of the two who had survived, the escape from indenture to the Schoharie, of how she had came to this farm. He in turn told of his grandfather's flight from France, his father's immigration to New York and his own childhood. When they later thought of the afternoon, they were each surprised at how much they had revealed of themselves.

Later, after they saw him off on the ride back to Albany, Aunt Schuyler said,

"He seems rather smitten, my dear,"

"I certainly hope so."

Aunt Schuyler smiled.

*****

It was one of those perfect winter nights, the air was still and clear, the deep snow crisp under foot. All the neighbors had come onto their stoops to watch the sport. Albany's young men were sledding down State Street hill past their doors. Spectators at every house cheered the more adventurous and hooted when they crashed in a cloud of snow.

Simeon Soumain stopped on his way up the hill, his sled under his arm.

"Lieutenant! Where is your hat? You will catch your death running about without it."

"Good evening, Madam, Miss Schoolcraft. Isn't this great fun! Manhattan is too flat for this. My cap flew off as I was descending. I'll recover it on the way back up."

"It must be wonderful to glide like that. You go so quickly!"

He held out his hand "Come with me!" Then, remembering himself, "By your leave, Madam?"

"Yes, yes, of course," said Aunt Schuyler, absently, pretending that something else was demanding her attention.

17

At the top of the hill, in the shadow of the fort, she looked down the quarter mile stretch of road and swallowed hard as Soumain surveyed her. "We need to cover your face; the breeze is quite stiff as we go. Can you wrap your scarf around? Perfect. No one could tell you from an Egyptian." Looking at her again, "Though I doubt that coat has an equal in all Albany!"

She was glad the scarf hid her blush.

"Here Dick, hold our steed while we mount. Now, can you scooch forward a bit Miss, that's it, bend your knees so I can get aboard. Good."

He sat close behind her, his heels tucked into the space beneath her bent knees, reached around her to grasp the tow ropes.

"My, this is as friendly as riding double!"

"Isn't it though. Now, to steer, we must lean a little, this way or that," he demonstrated, and with his arms on each side she had no choice but to follow, "but not too much or we shall crash. Ready?"

She nodded excitedly.

"All right, boys, give us a push, lively now!"

She heard the pounding feet, felt the lurch from the final shove. Then it was so quiet, only the soft sound of the sled against the packed snow. As they accelerated, the houses to the side became a blur. Her vision narrowed, focused on the English church ahead. They swerved around it, still faster. She found herself clutching his knees. Ahead was the Dutch church in the next intersection. Surely no horse could run so fast! The wind bit at her forehead and made her eyes water. She felt his cheek against her ear. Here was the Dutch church, another block to Market Street, and now they were slowing in the soft snow beyond. They somehow turned sideways and tumbled over and over in the drifts.

They rose to their feet, laughing. He watched as she brushed the snow from her coat, then suddenly caught her close and kissed her, right there in the street, with the whole town watching. Adrift in a hormonal sea she tried desperately, hopelessly, to respond as she wished.

He suddenly pulled away, panicked. "Oh! Miss Schoolcraft, I am so sorry. I don't know what…"

She placed a finger across his lips, a single, snowy mittened finger. "Yes, Simeon, that was very wrong of you, and you must never do it again." She paused, and then gave him a slow wink, "Unless we are alone!"

She pranced away awkwardly through the deep snow, laughing. He caught her in two strides; they stood close, their eyes locked.

"May I call you Margaret?"

"That would please me greatly."

She took his arm and they began to climb the hill together. She was sure no one could tell when he pressed her arm against his side, no one could sense the gentle squeeze of her free hand resting on his forearm. But then, she didn't care.

*****

They stood outside the elder Soumain's Manhattan dwelling, the day surprisingly warm for March. It was the house of a successful artisan, a nice but unprepossessing house. There were two doors with windows between showing examples of work. There was a sign over the left hand door.

Simeon Soumain
Silversmith
And
Jeweler

"Simeon, I'm terrified! What if he doesn't think I'm a good enough match for you? Does he know there will be no dowry, that dowries are unheard of in Albany?"

"I have written him that, but it is a long tradition here, and he is nothing if not traditional. If he does not love you as I do, I shall have to question his sanity."

They had been having this conversation, in various forms, for over a month.

"Simeon, I will not have you renounce your patrimony. I will not!"

"And I will not renounce you, so we are at a stand. Besides, my love, this can be nothing compared to how I met your father!

"Think of it. Here I am one day walking the streets of Albany with the most precious creature on my arm, the envy of every man, when I spy this really rough, grizzled character with an eye patch and ingrained powder burns down one side of his face coming toward us, looking as if he had just killed someone and now was ready for his breakfast. As I am trying to figure out how to disentangle myself to draw my sword against this threat, the girl of my dreams drops my arm, and runs to hug this apparition calling 'Papa, Papa!'

"So now I am introduced; he looks me up and down with his one eye, a look that says all too plainly, 'I've skinned one man today you whelp, I believe you'll be the second.

"Trust me, today will not be so stressful."

She was laughing as they climbed the steps to the right hand door.

Once inside, they had just begun tea with Simeon's parents, when his father got to business. "Now, Miss Schoolcraft, my son tells me that you two wish to marry. I must talk with your father about the dowry. Do you know what he might be prepared to offer?"

Simeon started to object but Margaret looked him into silence. She set her cup and saucer down carefully to conceal her shaking hands.

"I'm sorry, sir. There will be no need to bother him. I am my own dowry. A woman can bring assets other than money to a marriage. I am not yet twenty, but for two years I have overseen of one of the most famous houses in the Hudson Valley. I know how to provide a good home for a gentleman, something many girls waste years learning at their husband's expense. I know how to furnish it with taste yet not extravagantly, how to prepare a proper dinner, and I know how to direct domestics to do it as well. I know how to sit at table and be a proper hostess. At Schuyler Flats, I selected the menus, the seating, and the china; I set the maids to their duties. I directed the servants and the house slaves when to bring in the firewood and when to trim the shrubbery. I am fluent in four languages, halfway so with the

20

Mohawk tongue. I have sat at table with soldiers, merchants, fur traders, bankers and the governor's inner circle. I have conversed with farmers, tradesmen and sachems, Frenchmen too. I know them and they know me. I need not tell you what such entrée could mean to my future husband's prospects.

"There can be no discussion of dowry. My father is a poor schoolteacher and farmer in a frontier village. You know, probably better than you wish, that specie is scarce enough here in the city. In the settlements there is none, all is done through barter. A man who has two pounds pass through his hands in a year considers himself prosperous indeed. I am the eldest of four daughters; he must still feed and clothe those younger, who will not enjoy the advantages I have received. My five older brothers contribute to the home as they can, but they have their own families to look after as well."

"But you are now a part of Madame Schuyler's family, are you not? Would she provide a portion?"

"I am, sir, but by courtesy only. She has raised me since I was ten, out of Christian charity. Over the years there have been dozens she so blessed. All but a very few were members of her extended family, and I happened to be one of the lucky exceptions. I have no right to expect, or even ask, for more than she has already given. The very asking would demean us all."

Alexandria Va. May 1754

Margaret stood by the mizzen shrouds with Kathleen Browning, wife of the other lieutenant in the company and her very new best friend, the first friend she had really had since childhood, watching in the summer twilight as the sailors warped the ship against the pier in Alexandria. Kathleen was the only person Margaret had ever or would ever know who would presume to call her Meg. In retaliation, Kathleen had been truncated to Kate. They both treasured it.

It had been a Tuesday when Simeon had brought the news of his father's reluctant consent and of the impending transfer of the Independent Company to Will's Creek in Virginia. They had married on that Sunday with only Richard and Kate Browning as attendants. Simeon had insisted on the English church; he wanted to understand the words of his own ceremony. The next weeks had been a whirlwind of packing and goodbyes, of tears and the deepest joys she had ever experienced. The ensuing week aboard ship would have been restful if not for Rebecca Fife. Most of the wives had been good travelers; orderly, quiet and just a little seasick. Rebecca Fife had been none of those things. Once, she must have been a stunning girl, but years of hard living had taken a toll, one she refused to recognize.

Margaret could see Simeon and Richard on the wharf, waiting for them; the Company had preceded the women by a week. Ignoring decorum, the two ladies began to wave frantically.

At last the gangplank was passed, Simeon hurried aboard and took her in his arms. He felt her cling more tightly than ever, felt a shuddering sigh.

"My Dear, what is wrong?"

She squeezed him again. "Nothing now. It was a difficult voyage, but behind us." Then, collecting herself, "The people are watching. Come I will introduce you to the Captain. Later I will explain."

✳✳✳✳✳

As the full moon leaked through the flap of Browning's tent. The two couples relaxed, sipping Madeira, swapping stories of their journeys.

"That Rebecca Fife is an ugly piece of work, isn't she?" said Kate.

"Yes, but I did not handle her well," said Margaret. "Any slave at the Flats who showed such insolence would have been sold to Jamaica, so they never did it. Her insubordination took me aback. Our captain wanted only that she moderate her behavior—constant flirting among a crew of woman-starved sailors is bound to make trouble. Incidentally, gentlemen, you would be advised to keep an eye on her—she probably infected half the ship's crew, and she'll probably pox your whole company if given the chance, husband or no. But, instead of helping the situation, I allowed myself an argument with her and made it worse and now I know she hates me."

"She always has—you're the embodiment of all she wishes to be, yet knows she cannot. Besides, you're a decade younger and prettier than she could ever have been. Her problem is that she craves the attention of men, and knows only one way to get it.

"We were in a bit of a difficult position" Kate continued, "legally we had no authority over those women, yet as officer's wives, the captain and the army expected us to keep them in line. I for one am glad to pass her off to you all-knowing men. How much grief can she cause us?"

"Enough, said Margaret. "If not mutiny, then certainly violence amongst the men. I believe she could slip a knife into my ribs and think the world a better place."

"Oh Meg, surely you exaggerate!"

"I think not. I would not be surprised to find she had not already done it somewhere, sometime."

"Do you really think she is poxed?"

"Shouldn't wonder, the way she throws herself about. I thought I saw the light of madness in her eyes. But that's a concern for her dear husband, the most worthless soldier of the company, not me."

"And for us" Simeon added. "If she becomes too great a detriment, Captain Gates could always put her out of camp, but then she'd just follow us and yet be outside our control entirely."

✳✳✳✳✳

The parade was very small for all the commotion it caused. They stood, watching as the mounted company escorted the twenty prisoners to the jail through the crowd of jeering Virginians standing at the roadside. The prisoners wore the dirty white uniforms of French Regular soldiers. They looked about at the gathered crowds, clearly terrified. The two officers leading were pitifully young, still in their teens, and were equally afraid.

"Simeon, who are these?"

"French. Major Washington's captives. He caught them up the Potomac, spying."

"They look so frightened," said Kate, "I would hope a British soldier would show more pluck than this!"

Probably not, fear knows no nationalitie,s thought Margaret, then, aloud, "After the way the French have treated our settlers for years, they probably expect to be drawn and quartered before lunch."

"That seems extreme. Surely a noose will suffice."

Will's Creek Va, June 1754

The men were busy but morale was low. There were now troops from Maryland and Virginia as well as the two companies from New York here at the very edge of British America. There were more than 500 soldiers working and Rebecca Fife was making her presence felt among them. Futile fighting over her uncertain favors had brought complaints from of all of the commanders. Horatio Gates had at last had his fill of Rebecca. Browning had reported last night that she was to be expelled from camp.

The new fort was a massive undertaking. Every bit of growth that could provide cover for an attacker had to be removed, removed over an area that exceeded a gunshot from the stockade timbers. The flood plain around their tent below the postern gate looked as if a mad farmer had just cut his crop of giant corn; the stubble of stumps extended a quarter mile to the river. The ashes of burned logs still smoldered. Beyond, toward their junction, Wills Creek and the upper Potomac drew blue lines across the landscape, further yet, the dark forest rose. In the half-light of dawn, she could see deer drinking in the creek and once she had seen a she-bear with her cubs.

All of the officers had spread their tents in the plain below the fort on its raised bluff, in the narrow angle between the fort and the water. From here she could hear the carpenters Virginia had sent working inside the stockade, building new barracks and a storehouse for the three companies who were to winter over. Although she could not hear them she knew that the rest of the men were clear cutting the forest on the other side of the fort, away from the water. Rebecca Fife made that work more difficult too.

Major Washington had had several encounters with the French through the spring, the last being in July; he had lost badly. The interpreter he had had with him had not been up to the task and the surrender terms libeled the British efforts. He had signed them unknowing. His former prisoners in the

25

Alexandria jail were exchanged. That had been the last of increasing provocations by both sides for the summer. Now each was shoring defenses in preparation for the 1755 campaign season.

Margaret was in their tent, turning up the hem of her skirt. She should have remembered that the women of her early life wore them shorter than those of the town and silently cursed herself for the lapse. For the ten day's march from Alexandria to Will's Creek she had endured hemlines that were either wet or muddy, or both. Today she had vowed to alter the last of them. If the men caught sight of her ankles, so be it.

The shouting from the cooking fire before their tents filtered in.

"Get me put out of camp will you, you uppity slut! Where is that other bitch? I know she did it! I'll kill you both, I will!"

Kate, very much afraid, "I don't know where Mrs. Soumain is—please don't hurt us—we had nothing to do with this!"

Margaret felt cold. She found Simeon's pistol box. She snatched one and began loading. Still she heard Rebecca raging, Kate pleading. She bit the cartridge, poured powder into the barrel. She rammed the wadding and ball. Some powder for the priming pan. It took less than a minute to load. It seemed forever.

She dropped the ramrod onto the cot and stepped out of the tent, the pistol behind her back.

"Rebecca Fife! Get away from her!"

Rebecca, standing over a cowering Kate looked up, startled.

"Oh there you are you whore! You think you're just such a goody—I'll cut you so often that pretty boy of yours won't be able to stand the sight of you! You've crossed the wrong woman, you have, Rebecca Fife is not to be trifled with."

"Come then if you can."

26

She advanced slowly on Margaret, the dagger in her hand low, swinging in slow hypnotic arcs before her, savoring the impending revenge. When she was ten feet away, Margaret closed one eye, extended her arm and fired.

Kate screamed. Rebecca dropped where she had stood, the knife still clutched in her hand.

Margaret tossed the pistol onto the cot. She didn't bother to inspect the corpse—in her adrenaline heightened awareness she had seen the ball's impact. She knew that her aim had been true. She hurried to Kate, crouched on a log, weeping. She was beyond speech; she clung desperately, sobbing.

By now, a small crowd had gathered, summoned by the gunshot.

"What's going on here?" demanded Washington. He stood above the body, a bloody puddle was beginning to spread in the sandy soil.

Margaret rose. "I shot her, Major Washington. She was coming at me with a knife. She meant to kill us both."

"Are either of you hurt?

"No. Thoroughly frightened, but not hurt."

"And you loaded and fired without help?

"Major, I grew up in a settlement smaller and closer to the savages than Winchester. All the children learn to load very young."

He looked at her closely. "Are you all right, Mrs. Soumain?"

"Yes, as I said, we are unhurt."

"No, I mean are you all right."

"Oh. Yes. Thank you. She was a mad dog that needed to be put down."

Margaret moved to the body and took the dagger from the dead hand. It was a heavy old weapon. There were traces of gilding still in the spiral grooves of its hilt. She tested the steel against a stump.

"May I keep this?"

He turned to look at her, not quite sure what to make of this yankee, far outside the women of his experience. He nodded slowly.

Margaret knelt before her friend, still huddled on her log, crying. She took Kate's hands in her own.

"God, Meg, I was so scared! I'm such a coward, I couldn't do anything. You've saved me!"

"Kate, you did everything. I was just as afraid. You refused to give me up, and that was very brave. It gave me time to load. If you hadn't, she would have gutted us both."

"What are you going to do with that dagger?" Kate was starting to recover and Margaret was glad to get her thinking of anything besides Rebecca Fife.

"I'm going to carry it with me. We are among some pretty rough fellows, and the quality of our company is not going to improve soon. I never want to feel so powerless again. I must make a sheath for it, so I can wear it under my skirt. I can make a false pocket so that I can reach it. I know it can be done. I'll probably need your help with that—where I plan to wear it, no one else will be doing the fitting!"

*****

The Virginia winter had been the most dreary she had ever known. In all of her life the cold had come and it had stayed. There had been snow and it stayed too, until spring. Winter unremitting and so constant. Here, there had been cold days with snow, but then everything would thaw, the pounding cold rain would wash away the snow leaving mud. Everything was mud. The men tried, but it was always coming into the barracks on their boots. She was so tired of sweeping out the dirt.

Spring had finally come; rhododendrons were showing in the lower levels of the wood across the river. There was word of an army, a regular British army, landing in Alexandria and coming to them. Now, in mid May, a few companies had already camped on the plain above the fort.

It was a sunny day when they first heard the faint drums. Margaret and Kate hurried to the ramparts so they could see. The drums grew louder. They could hear the bagpipes, they could see regimental colors through the trees along the Potomac. There were mounted officers and soon men, rank after rank in perfect formation. Margaret had never seen a full regiment marching before; the train was a half mile long! The sun reflected from the polished musket barrels, the pure white breeches and red jackets were vibrant against the dark green of the forest, the blue of the river. This was only half the force, yet another regiment was coming too! The sight was impressive, stirring. Woe to any enemy who fell afoul of such might.

Brilliantly mounted men with the swagger of conquerors allowed themselves to be shown to their quarters, those Margaret had recently occupied. All of the colonial officers were again camping in the flood plain to make way. The men spread their tents with their compatriots above the fort.

"Here, Gates, where are we to settle?"

"We thought General Braddock in the center barracks, Colonel Halkett, your regiment in the right most one, and Col. Dunbar's in the left."

"See here, that won't do. We shall claim the left. To be on the right hand of God, what?" Halkett was immensely pleased with his jest.

"Where is that Washington fellow—oh there you are. See that the men are properly bedded. There's a good chap. And take my horse."

Margaret saw the Major's face darken. She imagined no one had ever mistaken him for a groom in his life.

*****

The fort, now named Fort Cumberland, was quickly becoming more empty. For six weeks the army had camped around it and now Simeon was leaving with the first 500 men, to escort the engineers who would cut a new road to Fort Duquesne. She and Kate stood before the gate, watching. They made a good show, less glorious than the regular army perhaps, but a brave one nonetheless.

As Simeon reached the opening where the road disappeared into the forest, he had stopped and turned his horse to face them. Too far for words, too far

29

even for faces to be read, he had removed his tricorn, held it over his heart and bowed his head. Margaret could only curtsey, deep and sincere. She was so glad he could not see her tears. She raised her head, he turned his horse and was gone.

"He is a good man." She turned to see Washington beside her.

"Yes, he is," wiping the tears from her cheeks, "Are you feeling better sir?"

Washington had been left behind by the army because an intestinal bug had laid him low.

"Considerably. I believe in a day or so I shall be able to follow. You know, there is no shame in honest tears. May I have the pleasure of escorting you and Mrs. Browning to your tent?"

As she took his arm, "Tell me they will be successful, please do! I am fearful of General Braddock's pride. He seems to be a stubborn, inflexible man. This wilderness is so different than the open parks of Europe where he trained."

"I can only offer him my best service, Mrs. Soumain. Whether he accepts it is beyond my control. It is hard imagine that such an army, the greatest ever assembled on this continent, cannot be successful. We shall be three to four times as many as the French and have heavier cannon besides."

"It speaks well of you that you continue—I know you have chafed under their attitude. You deserved more respect than they have shown."

"You do know it is just 'Mr. Washington' now? I shall have to seek honors without a title. I have resigned my commission rather than answer to some adolescent ensign. I am here now as a volunteer."

"You will be an asset to them—you have been over the ground they travel, and know far more of the woodsman's trade than they." She paused and looked closely at him. "Mr. Washington? May I speak freely, as a loving sister might?"

"I feel advice coming on," with a smile, "please continue."

"I have met many gentlemen in my life, sir, and none have so deeply impressed me as you. But do be careful in the pursuit of honors. Just as a woman wooed too closely may refuse herself to the one who seeks her most ardently, honors can be fickle, even, like the woman, unjust. Seek not the honors, seek instead to do that which is deserving of them and they will surely come to you."

"Thank you Madam," without a hint of sarcasm. "I am pleased to know that someone besides my mother is so certain of my future."

*****

It was a Tuesday when the first hints of the disaster reached them. Dozens of teamsters had burst from the wood, proclaiming the army lost. They had stopped only long enough to steal some food, and then kept running.

For two anguished days, men had come in small groups. Men, some bloodied, some without uniform coats or packs, some without even a musket or cartridge case. They were men panicked. Tales of half the army killed, even more of the officers, the artillery, the baggage, the war chest and Braddock's papers, the General himself, all lost. Surely, these were the deserters, the cowards. The army would soon arrive to give the true news. It might be bad, but not so bad as this!

Today, Thursday, they were coming. Margaret and Kate stood by the opening in the woods, watching as the first soldiers emerged. They were trudging, lost, eyes vacant, spirit dead. They were men transformed, and the transformation struck terror into the waiting women.

Where was Simeon? There were some of the men of his company, but not him. Perhaps he was with the ambulance wagons, yes, that must be it, he would stay with his wounded. Where were they?

There was Browning, his arm in a sling; Kate had somehow found him without Margaret realizing that she was no longer standing next to her.

Where was Simeon?

Richard was talking to his wife, she burst into tears, they were coming toward her.

31

"Meg!"

Suddenly she understood.

*****

The sun was hot on her face. She blinked and shielded her eyes. Anxious friends were gathered above her, the grass beneath was cool.

"Ah Meg, you gave us a scare! Are you all right?"

"I think—what happened?—Simeon?"

Kate slowly shook her head. "I am so sorry, Meg. Can you sit up, dear?"

Margaret, dazed, could only nod.

"Richard, we must get her back to our tent. A bit of brandy is in order."

Browning summoned two men passing by. "Here, you two, make a chair of your arms. Now Meg, let me help you to stand, that's it. Now sit. Good. Now you men, follow me."

Margaret, like the two soldiers, could only do as she was told. The world was suddenly a place she could not understand. She rode in her makeshift chair, one arm around each man's shoulder. Slowly thought was returning. The men were dirty, she became aware of a blood stain on one man's shirt.

"Are you wounded, soldier?" she asked.

No, that's from my mate Jack—he was a good fellow, ma'am, always with a quip or two. Not no more."

"I'm sorry." She regretted asking.

*****

32

Kate had stayed with her through the afternoon. The brandy helped shock her into thought. Some food was welcome but did nothing for the hard knot in her stomach.

Finally toward evening, "Kate, where is Richard? Why are you sitting with me? Surely he needs you."

"He had his duties. I think you may need me the more."

"Nonsense, Kate, listen to me. He needs you. Your devotion must lie with him. I can manage, but when this awful day ends you must be with him."

Kate, grateful but unsure, "Really? I am so worried about you Meg. You've had an unimaginable shock. You've always been so strong and to see you laid out on the grass like that..."

"Truly, I will be good. Now go."

After her friend left, she curled in a ball on the cot, sighed, and allowed herself to weep silently.

*****

It was early when she rose, prodded the fire and put tea on. Richard and Kate heard her stirring and joined her.

"Richard, I want you to tell me what happened."

"I think, Meg, it will be too raw."

"Tell me!"

Browning paused, "All right. Simeon was a little way from me, directing his men. He was one of the few who kept his head during the battle. A ball felled him, he died instantly and felt no pain."

"Thank you. That is what I will tell his mother. Now tell me what happened. I understand it will be hard for you too, but I must know."

Browning cast a pleading look to his wife, who refused to rescue him.

33

He took a deep breath. "Simeon was in the van, with the engineers. We were only a mile or so from Fort Duquesne. They saw a Frenchman and some Indians in the road ahead. His men gave fire and killed them. Then the woods erupted. The savages had taken position in the trees on both our flanks. There must have been a thousand muskets leveled at us! His horse, the bay, was shot beneath him, he took a ball to the fleshy part of his leg. The van fell back upon the main body. When I saw him he was using a musket as a cane, still directing his troops. The man standing next to me was cursing our situation, cursing our general, cursing all Frenchmen and all savages, when his head suddenly snapped back and he fell without sound or movement. All this time we were under fire, but we couldn't see a single enemy. All around us men were dropping; the fire was murderous and constant. Our cannon would not depress enough to dislodge them. Many were not even sure where the enemy lay and just discharged their weapons into the air in frustration. Confusion and panic were everywhere.

"Simeon came to me, pointing at the woods, he said, 'Richard we must break that line or we're lost! Ready the men for a bayonet charge.' Just then, the Virginia company made such a charge, they were nearly at the wood line when a company of regulars—under orders mind you—fired into their backs. Those they didn't kill, the savages did. I turned back to Simeon, he was down. He had taken two more balls, one in his chest.

"I went to him—he said 'Richard, I'm dying. Promise me two things. See Margaret safe home. Her people are in Albany,' and 'Don't leave me on the field. I'd rather the wolves scattered my bones than let those bastards have me!'

"After a time, as we were preparing retreat, I got him into a cart with some others who couldn't walk. He was still alive, in pain and couldn't speak. I could see the gratitude in his eyes. We saved as many as we could. We all knew that any wounded left behind would be murdered before dark, but we had no room for many. We could hear their cries as we left. Before we were out of earshot the scalping and murders began. We could hear that too.

"It must have been an awful ride. The road was terrible and the carts bumped around frightfully. I came to him again later in the afternoon. It was clear that the end was nigh. He gripped my hand, he said 'Your promise?' I said 'My word' and he closed his eyes. That was the last he said. He died a little later, still holding my hand.

34

"Understand, Meg, we were running for our lives—we were certain the savages were following close. We dared not stop. We had no shovels. We could not bury our dead. I had two men carry him into the woods and we sat him against a tree. I said a prayer over him, and we left. There was nothing more we could do! My best friend, and I just left him there!"

He fell into his wife's arms and began to sob.

Margaret went to him. "I am sorry Richard. It was unspeakably selfish of me to make you live it again, but thank you. I needed to know. You must know that I do not reproach you for anything and neither would Simeon. I thank you for all you did for him. He was lucky to have a friend like you to be with him."

She glanced at Kate, who signaled with her eyes. She left them alone.

*****

The army was running to Philadelphia. There was no more charitable way to describe it. It as a cowardly decision, a charge laid on General Braddock now that he could no longer dispute the claim. They were leaving the depleted New York companies at Fort Cumberland. Fewer than 100 men to hold a place that required 300, fewer than 100 men to protect settlers scattered over hundreds of miles of frontier. It would be a futile, possibly suicidal assignment.

The rest, all the fine Regular Army troops, were going to flee for their lives to the safety of the city.

Browning came to the women as they were sitting before the fire.

"Kathleen, I have found a man to escort you to Philadelphia. This" indicating the man standing with him, "is Lt John Montraville of the 48th Foot. He was with Simeon when he died."

"Richard I do not want to go."

"I know Kathleen, and I wish you did not have to. I will miss you, but you cannot stay. This place is far too dangerous. If the French come, we will be lost; there could be no other outcome. Then you would be either raped and murdered, or murdered and scalped, depending on whether you were caught by a Frenchman or an Indian. I could not forgive myself for allowing either. I can only prevent it by sending you away."

She opened her mouth to protest, but stopped, resigned. "Very well. Can you not come away too?"

"You know I have submitted my resignation but Gates will not accept it until a replacement is found. I am probably stuck here for the winter. I will come to you in the spring, I swear it. Shaking the dust of this unhappy place from my boots cannot happen too soon."

"Amen", said Margaret, then turning from what had been to what would be, "So, Montraville, what can we take and when do we leave?"

Boston, December, 1777

"Good afternoon, Mrs. Brush"

"And a good afternoon to you, Mrs. Warren. Had I known you were coming, I would have better prepared my quarters to receive you."

Mercy Warren and Capt. Carson had entered the cell, unannounced.

Mercy, looking about, "I'm not sure anything you could do would improve this place. Does a jail always smell so?"

"That has certainly been my experience. The nose quickly fatigues though, so that after a month or two it is scarcely noticeable."

"No matter, I've come to offer it a respite. Captain Carson has agreed to accept your parole for a night. You'll come with me to my home, get a good meal and a solid night's sleep. And a hot bath. I don't suppose you object?"

"Such an offer to one in my position cannot be rejected."

"You do understand, Mrs. Brush, that you are in Mrs. Warren's custody? This is most irregular, and I do not approve. Persons more powerful than I have decreed it. If you fail to return by noon tomorrow there will be consequences."

"Yes sir. You have my word that I shall appear as required."

The uneven cobblestones beneath her feet felt so different that the flat stones on the cell floor. The fresh scent of the city surrounded her. There were people, hurrying, free people, everywhere, everywhere the sound of horse carts and squealing pigs, even chickens. A dog barked. It had been so long since she was a part of this world.

"You know, that place looks really grim on the outside." She had turned to regard the warehouse-prison from the street as they walked away. "But not so grim as it is on the inside." Then, "Please tell me Mrs. Warren, why you are so solicitous of me"

"May we *tutoyer* each other? Please call me Mercy."

"And I am Margaret. But why? Our politics, or rather our 'political economies' as Mr. Locke would have it, are so very different."

"They are, but I believe that on a more fundamental level, we disagree not at all. As I mentioned, you have many friends among us Margaret, and they wish to know that you are well. General Schuyler and his wife both speak very highly of you."

"Probably Kitty more than Phillip. I've known him for decades. We were never close, but I lived with her for a year or so during the old French War while he was away.

"I must ask, without seeming ungrateful, are you attempting to turn me rebel?"

Mercy met her eyes. "Yes, although, we do prefer the term 'patriot'"

"Thank you for your honesty. Why me?"

"I see an intelligent woman of immense physical courage. You would be an asset to our cause. And, I suspect that, having seen the British officer class far more than most, you know their opinion of colonials, of all of us, including you. Given that they are so dismissive of us as individuals, can it be possible that they, and their masters, think any more highly of us collectively? I believe we shall never receive just treatment from the Crown while such an attitude continues."

"But is it George III who errs, or his ministers?" asked Margaret. Even if it is the King, would not a good king rectify these things?"

"Perhaps, but then the next one after, who might not be so good, could reverse all by fiat. I think that in all of history a very good man seldom rises in palace intrigue, at least not with his goodness intact."

38

"You know, I can accept that there is a sort of contract between the ruler and the people, as Mr. Locke says. I am married to a lawyer after all. Logically, there is no reason why a king could not be so bound. I do wonder though why any ruler would consent to such a bargain so clearly not in his own best interest."

"We are both lawyers' wives," said Mercy with a laugh. "Interesting how that mode of thought rubs off on us, isn't it?"

"I question whether such a contract could be valid, Mercy. If made between men, if one party or the other has a complaint of malfeasance, he takes his case to a recognized third and asks for relief. To whom can man or king take their claim? There is no competent third party. An appeal to constitutional law is a slippery thing; the interpretation of it is left to judges whose offices are in the king's gift—which gives no comfort to the man if he is ruled against. If we can judge a king, then how can that king in turn judge us? I mean, there must be an order to society, don't you think?"

"Well, a man and his wife often judge each other, sometimes harshly, yet in love and friendship. It can be a two-sided arrangement. Each accepts the other's opinion and seeks approval. And so I think can it be between a ruler and the ruled."

"But," Margaret interjected, "without a king, would not the people dissolve into anarchy? Why would they not, if there is no social order?"

"Social order and political order are different things. Do you believe that the people crave anarchy? I cannot because it is contrary to their interests. A farmer will carefully tend his fields because they yield more grain if he does. It would be easier for him to neglect them, or steal from his neighbor, but besides being a violation of the laws of God and man, it is an unreliable way to provide for his children, a need which all but a few depraved souls recognize.

"It is possible to be a republican without being a leveler," she continued. Clearly, all men are not equal in their abilities or their estates, and that will never change. Some are able to contribute more, and deserve more reward for it. Conversely, because they receive more benefits of society, their debt is the greater to it."

"Is that not circular?"

"No, it is reflexive. You are repeating in your mind arguments that have been convulsing Massachusetts for a decade, and answers don't come easily. Some of us have determined that a body of just men can perform the functions of kingship, that is, government, without an individual to personify those duties.

"Listen to us! Mere women discussing political theories like philosophers while everyone knows our little heads are stuffed full of only recipes and thoughts of damask." Mercy stopped to look in a shop window. "Margaret, doesn't that look good? Come, I want one of those sweets!"

*****

Margaret felt clean for the first time in months. The hot bath, the warmed towels, the scent of perfumed water brought the lassitude of ease. She dressed, a clean dress, slowly. Mercy's girl proved herself a magician with hair who transformed Margaret's neglected tresses into something presentable. She had not felt so much like a lady since arriving in Boston.

"Mercy, I cannot thank you enough for all this kindness. You have been a Godsend."

"You're welcome. Would you care to join my husband in the library? It will be just the three of us at dinner tonight. I thought I'd not subject you to my husband's friends just yet—or my brother. They can be quite vociferous in their opinions. I'm afraid the talk will be of politics. As you know, he is president of the provincial assembly; conversation tends to be of work."

"I think that would be fine—I'm learning there are more shades to this rebellion than I knew. The 'patriots' I have encountered in the jail have not been perhaps not the best exemplars of your cause. Captain Carson seems to bear particular enmity."

"He has suffered in this war, as have many. His wound will never heal and gives him pain. As well, his father suffered greatly from Mr. Brush's sequestration. He fell ill and died soon after and Carson blames your husband. He was once a very gay fellow."

40

"That explains a good bit. I shall have to make an accommodation for his behavior. I was once quite gay myself, although I do feel so much lighter tonight! Perhaps Mr. Warren will now help reform my opinions as you have reformed my mood! Although, as you know, my husband's beliefs must be mine, publically."

"Yes. I suppose I would rather you were a reluctant royalist if you can't be an active patriot!"

Later, after a good dinner, a truly hot dinner, with wine and nuts, Margaret was feeling relaxed and replete. As predicted, the talk turned to politics.

"Margaret and I were talking today, James, of the covenant between ruler and man. The question arose, 'how may disputes between them be resolved and to what court may they bring their suit?'"

"Well, my dear, let us assume that they have competent representation. Any good attorney will try to get the parties to come to accommodation before pursuing a suit at law. In the case that I'm sure you were discussing, it is difficult to have an accommodation when one party refuses conversation. For ten years, various colonies sent petition after petition to the crown, as is their right under the British constitution. They were asking for redress of wrongs, yet in every instance, the petition was ignored or else an even more punitive legislation was passed as punishment for the act of petition."

"I agree, James," asked Margaret, "that London did not act wisely in response to just complaints, but is that ample reason to take to arms? "

"Resort to arms is always unsatisfactory. Even if you set aside the loss and suffering attendant, it becomes a test of strength, not of right.

"Your question, Margaret," he continued with a twinkle in his eye, "Indicates that you hope for the clouds to part and some sort of *deus ex machina* to descend, to chastise King George for his intransigence, and also we colonists for our refractory conduct. Then we could all return to the *status quo ante,* to the happy days of 1763 when Britons and Americans alike rejoiced and lived in harmony. Alas, the past few years have diminished my faith in mechanics! Sometimes, there is no alternative to arms, as unsatisfactory as they may be.

"The crown has three choices when petitioned by the people, just as in any contractual dispute. It may accede to the plea, it may offer compromise, or it may call upon the powers of the state to stop up the mouths of the petitioners. This, this king has chosen to do. What choice have we but to fight? Are we to be slaves in our own land?

"James," said Mercy, "there are but three of us here. You may stop speechifying now."

"I'm sorry, my dear, I do tend to be carried away, don't I?"

"James," said Margaret, "I see no need for apologies when the enthusiasm is honest—as yours is. I respect your fervency but I remain unconvinced that yours is the very best course. Does it not lead to the sort of rigidity you condemn in our King?"

"Ah, Margaret, have you ever read a thing called Candide by M. Voltaire? No? Then I shall send you home with a copy. It speaks to the 'very best course' idea. I do think you'll enjoy it."

As they were retiring, Mercy said, "Good night, Margaret. This has been a most pleasant evening. Like you, I am learning that our foes are more variable than I had known. I will arrange another like this soon, one where you may meet more of our friends."

"I should like that very much. James is a charming fellow. My wits have not been exercised so in months! I enjoyed myself immensely. Thank you again and good night."

She climbed into the soft warmed bed as content as it was possible for her to be. She wormed her way down into the bedclothes and slept soundly for the first time in months.

*****

"Margaret, pack your things! You're coming with me."

"What do you mean, Mercy. Am I released?"

"No, but Captain Carson will be here in a moment to accept your parole. You are coming to my house to serve whatever the balance of your sentence

42

may be. Margaret, James and I have extended ourselves to obtain this. I pray you will not be so inhospitable as to embarrass us?"

"Lord no, Mercy. I could never be so ungrateful. Even had you not been so kind, I would not break my word. Nor even if I stood alone on an open road. I shall be at your command."

"Now, get packing! I'd rather leave this place. I truly don't like it here."

"Nor do I."

Carson appeared as predicted and grudgingly accepted Margaret's word that she would not flee the city, that she would be bound by the Warrens' instructions, and that she would engage in no spying.

Light snow was falling as they walked out into the gray cold December afternoon. It was a glorious day.

Quebec, July 1759

They first heard the artillery just before noon. The guns of Pointe Levis on the south bank began to fire sporadically across the wide St. Lawrence into the lower city. Those on Isle d'Orleans and the east bank of the Montmorency River began to pummel the redoubts at the little river's mouth. Although they could not see them from the island, cannon further up the river above the falls began to blast the French lines at the top of the river embankment. Three warships dropped down close and added their voices to the rest. General Wolfe had landed further to the east a week before. The men had spent the time pushing the lines to the river and in building gun emplacements. During that time she had scarcely seen Montraville, who, as Wolfe's chief engineer, had been fully occupied in that work. It had been a brief, passionate visit, only one night as he sped from one camp to another.

Her servant Sally rushed into the tent. "Oh Ma'am. Come quick! I think they're attacking!"

Margaret grabbed her telescope; they ran to join a group of women lining the northern shore of Isle d'Orleans. She found a good spot in the growing crowd and leveled her glass across the St Lawrence.

"Where away?"

"There, over below the point."

She found them, a squadron of little boats inching across the water from Point Levis. They would have a two-mile row before they reached the beach. Soon other boats put off from the island near where she stood, their departure staggered so as to all arrive together.

She scanned the boats.

"Look, Sally, there are the Royal Americans." She handed over the glass.

"Here, see if you can find your husband, in those boats on the left." She pointed and helped Sally aim the telescope.

"Where? Oh, there he is!" As she found him, "I'll bet he never planned to row a boat when he joined the army!"

The attack had been planned for high tide so that the current would not impede them. As the boats reached the ships, more boatloads of men joined. She knew the plan called for 8000 men to land, to take the two redoubts and then scale the steep grassy banks to the highlands, there to establish a foothold from which to launch the attack on Quebec itself.

It was risky, attacking the strongest point of the French defensive forces, but Montraville had confided that General Wolfe was growing frustrated with the pace of the siege. Now, on the last day of July, the season was drawing to a close. In six weeks the city must be taken or the siege abandoned. Any longer and the English fleet would not make the dangerous thousand-mile voyage down the St. Lawrence before winter ice entrapped them. The prospect of marching this army south to Albany through the snow was not pleasant either. Nor was the thought of the official inquiries that would surely follow such a failure.

General Wolfe was riding high after his role in the reduction of Louisburg on Cape Breton Island the year before. He and Lord Amherst had directed the removal of a major thorn from the side of British-colonial shipping. Without that port, French cruisers had no base from which to prey upon shipping to the northern colonies. The mouth of the St Lawrence had been laid open. It had been Wolfe who led the first landings there, he who destroyed the trapped men-of-war. It had been Montraville who directed the siege works.

She had watched as the worm-like trenches crawled toward the fortress, each night adding hundreds of feet, periodically opening to a new battery and all the while, the great guns loaned by the warships fired over their heads, battering the walls. It had been a relatively bloodless conquest, a few hundreds out of the thousands engaged on each side. The ultimate capitulation was the high point of an otherwise dismal half-decade for British arms in North America. Between Braddock's defeat and the fall of Louisburg there had been precious little to cheer. The settlers had been driven back to the coast, the colonies still clung to their insular jealousies.

The Iroquois were beginning to wonder whether they had backed the wrong horse. One incompetent commander after another had been sent out to bungle yet another campaign. One army after another went forth in confidence and returned in failure. Many more never even managed to set out, wasting their opportunities as their commanders quarreled over precedence.

James Wolfe had been different. A hypochondriacal mere wisp of a man, his iron determination seemed to have been placed in the wrong body. His was the first army that had actually managed to invest Quebec in two hundred years, and he was not about to let this chance pass by. Yet time was running out.

The boats were further away now, just bristly black dots on the water. The cannon fire from the batteries across the Montmorency continuously battered the two redoubts built at the foot of the steep bank. A cloud of thick smoke was forming in the clear summer sky above them.

When the boats reached the edge of the tidal flat at the base of the embankment, they would have a 150 yard dash to the redoubts, and those taken, another 50 to the base of the grassy slope.

Then things began to go wrong. The boats from Point Levis stopped short of the beach. She could make out men jumping out, standing in shallow water as they heaved their boats back into the river.

"They have struck a shoal," Margaret reported to those around. "Now they have to find a landing space."

The boats milled about for much of the afternoon, searching. On the bluff, Montcalm was busy arranging his forces to accept them. This was not going well at all. The clear afternoon sky was beginning to fill with clouds. The tide was ebbing, more and more of the tidal flats were exposed with each passing minute, the strand becoming wider. With her glass, she could see the French abandon the two bastions, scurry up the bank to join their comrades.

That bank is so steep those men are using their hands to climb it! How can an attack be mounted there?

Finally the boats reached the far shore. Men poured out, advancing slowly, with difficulty through the mucky tidal flats. When they finally reached the solid ground they were winded. The little red dots that were men paused at the captured redoubts, then, without waiting for reinforcements to join, dashed for the slope. French musketry on the heights began to cut them down.

The slope began to change from grassy green to red as the soldiers clambered up it, one hand grasping at clumps of weeds, the other clutching a bayoneted musket. The threatened summer storm broke. The sounds died away as damp gunpowder stilled the cannon, silenced the muskets. A faint roar from the attacking men reached them from across the water.

She could see the tiny red, antlike army struggling upward. Here one would slip, starting an avalanche of little red bugs as he slid down, taking more and more with him as he fell. At the bottom, most of the dots would begin to climb again, a few did not. Those not moving at the bottom were multiplying.

Here and there, a man would reach the top, only to be swarmed upon by the defenders. His body cast down upon his fellows, a new avalanche would begin.

The women on the island watched, fearful yet fascinated. All were army wives, most had a husband somewhere in this debacle. None had ever seen such a battle.

"This must stop! Surly General Wolfe must see that they cannot take that bluff!"

As if he had heard them, the sound of a bugle calling 'retreat' floated across the water. The dots, most of them, returned to their boats in good order and began to row back in the dusk.

Sally, her face white, "Ma'am, what shall we do? Those men…"

"Come Sally, we will meet the boats. We can perhaps help them. The wounded."

*****

Something was afoot. Men silently entered boats on the back of the island and disappeared into the evening. The great guns on Point Levis fired as they had for two months since the army had arrived. Margaret had no idea of the plans for the first time all summer. She had not seen much of Montraville in the month since Montmorency and he had been more close-mouthed than ever. Expectancy tinted the air. Did the enemy know how desperate was this troop movement?

The next day, mid morning, they could hear the sounds of battle from beyond the thirteen spires of Quebec. It was loud and it was short. Had the army succeeded? Someone must have been routed for the fight to be done so quickly. The white flag of the Bourbons still flew above the city, yet there was no cannon fire.

The afternoon dragged on, the women on Isle d'Orleans fretted. Finally, late in the day, the Union Jack rose above the fortress.

*****

By now, three days later, everyone knew the broad strokes. The army had found a neglected path up the cliffs beyond Quebec, had climbed in the dark, had formed on the Plains of Abraham before the city by dawn. Montcalm, not trusting the ancient walls of the city, had brought his soldiers out of the city to stand and he had lost. He was dead, Wolfe was dead, the city had fallen.

Margaret had been dreading facing Montraville, but he came to her. They embraced, kissed.

"John, I am relieved that you are safe. How could you leave me in suspense so long?"

"There was much business in quieting the city, I expect even you would know that."

There was no good way. "John, I am with child."

He exploded into rage. "You stupid colonial sow! How could you do this to me?"

It was the reaction she had feared. "I believe I was not alone in this! We must marry."

"What, did you really think I would marry the likes of you? You have no money, no connections. You would be worthless as a wife. You're even stupider than I imagined."

"But you promised…"

"A gentleman is not required to honor promises made while wooing. Any advantage may be pursued without dishonor."

"I have followed you for three years on the basis of that promise. I'm a thousand miles from my home! Only a cad would expose a woman so!"

He slapped her.

She turned her back, the blow had made her cheek sting and her eyes water. She found her hand in her pocket, untying the thong that secured her dagger. In that moment she became a mother. She let him live.

He raged at her back, "You're nothing but a damned army whore! It is not your place to judge me. Do you think I care a snap about your opinions?"

She turned to face him, icily cold. "Very well then. Am I to be cast out to starve and freeze?"

"I care not what you do. Find yourself a greasy French pig to support you! You'll see nothing from me, not now or ever! Can you grasp that? I'll send my man tomorrow for my things. I'll not come here again."

"We agree about something."

He doubled his fist and struck her belly.

She collapsed on the ground breathless, disoriented by the pain and the shock.

"How could you?" she gasped, "Your own child!"

"I'll have no half-breed bastard of mine running about the world."

He turned on his heel and left.

*****

Sally came in to find her mistress curled in a ball on the ground, weeping.

"What has he done? Are you allright?" little flustered nonce words. "Here, let me help you. I heard, Ma'am, everyone did. What can I do? Come, sit."

After a few minutes Margaret began to recover. "Will my baby be harmed? He struck my womb."

"I don't know Ma'am. We can only wait till the baby tells us. If I had not been here, I could not believe any man could be such a brute!"

Margaret laughed, a mirthless laugh. "Aren't we a pair. You a widow and me to be a mother and not a man between us. God! I hate officers! My life would have been so much sweeter if Simeon had lived and John had died in that awful cart!"

"Fitzgerald was only a corporal, ma'am."

"Forgive me Sally, I did not mean to impugn him too. I'm over-wrought." She paused as composure began to return. "Well, I have brought this problem on and now I must live through it. Will you stay? You know I won't be able to pay you anything."

"I will, ma'am. I have no place to go either. Two of us together will have a better chance of survival. He has used you terribly but now we must prepare for the winter. I've been told they are brutal here. Anything of value here must be gone before his man comes in the morning; he will be under instructions to take everything away."

"I'll not steal, Sally. If we take his things, he might cry 'thief' and have us arrested."

"He could and he won't and he owes you. He knows better than to call attention to this. It would be an advertisement of his base character. Besides, he tried to steal your baby. Things must be converted to sterling or francs or whatever passes as money here. By January, a bauble won't buy you a shank of pork, but cash will. Now, what is there that we must hide?"

50

"He has my husband's pistols, I gave them to him and he carries them. Besides them, there are only a few pins and rings, the telescope, doodads like that."

"Well, then the pistols are all he's going to get from you and it's a pity he gets even those! Let's gather everything else. We'll find more than you think. I will take them tomorrow and bring money before evening."

"How Sally? How does one do that?"

"It is better that you not know. Now, you must not be here tomorrow either."

"Perhaps I shall take a walk by the river. I do have much to think about. How could I have been such a damned fool!"

"You will take great care by that river, Ma'am? The rocks can be slippery." Sally looked at Margaret searchingly. "I pray I have not misjudged you."

"I shall be here in the evening."

"As will I. You have my word on it."

"A good woman's word is more valuable than a gentleman's, it seems." She managed a wan smile. "You have mine that I shall return from my walk. Now that we have made a pact, we must act."

An hour's work produced a small pile of metal work. They sat on the cot with the loot on a cloth between them.

"It looks so pitiful, all my wealth, there on that little rag. How much, Sally, is there, do you think?"

"Probably fifteen or twenty pounds worth, I think. Some of the silver work is quite nice, should fetch a penny or two. In normal times it would feed a family for a year, but these will not be normal times." She shrugged. "It will have to be enough."

*****

Up close, the ruined city revealed itself. As the boat drifted to the quay she could see the blasted empty houses, the burned stone commercial buildings. The artillery on Point Levis had done its work.

The British army was collecting itself from the drawn-out summer positions, separated by miles and water, into the shell of Quebec for the winter. The city and immediate countryside were all they held; Canadian partisans and their Indian allies lurked just beyond. Work parties were heavily guarded yet still attacked. Every lone sentry knew that tonight might be his last turn of duty.

Margaret and Sally, all of the women from the camp on Isle d'Orleans, were being ferried across the harbor basin this chill October morning. Each held their small bundle, the sum of their possessions. Behind them hundreds of small boats crossed and re-crossed the water. Ahead, the pier was filled with bustling people, shouted commands, the sound of wheels grinding on the stone pavement, piles of goods destined no one knew where. There were very few horses. All of this materiel must be moved up the steep road to the upper city by human power.

"What shall we do Ma'am?"

"I'm not sure—we must find quarters soon. There'll not be much to choose among and they will fill quickly." She gestured at the river traffic.

She saw a captain in earnest conversation with a nun. Each had something they desperately needed to convey, neither spoke the other's language. She watched for a moment.

"Follow me." She took a deep breath and interrupted them.

"May I help?" She said in English and then repeated herself in French. They both launched into a long simultaneous spiel. She held up her hand. "One at a time, please! Ladies first," she said to the captain, and turning to the nun, speaking in French, "I will translate. What shall I say to him?"

Gratefully the appeal came out. Margaret listened, nodding. She asked for a clarification, then, to the captain, "She asks for a work party to help with the heavy items, to move them from the ruined convent there" she pointed, "to the upper city, to the Hotel Dieu, the hospital. She says the sisters have done

52

almost all they can, but some things are too much for their strength. And she offers the hospital to your sick and wounded."

"How many men?"

A side conversation. "She thinks six or eight might be enough."

"Done. Go to the convent, I will send a corporal and a party. And thank you. I so wanted to help the woman, but knew not what she wanted."

Margaret relayed the message to the nun, adding anxiously "I—we can come with you if you like. We'll help any way we can."

"Have you no men?"

"We are both widows. I am Margaret Soumain, this is my friend, Sally Fitzgerald. I'm not sure how I should address you. The regiment have granted us rations for the winter, but no shelter. We will do anything in exchange. Can you help us?"

"You may call me Mother Superior. Let us see how this day progresses. You have been kind so far, but Hotel Dieu has no place for idle hands."

"I shouldn't think there is any place in this city for idle hands," said Margaret, looking about her at the ruins.

"You speak French like a Canadian."

"I was bred in Albany. My tutors were Montrealers."

✳✳✳✳✳

In the gathering evening, Margaret sat on the steps of the hospital, bone tired. Seven times, she and Sally had laboriously pushed the little cart up the steep road, and six times controlled its perverse urge to careen downward. Seven times they had loaded and unloaded.

Mother Superior came to her. "You are with child."

"How did you know?"

53

"This is a hospital. We see these things. When?"

"March or April, I think."

"When was your husband killed, my dear?

"Oh! Mother Superior, I fear I may have given you a wrong impression of me. You see, my husband was killed in '55, with Braddock on the Monongahela. My baby's father was another man, one who promised matrimony, but refused it when it mattered most."

"An officer?"

"Yes, I was very foolish; I trusted him and came here with him. When I became pregnant, he repudiated me. Sally's husband was killed in July, at the Montmorency. I pray my past will not disqualify us from your mercy."

"When did you meet him, this bad man?"

"It was just days after Simeon, my husband, died. They had been together at his end."

"So he pounced upon you while you were grieving? Looking at you I can see how a man might do such a thing."

"Yes, I guess he did, although it was some time before we took up."

"Your Mr. Shakespeare has a phrase, *"Plus péché contre puis pécher"*

Margaret smiled, "'More sinned against than sinning.' I would not have expected to find King Lear here."

"I find Shakespeare a concentrated course in humanity. He has been quite useful to me over the years. In a hospital, one sees enough of human frailty. Little can offend me anymore. Certainly not this. Sally is rather your maid than your friend, then?"

"Both, really. We stay together, even though she knows I cannot pay her. She has been a blessing these last weeks. She always was, but more now."

"It speaks well of you as a mistress that she remains. You have worked hard today, both of you. There will be a place for you here, if you will work in the wards, and translate for me. I shall need someone like you, for I cannot be sure that the English officers will render my words correctly. You have been honest with me about how you came. You were honest about something you had reason to fear would be to your detriment. You, I think, I can trust."

$$*****$$

Margaret sat in the garden of the Hotel Dieu, in the first warm sun of April. At last, after the hard winter, the hunger, the days of the sick coming to the hospital, many of them to leave in a shroud, the small victories as one returned to duty, at last the idea of spring! Little Fanny had found her breast; she felt a contentment denied to the males of every species.

A soft voice behind her, "Margaret? Is that you?"

She turned and tried to make out the features of the two men, the afternoon sun behind them masking their faces.

"Hannes, can that be you? Oh my God! It is! How…"

"We came for you."

She rose hastily and went to them. Fanny protested the interruption. "Boys, I would like you to meet your niece, Frances. Fanny, this is your uncle Hannes and your uncle Christian. Would you smile for them?"

Fanny regarded them solemnly but soon found her previous business more pressing.

"How did you get here? There are French all about."

"From Ticonderoga we joined a scout that was sent to bring dispatches to General Murray. We saw plenty of Canadians after we got to Sorel, on the St Lawrence. We stayed away from the forts on Richelieu River. They do seem to be coming this way. We stole boats at Cape Rouge and finished by water. But how are you? We got your letter in December, but it was too late to travel. Did you manage to stay warm, have enough food? This city looks a ruin! Papa wanted to come, we wouldn't let him."

55

So they continued, siblings who had not seen each other for two years, jabbering excitedly. Margaret felt lighter than she had in months.

*****

The cannons on the walls were booming.

Margaret and Fanny sat in a storeroom deep in the basement of Hotel Dieu. Another mother, her broken leg propped on a cushion, held her own child, just weeks older than Fanny. Two septuagenarian Sisters sat in a corner working their rosaries.

Out on the Plains of Abraham, the second battle for Quebec was raging. The remnants of the army which had taken the city seven months before had marched out to meet the French, the Canadians and Indians coming from Montreal to recapture their capitol. There were two of them for every Englishman. Her brothers were among a company of volunteers marching with the army. Their rifled flintlocks stood in a corner of her room, neither their accuracy nor their slow re-loading time were wanted in this encounter. They had drawn muskets and bayonets from the armory.

The Mother Superior, breathless, rushed in. "Margaret, I'm sorry my child, but we need you!"

"But Fanny? What am I to do?"

"Let me take her, Margaret," offered the other mother. "I'm wet enough for two! I can't walk on this broken leg. She'll be safe from all those nasty cannons shooting overhead." Doubtful, Margaret let the other mother take her baby.

"Are you positive? She can be fussy…"

"Hungry babies are never fussy, just hungry. Now go."

"Margaret, please. Follow after me. The wounded are coming in quickly. I must return. Hurry!"

The babble of voices filled the entry hall of the hospital. Dozens of men, bloodied and in pain, stood waiting for aid. More lay on the floor where the litter bearers had left them. Most were English. The French had held the field and only those who could be taken away by their comrades came here. Those abandoned were now being murdered by the Canadian Indians. Here and there stood an unlucky soul in a French uniform. Even an occasional Indian was drawn here by a lifetime of associations with the ministry of the nuns. Everyone carried weapons of some sort. By tacit consent, there was no war in these walls. These were soldiers, English and French, Canadian militia, Indians, all in pain and very afraid. While each had believed, as soldiers must, that the man next to them might be hit, their own mortality had never been considered. It now looked into their eyes.

Many of the wounded had walked themselves there and required only a quick dressing before being sent on their way. Some of the slightly wounded chose not to come at all; most men were terrified of the hospital. It was a place to die. Other than setting bones and controlling bleeding, most of what the Sisters did was merely palliative. There were no medicines other than a chunk of willow bark to be chewed, a mild analgesic that barely dented the pain of the injured.

"Margaret," said the Mother Superior, "The slightly wounded go to the dining hall. Surgery is set up in the dispensary, broken bones and stab wounds. The others," she hesitated, not wishing to pronounce upon those already without hope, "Father Joachim is working in the hall toward the chapel."

Margaret nodded, "Go do what you must, I'll try to get some order here." She turned to face the men, stamped her foot loudly on the stone floor and ordered, "Silence!", and then repeated the order in French. So it would be all afternoon; everything said twice so that all could understand.

They were soldiers and responded to the accustomed order.

"Now, listen to me. The Sisters will see each of you as soon as they can. All those who wish to be seen and then return to their regiments, line up against that wall. Move now, lively. Very well, the first four, go with this Sister, she will direct you.

"Are there any able men here?" A half dozen hands raised. "Good. You are now stretcher bearers. You two, come with me."

She began to move among the men on the floor, questioning, comforting, directing them toward their fates. Gradually the hall began to empty, the prone men came to be in orderly rows. She sent five men to the priest.

Periodically, a Sister in a bloodied apron would come from one hallway or another, the line of ambulatory would become shorter, the bearers would take another to the dispensary where the most skilled nurses cleansed and bandaged the deepest wounds, the penetrating stab of the sword or bayonet, the path of the musket ball. There bones were set or the mangled limbs sawed off. If gangrene and shock could be avoided many of these would survive. There were no doctors.

It was in the early afternoon when they brought the Mohawk warrior to her. He was very young, still in his teens. When he saw her he began to struggle violently on his litter, so violently that the bearers had to set him down and restrain him. She knelt beside him and placed her fingers softly on his bare chest.

"Brave one," she said in her broken Mohawk, "Brave one, why do you struggle so? Will you speak with me?" She found his eyes and willed him to look at hers.

"I am called Margaret. What is your name?"

"I am called Eksa'a Ron:kwe."

Eksa'a Ron:kwe, Half-man? Had she misunderstood him? Indian names, she knew, usually had some basis, either in the character, the physical or in accomplishment. Sometimes they were ironic and occasionally quite ribald. But Half-man? This fellow was as well muscled as any she had ever seen. The fine narrow face betrayed some European dalliance in his ancestry.

"Half-man, I have been told that a warrior, when he is captured by an enemy, will suffer any treatment without complaint and by his quiet carriage show his courage. Have I been told correctly? Will you show me your courage, Half-man?"

The guttural Iroquoian language had lowered the pitch of her voice. The request, spoken so softly, so pleadingly, could not be denied by testosterone. She felt the tension beginning to leave him. "Have you a woman?"

58

"There is one in my village."

"What is her name?"

"She is called Yokennoren Akennha'kène."

"Ah, is she soft and warm like a summer rain?"

"Yes, but I must prove myself a man here to satisfy her father."

"Well, I think you have done that! A coward is wounded in the back, you were not. Now, today, I want you to think of her. Do not make her grieve. Allow these kind people to help you, and you shall see her before the leaves turn. No one here wishes to harm you. They have much magic here to cure your leg. May I look at your wound?"

She saw the fear return to his eyes. "What is wrong, Half-man? I will not hurt you."

She began to lay aside his legging, he moved his hand feebly to stop her. She swatted it away. He lay still, resigned to his fate. There it was, high on his inner thigh, one of those ugly, three-cornered bayonet wounds, this one with considerable tearing. It was bleeding well, but not profusely. The femoral artery must be undamaged or else he would have bled to death long before this. She slid her fingers between his legs, probing for an exit wound. There, open and oozing. His body began to betray him. Suddenly, she understood.

"Well, Man" she said slyly, deliberately omitting the prefix, "I think that Yokennoren Akennha'kène will be very glad to see you again." She was surprised to find herself blushing. "Yours is a good wound, if we can prevent the mortification, you shall be as good as ever, with an interesting scar to show. It requires more skill than I have to heal you. I will take you now to another who has great magic to clean and bind it. Now, Man, it will hurt when she cleanses it, it will have the sting of a thousand bees, but that will soon pass. I must remain here to help others but I shall visit you tomorrow. You will be the man for Yokennoren Akennha'kène?"

There had been no end to the wounded. They came to lie waiting in the hospital corridors as the women tended them as well as they could. The ambulatory shuffled about, heads down. The English army had retreated

59

behind the city walls. Still the cannons fired. Margaret saw Fanny only during one brief respite. She had needed desperately to nurse. It was nearly midnight when she finally sat. She fell asleep with Fanny at her breast.

✳✳✳✳✳

The road from the hospital at Sacre Ceour to Quebec City, only two miles away, led through a patch of thick woods. Yesterday this place had seen fierce fighting between the armies as the French again tried to take the city from its enfeebled defenders.

She was tired. The wounded soldiers packed the two hospitals to overflowing. The Sisters worked in ceaseless shifts giving the little aid that their medicine could provide. At night wagons had carried away the dead. The wards were filled, even the hallways were choked with men bedded on nothing but blankets. Margaret and Sally had spent the morning searching for wounded on the field, working through the scattered drifts of spring snow, the muddy half thawed ground, looking for signs of life among the piled bodies.

Now, she and two Holy Sisters were walking back to Hotel Dieu, through this wood. The little donkey Ferdinand was dutifully pulling the cart of bandages needed there. Un-escorted, the Sisters had enjoyed free passage, protected by their God and their habits. They didn't notice the man until he was very close to them.

He stood in the road, a pistol in his hand. He wore a torn and bloody red coat.

"Halt! Well looky here what the road has brought me. Give me your money!"

Margaret stepped forward. "We have none. We're from the hospital—all we have are bandages."

"Not all—some men only want money, but Ole Bill is a yielding chap, he just takes what the world brings to his door. Lemme see, shall I keep them virgins, or this one here. That one's kinda old and fat and that one's too boney." He leered at her; his teeth were rotten and broken. "I think maybe you'll do me better than them. You must know a little how to please. I

60

believe I'll just take you!" He grabbed Margaret's arm. "Yup, you'll do me real good. The rest of you—run!"

"Run, Sisters, run!"

The alcohol on his breath struck her. She felt cold. Her one hand untied the thong holding her knife. He watched the retreating nuns for a moment, then began to raise his pistol. His fingers contracted involuntarily as the point of her dagger entered his belly, thrust upward. She buried it to the guard. The ball splintered a tree twenty feet away.

She pushed him away, sweeping the blade sideways as she withdrew it, widening the wound. Clutching his gut, he swore and lurched clumsily forward. She stepped aside and swung the heavy hilt against the base of his skull as he passed. He grunted and fell hard, twisting as he reached for her. He rolled onto his back and lay stunned and gasping.

Margaret stood looking down at him. She recalled a hundred overheard conversations, the officers discussing their craft. "Always be sure of your man," the soldiers had said.

She bent down and jabbed the blade into the side of his neck and sliced upward, severing carotids and windpipe. She watched until the blood flowing from his neck ran without foam. It did not take long. She wiped her knife on his jacket and carefully re-sheathed it. The muscles in her arm twitched from the unaccustomed effort.

"Thank you, Simeon," she whispered.

Sister Marie Lisabetha, too heavy and un-used to exercise, had not gone far when the sound of the pistol shot stopped her. She turned, fascinated, watching the struggle. Ferdinand had come between; she could only hear the muffled sounds. Then Margaret had stood above the cart.

"My child, are you all right?"

"Yes Sister, he will trouble us no more."

"Oh, my dear, is he dead?"

"Yes." Margaret walked to her. "Sister Marie Henrietta runs really quickly, doesn't she!"

They both thought this extremely funny.

"What shall we do now? Do you think it is safe to proceed? Where did you get that knife Margaret? Was he carrying it?"

"No, It's mine. I have carried it for years, for this whole war. I think we are safe. What are the odds that two footpads will be in this little patch of wood? Come, these bandages are needed at the hospital, and I really need to get back to my daughter. I'm becoming uncomfortable again."

They had not gone far when they heard shouts and pounding feet behind them. Sister Marie Henrietta appeared with a half dozen Grenadiers, some with their jackets unbuttoned, some without their mitered caps. It was a hurried rescue party.

"Margaret, are you safe? Where is he?"

"Over there. He won't hurt anyone."

✳✳✳✳✳

"Margaret, my child, you are a puzzle. Yesterday, with the Indian, you were the picture of womanliness, today, they tell me that you have killed a man in the most efficient and ruthless manner possible. How can both of these be within you?"

Mother Superior had come into the little room Margaret and Sally shared in the Hotel Dieu, concern in her tone. She sat on the little bed half facing Margaret.

"I only did what I had to do, Mother Superior. He was going to shoot Sister Marie Lisabetha in the back, he was going to kill me after he had had his pleasure. As for Eksa'a Ron:kwe, I was sure he was going to kill himself."

"I doubt it not. It's your soul that has my concern. Murder is unwelcome in God's eyes."

62

"In most eyes, I suppose, but this isn't murder, I don't think. Perhaps I was God's instrument to save the good Sister?"

"You verge on blasphemy, child. It is presumptuous to suggest that you know His will."

"Forgive me, I was being glib without right. You know I would never disparage your faith, Mother Superior."

"But you do not share it?"

"Respectfully, I cannot. I was bred in the Dutch Church, where all ornament is eschewed as sacreligious. It is too much a part of me to be changed. But I do not doubt your sincerity—of all the Sisters here. It is just too foreign for me."

"It bothers me also that you carry a weapon here. This is a hospital."

I have never carried it when within doors, Mother Superior. I have seldom felt so safe as when I am here. But this was a journey out in the violent world; I needed it."

"You did, but did the fact that you had it make you reach too quickly for it—could you have resolved things with words if you had not that choice? Might not Our Father have sent other protection? And, where did you get the knife?"

"Perhaps He might have, we shall never know. As for the dagger, I took it from one who was intent on killing me some time ago. As I said, it can be a violent world at times. This is a war, and war unleashes the worst in us all. I would have preferred not to kill either of those people, yet I sleep well.

"For all of my life, there have been times when I simply knew what I must do, and I have done it, twice with fatal consequence. Is it wrong that I can be so certain in those times? Is it some kind of madness?"

"How do you know, my child? How do you know what you must do? Does a voice tell you this?"

"No, there is only a chilling certainty. It is much like a soldier who, when he receives his order, simply does it without question. 'March here, shoot this one...' He accepts that it is right because he must believe that his officer is in the right or he shall be paralyzed with confusion. I get a wordless order from a general within, and I do it. It is hard to explain..."

"Well, I could call this many things, my child, but not madness, I think. My concern is for your soul. What if this general of yours directs you to do something evil? Can you refuse these orders? You risk becoming a self-righteous judge of all, to your own great peril."

"I have not thought of this. I suppose I could always mutiny, but what of the discipline of my internal army if I should?"

"Aha, my child, you have found that which you fear most. There is a certain serenity about you, your defining characteristic, and it comes from that certainty you experience. You wish not to examine too closely lest you lose it."

Boston, January 1778

Margaret and Mercy entered the library together. A good fire warmed the room. It was filled with a half-dozen important-looking dinner guests, some of whom she recognized. James Warren greeted them.

"There you are ladies! Come, Margaret, let us introduce you around. It will be a few minutes before dinner is called. Might I fetch you a libation?"

"Introductions first, then a glass of Madeira would be nice, if you could James."

"Very well. Mercy, will you introduce her whilst I fetch?"

Mercy turned to the nearest group. "Mrs. Brush, may I present Mr. John Hancock and General Artemus Ward? Gentlemen, Mrs. Margaret Brush. Mrs. Brush is serving out her sentence with us rather than in the Ship Street jail. Her husband was the rather notorious Crean Brush. Now John, please play nicely."

"A pleasure, gentlemen. Mr. Hancock, I understand that you suffered significant losses due to my husband's activities and I sincerely hope you are able to recover them once this war is past. Please remember that my husband was acting under the direct order of General Gage. As I'm sure General Ward would remind you, a man under orders sometimes must do unpleasant duty."

"I had no idea Mr. Brush had such a charming wife." Margaret acknowledged the compliment. "Shall we agree to a truce for the evening? Perhaps avoid all mention of this war?"

"Well, sir, we could, but I think we should both find that rather tiresome. Could we instead agree that when we discuss the events of the day, as I'm

65

quite sure we will, that we remain somewhat detached from the personal?" She paused to survey the room. "From the look on everyone's faces, I presume we shall be celebrating General Washington's victories at Trenton and Princeton?"

"Yes. I hope that will not make you uncomfortable?"

"No, I think victors deserve their moment. Driving Cornwallis and Howe out of New Jersey is a significant achievement for you...patriots."

"You almost said 'rebels,' didn't you? From your accent, I judge you to be American?"

"Yes to both. I was born near Albany. Habits of speech can trip us so."

"Yet you stand with the oppressors?" said General Ward.

"I stand with my husband, sir." She flashed a warning edge in her voice and then sheathed it again. "I do deplore this war. I have seen too much of it in my life. I'm also not convinced of the necessity of it. We agree, I think, that Americans had righteous complaints of mistreatment by the government, but I remain unconvinced that all constitutional means had been exhausted before Lexington."

"But now, since that day, are not constitutional questions moot?" asked Gereral Ward. "Once the fuse was lit, by whom is immaterial, is there any way to put the powder back in the keg?"

"Moot is probably a good word for it, General, but I'm not at all sure about immaterial. The country was already whipped to enthusiasm by the incendiaries of the mob. London was intoxicated by hubris. Good reason had already fled not to be seen again while armies are in the field."

"Incendiaries of the mob? Did I hear my name called?" A passing gentleman stopped to join the discussion.

"Sam!" said Mercy. "Allow me. Mrs. Brush, Mr. Sam Adams. Sam, Mrs. Margaret Brush. Don't be so thin skinned, Sam. I'm sure Mrs. Brush was not referring to you specifically."

"I recognize Mr. Adams, though we had never been before introduced. Truth be told, sir, I was thinking of you. You do have admirable skill at exciting an audience. I confess I wish you had had other aims than you did. How do you find governance, now that you have the reins?"

"Lo, Mercy, you have found an honest woman! In truth, madam, I find selling apples not nearly as much fun as upsetting the cart. All these voices, pulling first this way and then that makes one wish for a corrupt royal governor and his circle of sycophants!" He winked at Margaret. Everyone laughed.

"Mr. Hancock, you are a merchant. Was it not to your advantage that your ships sailed under British colors and had protection of the Royal Navy?"

"A small one, madam, but more than offset by the fact that there were hundreds, nay thousands of ports to which we could not go. The fellows in London reaped the great profit by importing goods and then re-selling them to us, a captive market, thereby engrossing several hundred per centum. I see James approaching with your Madeira. It would cost him only half as much if we could fetch it ourselves from Iberia."

"But what of manufactures? Don't we import our iron, gunpowder, glass and furniture because we are unable to make it here as well?"

"We did, largely because the law required us to. We have already begun our own powder manufactories, the skill of iron will come, so will the glass. It is far cheaper to import a cabinet maker than a year's worth of his work. We're not wanting in the raw materials."

James Warren joined them, a glass in each hand. "Your madeira, ladies. Come, there are others I would like you to meet. Gentlemen, will you excuse us? You can't be allowed to monopolize the lovely ladies."

The Great Carry, NY August 1760

The five of them, Margaret, Sally, Fanny, Hannes and Christian were walking the road from Lake George to Fort Edward. It had been three weeks since they had left Quebec. The summer months, with their fresh vegetables and meat on Isle d'Orleans had restored them. Fanny had grown. They had followed the army through subdued but hostile territory up the St. Lawrence to Montreal, where by a miraculous bit of timing, three armies that had travelled thousands of miles on different paths had all arrived within two days of each other. Montreal was doomed, French Canada was doomed. Quebec to the east was sealed. To the south a second advancing army had rolled up the forts on the Richelieu River from Lake Champlain. The largest army of all had come through Oswego and down the river to bar any flight to the west: there could be no new capitol established at Detroit to command the Great Lakes, connected and supplied via the Mississippi to New Orleans. There could be no escape. The French army, the only French army, was trapped. It had taken only two days of negotiation to draft the capitulation of half a continent. The war had been over.

They had walked a few miles to the little village of Chambly, on the Richelieu, where Christian found some of Col. Bradstreet's para-military batteau-men with whom he had served for three years and had gotten them passage on a boat returning to Ticonderoga for supplies. With Hannes and Christian as two of the six oarsmen, the women and baby resting comfortably in the stern, they had rowed up the river, past the burned forts at St. Jean and Isle aux Noix and into Lake Champlain. They had stopped for a night at the ruins of Fort St. Frederick, blasted to rubble by the retreating French, partly to deny it to English use, partly from spite; the enemy simply could not have it.

They were welcomed by the men at Crown Point, the little English fort new-built beside the ruins, for they were among the first to bring news of the

68

capitulation southward, and men were glad to exchange a meal for news of it. From there it had been a half day to Ticonderoga at the south end of the Lake. Now they had entered the theater of the war that had dictated their lives for the last five years. Christian had made this part of the journey dozens of times as supplies and men were ferried northward. Margaret had thought Lake Champlain the most picturesque place she had ever seen. The tiny islets of Lake George, their rocky bases showing between the crowded trees, had made her revise her estimate. An afternoon squall had driven them ashore at Sabbath Day Point, where in 1757, 400 men were massacred while the survivors could be counted on a widow's fingers. They had rowed through the ensuing moonlit night down the calm lake to Fort George at the southern end.

A brief nap, then daylight had awakened them to the ruins of Fort William Henry, where those who had survived the surrender and that massacre had been chased naked down this same road to Fort Edward. It was here that Hannes and their brother Lawrence had fought in the only meaningful victory of the early war in 1755, here that Hannes had labored to build William Henry and a half dozen other smaller strong points, designed to protect the communications with Albany, fifty miles to the south. They were travelling the invasion route from Albany to Montreal or the reverse, and for some years, it had appeared that the French would be the ones to make use of it.

Margaret wiped some sweat from her forehead. It was a hot day.

"Hannes, you were a soldier, what does a soldier do if he is given a bad order by his officer? Must he obey it?"

"It depends. Is he militia or regular army?"

"Does that matter?"

"Oh yes. A militia man would simply refuse, or ignore it. If he could find enough fellows who agreed with him, they would elect a new officer. If he couldn't do either, he'd just leave for home. A regular, on the other hand, has few choices, none good. He could obey and be damned by God, or refuse and be hanged by his officer. He could desert, but it's harder for a regular to do. He is in conspicuous uniform and doesn't know the country well. He sticks out and there will be a reward on his head.

"Is this the question that has had you in a brown study all summer? Whether or not a man must always follow orders? And what's a bad one?"

"A bad one would be, say, to turn out a widow into the cold of December, to burn up a church filled with orphans, something that repels the soul.

"I've been thinking of something the Mother Superior said to me. How do we know the thing we plan to do is the right thing? I mean, how can we know that we are doing a good thing? Anything may seem so, but our knowledge is imprecise. I thought following Montraville was a good thing, yet it placed all our lives in peril. Everyone must be able to produce a hundred such cases; how can we be certain?"

"Think of your life when you began to follow. You were a young widow with no money coming in except the uncertain pension, no place to live, unless you elected to come back to Schoharie. That would have been a waste after all of your training, and you wouldn't have fit in there anymore anyway. Following him was not a perfect situation, but it was better than other choices you had then.

"As for being certain, we can't be. Don't all of those books you read give you a hint? Can't all of those friends of yours, who have read so many?"

"No, all they can do is dress the question in a fine waistcoat and send it to a ball. Bookish sorts are wonderfully good at raising questions, blessedly poor at answering them. Listen, Hannes, you're a carpenter. There must be times when you're building, that you could put a brace here or a timber there, but you do it this way instead of that. How do you choose?"

"You do what you think is best for the way the owner wants to use the building. There is seldom a single answer for how it should be done. Dozens of ways could work. You build it the best way you know. Perfection is God's province, not ours. I'm not sure that right and wrong lie in our territory either. Maybe we should just try to do the best we can."

"You should write books."

"Fat chance of that! Besides, if you hadn't followed Montraville, you wouldn't have this little one." He extended his finger to Fanny, riding in a sack on Margaret's back. She made happy baby noises, wrapped her little fingers around his, pulled it toward her mouth. "Surely, she is a good thing?"

70

Albany, August 1760

"Margaret, my dear, it is so good to see you! Come, give us a kiss. Is this the little one? Why, she's the image of you." Margarite Schuyler rose from the chair in her parlor to pinch Fanny's cheeks.

"And wonderful to see you as well, Aunt Schuyler. It is unspeakably good to be among friends again."

"Do let me hold her." She turned to Hannes and Christian, "Gentlemen, thank you so much for returning the prodigal. I imagine she was as refractory as ever. And who is this one?"

"Aunt Schuyler, this is my girl, Sally Fitzgerald, another widow. We have been together for three years now. She's wonderfully inventive; I could not have survived Quebec without her."

"I'm pleased to meet you, Sally, and you have my thanks as well. Boys, do you remember the kitchen? Good. Refresh yourselves there, we'll figure where to bed you all later. I'll hear no talk of your not spending the night after your journey. Now, Margaret, sit, and tell me of your adventures and what you will do now."

"That's just it, Aunt Schuyler, for months my plan was to get to Albany. Now I find I don't know what to do, much as when I came home the last time."

"No matter, just as the last time, I have the plan for you. Do you remember Colonel Bradstreet? Well, he's setting up household here. He needs a proper woman to run it, and his wife refuses to come closer than Boston, even finds that too raw for her sensibilities. You're just the one he needs."

"Of course, I remember him. He came to Kitty Schuyler's often. An agreeable fellow. Will he have me?"

"He came to Kitty's far too often according to the gossips around here! He's coming to dinner today, so are Phillip and Kitty. I shall propose the match. Now," looking Margaret up and down, "You and Kitty look the same size still...Annetje..." she called to the girl who materialized beside her, "Run to Mrs. Phillip Schuyler, tell her that Mrs. Margaret Soumain will be joining us for dinner today. She has just arrived in town without her baggage, and needs a proper dress. Ask her to send one directly, and return with it. And set another place for dinner. Margaret, leave Fanny with me, I get to be the grandmother for an hour. Wash the road off you and get ready for dinner. Annetje will be back in time for you to dress."

Albany, March 1765

"Mrs. Soumain!"

"Yes, General Bradsteeet?"

"I think a dinner is in order. Would Tuesday be convenient?"

"Of course, sir, as you wish. For how many shall I plan?"

"I think eight, and you must count yourself as among them."

"Thank you, sir. Who shall there be?"

"The usual lot. Kitty Schuyler will be coming of course, what with her husband still in England. Mayor Douw and his wife, Sheriff Schuyler and his. Then there'll be a fellow from New York, an Irishman named Brush. A lawyer, sits in the Provincial Assembly. Kitty recommends him. He's in town on some sort of business for the Governor, and Kitty insists that he must not find us all barbarians."

"I shall then leave the hominy fried in bear grease off the menu. Have you any preferences? And how many courses shall there be?"

"Please do that! Lord, how do you think of these abominations? Five courses, I think should suffice. We may not be savages but neither are we kings! I'll trust your judgment on the menu."

"Very good, sir."

"No bear grease. Oh— Mrs. Soumain? Lay in some more port—the last bottle seemed a bit off."

"Certainly, sir."

✶✶✶✶✶

Eight, she thought, *is an awkward number for dinner.* No matter how divided, there were unequal numbers of each sex in the side chairs. The General took the head, of course, and she the foot. Kitty Schuyler sat to his right, even though she ranked far higher than did Margaret. By rights Kitty deserved the end of the table but the symbolism would not be lost on the gossips of Albany. Crean Brush sat to Margaret's right. Mayor Douw was to the host's left, his wife was at Margaret's. *Ah the protocol of seating!* Poor Sheriff Schuyler sat sandwiched between his cousin and Mrs. Douw, who seemed never to run out of words, just the thoughts behind them. His wife sat across and Margaret felt badly for her. The Mayor, despite being a good conversationalist when by himself, was notorious for his silence when his wife was present. Mr. Brush did his best to engage the ladies to either side.

"Tis true, Mrs. Schuyler, that the Irishman has a reputation of fondness for the bottle. It cannot be gainsaid. I think, though, that his defining characteristic is not bonhomie, but a sort of melancholy. Before we condemn him as a worthless lout, let us examine his life. On my farm near Dublin, he lives with 100 of his brothers and cousins, and their numerous families. After the home farm is deducted, that leaves well less than three acres for him to till. From this he must scratch a living for more children than any man should have. Suppose, unlikely as it is, that he arises early and goes to his patch. By noon there is nothing left for him to weed; he had pulled them all yesterday in any case.

"He returns to his hovel, which he has not the wherewithal to repair. He and his poor exhausted, harried wife either stare at each other in boredom or they make another child. Or they get drunk to pass the day and then make another.

"Mr. Brush!" injected Mrs. Schuyler, blushing. "Such talk!"

74

"Apologies madam," He glanced at Margaret and was relieved to see that no apology was necessary. "The root problem is that there are just too many of them and too little for them to do. Would that Ireland could export some to the colonies, but they will not go. They are devout Catholics, and the village priest reminds them every week that it would be a sin to abandon their homes. The ignorance and folly of an Irish priest cannot be exaggerated. Many are barely literate."

"You are not of that faith, Mr. Brush?" asked Margaret.

"No, I'm a Church of England man, myself. My family, you see, has only been in Ireland for 100 years, about as long as many have been here. They came at the request of Cromwell during the Protectorate, colonists, really, just as some came to America."

After dinner, she took his arm as they proceeded to the parlor.

"Will you be returning to your farm someday, sir?" she asked.

"God willing, no. Ireland has too many unhappy memories. I'm a widower, you see, Mrs. Soumain. My dear wife died of childbirth and I did not take it well. In truth, I became as morose as my Catholic countrymen. I ran to the sunshine of New York."

"What of the child?"

"My daughter is there, she's just six years, yet I scarcely know her. My wife's family could not bear to part with her, so she stays with them. My wife's brother manages my property. The proceeds go to my daughter's support. In truth, when I left I was not fit to be a father." Self reproach hung in his speech.

"I can't imagine being separated from my daughter." She patted his arm. "It must be awful."

"You have a daughter, Madam?"

"Yes. In fact, I must abandon you in a few minutes to see her to bed. I hope you'll excuse a brief absence?"

"Of course...Mrs. Soumain...I know I ask too much, that I would be intruding, but might I help...put a daughter to bed?"

*****

She sat alone with Mr. Brush in Kitty's parlor. This was the third time this week they had dined. He had been coming to Albany every month since spring. Kitty always insisted that he stay with her. She and the General had vanished into the house somewhere.

"I feel slightly awkward when they do that," he said.

"You do know you and I are just here as a blind to silence the tongues in town?"

"Is Mr. Schuyler going to burst through a door and demand satisfaction?"

Margaret laughed. "No. He's in England, and she has as many grounds for complaint as he might. They have an understanding."

Changing the subject, "Your name is very unusual, Mr. Brush."

"It is. I invented it."

"Sir?"

"In Ireland it is spelled C-r-a-n-e. It's an old family name. I found no one here could pronounce it correctly, so I jumbled the letters to help them."

"Successfully?"

"Not really."

"Say it."

"Crean." She listened closely.

"Again."

"Crean."

She sifted through vowel sounds in her mind. "There's nothing quite like it in English…Crean," she tried. "No… " She tried again.

"Crean."

"That's it! I think I shall have to marry you. You're the only person on this continent who can say my name!" He planted an enthusiastic kiss on her cheek. "I hope that was not too forward..."

"Mr. Brush," she said gravely, "You missed the mark. Allow me to demonstrate." She put a hand on his cheek and corrected his aim.

A silent moment later. "Wait! Were you serious?"

"Mrs. Soumain, I have never been more so."

She examined his eyes.

"I think, Crean, that a gentleman should address his future wife by her Christian name."

"I agree, Margaret."

They smiled at each other and there was another long silence.

Boston, January 1778

"Come, Margaret," said Mercy as she led her guest away from Mr. Hancock, General Ward and Mr. Adams. "There are more people I wish you to meet." They joined another group standing near the fireplace, glasses in hand.

"Margaret, may I present Mr. Elbridge Gerry and his wife Ann Gerry, and Mr. Francis Dana? Elbridge, Ann, Francis, may I introduce Mrs. Margaret Brush? Mr. Dana is going to join Mr. Gerry in representing Massachusetts in the Continental Congress."

"A pleasure, Mercy, Mrs. Brush. We were just discussing the form of government we should have after this war. Surely it must be a republic of some sort, but who will electors be? The mob is unqualified for the job, clearly."

"How can it be limited?" responded Mercy. Have they not suffered as much as we, perhaps more than we?"

"In some cases, yes. But the functions of government require judgment, and many of the mob do not have that. They are better educated here in Massachusetts than other colonies, and I would shudder to trust matters to their vote. Their heads are turned faster than a boy's at a female seminary. Any demagogue can lead them into madness."

"Be careful that you do not condemn yourself, Francis." Mercy responded. "I expect some in New York would accuse you of that which you decry."

"I think the hard nut shall be the relations of the various colonies to each other and to the united government. Ignore for a moment how the delegates are to be selected. How do tiny colonies like Rhode Island sit at table with monster Virginia comfortably? May the national government tax?"

"It must, I fear. The lessons of the last war should not be forgot. King and Governor appealed for money, men and materiel; colonies responded if they felt threatened, otherwise dithered for years. No effective government can operate on such a system."

"We hear that we cabal to establish a new monarchy—that General Washington would make a suitable king!"

Margaret spoke for the first time, "I think not. The man I knew would never accept a crown. He would find the very idea reprehensible."

"You <u>know</u> General Washington?"

"I did. We wintered together at Fort Cumberland during the old war. There were only two ladies with the garrison, we were ever so popular. We messed with him frequently. Men can change over the years, but not, I think, on something so fundamental to their character.

"Besides, a monarchy, even a constitutional one, would make a mockery of all you have espoused for a decade. Your people, the 'mob' would not tolerate it, not for long, and then you'd be back where you are today, except weaker. But I do agree with Mr. Dana that your proposed government must tax. I think you need to consider your future position. You will be assuming a place among the community of nations, and you must behave like one or the others will certainly try to annex you in one way or another. You would make this continent a seat of constant warfare, as Europe is.

"But even more critically, you are now engaged in a civil war and they are of the worst variety of a very bad thing. People are hurt, in mind, body and property. My husband and I have been impoverished. Many good folks of all philosophies have as well. My firmest wish is that it should end. It has pitted brother against brother, friend against friend. One of my brothers and his sons all fought for the King at Saratoga. Another of my brothers and two sons of yet a third fought there with General Gates. The brothers were close through childhood, there being only a few years difference in their ages. Now they would shoot each other at sight. I expect that you could give similar cases.

"I have heard you discussing the form of government you wish to establish. It is right that you should give that serious thought, but right now, today, you should be concentrating on how to win this war if you can. To ignore the

79

question of today is to ignore those you ask to sacrifice in you armies. In my experience, men in the field have a very low opinion of legislatures. They suffer bad food, late pay and supply shortages while you debate philosophy. All the philosophizing in the world will be meaningless if those men do not succeed."

"You say you want the war stopped, yet you urge us to support the army?

"You are engaged in a war. You must give it your best efforts, or get out of it. There is no middle ground."

"Things are never as simple as they may appear. A close examination reveals all sorts of conflicting interests."

"I would suggest, Mr. Gerry, that things are rarely as complex as some wish to make them."

"You are a friend of the Crown, correct?"

"My husband is an officer of the Crown. I go where he goes."

"Have you no personal preference?"

"Have you ever met a lady who did not, sir? The mystique of a woman is that she will not tell you what it is!"

Albany August 1765

Margaret sat at her dressing table, her hands shaking slightly as she prepared for the ceremony. "Blast it! Kitty, come help me with this comb. I simply cannot get it right."

"That's because you're as nervous as a young girl. One would think you'd not been married before! Crean is pacing about downstairs like an anxious father-to-be! General Bradstreet is cooling his heels at your door to escort you down, the minister is just arrived. I think Fanny is the only sane one in your family!"

"You and Sally are the only calm ones, certainly. It's good that Fanny is so fond of Crean, isn't it. Has she been dressed?"

"Stop fretting. Sally will have her ready in good time. You know Crean dotes on her, he's already talking of tutors and dancing masters and who knows what else when you get to Manhattan. Speaking of Fanny, turn around, Margaret, your little flower girl has arrived."

Five year old Fanny walked carefully in to the room, her natural ebullience subdued by the most gorgeous dress she had ever worn. She looked up at her mother, her blue eyes wide.

"Mama, you look beautiful!"

"Thank you dear, I believe I shall be the second prettiest girl there. Now, come sit my lap for a minute. Do you know your part for today?"

"Yes Mama, I'm to walk in front of you and the General, then stand beside you while the minister talks and not fuss if he says too much. Then we shall have a party."

"You do have the important parts! Fanny, you do know that just because Mr. Brush joins our family that I love you no less?"

"Yes, Mama. At the party, may I call him Papa?"

"Well," Margaret's eyes were moist, "I think you shall have to have a serious, grown-up conversation with him about that, but I suspect that he will not mind."

Boston, January 1778

It was late. James, Mercy and Margaret were sitting in the Warren's library as the servants cleared away the orderly debris of a successful evening.

"That was a lovely dinner, Mercy. I had a wonderful time. Your friends are all such interesting people."

"I hope you understand now that we are not all foaming-at-the-mouth regicides?"

"Yes, I confess that my estimation of 'patriots' has risen these last weeks. I find that, among the better sort, there is only a sliver of difference between a loyalist and a patriot. The sliver of independency is a very sharp one. I don't think that a person can be persuaded one way or the other by logic. It is a passion that grips the gut, not to be shifted without physical effort."

"I didn't realize that you knew General Washington! Are there any more surprises?"

"Well, my first husband was a lieutenant in General Horatio Gates' company. He was a captain then. Colonel Browning, from General Washington's staff, was my husband's best friend. His wife was the other lady at Fort Cumberland. General Gage was there for a time too, a Colonel.

"Is that how Mr. Brush came to be attached to General Gage, through you?"

"Not really. He sat in the New York Assembly and was heavily involved in the disputes with New Hampshire about the conflicting land grants on our eastern border. He came to know the General in that way."

"How came you to Boston?"

"When the New York Assembly adjourned in 1775, he felt it a duty to report, to offer his services. He is Irish born and feels a strong attachment to the Crown."

"He certainly was assigned the most odious of duties, the seizing citizens' goods!

"My husband knew he would be unpopular but felt duty bound. He also knew that some men were overzealous in their duties. He did all he could to control them, but it was not always possible. He was under orders to do as he did."

A knot in the fire popped and they all watched the flames for a moment.

"I noticed that while you asked questions this evening, you did not dispute the answers. Was everyone so convincing?"

"No, but consider my position here. I am, legally, a prisoner of war. Now I know and deeply appreciate, Mercy, that you and James have been more than kind, and I think of you as friends, and I hope you feel the same way about me. But I am, nonetheless, bound here. It is not my place to try to persuade you or your guests of errors. It is better that I should try to learn and understand.

"Consider Mr. Hancock. He lamented that ports of Europe were closed to him, and they were, if he chose to land his cargo at Boston. Yet we all know as much passed through other small ports without any duty and no questions asked. He made good profits from smuggling, as have most merchants here. That Madeira you're sipping is probably illegal and James wouldn't have saved a schilling if he had bought it through regular channels. The evening's entertainment would not have been improved had I mentioned that to him then."

"James, you would not ply our guests with smuggled brandy, would you?"

"Never, my dear!" said James Warren innocently.

"As for Mr. Gerry and Mr. Dana, I am not competent to advise them, other than to say what they must know full well, that any attempt at monarchy here would certainly fail. Inventing a government must be breathlessly exciting, and difficult.

"Something I have come to understand lately is that there is not a clump of identical people here, rebels all, and another clump over there, all loyalists. It is like Isaac Newton's rainbow, a spectrum of people. Over here," she held her hands apart like an angler describing the fish he failed to catch, then looking from hand to hand, "you have the zealots, motivated by vengeance and old grudges as much as anything, wishing death and desolation to any who do not fully agree with them.

"Here," she moved her hands to shoulder width, "you find folks such as we; who have different ideals, but respect those of the other. And we understand that this country, however it is structured, will require all of us." She looked at her left hand, and moved it an inch or so further left. "Perhaps Mr. Adams is more here."

They all laughed.

"But here, in the center," she made circular motions with her hands, palms upright, "Is the great mass of the people. They just wish the whole business would just go away without harming them. They just wish to plant their wheat and milk their cows and raise their children."

"Margaret, what do you see as the outcome of this war?" asked James.

She hesitated. "What I say will not leave this room?"

The Warrens nodded.

"I think that if you can hold this rebellion together, it will succeed. The cost to England is simply too great for them to pursue it indefinitely. Now that France has joined you, England will be limited in the numbers of men she can spare. She will need to retain a sufficient force to repel any French landing on the channel. Every man of hers incapacitated will be irreplaceable. Right now neither Washington nor Clinton dares risk a pitched battle because either might lose, and that would decide the war. Washington dare not lose because he has only one army, and could never raise another. Clinton can't lose because he has the bulk of the British army here, and their defeat would leave the home island vulnerable to attack.

85

"This will continue as a war of attrition until the British public tires of it and demands it end. Until then it will be chase and skirmish and frustration. It's bloody and messy and unsatisfying, but it is effective, and General Washington fully understands this. I think that many here do not appreciate the man that he is. I have never met a British officer who was his equal. Remember that the best officers of the Army will not serve here; there is no glory in it for them. For that, an officer must go to the continent and fight Frenchmen or Austrians or whomever. Your Continental Army and militia are seen as a mob of peasants. If a man succeeds against them, then of course he should have. If he fails, he is damned and his career is over. Losing to such would bring ignominy.

"That, is what I think will happen."

The conversation began to lag as they all reflected on an enjoyable evening.

"I liked your image of the spectrum, Margaret. You have the soul of a poetess."

"A poor one! No one published anything I wrote, nor would they ever."

"Isn't it strange that we dismiss the abilities we have and envy those we don't?"

"Yes. I wish I could sing like my daughter. I just croak along like an old frog with a bad cold."

Seeing her glass empty, "Well friends, I think I shall call this a complete evening. Thank you again and good night."

"James still has a swallow of his brandy yet, I think I shall sit with him for a bit. Good night, my friend."

New York, April 1775

Crean Brush hurried into the parlor. His face was flushed, he was out of breath. Margaret and Fanny looked up from their needlepoint, alarmed. "Margaret, it's time. The Assembly has adjourned. These men will never meet together again. Isaac Sears and his cursed Sons of Liberty have the mob so worked up that it is impossible to get anything done. We have tickets on the morning Hartford coach. It's not safe for a loyal man here in the city any longer, nor for his family."

"But Papa, tomorrow is my birthday! We had a little celebration planned! Must we be so precipitous?"

"Yes, my dear we must. I was accosted on my way home by a gang of rowdies and you know what happened to Governor Hutchinson's house. Feeling runs higher now than it did then. I'll not have either of you in such danger. I'm sorry for your party; we shall have to honor your birthday in the coach child, perhaps at Norwalk or some such. Now you must both go and pack."

Margaret examined his face closely. "You are truly alarmed, aren't you." It was not a question.

"Yes." There was none of his accustomed Irish banter in the reply. "These damned rabble rousers will not moderate their tone. I fear the army will be soon called out to settle them, and once the blood flows, I know not what will happen, except that more will follow, and I'll not have it either of yours. Civil insurrections are a terrible business. We have seen some if this in Ireland, with the bodies of gentlefolk lying dead next to laborers and sailors, their families too. There is no longer any right or wrong, only foes and precious few friends"

Packing did not take long, the house had been rented furnished for the legislative season and most of their things had been sent ahead to the house in Westminster in the Hampshire Grants. Faithful Sally had seen to most of the rest.

Fanny came into her mother's room to find her dressing the edge of her dagger.

"Mama. What are you doing?"

Margaret set the stone on the dresser. "I fear you are fated to see a side of your mother that has lain dormant almost all of your life." She put her foot on the seat of a chair, hiked up her skirt and carefully slid the knife into a sheath strapped to her thigh. "I don't see any good coming of these troubles. Actually, I think there is a fair chance of civil war." She sat on the bed, patted a spot for Fanny beside her.

"Now, tell me, what was really so important about tomorrow?"

"Tom Lansing hinted he might call...Can you not get Papa to put off our leaving for just a day?"

Margaret shook her head sadly. "No, Honey. He is adamant, and he is right. Those are two things difficult to argue against. I was five years older than you when my war came and I know this will be very hard for you to understand now. Believe me, there is a lifetime between fifteen and twenty for any girl. I hope yours will not be as tumultuous as I foresee. Tom's parents may forestall visiting tomorrow at any rate. The streets are truly not very safe."

"But Mama..."

"No, Fanny."

Fanny opened her mouth to protest, but paused. "I'm whining, aren't I?"

"Just a bit, but you're quick enough to realize it. Many your age would not."

"Will Westminster really be any safer than here?"

"Probably. It's easier to assault someone you don't know than someone you've seen in church your whole life. Here in the city, there are clever men who can raise a mob for whatever cause they wish and there are many people you don't know. Our neighbors in the countryside tend not to be so clever."

"I think I'll go apologize to Papa." She rose and moved to the door.

"Fanny?" She paused as her daughter turned to face her. "I love you."

"I know. I love you too, Mama."

Boston, June 1775

This warm June night, Fanueil Hall was filled with officers in their best uniforms, ladies with their hair high and powdered, civilian gentlemen of the best sort. All the candles of Christendom lit the galleries and the alcoves beneath. The mirrored chandeliers reflected their light through the room. On the dais a string quartet played the latest of Haydn, interspersed with spritely dance tunes. The young danced in the clear center floor, their elders watched from the sides. There was no thought, at least for tonight, of the rebel army barricading the isthmus which connected Boston to the mainland. No quixotic rebellion would be allowed to dampen the celebration of this King's birthday.

News of lynchings in western Massachusetts had caused the Brush family to redirect their steps toward Boston instead of Westminster. People were sorting themselves by their persuasions. The disaffected were leaving the city, the loyal were moving in, neither felt safe in the minority. The British army held Boston secure.

"Why Mrs. Brush, it is so good to see you again! I had no idea you were in Boston!"

"It is good to see you as well, Mrs. Gage. We have been here for some weeks. We came just before that Lexington unpleasantness. How goes it with the General? Mr. Brush had an audience with him just the other day and said he seemed well but harried."

The two ladies had become acquainted in the years before while living in New York. Even though they had much in common, they had never become friends. Besides being American born and married to Crown officials, they shared a given name and even the same birthdate.

"I think that is an accurate description. These levelers in the country are a sore trial. God help us if those bumpkins ever start writing laws! The effrontery of them to even imagine that they could!

"Did your daughter come with you? What is she now, twelve or so?"

"No, she's a full fifteen. She's here tonight, there in the gallery, the blonde one by the third pillar, talking with those two ensigns."

"Oh isn't she a picture! I see the resemblance with her mother. She'll break the hearts of half the army if the boys aren't careful!"

"Ah, Crean, there you are. You remember Mrs. Gage? Mrs. Gage, Mr. Brush."

"Of course." A bow and a kiss for the proffered hand. "Lovely to see you again. I'm afraid I must drag you away, my dear, the General wishes to have Fanny presented. He's never had the pleasure, that he recalls. My apologies, Madam. Will you excuse us?"

Margaret glanced to the gallery to locate her daughter. The two ensigns had been replaced by a captain old enough to be her father. She tried to break away, but he held her firmly by the forearm. She looked pleadingly to her mother.

"Damn him! This will never do. Hurry, Crean."

"What is it Margaret?"

"Montraville."

His Majesty's Chief Engineer for North America was surprised to be shouldered aside by the two parents, their backs to him.

"Fanny, my dear, General Gage wishes to meet you, and introduce you to Generals Howe, Clinton and Burgoyne. You must go now. Mr. Brush, would you be so kind as to present her? I will have a few words with Captain Montraville."

"With pleasure." He paused, knowing his wife well enough to wonder for a moment if there might be bloodshed. "Won't you join us?" Margaret shook her head. Fanny took his arm and he whisked her way.

They heard her say, perfectly voiced so that they but few others could hear, "Thank you, Papa."

91

She faced him. "What are you doing John?"

"I wanted to see my daughter, Margaret."

"It's Mrs. Brush to you, Captain!" she snapped. She continued, her calm demeanor and soft voice so at variance with the import of her words that it disoriented him. "She is my daughter, John, not yours. Mr. Brush is the only father she has ever known. It has been he, not you, who has loved her and nurtured her and educated her. For fifteen years you pretended that she did not even exist. Now that she has become the beautiful young woman, you want to swoop in and take credit? Not in this lifetime! Stay away from her, John or I will tell the world of your deeds in Quebec." Her voice became threatening. "I have never told anyone, but I will. The rebel papers will love to spread tales of your barbarous behavior. Have you forgotten that you tried to murder her in the womb? They'll love to tell of a British officer so brutish—such wonderful propaganda they will spread. You'll not have a friend between Florida and Nova Scotia."

She saw his color rising. "Allow me to save you from some troublesome thoughts, John. While I know that while you would not do the deed, I also know you are not above suborning murder. Know then that there are several sealed letters distributed among friends throughout the Colonies, to be opened in the event of my untimely death. The story is contained within, and you are named as my murderer. Wish me long life, John."

She turned her back and went to rejoin her family.

"Is that him?"

"Yes, Fanny. I'm sorry you had to meet him that way. Are you all right?"

"I think he raised some bruises on my arm. With long sleeves, no one will notice. You know, I used to wonder what he was like; no more." She hugged Crean's arm closely. "You are my only Papa, and I would not have it any other way. Now, let's go meet some Generals."

*****

"Ah! Brush, there you are." Thomas Gage was feeling expansive. "Gentlemen, May I present Mr. Crean Brush, his wife Margaret and this must be their daughter Frances. I say, Brush, it must be pleasant to be among such fetching creatures daily!

"Brush has been handling a particularly touchy project for me, sequestering military stores belonging to rebels but located in storehouses within the city. It has not brought him popularity, but does come with my thanks. I commend him to you gentlemen should you require a discreet and loyal man."

"Tell me, Brush, do you give receipts for these goods?" asked General Burgoyne.

"Yes sir, I was bred in the law. Everything is quite regular."

"Then I should think the signature of a King's officer would be quite as satisfactory as a bank note! But can these bumpkins even read it?"

"Actually, sir, literacy is quite common here, more so than in England, I believe."

The press of those seeking an audience moved them along. Margaret saw a young fellow waiting for Fanny to be liberated.

"Fanny, would you care to go make some friends more your own age?"

She called "yes" over her shoulder as she took the boy's arm.

"When I find out which of her tutors showed her that thing with the fan, I'll half his pay!"

Margaret flipped her fan open and peeked coquettishly over it. "Why, Mr. Brush, whatever do you mean?"

"Oh—You too? We shall have to continue this conversation at a later time."

"You are a wicked, wicked man, Mr. Brush"

"And you are a saucy wench."

"As you say, M'lord."

93

The quartet began to play a new piece. He extended his hand, "Shall we?"

She smiled and placed her hand lightly upon his. "We shall."

They began the minuet, that most elegant and graceful of dances. As she honored the bystanders she caught a glimpse of Fanny smiling. She winked back.

*****

Later the three walked home in the dim glow of the new whale oil street lamps. There had been a summer shower during the ball, the wet cobblestones shone with the low reflected light of a rising full moon. Fanny had a parent on each arm. "Hold tight on your side Crean, I fear she will float away if we lose our grip!"

Crean said. "Well, Fanny, I take it that you enjoyed yourself tonight?"

"Absolutely Papa! There are some very nice young men in this army who are wonderful dancers, and witty besides!"

"The girl is introduced to not one but four generals in an evening, is petted and caressed by them all, yet what she recalls are some young fops who turn a pretty minuet! Whatever is to become of us."

"I suppose I will tell my grandchildren about meeting them. That General Burgoyne is a dashing fellow."

"So, of these young ones, did any strike you?"

"Yes Mama. His name is Tom Jennings, an ensign in the 43d Regiment of Foot. He asked if he could call, and I told him yes. I hope that is all right—I hope you'll not ask him a lot of questions and embarrass me."

"I think you'll find that your Aunt Sally will be hovering about, being very careful to keep you all well supplied with tea and biscuits. She'll know more about him than you by the end of the assignation! When is he coming?"

"It's not an 'assignation' Mama—oh, do say she won't! Papa, say something!"

"Not even those four generals would get involved in this, and I applaud their judgment."

*****

They were awakened by the sound of cannon-fire.. One of the warships had dropped down to begin shelling the rebels building fortifications atop Breed's Hill over in Charlestown. Sally had found a hatch leading to the flat roof of their rented house. One at a time they had climbed the rickety ladder leading up from the attic. From there they could see the rebels, barely a mile away. The British troops were loading into boats at the commercial wharf to be ferried across. They saw them form just a half mile from where they stood. They watched as the first ranks advanced toward the rebel lines, heard the first rebel volley that felled half the men approaching. They watched the Royal army retreat, reform and advance again, only to be decimated yet again by more disciplined musketry.

Margaret and Sally looked at each other, each recalling a summer's day sixteen years before.

"We'll go, Sally. Crean, you should get to headquarters. They'll need a man of your abilities there. Sally and I will go meet those returning boats. There are many wounded."

"I'm going with you Mama."

"No, Fanny, there will be things there that you should not see. It will be too raw. You are still too young."

"Mama, I coming with you. I can help."

Margaret looked at her daughter. "You always were a willful child."

"Mama, I know I can do something. Those brave men, they deserve all we can give them."

"However you may imagine the returning soldiers, this will not be it. There is nothing the least bit romantical about a defeated army, even less about wounded and defeated soldiers."

"Mama, I'm going with you."

95

A pause as Margaret considered. "Against my better judgment. If things become too much for you, you must tell me. What you're about to witness can scar you for life. You will tell me?"

"Yes."

"Stay close. Watch what I do, try to do the same. Keep talking, to them or to me, but keep talking. Can you?"

"Yes."

"Come then."

*****

The wharf was a scene of confusion. Some men labored to clear a space in the center, others were erecting tents for the surgeons. A group of them huddled near a corner.

"Dr. Dagliesh!"

"Mrs. Brush! Normally I would ask to what I owe the pleasure, but we are rather busy at the moment. This is no place for a lady!"

"Perhaps not, but it is a place for a woman. We are here to help you. We watched from our roof. I saw half a regiment felled in the first volley, more in the second. You perhaps do not realize the extent of the wounded. You need us"

"I don't think I can allow that. You have no idea what this place will become in just minutes! Things not suited for a female to witness."

"My servant and I have witnessed it twice already at Quebec. We know what must be done. We can sort the men as they arrive. That will save you valuable minutes on each case. Now, where are your loblolly boys setting up? Where is the surgery, what shall we do with the dead? You must deputize us so that the men will obey."

"This is most irregular." He paused as he sifted through objections. This damned woman was pertinacious, and right besides. "What will Mr. Brush say? You say you and your girl have done this before, but what of that one—she is only a child!"

"I am cursed with a very stubborn daughter, Doctor, Surely you know what that can be like. She will not leave. I will take the responsibility. Now, tell us where we should send the wounded, get to your surgery and we will send you your customers. Penetrating wounds and amputations to you, the rest to the assistants, the others somewhere you have not yet identified."

Thus began an exhausting afternoon. As directed, Fanny stayed close. Her gentle touch and youth had a calming effect on the men. After several hours among the groaning and shrieking wounded and among the silent dead, Margaret realized she had slipped away. Looking about, she found her a little ways off, holding a poor soldier's hand, assessing his injuries. Fanny brushed a strand of hair from her face and gave her mother a wan smile. Margaret nodded and smiled encouragement, proud of her daughter, yet worried of what she might yet encounter.

Toward evening, the influx of wounded slowed, then stopped, the open space began to empty. In the gathering dusk Sally came to her, her voice urgent.

"Fanny needs you. Over there."

She was sitting on the steps of a commercial building, her hands clasped between her wide-spread knees, staring at her blood spattered shoes.

Margaret sat beside her daughter. "Honey?"

"There's a wagon in the back. I saw it. Filled with mangled arms and legs. All sawed off. There's rows of dead men." Her voice came flatly, without emotion. "He died Mama, he looked at me, he smiled, and then he just...died."

"Who did?"

"Tom Jennings. I danced with him two weeks ago. Sunday, he came for tea. Now he's dead. I don't understand."

Margaret pulled her daughter close and waited for the tears to come. Finally they too passed. She sat silently, her head resting on Margaret's bosom. Dr.

Daghliesh approached. Margaret smiled and waved him away. He bowed his thanks. Margaret nodded back.

Fanny pulled herself erect.

"Is this what war is like? Mama, why do they do it? Why do men war?"

A deep sigh. "I truly don't know. Some do it for a cause, some for glory, some for money. Some surely do it because we women reward them for it. They are such craven creatures, men. They'll do almost anything if a woman hints she wants it. Think of how we fawn over the returning heroes ignoring those women among us who no longer have a hero to fuss about."

"God, I hate those damned rebels!"

"There is a girl, probably not ten miles from here tonight, cursing the damned redcoats, hating them for killing her man. Her grief is identical to your own. It is not a man who killed Tom, or that rebel fellow either, it is war that caused them to march and shoot, it is war that killed them both. It is war that makes women weep. It is such a terrible business yet we still do it. Fundamentally, no one can say why.

"Come. We're not needed here any longer. Let me take you home. You did well today, Fanny."

Fanny laughed mirthlessly. "Daughters are just as craven as men, it seems! When we get home, can I have some brandy?"

"You, who always hated the taste of it?"
"Today, I have learned that there are things I hate a good deal more."

Boston, January, 1778

Mercy waited, listening for the door to Margaret's room to close. At the sound, she turned to her husband. "I don't think I shall be able to complete my assignment. She is far too thoughtful to be easily swayed."

"Don't tell Mrs. Browning just yet, Mercy. Margaret is right that the difference between a loyal man and a rebel is a matter of faith, of emotion. Events may provide the epiphany that logic cannot. In the meanwhile, she is the second most delightful woman I have ever met. Her loyalty to a lost cause is rather poetic, don't you think"

"She isn't loyal to a cause, James; she's loyal to her husband. She'll not ask for new cards while he breathes."

Boston, March 1776

The weather and the mood fit each other well. The cold March rain blew in sheets across the wharf. The feeble light from a sliver of waning moon was obscured by the heavy clouds. A few wind-tossed lanterns lit the ship where men were loading confiscated goods for the voyage to Halifax. The British army was evacuating Boston. Rebels had positioned cannon on the Dorchester Heights and could now bombard half the city. After a short demonstration, General Washington had granted them a few days' grace to run before, he swore, he would level Boston.

Margaret reached up to caress Crean's cheek. "I hate this separation. You will be careful?"

Crean looked down at her. His tried to conceal the anxiety he felt. "It will be but a week or so. Lading will be done by morning, then we sail. We shall all be reunited in Halifax. You take a care as well."

A sailor's urgent voice came from the longboat waiting to take her out to the warship anchored in the harbor. "Hurry Ma'am, or we shall miss the tide! The captain will leave and we have orders!" She knew she would be the last to come aboard.

"Yes, just one moment."

They embraced. "I love you, my darling."

A gust of wind swallowed most of his throaty reply. All she heard was "...love you as well."

She hurried down the rain-slicked stone steps, A sailor's calloused hand guided her to the sternsheets. Orders shouted, the boat was underway. She turned to look up at Crean on the wharf, he blew her a kiss and then the storm swallowed him.

Halifax, April 1776

Sally hurried between the rows of tents, her face distressed. She was surrounded by loyalist refugees; more than 3000 civilians had been deemed important enough to rate transport in the evacuation fleet. Thousands more who had requested it were not. The tents stretched off nearly to the harborside. Hundreds of tents, thousands of civilians, living where there had been nothing but stunted cows a week before. The army was good at this. Latrines had been dug, tents erected, food distribution organized, medical tents set up, all with impressive speed, and all under martial law.

She burst through the tent flap. "Ma'am, Mr. Brush has been captured! It's here in this Boston newspaper!"

Margaret snatched the paper and quickly scanned through the article. *The notorious Crean Brush...brig Elizabeth surrendered after exchange of gunfire...gallant Commodore Manly...taken to Portsmouth...sentenced to Boston jail...miscreant rightly deserved harsher...* She hadn't realized she had been reading aloud.

"At least he's not lost at sea," said Fanny, in a vain attempt to put a good face on events.

"True, knowing is better than not. I wonder what indignities those rebels may have heaped upon him. He hadn't much money with him, they'll have taken it all—I wonder if there is a way to get him food—prison fare is notorious."

"Poor Papa, he will not do well in a jail. But what will we do, Mama?"

"Rumor has it that the army will invest New York this summer. That makes sense—it's the old strategy to divide the colonies at the Hudson. All of us will go with them. Leaving us here would be condemning us to freeze. This place could not house us all by winter, and it will be far cheaper for the army to support us there. Once they capture the city, I suppose we will be able to find good rooms before the cold. Housing will be very dear, and soon food as well. I'll have to find a way to get him some decent food. Mr. Brush will have some pay coming. I think we'll be able to claim that, and I have money. We will have to live carefully to make it last. Not as bad as Quebec, is it, Sally?"

"No Ma'am. I think it would be wise if people somehow came to believe that Mr. Brush had the money with him. Surely it would be safer."

"You're right. Fanny, I know this will be strange to you. Your life so far has been so orderly and safe. For the next while it will be neither. In a village this size there are certainly cut-purses, ruthless ones who would slit our throats for what we have. Sally and I were in similar circumstances when you were born. I hope you will be pliant and follow our examples. For the short term, we are pitiful penniless women dependent on the army for our existence. We are playing a role, as in one of those theatrics you enjoy so. Can you do this?"

"I guess I can. Mama, I'm confused and frightened!"

"Good. There is plenty of reason to be. And cultivate that—you should react to things as a frightened girl would. That's your role. And you really must stop celebrating your birthday in such outlandish places!"

"Oh my, I had forgotten! Happy birthday Fanny, dear. You're sixteen!"

"Thank you, Aunt Sally. Just over a year ago I was dreaming about the splendid coming-out party this would be. It's turned out to be not so wonderful, but not one I will forget! I only wish Papa could be here too."

Boston, November 1777

She stepped to the single window of his cell in the old stone warehouse the rebels had turned into a jail. In the early November dusk, she looked across the wharves toward Boston harbor.

"Now, Crean, it is time. It must be tonight." She moved to the wall beside the door where no one could see and began to disrobe. "Here, take this. Now, listen. There is a boy holding a horse for you at the corner of North and Fleet streets. I gave him half of a pound note and promised you would give him the other half. Your name is Mr. Johnson. Here is your pass." She handed him a wine bottle. Take a deep drink, rinse it around in your mouth to give you a boozy breath. If anyone questions you, you are a reveler damning the Pope and Guy Fawkes. When you are out of this prison, sprinkle some on your clothes. The scent will convince them. Take off the dress before you pass the guards on the Boston neck. Get rid of it and the pass. If you are found with then later, they will condemn you as a spy. You know what to do from there. The Post Road is well marked. Here, take this purse."

"This is not right! I cannot allow this."

"We have had this discussion before, we will not have it now. You know you must, it is your duty. You are needed in New York, I am just another dependent mouth. Fanny and Sally need you there as well. Go. The guards here will be well into their whiskey jug; the citizens are already in the streets making fools of themselves. Kiss me, and go."

Crean Brush had been married long enough to know that there were times to argue, and that this was not one of them. He took the dress, kissed his wife and was gone. She listened intently for several minutes, hoping for what she would not hear. The jail and the streets were silent except for the sounds of celebration.

She surveyed the sparse room, the heavy wooden partitions, a couple of mattresses on the floor, a poor chair and a worse table. A necessary pot stood alone in one corner. She sighed and sat in the chair, laid her head on her arms, and began to wait the long night.

Book II

1778

The lilacs were blooming, a robin proclaimed his lust from a branch just outside the open window beside her. There were voices from the entry hall. Margaret looked up from her book, one of those penny dreadfuls Mercy wished she wouldn't read. The voices were familiar but strange. Who had come?

The hallway door opened. Margaret tossed aside her book and rose.

"Kate Browning! What are you doing here?" Then, seeing her friend's face, "What's wrong? Fanny?"

"No, no, Fanny is fine." She took Margaret's hands and led her to a settee. "Meg, please sit. I seem to be fated to bring my best friend the worst of news." She took a breath and steeled herself. "Mr. Brush has killed himself."

Margaret sat motionless, pale and silent. She heard Kate faintly, far away, coming closer.

"Meg? Can you hear me? Are you all right?"

"What happened?"

"I'm not totally sure. I've brought you a letter from Fanny." She handed over the thick packet. As Margaret broke the seal, a second sealed packet fell to her lap. She read the first.

Dearest Mama—

Papa has shot himself today. Aunt S. and I were in the kitchen, he was alone in the front room. We heard a shot, hurried in and found him. He had been angry with Gen. C. for not raising loyalist companies, but the last few days he seemed quite calm—his old self. He left three notes, For Aunt S., for you and for me. I am enclosing yours.

Aunt S.'s was filled with instructions. He had taken pains to ensure we were well provided. He had ordered wood and food for us, paid rent ahead. We will be well and comfortable for some time. Aunt S. has been wonderful.

To me, he expressed love and affection, apologized, but said it was something his duty required that he do. I don't understand. He was surely the best Papa a man could be, yet he betook himself from us.

I hope they will let you come to us. I do miss you so.

Your loving daughter

F.

She looked up at Kate. Plaintively, "I want my daughter."

"I can take you to her. It's why I came myself. Mr. Brush's death releases you. I brought the order from General Washington."

Margaret picked up the second letter and examined the seal. "It's from Crean," she said as she broke it.

My Dearest Wife

My only regret is that I shall not see you again in this life. I have come to realize that I must do this. The rebels will never free you whilst I live; the government here has no further use for me, for anyone other than abject servants. I am saddened that your sacrifice was in vain. I must redeem you from that terrible place. You deserve so much more.

108

I have provided for our daughter until you can come to her. Sally is ever faithful, a second mother to her, and she will be safe.

You have my most sincere thanks. You saved me, and now I must save you. Know that my heart is not troubled. I do so love you.

Your Husband, devoted unto eternity

Crean

Margaret wiped a tear from her cheek. "Did he know I was paroled?"

"Yes, I got word to them."

"How did you...the letters, they were through you?"

"Indirectly. We have much to discuss. Then Edward and I will escort you as far as we dare go. The last miles you will have to do alone, but I have a pass for you to use."

"Edward? Your son? I haven't seen him for, what, seven or eight years?"

"He's taken your release to the Commandant and should be here soon with your paper. He's twenty-two now."

"I'm overwhelmed. This is so much...when can we leave, I want to see Fanny...Mercy and James have been so kind...Has anyone been so loved..." She rose and moved to the open window. The robin, startled, stopped singing and flew away. She took a vicious pleasure in it. "I don't deserve it. Help me, Kate!"

"You know I will. We can leave whenever you are ready. We'll coach to Hartford, then, I'm afraid it will be horseback for us to the Hudson at Peekskill. Those roads are barely passable for a coach in August. We can't go further south; if I were to be captured, Richard would be compromised. You should go talk to the Warrens—they do know why I am here."

*****

Margaret dressed in the half light of dawn. It was the work of minutes to pack her few things into a single satchel. She found the Warrens downstairs, bleary eyed. Early mornings were foreign to them. They had barely time for greetings when the hoof beats, the rattle and creaking announced a coach at their door. A tall young man in the uniform of a Continental captain guided Kate out.

"Good Morning, all! It seems we shall have a gorgeous day for travel. Are you ready, Meg?"

"Will you be this chipper each morning for this trip?"

"Depend upon it. It's constitutional. It didn't bother you the last time we travelled."

"I was twenty years younger. I have since adopted the hours of civilized folk."

"No one has ever alleged travel to be civilized."

"I didn't realize the stage stopped here. James, do you have a sideline I was unaware of?"

"This one is ours till Hartford," said Kate. "I rented it in the name of the Continental Congress. The best part is that we get fresh horses at each stage. Two days to Hartford, imagine it!"

After a quick round of good-byes, thanks and promises to visit after the war, Kate and Margaret were handed in. As they took their seats, Edward passed a sheathed sword through the window "Mother, will you keep this safe for me? If any ruffians manage to get inside, you'll know what to do with them!"

"Aren't you riding inside?" asked Margaret. She noticed he carried a brace of pistols.

"Not today. Meg, you and I have much to discuss; but, until we are clear of the city, let us relax and enjoy the ride."

A cry and the crack of a whip and they were off, trotting bravely through the streets of Boston, boys and dogs running after, falling away to be replaced by others. Margaret felt quite regal as she watched the buildings pass. As they gave way to farms, one after the other, she turned to Kate.

"Now, Madam, will you explain to me how you are able to get letters in and out of New York? Does Fanny know you're a spy?"

"I'm not, really. And Fanny knows only that if she takes a letter addressed to a Mrs. Williamson in Eastchester to a certain store, it will find its way to you. Sometimes letters from Mrs. Williamson find their way to her."

"If you're not a spy, then what? A spy…"

Kate held up a hand. "Some thoughts are better left unspoken. Meg, over the next days I will tell you things that will literally put my life in your hands. I will do this because I trust you and I want you to help me."

"You want me to spy for you."

"I do."

"How many spies are in New York?"

"A dozen or two, that I know of. There are others. Probably as many as there are British spies in Boston."

"Will you ever tell me who?"

"No."

"Is Fanny is one of them?"

"She is not. Listen, Meg, I will never lie to you, but there are things I simply cannot reveal. When you touch on those, I will refuse to answer. Is that fair?"

"Very well." They rode in silence for a minute. "Were Mercy and James working at your direction?"

"Yes, at first anyway. They really did enjoy your company, you know. I wanted to remind you that there are good people in favor of independency; you already knew of good people who want reunion. I think too many loyalists judge us all by the behavior of the least of us. They then act as badly as do those, causing all patriots to judge all loyalists badly. There are lynchings and atrocities, humiliation, and dis-appropriation on all sides, and many of us detest them all. This new nation we're building needs all the ablest citizens together. You're one of the ablest citizens I know."

Kate let her friend digest this. Nearly a mile passed before Margaret spoke. "This leaderless democracy you're trying to build—in all of history it's never been done on such a scale, a whole continent. Is it not prideful to think it can be made to work?"

"It's exciting, it's fascinating, to watch brilliant men work through it. Rather humbling than prideful, I think. What is prideful is London thinking that they are the only ones capable of rule. You know they think we're all peasants. I think King George's reaction to us is fundamentally designed to put the servants back in their place."

"Does Edward know what you do?"

"He may have guessed, but he'll not be told—he can't be. Neither could Fanny."

There followed another long silence. They passed on between new-plowed fields, the scent of fresh earth and manure wafted through the open windows.

"Kate, have you noticed how many fields are being plowed by women and boys?"

"Yes. Where, do you suppose, are the men?"

"You're testing my spying, aren't you? The men, I suppose, are off to the war, or are never coming back from it. One farm in ten, do you think?"

"About that. You have a good eye."

Another long silence, the comfortable silence of long-time friends.

"All of my adult life, I have been following the army. I begin to believe that there can never be an end to conflict. It's all I've seen for so long. You and Richard were wise to chuck it and enjoy life at Yale College. Is he still doing Latin and Greek there?"

"He was, until lately. He wants to be back there again. So do I."

"Do you know what I want, Kate? I want this damned war ended. I'm sick of war, I'm sick of soldiers and soldiering, and I am sick to death of all they soldier for! I'm sick of widows and orphans and grieving mothers. I'm sick of men with half an arm or no wits.

"I just want to go up to my house in Westminster. There is a place there, you can stand on a hill looking over the river and see for miles. I want to stand there and watch the birds. In spring and autumn, the pigeons come in such numbers, thousands, thousands upon thousands. There are so many that when they pass in their silent flight their shadow is as cool as the shade of a stone wall. They flow in graceful curves as the flock follows the river. It's a minuet in the sky. I want to bounce a grandchild on my knee, I want to show him those birds. I want to grow roses. Will I ever?"

"Help me end this war, Meg. Then perhaps we can all see those birds. You can help make fewer widows and orphans, fewer maimed. You are quite wise enough to know how this war must end. Help me bring that end sooner."

"I don't know what to do, Kate! For the first time in my life, I simply don't know what I should do! Here I am a widow with more freedom to act than I have enjoyed for years, yet I feel incredibly constrained. Will I be dishonoring Crean's memory if I do this?"

"I never knew him well, but I do believe he was an honest and moderate man, the sort of man who would have eventually joined us himself had it been allowed. I think you know, Meg, but you're just not ready to hear yourself say it."

Margaret smiled thinly. "Perhaps." She turned to watch a woman pause from her plowing to wipe the sweat from her face.

Kate too turned to watch the world passing. The rhythmic sound of the horses' hoofs counted the distance. They rode in silence for another mile. The soft spring air carried the scent of wildflowers. It was a good road.

"What is it you would have me do?"

113

"You know people. You talk to them and they talk to you. I would have you tell me what they say, what they are thinking. The sort of words that come out of their mouths during normal conversation and what you think about them and about their words. I wouldn't want you to steal documents or poison the wells or anything like that, just carefully observe your surroundings and tell me those things that are important. Could you do that?"

*****

They ate their lunch under a tree in Westborough while the horses were changed. Mercy had sent along some cold chicken and biscuits and a bottle of wine in a hamper that had ridden on the floor between their feet.

"Aunt Margaret, you're very quiet today. Did we rouse you too early?"

"Well, Edward, I've been thinking of Fanny," she lied, "of how she's getting on."

They watched as a fresh team was hitched to their coach. The driver checked over his rig and looked expectantly toward them.

"I see the coach is ready," said Kate. We must be off. We need to make Sturbridge by nightfall."

"Do you have a favorite inn there?"

"We'll be staying at friends' houses, just as we won't be eating in any of these awful places along the way. Our passage must be as little noticed as possible."

*****

They had been riding a full hour before Margaret spoke. "Very well, Kate, here are my conditions. I'm not sure you will find them acceptable. I will help you, to the extent it will reduce the blood-letting. For instance, I will not tell you that a company is to forage in Westchester tomorrow so that you can send a regiment to ambush them. I would tell you if a regiment was being sent to ambush the company you were planning to send. Neither action would help end the war, only to kill people. I would tell you,

114

however, if I came to know that the army was in quarters for the winter, or that some general had been recalled.

"I want the war to end and I want the people to settle into peaceful employment. I believe that means there should be as little actual combat as possible. To that end I would be at your service."

It was now Kate who rode lost in thought.

"I think that would be acceptable. May we make a pact that the one may rely absolutely on the other's word? No lies, only omissions?"

The two friends searched each other's faces as intently as lovers, each praying to find no hint of deception. They nodded together, and exhaled.

"How am I to send to you?"

"Ah, that will take some time to explain." She rummaged in her portmanteau. She handed over a book, the cover worn from long use, a portion of the title 'Gulliver's' barely discernible on the spine. "Here, take this book, never lose it. Read the inscription."

Margaret opened to the title page and there read:

'To Margaret Schoolcraft
on the occasion of her eleventh birthday,
from her friend,
Margarite Schuyler.'

"Kate, I've never seen this book in my life! I've read it often enough, but not this edition. Yet, that is her hand!"

"I know. That is your treasured gift from your patroness. You've carried it with you always. We have some people who are wonderfully skilled. I gather getting the wear right was a challenge. I have the same edition of Gulliver. When you send a message, you will represent each word by three code numbers indicating the page, line, and word, separated by commas. I can then take my copy, find the indicated page etc, and the word you mean. No one will be able to read the message unless they know both the code and the correct edition of the correct book."

"But won't a message of all numbers look just a bit suspect?"

"It would, so that's why you will write a newsy sort of note, as between friends, with wide spaces around the text. It should be devoid of all personal reference, and it would not hurt to disguise the gender of both the sender and the recipient. Your hand is sufficiently masculine to protect you.

"Now then, I will give you two vials of a special ink, sympathetic ink, they call it. The first will be invisible when it dries. You'll put your numbers in the blank parts of the paper. The second vial will make messages from me visible. I'll show you when we get to Peekskill.

"Now, pay attention, dear student, we have only three days, and there is much to teach you. Never forget that this is dangerous. You could be hanged, as could I, if they could but catch me."

"That's why Edward is so armed—the coachman is probably not the regular driver either, is he?"

Kate smiled and shook her head.

*****

"Kate, this road is bloody awful!" She grunted as her horse stumbled. "Now I understand why we left the coach at Hartford. I shall be a very sore woman by day's end. Is all this escort really necessary?"

The two were riding stirrup to stirrup up a steep road, little more than a path through the wood. The dappled late spring sunlight filtered through the new-leafed trees close beside them. They were surrounded ahead and behind by a company of Continental cavalry.

"There's been a Tory band terrorizing folks around here of late. A regiment has been up here all spring, catching them one-by-one. You saw how some in that last village glared at us as we passed?"

"Are we really important enough to be so hated?"

"Symbolically we are, even though as people we're insignificant. If they but knew who I was, I'd be of value as a hostage to compromise Richard. Face it Meg, as women, we're seen only as a means to control our husband's

116

actions, as a tool to make them do as our enemies want, against their will. That's the only reason you were jailed in Boston, to make Mr. Brush return, even though he was under strict orders from General Clinton not to leave New York."

"Was he really? Even though the General would not employ him? I didn't know that!"

"Oh yes. He was watched, and he knew it. Clinton wanted him to know. He chose the only way he could to free you. It was very romantic, and very brave."

"You were always the romantical one, Kate. He more likely thought of the most practical method. I know he loved me, but he thought like a lawyer, and would have found a means to win his suit at law, through an appeal."

"Meg, I swear, sometimes I think you're positively cold-blooded."

✳✳✳✳✳

The little bell over the door tinkled as Margaret entered the book seller's shop on Murray Street. The place was dimly lit and had the comfortable smell of old books, of leather and glue and dust.

The old bookman himself sat behind a low counter, working his accounts. He was a dry wisp of a man with a receding forehead and a sharp nose. He looked up over his half-glasses and the light from the window shone on his bald dome. Strings of gray hair brushed his collar. "Good morning, Madam, Thaddeus Kimble at your service. How may I help you today?"

"I'm looking for Cicero's <u>De Re Publica</u>, in the Latin. A friend told me you might have such a thing, being so close to the college."

"Hmm, let me see. You know, I just the other day picked up a nice collection from Mr. Pine's people. Did you know him? Lovely man, almost kept me in business by himself. No? No matter. I don't see so many women reading the Latin. Most of the gentlemen students of the college prefer the English, so they can fool their professors, even though they can't. Now, let me see. I haven't gone through the whole lot yet."

He rummaged through a box on the floor behind him. "Here's a nice Latin grammar, might that be of interest?" He handed the book across to her and returned to the box. While he searched, mumbling "Cicero, Cicero," to himself, Margaret quickly opened the book and inserted a folded paper. Kate would know that she had arrived safely.

She waited until he looked up. "I'm afraid there's not a Cicero to be had, Madam. Would that grammar perhaps suit you?"

"So sorry, but I already have one that I'm used to. It's a 'the bear you know' sort of thing. Perhaps one of those gentlemen of the college might choose it?" She handed the book back. "Could you keep an eye out for a copy? I live just around the corner so it's a small matter for me to stop back from time to time to see."

"Certainly, always happy to help a true scholar. Might you be interested in my lending library?" He gestured toward the back wall of his shop, covered to the ceiling with bookshelves. "I keep most of the popular novels there for lighter reading, plus some histories and such. You can borrow a book for a week, one at a time. It's £2 the year, though for a scholar such as yourself, I could waive the fee."

"That sounds most attractive, Mr. Kimble, thank you."

"Fine, just enter your name here in the book and then you may select as you please."

She smiled and signed her name, 'Mary Stephens', bright and clear. Her hand didn't even shake.

*****

The knock at their door came in the early afternoon. They had been expecting it for days. All morning, soldiers, British and Hessian, had been arriving at their neighbors' doors, bearing an order from the Barracksmaster, an order requiring the residents to provide shelter and food for a certain number of men. Those men were arrived to claim their quarters. New York faced a serious housing crisis. A city of 25,000 before the war, it had grown. Those, rebel and loyalist, who had fled the occupation by opposing armies were more than replaced by the influx of loyalists from Charleston and Philadelphia and from the hinterlands of New York and New Jersey. The

118

25,000 soldiers exceeded the available barracks by thousands. Men were living in tents north of the city, beyond the Negro Burying Ground, but armies in tents do not long flourish. To exacerbate affairs, there had been a disastrous fire in winter that had destroyed a quarter of the city's housing. There was no room. An order had come from the military governor that the citizens would provide for his soldiers, in proportion to their means and the spaces in their homes. A week before, a gruff captain and a portly sergeant had inspected the homes in the neighborhood to determine how many men were to be assigned to each. Now their boarders had arrived.

There were two of them, fresh-faced ensigns, Mr. Litton and Mr. Lawrence. Young and dull and arrogant, they affected the latest London fashion, the languid drawl of the smart set.

The taller, more handsome one looked about, and with a sneer, "Here, this room, in the back of the house, is not acceptable. I wouldn't have my valet sleep here. Mrs. Brush, show us the others."

"There are no others. I do not believe, young man, that as an ensign, you even rate a valet. Should you have one, he may sleep in the barn. We have no animals to disturb him. This order," she waved the paper at him, "says merely that I must board you, it does not specify how. It does not specify that I must enjoy it, nor does it require that you enjoy it either. There are rules in my house, and you will obey them. I am twice widowed by officers ranking far higher than you. If you will accept that I know much of the army, we shall get on so much better. Are there any questions?"

"No," he replied, surprised, sullen and beaten.

"Very well then, gentlemen. Here are the rules. You are not permitted on the second floor under any circumstances. There will be no drunkenness. If you return here inebriated, you will sleep it off in the barn. You will eat when we do, or take cold rations. There shall be reasonable quiet between sunset and sunrise. My daughter and my maid are to be accorded the same respect that you accord me, the same as you would grant and expect of members of your own families. You will use the rear door. On those terms, we shall get on well. On other terms, you will find your stay here to be uncomfortable."

"Madam, I shall have you know that my grandfather is Sir James Litton. I shall not be ordered about by a colonial."

"That you refer to your grandfather tells me that you are of a junior branch of the family. You are a commoner, sir, just as I am. We are equals, you and I, except that this is my house, not yours. An Englishman's home is his castle and this one is mine. It may be less spacious than you might desire, but this room behind the kitchen, is warm, the roof does not leak. That, I think, is an improvement of your present situation."

*****

There was always a bustle around City Hall, the army headquarters. Governing the colonies, even though now reduced to a handful of seaports, seemed to require just as many men as it had before the war began. The lobby was filled with people, officers rushing to and fro on most important business, civilians of all ranks, rubbing shoulders with those they wouldn't acknowledge on a street, all seeking some favor. Margaret had been a weekly visitor for a month, joining the line of loyalist refugees who clogged New York, mostly begging for a position or perhaps a pension. She was one of the latter. The cost of everything was ruinous. Sally had once again reminded her that the household funds were being depleted far too quickly.

She found a seat on a narrow windowsill and waited. Her attention was drawn to an excited Hessian colonel, loudly repeating "*futter*" to a confused British colonel. With a sense of *déjà vu*, she entered the fray.

"Colonel, if I may," she put a hand on the Hessian's arm to interrupt him, "he wishes more fodder for his regiment's horses. The allotment given will sustain only half of them. I am Mrs. Margaret Brush, sir. I can translate if you'd like." She turned and repeated her offer to the German. One or the other might give a gratuity.

Fodder was only one of the Hessian's problems. The long list of complaints and requirements tested her vocabulary. The discussion had continued for nearly a quarter hour when she noticed the room had become silent; the soldiers all stood at attention. She turned to find herself facing General Sir Henry Clinton, commandant of His Majesty's Troops in North America and Military Governor of New York.

She curtsied. "Good Morning, Your Excellency. I am Mrs. Margaret Brush. Perhaps you might recall that we had the pleasure of meeting in Boston

120

several years ago. I have been seeking an audience, sir, to speak of my late husband's pension."

"Ah, yes. That would be Crean Brush? A regrettable thing about your husband, he was a useful man, and loyal. I gather you speak German, Madam?"

"Yes, sir. Also French and Dutch."

"I did not know you had returned to New York. You were held hostage in Boston, if I recall?"

"Yes, but with my husband's death, I was useless to them. They sent me packing overland. My family was here, I had to come to them."

Sir Henry turned to the aide who followed him everywhere. "Drummond, set an appointment for Mrs. Brush with Major Andre." He turned back to Margaret, "Mrs. Brush, I expect a woman of your proven loyalty would have no concern in describing conditions in that pestiferous city to him? He is my man for intelligence."

"No, sir, I would be happy to serve in any way I can." She was learning to control her face well. "About that pension, sir?"

"I shall have a man look into it for you, Madam."

*****

"Eyes front, Mr. Litton, if you please," said Margaret, as Fanny, standing beside him, reached in to place the requested sugar bowl on the table.

"Yes Madam. The temptations of nature are a terrible thing, are they not?"

"The temptations are not so terrible, sir. Yielding to them is. Indecorous response is deplorable. I will expect you to display more respect for Miss Brush another time."

Ungracefully, "Yes Madam, Miss, so sorry." He looked as if he had just been dressed down by his officer.

Later, as Sally was brushing out Margaret's hair for bed, "Oh-oh, a grey hair Ma'am."

"That comes from having a nubile daughter and a lecher in the same house. Pull it out."

"Mama, you were awfully hard on him tonight. He really is a nice fellow, and good looking too."

"Good looking or not, he had it coming. There's something unnatural in the way he looks at you. He was inspecting your bosom at close range; a gentleman would have been looking at your face. Men, especially young ones, tend to mistake the simple kindnesses of a girl for affection. Do be careful around him, Fanny."

"She's right, Miss Fanny, Sometimes, when you're not looking, I swear I've caught him drooling. I don't like him. His friend is as bad, just more timid. He'd follow Litton into hell for a basket of apples and a smile."

"Oh, you're both exaggerating, I'm sure. They're officers in the British army for goodness sake!"

"Not all officers are gentlemen, honey."

*****

City Hall was strangely quiet. There was a French battle fleet cruising outside the harbor, just fifteen miles from the spot Margaret stood. If they should pass the bar at Sandy Hook, the city must fall. The Royal Navy had but half their force and would be overwhelmed. Soldiers had been deployed to the beaches of Sandy Hook to discourage the attempt. The French were invisible to the residents, but everyone knew they were there. The rumors multiplied their strength and ferocity. The crowds clamoring for some special consideration had stayed at home. Why seek favors of a government that might not well exist tomorrow? She found the office on the second floor, and entered.

Major John Andre was a pleasant fellow, a decade younger than Margaret herself. He was tall and handsome, his preliminary conversation was as smooth and urbane as anyone could wish. "Now, Mrs. Brush," as he turned to business, "what can you tell me of Boston? You don't mind that I keep a record?"

"Not at all. I doubt that I can tell you anything that you don't know from other sources, but I shall certainly try. Understand, my view was limited to what I could see from my cell window, a tiny thing. I could see the docks on the east side of town, Castle William, or where Castle William was, a bit of Noodles Island, and the outer harbor."

"How much of the old fort was left?" please."

"The army destroyed it during the evacuation in '76. I remember that we could see the smoke from our ship in Nastasket Roads. They've been working to rebuild it."

"How successful were they?" Major Andre scribbled some more in his notes.

"The fort was completely thrown down. They have built some batteries there since. I could see the lighters bringing supplies out. There are, or were, about two companies of men working, also a garrison, again, a couple of companies. It looked like a barracks was being thrown up on the landward side, where the gardens used to be."

"How heavy are the batteries?"

"Fairly large, the boats were heavy laden. It was hard to tell from the distance, but I should say twenty-four pounders, at least."

And so it went, for an hour. She told him nothing that anyone with eyes could not see or that he should not have known. Above all, everything had to be accurate. She understood that this was a time to establish creditability.

"How came you to New York? I understand that the rebels released you, but what ensued?"

"I took coach to Hartford, then I bought a horse, a poor thing. She gave out in Westchester. I left her with a farmer and walked from there."

"Do you know this farmer's name?"

"I don't recall it. He gave me some food and a spot in his barn for the night in exchange; I thought I had the advantage of him."

Andre paused, for the first time not completely sure. He rose and began to pace the room. "Mrs. Brush, if I were to ask you to do a further service for your King, would you oblige?"

"If I were able, sir, certainly. What service have you in mind?"

"First, I must have your assurance that this will not leave this office." Margaret nodded her agreement. "As you know, New York is filled with loyalists; it the safest place in the colonies for them. But there are certainly spies among them, and besides, I find it difficult to give the General accurate information of their mood. The refugees from New York have different aims than those from Pennsylvania, who differ with those of Massachusetts. I wonder if you might, as you circulate among them, observe and give me a sense of their desires. Could you tell me what you hear, be a sort of ear for me in that realm?"

"You want me to inform on them? She said lightly, hoping her face did not reveal her excitement.

"*Inform* has such an unpleasant connotation. I should not wish to know that this man damned his King and Sir Henry, or that that one was having an affair with an officer's wife. Rather, I should like intelligence of their broader political economies, as a group. Somewhat as a scholar might report the mood and intrigues of Charles I's court. You would be writing current history. A gentleman could never ask anyone, let alone a lady, to really spy. Besides, you Colonials aren't really the enemy, are you?"

"Major, I must be sure I absolutely understand. You would like me to make an effort to mingle among my friends, go to their houses and gathering places, and collect information that I am to pass on to you?"

"You are correct. You'll do it then? Your daughter, too. I understand that she also has a wide circle of friends."

"I shall be glad to help the cause in any way I can, sir, but know that the loyalist community may come to think I might be spying for the rebels. They are a suspicious lot. I must know that I...we, if Fanny so chooses, enjoy your absolute protection. You understand there is some risk involved?"

124

"I should think it minimal; they don't tar and feather ladies."

"No, but they do savage reputations. That would render me ineffective in this quest. How would I report? Clearly I could not visit you regularly, as pleasant as that might be. People would soon divine what I was about and shun me."

"There is a way." John Andre, sensing victory, had stopped his pacing directly behind her. She kept her eyes focused on his empty chair. "Do you know Kimble's bookshop? Yes? Good. If you were to go there, I will give you the sign and countersign, he's is a good man, as loyal as Sir Henry himself and discrete. You may leave a sealed note with him, and it will find its way to me."

Margaret felt herself paling. Had she been already exposed? Clearly Andre had already made inquiries about her and about Fanny too. Kimble was playing a double game—but to which side was he most attached? She forced herself to composure before Andre could return to face her.

"I would need a written direction from you, sir. You are a soldier and this is a war. As regrettable as it would be, there can be no guarantee of your survival—I must have that protection. As a soldier, you must understand the need for explicit orders. Fanny would also, if she were to agree. You see my point?"

"Yes, yes. You'll do it then?" He was unbecomingly eager.

"I must consider, sir. Fanny will of course make her own decision."

Then he changed course, "Do you enjoy the theater, Mrs. Brush?"

"Yes, certainly."

"Some of the other officers and I are presenting She Stoops to Conquer at the John Street Theater. I'll give you two passes for tonight. Would you care to come?"

"I've heard that it is a wonderful new play, but sold out—how shall we get in?"

"I'll write you backstage passes. You will watch from the wings and get to see all the machinery of the theater. Do come, please! It really is exciting! I shall be somewhat busy, directing the placing of stage dressings, but it shall be great fun."

"But two women cannot just walk the streets at night, it is not done, nor is it safe."

"Done! Barlow!" he called. A lieutenant appeared from the outer office. "Barlow, you are to call for Mrs. Brush and her daughter at 7 o'clock tonight, and escort them to the theater. You will watch the play from the wings, and then we shall escort them home." In his mind, the evening was set. Rhetorically, "Until this evening, Mrs. Brush?"

*****

Margaret walked home, lost in thought. She was glad the two annoying Ensigns had been ordered away to Sandy Hook. She climbed the stairs to her bedroom in the front of the house and sat on the bed. Sally appeared, as she should, and instantly sensed that her mistress was troubled.

"Sally, would you fetch Fanny for me?"

When they came into the room, Margaret said, "Come, sit with me, I must tell you both something that will put our lives in peril. I must tell you as I already have done so, without thinking things through carefully enough. Sit, please." She took a deep breath.

"Since I came back from Boston, I have been spying for the Americans."

Fanny stared at her, mouth open. "Mama! How could you? How can you? What would Papa say? I--I don't know what to say myself. Mama, I..." Fanny rose and went to the window. She looked at the street below for a long time. Three drunken soldiers staggered down the center of the street, bellowing the most bawdy drinking song in the English language. She stepped back quickly as one of them saw her and began to point and call to her. Finally she turned, and in a small voice, "Why are you telling us this now?"

"Two reasons. Firstly, if I were to be discovered, you would be tarred with my brush. I have only lately come to understand this, and I want you to be

126

prepared. I know this is overwhelming. This is not fool's play. I think your Papa would approve. He had come to be dissatisfied with the way the war was being conducted and wanted it ended. So do I, so does any thinking person. I believe it will end, ultimately, in independency. Believing that, I wish to have as few killed as possible. That means ending rather sooner than later, and hopefully without major battles with huge butcher bills. It means trying to stop us from robbing each other, from assaulting our neighbors and from killing our friends under guise of a great cause. In the neutral ground, in Westchester, farming and trade have all but stopped. Both armies prey upon the people, the men prey on each other too. People are hungry, babies are crying. The people do not deserve to be despoiled because of our politics. Stopping this madness seems to me to be right.

"But today, things changed. You know I had an interview with Major Andre? Well, as it turns out, he wants us, you and me, Fanny, to spy for him, too. He wants us to observe and report on the Loyalists in this city. He wouldn't call it spying, but that's what it is. Then he revealed that the person through whom I have been communicating with the Americans is also working for him. Now I don't know if I am compromised or not, and I'm not sure how to contact them for direction. I'm a soldier without an officer."

"Ma'am," said Sally softly, "I'm with you. I have not wanted to speak, it not being my place, but I have become so disgusted with these Englishmen— those two supercilious hacks we are forced to shelter have only confirmed it."

"Supercilious, Sally?"

"I read books too, Ma'am. Being with you has taught me that. Have you no way of communicating?"

"I can't think of a way, except to go to them. Then we would all have to leave, to run, and our usefulness would end. I admit to being stumped."

"Mama, could I go? We could have a disagreement, I could go to visit friends…"

"No Fanny, you couldn't. You are too transparent a soul to lie your way through the sentries. You are too young and too pretty—there are just too many extra risks for you."

"But, Aunt Sally, what are we to do?"

"Ma'am, do you know the person there to talk to? Are they trustworthy?"

"Yes to both, Sally. Somehow we need to get up to Peekskill. Oh, by the way, Fanny, one of those supercilious officers will call for us at 7 o'clock tonight. We are to be Major Andre's guest at the theater this evening. I have learned that a part of being a spy is pretending that nothing is unusual."

"The theater, Ma'am? Do they have costumes there?"

"One would think so. We will be backstage, I'll look to see. Why?"

"Because, properly dressed, I could go where Fanny cannot. You certainly can't go; either of you would be instantly missed. A lady's maid can vanish for days. We're even invisible when we're in the same room."

As they watched, her shoulders became hunched, her chin jutted forward, her eyes narrowed. "I think, Dearie," she cackled, "that tis time Granny Fitzgerald visited her nephew Gerald—yes indeed it tis. 'e lives in Yonkers, don't cha know—that wife of his is a piece of work, let me tell ya. Laws, always in the fancy clothes 'n such, costs 'im a fortune, it does. My faith, in my day ladies never carried on so, tis shameful, that's what it is!"

Sally rose painfully and shuffled to the door. She turned and bowed to the assembled audience. Margaret and Fanny applauded with delight.

"It's not Granny Fitzgerald, Sally, its old Mrs. Williamson of Eastchester. That will get you an instant audience when you arrive."

"See about those costumes, Ma'am. Something old womanish."

"But won't they be under lock and key?"

"Nothing is locked if I don't want it to be."

"But Aunt Sally, how can you—"

"Fanny, I learned twenty years ago that one does not ask Sally how she knows things. You really don't want to know, and she won't tell you anyway!"

128

*****

In the half-light of dawn, Sally made her way down the alley to the stage door of the theater. At that hour, no one was stirring. After a performance last night, the players would be well asleep. As expected, the outer door was not locked; who would break into an empty playhouse? She stood, waiting for her eyes to adjust to the gloom. Margaret had reported that the costumes were stored in a room along the wall to her right. She felt along the wall and found the door. She slipped inside. There were two dirty windows, high on the wall. She settled herself to wait for daylight.

The rising sun revealed rows of chests, heaps of costumes. *I've seen better order at a militia drill*, she thought. Poking through the piles, she found a long gray shawl here, a ragged dress there, best of all, a shaggy gray wig in yet a third place. She tried to think of a play featuring an old beggar woman. She was about to slip out when she heard the outer door open. Her treasures in her arms, she ducked behind a low counter and waited. She heard male voices, two or three of them. They came closer and stopped just outside the door. Would they never take their business away? She heard laughter. Her heart was racing and her legs began to ache. She struggled to settle herself more comfortably. She tried to will herself to calm, all without making a sound.

After what felt like a lifetime, she heard the curtain drawn back and footsteps across the stage, fading as they moved toward the back of the theater. Still she waited. Had they all gone? Another lifetime of silence. She rose and placed her hand against the door, then her ear. Silence.

She slipped out of the room, made the dozen steps to the outside door, and was away into the alley unseen, grinning.

*****

The servant had seen some strange folks at her mistress' door, but none quite like this old hag. Before she could shoo the gap-toothed creature away, it spoke.

"Gracious, Dearie, its Mrs. Williamson of Eastchester for Mrs. Browning. Now be a good child and tell her I'm here! Run along now, don't be keepin

129

an honest woman a'waitin on yur stoop. Gw'on now, tell yur lady I'm a'standin, Have important news for her I do!"

The poor girl was in a quandary. She knew that her mistress sometimes saw the most peculiar people, but this one had "thief" written all about her. "Very well, wait here." She snatched up a silver salver from the hall table and left with the message.

Sally heard voices in the next room, then the girl was back. "Mrs. Browning will see you now. Follow me, please." She put the salver back.

Sally was shown into the parlor. The lady of the house stood across the room, beside the hearth. A pistol lay on the mantle beside her. She was curious to see who had purloined one of her identities. Sally was relieved to see that it really was Kate Browning who greeted her.

"Afternoon to ya, Madam. I got a message for ya. Jest for you." Her eyes darted to the servant.

"You may leave us, Sophie." As the door closed behind Sophie, Kate watched as the woman began to unbend. "Do I know you?"

"Yes Mrs. Browning," the cackle was gone. "I bring a message from Mrs. Brush."

"My God, is that you in there Sally?"

"It is, ma'am. I could not risk a paper, so I've the message memorized. Pray let me deliver it completely before you ask questions. Shall I begin?"

Kate nodded, annoyed, wondering what could be so important that the usual channels would not have sufficed. There was tremendous risk in coming here.

"Mrs. Brush reports that she had an audience with Major John Andre two days ago. During that audience, he asked her to infiltrate and inform on Loyalists in the city. She was to communicate with the Major through Mr. Kimble at his bookstore. He was described to her as 'a good man and loyal.' Mrs. Brush is uncertain how she should proceed."

Kate was clearly shaken by this news. "Sally, has Margaret explained who Kimble is? Has she gone back to the store since?"

"No, Ma'am, and she says that she will not without direction from you."

"Good! She was right to send you, and you were very brave to come. Had you any idea what she was about?"

"I have now, but not before. She told Fanny and I that day. She returned from that interview quite disturbed, and said that she had to tell us for our protection."

"Yes, I see that. From your being here, I take it that you are with us. What about Fanny?"

"I don't know. She will never betray her mother, and betraying any of us would endanger her. She is still young, and dashing officers do turn her head. Let us say she is neuter."

"Does she know that you were to meet with me?"

"No, only that I was to come here."

"My friend has become cautious, and that's a good thing. Tell Meg that I will send someone she knows personally with a new plan. The password shall be... 'barnacle.' Until then she is to lie low and not draw attention to herself, to any of you. I will have to think about this informing on the Loyalists. It does open interesting possibilities. I'm sorry, Sally, I must send you back to New York tonight. You'll have a brave escort. But for now, I have much to arrange. Would Mrs. Williamson care to wait in the kitchen while I work? You should eat. Don't reveal yourself to anyone."

Kate watched as Sally again transformed herself into Mrs. Williamson. "Surely Ma'am, whatever yur ladyship requires, y'll find Mrs. Williamson ready to oblige."

*****

Mrs. Williamson sat in the stern of the little boat as the two men rowed with long sweeping strokes, pausing between each to listen. The Royal Navy had two frigates and a ship of the line posted in the Hudson between Manhattan

131

and Peekskill. The ebbing tide carried their boat quickly downstream. It was a clear night; the cool useless light from the stars barely revealed the two men within arm's reach. There was no moon. She pulled her shawl closer about her. She had no sense of how quickly they were moving, nor of where they were. She had been ordered to absolute silence by this duo, muscular determined men who expected to be obeyed. Had they not been introduced as Bill and Tom by Mrs. Browning, she would have avoided them both.

Once she had felt the loom of a ship; the men had silently altered their course away. There was the sound of a boat's crew, rowing clumsily, noisily. Again they altered course. The sky had begun to lighten when they stopped rowing and boat touched the shore. She could see trees silhouetted against the eastern sky. One man jumped into the shallow water and pulled the boat higher. His companion joined him and pulled it further. They reached out to her.

"Come Missus," one whispered. "The next few yards are the most dangerous. Once on the road we will not appear suspicious."

They crept to the edge of a field; the corn needed harvesting.

"We must part here, Missus, you go ahead. The road to your right leads to the city. Can you walk that far?"

"Don't you worry about me, young man. I may be slow but I get there." Mrs. Williamson's cackle was hard to maintain while whispering. Sally shuffled off, leaning on her stick.

It took her an hour to walk the mile to the house. She slipped into the barn, and several minutes later, Sally emerged; she walked briskly to the kitchen door and entered. It was just time to stoke the breakfast fire. She was bone tired.

"Here you, woman! Get that fire going. I'm wanting tea!"

"Yes, Mr. Litton. The house is just rising."

✳✳✳✳✳

"Excuse me, sir?"

Ensign Litton, blocking the passage into the dining room, grinned down at Fanny. She stepped to the side to go around him. He stepped in front of her again, still with that taunting grin.

"Let me pass, please, Mr. Litton. This tray is rather heavy."

"Now, lass, wouldn't you rather talk with me than deliver breakfast?"

"Less than you might believe. I'm hungry, sir. Aren't you?"

"For your conversation."

She turned and set the tray on the kitchen table. He stepped close behind her; she could feel his hot breath on her neck, his hands on her hips.

"You haven't given me a kind greeting in days. You should be more..."

"This greeting isn't so kind either, sir, so we are even. Step back please, that I may do my work."

He didn't move, so she elbowed him in the gut. He jumped back, surprised, unhurt and laughing.

"That's the best compliment you've given since I came here. Now, how about one a little more personal?" He leaned in for a kiss.

"MISTER LITTON!" Margaret appeared in the doorway. "Unhand her this instant!"

"Can't a gentleman have a little fun with a wench?"

"Not in this house, and certainly not with this girl. Either sit yourself for breakfast, or get to your duty. I am indifferent as to which. Shift yourself, sir!"

"That's the trouble with you Americans—you don't know how to treat with your betters."

"I know that quite well, sir. I remain unconvinced that you are one of them."

"I'll have you know, Missus, that I have three thousand pounds a year!"

133

"My congratulations to your father on his good fortune. Perhaps the next commission he buys for you will have some manners attached!"

"You insult me!"

"Yes."

Litton stood, his face contorted, uncertain how he could emerge victorious. Fanny thought for a second that he was going to attack her mother. He stamped his foot. "Come Lawrence, let's leave this old harridan and her nest of harpies." He jammed his tricorn onto his head and stormed out; he slammed the door. Lawrence wrenched the door open and followed him outside. He slammed the door too.

*****

Thaddeus Kimble was about to close his shop for the day when the two men entered and asked about his lending library. They were big men, but quiet and respectful. He was hungry, but £2 was £2. He carefully explained the program and showed them where to enter their names in the membership ledger. As he pointed to the page, he looked up just in time to receive the blow on the point of his chin. It was a powerful blow. It would have staggered a man far larger and stronger. Kimble fell to the floor. He grunted as the man sat heavily on his chest, his knees pinned Kimble's arms to the floor. Still dazed, he felt hands compressing his throat. His forearms flailed futilely. Unconsciousness came in seconds, and then he was stilled.

The other man had begun tearing the pages from books, showering loose paper on the floor around Kimble and his assailant. He tucked Kimble's purse into his shirt; he found a container of whale oil and began to empty the contents around the counter.

Once certain that Kimble was quite dead, his assassin rose. He took a button from his pocket, a button torn from the uniform of a Loyalist regiment. He closed the man's dead fingers around it. He searched the books behind the counter. He rifled the contents. He found eight notes that seemed to satisfy him. He placed them in the ledger and wrapped the book in a cloth. He tucked the bundle under his arm.

"Ready?" asked the second man.

"Do it" said the other. The lighted oil lamp crashed to the floor; its flame spread quickly among the loose pages. They watched for a minute to make sure the fire was well begun. They left the shop quietly and were three blocks away when the alarm was sounded. The fire brigade did a fine job; it saved the buildings on either side of the shop. Kimble's shop was a charred shell.

The next day, the night watch found Kimble's remains. The button, preserved from fire by his closed hand, convinced them that the fire had been started to conceal a robbery and murder. Kimble had struggled manfully, for such a small fellow.

$$*****$$

Fanny awoke parched. The house was blacker than pitch. She wondered whether she was coming down with a fever. She padded barefooted to the kitchen for some water. She worked the pump and filled her cup. Without warning a strong arm encircled her waist, pinning one arm to her side. A hand covered her mouth. She felt herself being lifted into the air. Her cup fell to the floor. She struggled, kicking. The table upset with a crash.

"Quick, Lawrence, get her feet before she raises the house!"

Lawrence grunted as she kicked him, then pinned her knees against his chest. Her free hand grabbed at door jams, hallways, anything to force her assailants off balance. They carried her out across the small yard. In the moonlight she saw the tufts of grass growing between the rotting boards of the derelict shay, unused for a decade. She tried to bite the hand across her mouth, to call out. They carried her into the barn and threw her onto a pile of old hay. They hadn't had animals since her papa had died. She grunted as Litton threw himself on top of her and again covered her mouth with his hand, stifling her cries.

"Get her ankles, Lawrence, damn you, hurry!" She could feel his growing excitement as she thrashed violently. Lawrence lit a small lantern. He bound first her ankles, then her wrists with coarse ropes. She lay, spread-eagled and struggling. The dry straw poked into her back and buttocks. She managed to bite the hand over her mouth. Litton swore and gave her the back of his hand. She spit blood from the cut inside her cheek, explored her teeth with her tongue.

"You little bitch! Bite me will you! Not so high and mighty now, what? Go along and this will be so much the easier for you!"

He pried at her jaw, he pinched her nose closed until she opened her mouth to gasp. Lawrence, at her other side, forced in a foul tasting rag. She thought she was going to gag. Litton stood, looking down at her in the flickering candle light.

"Cry, damn you! Beg mercy!" She swore at him with her eyes.

He struck her again. The blow disoriented her, her body lay still as her brain struggled to formulate commands.

She felt hands exploring her breasts, she felt a hand caressing her thigh, trembling as it moved higher and higher. The realization shocked her into consciousness. She jerked away as she might; they laughed. She began to working her tongue and jaw to eject the rag.

"Stop right there, you son of a bitch!"

Fanny lifted her head to see Sally burst into the circle of light, the heavy poker from the kitchen fire in her hands. Litton sidestepped her first swing and grabbed the poker at the end of its arc before she could raise it again. He landed a punch full on her face. Sally fell hard against the wall. He advanced on her, the poker raised.

"Litton! Drop it. Not one step."

She saw her mother at the limits of the light, the pistol in her extended hand pointed squarely at Litton's midriff. Her voice was low, almost soft, but laden with menace and imperative. It was a voice she had never heard.

There was a thud beside her as Lawrence, rising, lost his balance and fell against the stall partition. He soiled himself.

Litton froze, staring at the gun. The poker dropped uselessly at his feet. The black hole of the muzzle looked enormous. He had no doubt what would happen to him at this range if that black volcano should erupt. He didn't see the poker that Sally directed, forcefully, at his groin.

136

"OOO."

He dropped to his knees, fell to his side, then rolled onto his back, struggling feebly to find comfort, clutching himself. The sensation was so different than that he had been anticipating.

Margaret advanced into the light, away from the doorway. The unwavering pistol shifted to Lawrence.

"Sally, get behind me. You—get out of my house and take the garbage with you."

At that moment Fanny spit out her gag.

"Shoot them Mama, shoot the bastards dead!"

Margaret's face did not change. "There are two ways out of this Lawrence," still in the same deadly calm. She motioned toward the door with the pistol.

Lawrence finally noticed the pistol in her other hand, resting quietly at her side. He glanced at his friend, writhing on the floor. Humiliated, he helped Litton to his feet. They moved slowly toward the doorway.

Margaret called unnecessarily over her shoulder, "Sally—release her!"

She backed them down the alley to the street. She motioned again. "Now run!" They did. Lawrence left his friend far behind.

*****

"So, why didn't you shoot them?" Sally and Margaret sat at the dining table, nursing their morning tea. Fanny still slept upstairs in Margaret's bed. Her front bedroom had been re-made into a fortress. Through the night a heavy dresser had barred the door, the pistols, the poker, Margaret's dagger and Crean's sword had all been laid to hand. Either Margaret or Sally had been awake all night, in case the foolish duo should attempt the house again. Only Fanny had slept through. She had never wept about the attack.

"Twenty years ago I probably would have," said Margaret. "Had he achieved his aim I certainly would have blown his damned head off. With age comes some wisdom, and deviousness. As things now stand, we have the high ground. If I had killed them, I'd have had to defend a murder charge. This way, the weight of law will fall upon them.

"You know, of all the services you have performed for this family over the years, this ranks the highest—I don't want to think what would have happened if you hadn't distracted them. You have our undying gratitude. How is your eye—it looks terrible, all purple and swollen—can you see from it?"

"Barely, just a slit. A small price. I haven't been hit so hard since I ran away from my father. What do we do now, Ma'am?

"In all these years you've never told me so much about your past as you just did."

"It's past, Ma'am."

The two examined each other's faces. "As you wish."

Fanny came into the room, walking very carefully. "Oh, honey, how are you?"

"All right, I guess." A thin smile. "I hurt everywhere. Does my face look as badly as it feels?"

"It is a bit rough. I don't think anything is broken, though. Your nose is still nice and straight."

"Can I get you some tea, Fanny? Please, sit."

"Thank you, Aunt Sally." She eased herself into a chair.

"Mama, when you talked about spying, I said I wasn't sure—now I am. I want these damned British sirs the hell out of my country. I want to help."

"Fanny, I can't accept that today—you're angry and hurt, and that's not a good reason. It has to be a careful decision, because it requires careful action. If you feel the same in a few days, I will welcome your assistance, but not yet today."

138

"I won't change my mind."

"Probably not, knowing you. How early can you be ready to go to City Hall? Wear a good dress, but do nothing to disguise your injuries. We want all the sympathy we can garner."

$$*****$$

At 10:00 o'clock Margaret entered Major Andre's office. Lt. Barlow had looked up, surprised by her unexpected arrival. Then he saw Fanny, her face swollen and bruised, and Sally looking little better.

"My God, Fanny, what has happened to you?"

"The soldiers quartered with us tried to rape her last night. We need the major's help. Would you be so good as to announce us?"

Barlow disappeared into the inner office. After a moment, John Andre came out, Barlow on his heels.

"My dear Mrs. Brush, what has happened? Fanny, child, your face!" He took her hands. "Are you all right?"

"Sore, Major, but my two heroes foiled the attackers. Another time, I might not be so fortunate." She gave him an account of the events.

"That is why we came to you Major," said Margaret, "Those two will never enter my house again. Can you intercede with the Barracksmaster on our behalf?"

"Can and will. I must apologize on behalf of His Majesty's Army for this assault. Come, we're to his office right now. It's just down the stair." He took Fanny on his arm and the quartet swept through the lobby, past the curious eyes, until they encountered Sir Henry Clinton.

"Ah, Andre," as he met them near the door. "That Smithson matter, have you any results in that quarter?"

"Good Morning, Sir." Major Andre saluted, Margaret and Fanny curtsied, Sally gave a servile bob. "I have, Sir. I was just writing up my report when

139

this poor family came to me. With your permission, Sir, I will complete it as soon as I rectify this crime."

"Why, what has happened here? The Major gave a quick summary of the events.

"Very well, Andre. Two of my officers, you say?" He turned to Margaret. "Good morning to you, Mrs. Brush. I am embarrassed and aggrieved to encounter you under these circumstances. Is this the child whom I met in Boston?"

"I am, Sir. Thank you for your concern. Had my mother and her maid not intervened, I fear I would not be standing here today."

"Tell me, my dear, what punishment should be visited on these two?"

"I care not, General, as long as they are no longer able to reach me. I am fearful."

"You're more forgiving than I. Come now, first we'll get this quartering thing arranged, then I shall deal with them."

With a major on one arm and a general on the other, Fanny approached the office. They could hear raised voices within.

"That witch has expelled my two men, lawfully quartered with her. I demand you seize the quarters in the King's name! See how she likes sleeping in the streets."

They entered to see Litton and Lawrence standing self-righteously and wronged beside their captain, nodding in agreement. Margaret and Sally entered the office.

"There she is—she's the one! Evict her!" Their words tripped over each other. They fell silent as Fanny and her escort entered last.

The fellow at the desk, a mere captain, jumped to his feet. He had never been in the same room as his general.

"What's on here, Captain?"

140

"These two have been wronged by their landlady, and seek restitution, sir."

"I think not. These people are loyal subjects who have been assaulted criminally. Eviction shall be in the other direction."

"But General—she," Litton pointed at Margaret, "forced us from our quarters at gunpoint! She meant to fire upon us. That's the assault here! I demand that you turn her out!"

Clinton turned to Fanny. "Which is the one?"

Fanny extended her arm, pointing at Litton. Her sleeve rode up, revealing the rope burns on her wrist.

"Child, who did this to you?"

With a fine sense of the dramatic, she raised her other arm and pointed to Lawrence. More angry marks were revealed. "He did."

"General" protested Litton, who still did not understand, "She's but a stupid girl and damned colonial—that one's a maniac! You take their word above mine?"

Sir Henry Clinton looked from Fanny's small, damaged wrists to the two very junior officers. He passed summary judgment.

"Drummond—see that these two are transferred to General Grant's command. A visit to St. Lucia might allow them to redeem themselves. They'll not do it here. Get them the hell out of my sight. They're a disgrace."

Litton and Lawrence were very pale as they were escorted out. Fevers killed half the men sent to the Caribbean.

"Mrs. Brush, you say that you would accept other officers into your house?"

"Yes, Sir, it is my duty as a subject."

Very well. Captain, strike those two from Mrs. Brush's house. Find others who are gentlemen. This woman and her family are under my especial protection. It's the very least we can do after all they have suffered in this war."

✳✳✳✳✳

Captain Drummond knocked at their door just after lunch.

"Good afternoon, Mrs, Brush, Miss Brush. General Clinton asks that you call upon him at his office at ten o'clock tomorrow. He will send a coach. Would that be acceptable?"

"Generals never 'ask', Captain Drummond,." said Margaret with a laugh, "Of course, I shall be honored. Can you give me any hints as to why?"

"I cannot, Madam, but he did imply that it was a personal matter.

"Miss Brush, may I inquire as to your health?"

"Thank you, Captain. I am as well as I can be under these circumstances. I am blessed with two she-bears to protect me."

"She-bears, Miss?"

"You must be city bred, Captain Drummond. On this continent, one is taught not to trifle with a bear cub. The mothers are ferocious in defense."

✳✳✳✳✳

The carriage arrived precisely at ten. It was just half after ten when Drummond showed her through to the inner office. As the heavy door closed behind her the noise of the lobby vanished. She stood before the large desk, waiting.

General Sir Henry Clinton looked up from his last paper. "Ah, good morning, Mrs. Brush. How is Miss Brush this morning, recovering well? What those two did was shameful, bloody shameful."

"Yes Sir. Thank you for asking."

142

He indicated the paper he had just read. "I have been making inquiries of you."

"Yes sir."

"You have an excellent reputation—the way you helped your husband escape was something grand. Your German is quite good, by the way. I'm told that you once held station as the late General Bradstreet's chatelaine. Could you tell me of your duties there?"

"Well, sir, I managed his household in Albany for him. I hired the servants, got him food, saw to his domestic needs. He had his valet for the most personal ones, of course. I was privileged to serve him for five years, until I married Mr. Brush."

"I gather that your position is now somewhat precarious?"

"It is, Sir. We have some means, but with the cost of things lately, it is not an easy life. We are reduced to just the one lady's maid, who has been with me for over twenty years."

"Yes, yes, I understand. This city is like unto an armed camp more than a capitol." He appeared in deep thought, considering a decision actually made hours ago. "Mrs. Brush, I find myself in need of a woman to manage my household as well. I presume you know of Mrs. Baddeley? She is an excellent woman, but finds so large a house a bit much to manage alone. Would you be interested in such a position, subordinate to her but superior to all others?

"Why General, I'm honored that you would consider me. What would be the arrangements?"

"I'd consider it a captain's billet, £40 sterling the year. You'd live in, with all the advantages. Mrs. Baddeley would probably have you sit at table from time to time. She feels that my table has too many men." He surveyed her closely. "Is your wardrobe competent for such work?"

"Mostly, yes. I would need to adjust some particulars. What of my daughter? And would my maid be at my charge, or would you take her? I pay her £15."

"Would you bargain with the grocer this well? I'll increase you to £47,6s., your servant to be at your charge. Fanny would of course be welcome at table too. You will need to pass muster with Mrs. Baddeley before we can be fully engaged."

"Understood, sir. If you could provide an introductory note, I will stop at your house and speak with her now."

*****

She recognized the house as having once belonged to one of Madam Schuyler's nephews, one who did not share the family's disdain for ostentation. Originally a three story square, additions had been added successively to the rear, each being a floor smaller, like ducklings following their mother. Forfeited to the government because of the owner's politics, it now served as General Clinton's home. The aged slave who answered her knock looked vaguely familiar.

"Good morning madam, how may I assist you?"

"Good morning. I am Mrs. Brush. I bring a message from Sir Henry to Mrs. Baddeley. Would you announce me, please? May I ask, have you been with this house long?"

"Yes Ma'am, near fifteen years. I started with Master Schuyler way back."

"I thought so. He is a sort of cousin of mine. Your name?"

"I'm called Jupiter, Ma'am." He flashed a toothy smile. "If you will just wait here Ma'am, I'll tell Madam that you have arrived."

Margret heard voices, then scurrying feet. Jupiter reappeared, "Madam will see you now."

Mary Baddeley rose to greet her as she entered the drawing room. It was a modestly sized room sharing the front of the house with the parlor, she guessed, on the other side of the hall. Through an open doorway, she caught a glimpse of the dining room. There were fine mahogany chairs scattered about with studied carelessness, a settee, all upholstered in good damask. Other than the wall sconces and the gold acanthus leaf wallpaper, there were few decorations. Nothing about the room suggested that it was often used.

144

Mary Baddeley was scarcely older than Fanny, perhaps in her early twenties. Almost black hair and very blue eyes betrayed her Celtic heritage.

"Mrs. Brush, it's so nice to meet you. Sir Henry hinted that you might be calling."

"That was good of him. I come bearing a message." She handed the note. Mary took a moment to read it.

"He writes that you may be willing to come to us. I confess I would welcome your help. This house is much more than I am used to. Is not such a position beneath a woman of your station?"

"Honest work is beneath no one's station, Mrs. Baddeley. The war has reduced my options. I am recently widowed and marooned in this city and must make do until this conflict is ended. I have property in the Hampshire grants to which I shall return someday. How many have you in the house? About thirty?"

"In this house, with the stable hands, yes. The other houses have but a skeleton staff when we are not there. My father was a prosperous man for Ireland; we had about ten, usually, as I was growing. I find thirty a quite different affair."

As if on cue, raised voices floated through the open window.

"Oh dear, they're at it again. I suppose I must try to restore peace."

"I wonder, could I try to resolve this? To prove my worth?"

"Oh, could you? The stable hands I find especially trying."

The two women hurried through the dining room and out a side door overlooking the stable yard. There they found a white man beating a cowering slave with a stout stick.

Margaret raised her voice. "Hold, sir! What is the meaning of this?"

"This damned fool brought the pony cart back and now the pony is lame! He never checked the feet before harnessing."

145

"You are the stablemaster? What is your name?"

"Mr. Anderson—and this boy has it coming."

"This is indeed a serious matter, but before you damage your stick, Mr. Anderson, let us probe the issue. Boy, what is your name?"

I'se called Cato, Missus."

"Very well, Cato, did you check the pony's feet before you harnessed her?"

Cato paused for a moment, wondering how truthful he needed to be. "No Missus, I didn't do that. I swear I didn't know I should."

"Very well." She wasn't sure that she believed him. "Now Cato, the coblestones are very hard on an animal's feet, and you must take particular care about them. This is what you're going to do before you take any animal out for work. You will carefully inspect each foot. Always.

The slave started to protest. "Wait—there's more. Do you have a hoof knife?"

"We don't allow that here Ma'am."

"Understood, Mr. Anderson. Here's what you are going to do. For the next three times that Cato here takes an animal out, you will stand beside him and show him what to look out for. Cato, you will learn this. Then on the fourth and fifth and every time thereafter, you will carefully inspect the animal's feet, report any variance to Mr. Anderson, and rely on his discretion." With just a hint of menace, she continued. "I shall never have to speak to you again on this, will I? Do you understand?"

"Yes, Missus." His relief that the beating would stop was palpable, balanced against his certainty that this strange woman would as soon sell him to the Caribbean as not.

"Mr. Anderson, is this acceptable to you?"

"Yes, Ma'am," grudgingly.

146

"Very good. Continue your duties."

She turned on her heel and led Mary Baddeley back into the drawing room.

"Mrs. Brush! That was wonderful! I'd have been arguing with them for half an hour and still not gotten Anderson to stop beating that boy."

"He may well start again when he thinks we can't hear. There are some things among the servants that they will never allow us to understand; any attempt is not only fruitless, it diminishes us.

"Anderson bears watching. A man who beats the help probably beats the animals too. I have observed that there are only two reasons why a servant fails to do work properly, and they are both the master's fault."

"And these two reasons?"

"The first, as may be in this case, is that he has not been properly taught. Servants generally want to satisfy, we all do, but if they don't know what they are to do and how to do it, they will fail. It's the master's job to see them properly instructed."

"And the other reason?"

"Just pure cussedness. Such a one will not please and has no wish to. That lies also at the master's feet, as he should never have brought a malcontent into his house to begin with."

Mary Baddely laughed. "I think you will do quite well here. I shall welcome an ally."

"You shall have two of us. My daughter Fanny will come too; she's just eighteen. I think you two will get on famously. Sir Henry has agreed that my maid shall also come."

Margaret sensed Mary tense at the mention of Fanny. "Mrs. Baddeley, know that we come as friends. We shall present no threat to your position, I swear it. Neither of us. Sir Henry is my employer, and shall ever remain as nothing more."

147

"Is my cattiness showing? Inviting an attractive woman of Sir Henry's own age into my house, along with her fresh young daughter, whom I have seen, by the way—you two are a formidable competition."

"You would not be a woman if you had none. If I can ease your concern, will our coming be agreeable? Think about it. I do desperately need this position. We are only in competition if there is a game afoot and there is none. I still grieve my husband; Fanny has a young fellow in her heart.

"May we then be friends?" Mary nodded, slowly. "Good. Now, when shall we come, and where shall you put us? We have so many details to discuss!"

*****

The young man was waiting for her when she returned from her interview. Fanny had applied powder to hide her bruises, with some success. Margaret could hear them laughing in the parlor as she entered the hall.

He rose and faced her as she came into the parlor. "My God, Edward Browning! Are you mad?"

"Possibly, Aunt Margaret."

"Get away from those windows! Listen Edward, we may need to conceal you at a moment's notice. You have no idea of the danger to which you have exposed yourself! Do you have a plausible identity here?"

"Allow me to introduce myself, Madam. I am John Thompson of Newark, purveyor of fine fruits and vegetables. I supply several of the markets in New York. I have a boat crossing the Hudson every few days."

"Is it real?"

"Yes, Aunt Margaret, I've resigned my commission that I might feed the hungry."

"If there is a knock at the door, you must become a suitor, concerned over Fanny's injuries. Take your leave quickly and get away. There may be officers here at any minute for quartering. She turned to Fanny. "You, my dear, shall be indisposed." Then, turned back to Edward, "Did Kate send you?"

148

"The word is 'barnacle,' Aunt Margaret."

"Very well. We have a great deal to discuss. Fanny, I know I told you I wouldn't accept your decision yet, but events have preceded us. Are you still willing?"

"I am, Mama."

She looked carefully between the two young people. They had known each other intermittently for years. She wondered if there were not other influences upon her daughter. She dismissed the thought as unworthy.

"Tell me what you have, Edward. Fanny is with us."

"I think, Aunt Margaret, that you should visit Mr. Brush's grave at St. George's from time to time. You will find that a new bench has been installed there, at a convenient spot, where you may sit and reflect. There is a small gap at the top of the leg on your right, just the size to hold a sheet or two, folded octavo. At some times, you may find a message there, at others, you may chose to leave one. You'll not know who leaves them, nor will they know who responds. The contents will be created and read as you previously have done.

"When you have left a message, draw the shade over the center window of your room upstairs. Someone will notice and retrieve it. When there are instructions, someone will have thoughtlessly left a brick on your front stoop. Once you have retrieved the message, place the brick off the side."

"The depository is all very fine, Edward, but the signaling will not work. We shall be leaving this house tomorrow to enter General Clinton's."

"What! Mama, when did this happen?"

"About an hour ago, Fanny. I hadn't a chance to tell you yet. We're all to live in, with full privileges, including table. I know, Edward, I have exceeded my instructions, but this position is a gift not to be refused. I shall have almost daily conversation with Sir Henry, and be uniquely positioned to know his plans. It's beyond anything that could be dreamed. What started as simple course of observation has become much less simple."

149

"Yet you asked if I were mad Aunt Margaret! This is a *fait accompli*?"

"It is. All that remains is to devise the signaling, something as elegant as this bench. Persons lounging about would be noticed. You can't have his house under surveillance, Edward."

"Surely not. Who procures the food for the General's household?"

"Cook, probably. Is your produce good enough for a general's table? I'll be able to influence from whence it comes."

"I am cut to the quick that you should doubt the quality of New Jersey's finest foods! I can supply milk, butter and eggs, too.

"Ma'am," said Sally, "you could write a shopping list to be given to the grocer and you, Mr...Thompson, could produce an invoice of things delivered. No need for this bench at all. Do you use similar documents for the others you supply?"

"Yes!" Excitedly.

"All the better. There can be no better hiding place for a document than the midst a bunch of similar, usual items."

"A fine nest of spies you have grown here, Aunt Margaret"

"Isn't it? I would entrust each with my life."

"You already have."

They all froze at the knock at the door. Sally eased back into her servant's role. She looked around quickly to see that all faces were prepared, then went to answer.

She returned quickly, clearly distressed.

"It's Montraville! Is he to be our new boarder?"

Margaret softly swore. "Damn him! Of all the men in the world! I should have known he'd try to insert himself. He's a great friend of Major Andre's beside. Edward, you'll need to get your persona on, and pray for luck. He

150

knew your father and you do look like him!" She paused. "He is not a fool. If he presses, you are your father's nephew, the family divided over the rebellion. Say nothing more than you have to. He will have heard our voices and know a man is here. "Ready?" Her glance flicked from one to the next. Nervous nods. She motioned to Sally.

Montraville entered. He hurried his greeting and crossed directly to Fanny.

"Miss Brush, I hope you are well? I heard of last night."

"Captain, may I present Mr. Thompson, a friend of Fanny's? Mr. Thompson, Captain Montraville.

"Yes, yes, Thompson," as they shook hands. "A pleasure," dismissively. He was about to drop hands when he took a second look. "I say, Thompson, have we met before?"

"I don't believe I've had that pleasure, sir, perhaps you might have seen me around the town somewhere."

"Mr. Thompson, it is a shame that your business calls you away,: said Fanny. Shall you be in the city for long?"

"Only a day this time, Miss Brush. I must be getting back to New Jersey before my manager gives the store away. So nice to have met you Captain, Mrs. Brush, Miss Fanny." He bowed himself out.

Montraville stood looking at his back for a moment, then shook off the feeling that he had seen the man somewhere.

He turned toward Margaret. "Well Margaret, It appears that I shall be your new lodger. May I be shown my quarters?"

"John, This attempt is as pitiable as it is transparent. Your infiltration of our family shall fail, as we are moving out tomorrow. You're welcome to the place."

"Say what!" Crestfallen. "Where shall you go?"

"To Sir Henry's."

"But how?" Then, struggling to put the best face on events, "Very well, Margaret, I shall endeavor to protect your belongings in your absence. You should not be so hard—I really do have concern for you all. It is natural."

"I'll not have that discussion, John. Know that the house is rented furnished from a rebel widow, fled to Norwalk. Rent is paid through the year end. What arrangements you make with her beyond are not my concern. Everything of ours shall be removed by the General's people in the morning."

✳✳✳✳✳

Margaret and Fanny sat in the parlor, working their needlepoint. It was a long, narrow room, extending the full depth of the original house. A massive fieldstone fireplace was centered on one long wall, a mural of French pastoral wallpaper faced it. A harpsichord and other paraphernalia of music and a couple of straight chairs rested near a front window, a sitting area at the rear of the room allowed two conversations without either disturbing the other. Mary Baddely practiced at a new tune on her violin. The sounds of street traffic floated through the open windows. General Clinton entered, unbuttoned his coat and sank heavily into his chair. Mary set down her instrument.

"You look tired, Sir Henry. A long day, sir?"

"Another. That blasted William Franklin and his friends are a pesky lot, always on about this 'Loyalist' army that they want. He insists on civil law as well."

Margaret looked up from her sewing. "Would you like some privacy, Sir Henry?"

"No need, Mrs. Brush. After such a day I crave a little domesticity. Please stay."

"Is there any crumb that you could give to them? I hear that the Loyalists are frustrated that they have neither role nor say in the war."

"The lout can't seem to grasp that I can't have some fool judge meddling in my officers' affairs. Can't have an independent command mucking things up either."

152

Clinton looked at her for a moment, then said, "Mrs. Brush, you're a woman of good parts. Do you hear comments among the people about events? I know you were going to report to Major Andre about such things but could you share them with me instead?"

"Yes, sir. Few can avoid talking, I know people among the second rank of the King's friends, not Mr. Franklin, but those who might be called his staff—colonels and smaller merchants and such."

"How about you, Fanny? Could you share as well?"

"I hope I would be of service to my country!" Henry Clinton smiled benevolently at his own little spies.

"Sir Henry," said Mary "Fanny and I have been working up a new piece. Would you like to hear it?"

"With pleasure. I didn't know you played, Fanny."

Fanny moved to the harpsichord, Mary took up her violin. After a nervous glance, they began the slow movement of a Haydn sonata. Henry Clinton sat back in his chair, his eyes closed.

When they finished, he applauded. "Lovely, ladies, just the thing for my mood tonight. Slow and reflective, but not a bit sad. You play well indeed, Fanny. You know, Mary, having her here will open new repertoire for us— all those keyboard trios! There are some glorious ones. I must polish my 'cello."

*****

Generals, Margaret thought, *do not make good debaters. It's not a skill they usually need.* She looked around the table at the gentlemen. Besides Sir Henry and Major Andre, they were an assemblage of civilian leadership of the Loyalists. Governor William Franklin of New Jersey, Governor William Tryon of New York, the Reverend Charles Inglis, Chief Justice William Smith. All had come through the autumn afternoon for dinner and then discussion. They were excited and impassioned. Sir Henry however, was becoming frustrated with them and with this discussion of which he had lost control. Mary and Fanny looked just a bit uncomfortable.

This had been the first formal dinner for which Margaret had assumed responsibility; Mary Baddeley would get the credit if all went well, but it was her work, and she knew she would be blamed if it were to fail, as it looked it might. Things had been going so well, the food was well received, the service impeccable, the wine had flowed. All had been conviviality until Franklin threw good breeding to the winds and began to plead for coastal raiding, something of which he wanted more. Much more. There was no way she could speak. This was a gentlemen's conversation. By convention, it should have been delayed until the ladies had left the table, until the brandy had been served. Franklin plunged ahead.

"With all respect, Sir Henry, we must take this war to them! We sit here in New York while they rule the hinterlands. They practice the utmost cruelty upon anyone who does not cry 'independency' at the top of their lungs. Let them feel the hand of British justice on their throats, that's the only way their little rebellion will be quelled. These people will never return to their duty while we treat for conciliation and offer pardons. A firm hand, that's what they need!"

"Governor Franklin, do you question the King's judgment?" asked Andre. "You know London sent the peace commissioners to Philadelphia. It was not something any of us wanted."

"King's decision or no, it was poor policy. They won't respect our arms while ambassadors are pleading peace, nor will they believe ambassadors while the army promises retribution. The government must choose a path and then stay the course. For me the best way is to strike hard, punish them as they'll not forget.

"Sir Henry," injected Rev. Inglis, "What can be made of this unholy French alliance they have entered? Clearly the mob is disturbed by the prospect of enforced Catholicism and dependence on an empire they all worked so hard to defeat. What can be made of the discontent?"

"I do not war with the mob, Reverend, I war with Washington's army."

Margaret felt Mary's hand on her arm, beneath the table. She turned to the panic-stricken hostess, who mouthed "What shall I do?"

154

"We retire" Margaret mouthed back. Mary thought for a second, then nodded and stood.

"Gentlemen," she waited for quiet. "If you will excuse us, I'll have the brandy sent in. Ladies?" The men all rose as she led the women to the drawing room.

Mary spoke first. "Well, that was surely something!"

"Yes, Mr. Franklin is clearly insistent. One would have thought a politician of his stature would be more oblique. I wonder, does his father behave so?"

"Mama, did you get the feeling that they were performing for us?"

"I'm sure of it. Men are such peculiar creatures aren't they? I guess that's why women are supposed to leave the room before the brandy comes and the serious business begins."

Sir Henry's voice boomed under the door. "Blast it, sir, I can do none of those things without a navy!" Things were becoming heated. "I've told the Ministry a hundred times, yet my needs are ignored. They detach a couple of ships for a month and think that will overawe a French fleet here for the season. They promise a grand reinforcement and send 3000 invalids. How am I supposed to mount a campaign under these circumstances! My first responsibility is to hold this city. For even that I need more troops."

"Then arm the loyalists…"

The sound level dropped again.

****

It took Margaret nearly a day to complete her grocery list. The actual list, headed "For Sir Henry," was simply copied from the cook's poor writing. Potatoes, carrots, brussels sprouts, fresh fall crops for the General's table. The requirements of thirty people generated a long list. Coding the actual message had taken the longest of all. It was tedious business. She carefully folded her work, then gathered her drafts and burned them, watching the embers in the fireplace to make sure everything was destroyed. She carefully concealed her special inks.

"Mama, Mr. Thompson is here for you."

Very well, I'll be just a moment. Can you occupy him until I come?"

"I'll try."

"So sorry to inconvenience you."

Fanny stuck her tongue out at her mother. She skipped lightly down the stairs.

*****

"Sir Henry, will you join us this evening? I've found a Boccerini trio that looks interesting. I thought we might try to read through it tonight."

"I'm sorry, Mary, after another day of William Franklin I'd rather just sit. Perhaps you and Fanny might favor us with something. Be prepared that I might drift off."

"Perhaps we'll just work our needles then."

"Sir Henry, if I might ask, what is he on about today?"

"The same, Mrs. Brush, his civil law and armed loyalists."

"I don't think he is too concerned over the civil law issue, sir. Some of his people may be, but consider, martial law has been with us for four years now. Most have learned that it is a minor evil they can live under. Re-instituting civil government would be an upset all on its own. I don't believe loyalists want civil law so much as loyalist leaders want positions in civil government."

"You've been among these people, Mrs. Brush." He spoke in a strange mixtureof frustration and fatigue. "What is it they want?"

"I've been around politicians enough" answered Margaret, quietly, "to understand that they often will settle for less than they ask for; that what they ask for is sometimes not what they really want, and that sometimes they themselves don't know which is which.

156

"Mr. Franklin and his friends have suffered great reverses in fortune and position. They have had to abandon estates and livelihoods they have enjoyed for a lifetime. The financial losses are immense. They have discovered, some of them have, that they don't like dependency or poverty.

"That is not what drives them. In their prior lives, they were persons of stature: men bowed to them, ladies curtsied, their word could alter lives. They have lost that, they miss it, they hunger for it.

"They want to punish those who have taken it from them, to make them suffer as they have. They are like wounded animals, ready to strike blindly. The striking itself lessens their anguish."

"What then should I do with them?"

"I am only a woman, sir; my opinions would be of little value..."

"Nonsense, you are an intelligent person who has observed these people for some time. You have experience in public affairs. I'll wager some Machiavellian devices have been launched from your parlor over the years. I'd welcome your thoughts."

Margaret paused, ordering her words. "I don't want the Loyalists given free rein any more than you, sir, but for different reasons. Your objection is military, concerning the divided command. Mine has a different basis, no more correct than yours, but different.

"These people are hurt, angry and frustrated. If they were to be armed and set loose, there would be bloodshed and destruction on a scale yet unseen. The enemy would respond in a deepening spiral of violence. My country would become a garden of hatred. I've seen it happen regarding the savages.

"At some time in the future this war will be over. No matter how it ends, these same people would then have to set aside differences and live together. The level of hatred, if that hatred comes to exist, would divide this continent for generations. That, I do not want.

"On a more practical level, think about the people. I don't know the exact numbers, but these will do for argument. Say a fourth part are active rebels. Another fourth part are strong for the King. That leaves fully half the people either afraid to voice an opinion, or else too indifferent to form one.

"General Grey's raids in New Bedford and Martha's Vineyard were small affairs that destroyed a dozen houses, two dozen businesses and three dozen ships. If you burn their property, people will cease to be indifferent.

"The raids appropriated, 'stole' in the eyes of the residents, 10,000 sheep and 300 oxen. Half of those should have been the property of persons previously indifferent. The result of these actions raised a company of soldiers for General Washington in New Bedford, and a hostile island. Not, I submit, good economy.

"As for this civil government thing, I should ignore it. I hope I have given no offense?"

"No, no, on the large, I agree with what you have said. I have heard bits of this in council, though not so cogently. Know that, absent a direct order from the Ministry, I shall not release the Loyalists on the people. But God himself only knows what foolishness Lord George Germain will foist upon me next!"

"You said once that I should throw them a bone—what should that be?"

"Self respect, sir. Give them something to be proud of, for their wives to be proud of. Offices in your government or the Loyalist regiments. Participation will give a sensation of control in affairs. That would satisfy the lesser of them. You have no offices in your gift, unfortunately, for the greater."

"And the greater are so noisy."

✳✳✳✳✳

George Washington looked up from his hoecakes as Richard Browning slipped through the kitchen door, got coffee from the sideboard and seated himself across the table.

"Good morning. How are you today, Browning?"

"Freezing, Your Excellency. It's colder than Hell out there!"

"I never thought of Hell as a particularly cold place."

158

"You take my meaning, sir. I do have a good bit for you today though, that warms my soul. Odysseus believes he has found Clinton's strategic plan for the campaign!"

"This Odysseus must have rare access; he has been proven right before. Who is this, may I ask?"

"Of course you may ask, and of course, I can't tell you, as Kathleen will not tell me."

"She trusts him." It wasn't a question. "Very well, what says the man?"

"The plan is predicated on Clinton getting an adequate reinforcement, and an admiral with whom he can work. Odysseus is not sure he will receive either. He wants a 30,000 man field army, the latest figure is 6,600 are to be sent; Kathleen figures that will leave him about 11,000 short of his desire. She believes that the threat from France will be more important to the King than will be any threat from us.

"Do all professors have wives as prescient as yours?"

"I don't know. I just know mine is right far too often for my comfort.

"Anyway, there are four parts to the plan. First there will be some coastal raiding, in the Sound and in New Jersey. These are intended to hurt us a bit, but mainly so that men will want to stay at home, away from the army. For these he needs a cooperative admiral. Perhaps you will come down to the shore to protect it. He hopes you might. Then there will be an advance up the Hudson, sure to lure you out of New Jersey, if you haven't already obliged, onto the coastal plain where he figures he can defeat you. He envisions a massive, water borne transport to some place beyond our army, then a push southward from our rear to drive us out of our havens. Again, he needs an admiral who knows which end of a ship to point at an enemy. After he has whipped you he will shift the theater to the south, to Savannah or Charleston. He believes the war will be won from there. Again, an admiral. In essence, he plans to leave New England to wither because he cannot prune it, even if his Hudson adventure is successful."

"None can say the fellow doesn't have grand ideas. That he lays so much on the navy tells me he doesn't feel strong enough to come at us alone. Is Admiral Gambier to continue there, do you think?"

"There are indications that he will be recalled this year, but his replacement is not named. Command will devolve to Collier until a new man arrives. Clinton has sent a list of candidates to Germain, but both Odysseus and Kathleen believe that he aims too high. His choices are too able and too much needed in Europe to be spared for our little war. They would probably refuse the offer if it were to be tendered. Collier may be the best for the job, but he is still too junior. A very good thing for us.

"Don't forget that Clinton's heart may not be in this—he has been asking to be relieved of the command for a year. Kathleen thinks that he is being retained because half the Cabinet wants to resign too, and are not being allowed to. She can't see them granting some mere general a privilege they themselves are denied."

Washington fell silent, digesting his hoe cakes and his intelligence. Richard had learned to let his commander consider in peace.

"Does Odysseus think there will be an attempt on Albany, to open the Champlain corridor to Montreal?"

"Silent on that point, sir. I think the plan is just a flanking movement to drive us from our strong positions in the highlands. Clinton really wants us on level ground where he believes his chances better."

"I shall have to make a note of that. If Clinton does not get the support he wishes, how does he proceed?"

"Speculatively, sir, I think he will sit tight. He hasn't the troops for a frontal attack on our positions, nor for a move to the south, unless he abandons New York as they did Philadelphia last year. Such a move would be devastating to the Loyalists and to the Ministry as well. Their Parliamentary opponents would seize such a failure with enthusiasm, possibly turn them from office. If he detaches a southern army, he will positively be on the defensive in the north. The southern army would still be far smaller than needed to insure success. He might send Cornwallis. The two have come to dislike each other."

Any other news?"

"Nothing but bits and blobs, sir. Too nebulous to present now."

160

"Very well, Browning. Until tomorrow morning?"

"As you wish. Thank you, Your Excellency."

Richard Browning slipped out the way he had come.

✶✶✶✶✶

The final cadence filled the room. Margaret, the sole audience, watched the performers' rapt faces, enjoying the quick glances among them to coordinate an entrance, the swift, satisfied little smiles as something went well. She listened as Mary and Sir Henry began their last long downbow, as Fanny rolled her last chord, timed so that the small finger of her right hand depressed the last key just as the others reached their bow tips.

They sat with hands and bows suspended in mid air, none wanting to move or speak as the hungry draperies swallowed the last vibrations.

Mary spoke, softly, "Did we really just do that?"

"Bravo us! Something I'll surely remember!"

Now the floodgates were open. "Sir Henry, that was wonderful"..."That was the first time we got through the whole piece without stopping"..."When I first saw the part, I thought I'd never play that last movement"..."I made a couple of mistakes"..."I just left things out to get to the barline"..."Didn't detract"..."I worked up a sweat toward the end"..."Thank you for setting a more moderate tempo, Fanny"..."Could have been a hair faster, but I think something would have been lost"..."yes, more of my notes..."

"I must compliment you all. That was most wonderful. I feel like royalty, being the only one to enjoy it"

"You weren't Mama, we all did."

"Next time, let's do one of those old numbers so I can just drone away on the continuo. My fingers are feeling abused."

"You draw a fine sound from your instrument."

161

"Thank you. It's a nice one, by a fellow down in that little town where Stradivarii worked. Not one of the famous names, but a reputable man nonetheless. I paid £100 for it."

"Your fingers do deserve a break after that last movement. Do you want to play more tonight, sir?"

"No, I'm done. That was a splendid way to end the evening. Anything else would be anticlimactic. I plan to sip my port, meditate, then retire."

"You and Mary can go up whenever you're ready, Sir Henry. Fanny and I can put the house to bed."

1779

Margaret stood in the theater lobby, waiting for John Andre to finish his business backstage so they could leave together. Most of the play's audience had long since filed out, but she could hear Oliver DeLancey holding forth from the other end of the room before a small knot of people. Curious, she moved nearer.

"What we need is a general who knows his business! Sir Henry sits at home playing the fiddle, or chasing foxes. That's as close to being in the field this army has come. Meanwhile the damned rebels sit secure not thirty miles from here! Some of us are going to write to Lord George Germain to get a new man sent out, one with blood in his eye and iron in his spine. Who's with me?"

"Mr. DeLancey," said Margaret, "What, exactly, is it that Sir Henry should do?"

"Go up to the highlands and drive those rascals out! One bellyful of Royal lead, Mrs. Brush, and half of them would be on their way home before dinner! They've sat there for three years without the least threat from us. They sit there laughing while a Commission says 'please.' Then they laugh some more when the army threatens to hang them. They know it's all just words. We need actions! Am I right, people?"

There came a chorus of murmured agreement, a nodding of heads.

"When I said 'exactly,' I was hoping for something more specific. You want him to attack the enemy in the highlands?"

"Yes, sooner rather than later."

"How is he to get his army there for this attack?"

"I don't care! Send them up the river."

"Where are the boats and the seamen to take them there? Never mind, I'll tell you where they aren't, they aren't here. Sir Henry has been asking for naval support for two years, yet London does not deem it important enough to send a fleet to his aid. The French, however, do think it important and summer a fleet upon us each season."

"Then let them march."

"Let's see. March an entire army across Kingsbridge, three abreast, form them up, and march across Westchester. What, two days, do you think, or would it take three? All that time the enemy would know you were coming and be preparing for your coming. Let me remind you that up there in those hills are scores of men who support their families by potting squirrels at fifty yards. Do you think they couldn't shoot you at three hundred? Half the officer corps would be down before you were close enough to call a bayonet charge."

"Damned unsporting of them, picking a target, I say!"

"Those men understand that war is not sport. They have learned from the savages. Shoot a captain before the charge and the company mills about. Shoot a colonel and a regiment retreats. Shoot a general, the retreat becomes a rout.

"Your zeal is commendable, Mr. DeLancey. Forgive me if I have been blunt. The point I'm trying to make is that until the strategic situation changes, until London sends the men and ships and guns we need, there is no tactical solution to this problem. Write to London all you want, please do. Just don't ask for a new general. The one we have is quite good enough. Ask instead for the tools so that he may do what is expected. If enough voices are heard in London, if the clamor can be loud enough, perhaps the support will be forthcoming."

"Can the clamor ever be loud enough?"

"I don't know, sir. I just don't know."

✳✳✳✳✳

"You seem agitated this evening, Sir Henry."

Margaret and Henry Clinton sat in their end of the parlor while Fanny and Mary Baddeley practiced their music around the harpsichord. They could overhear but ignore their comments to each other as they worked, just as they ignored what passed between their elders.

"Lord George Germain again. The tone of his letters seems to imply disfavor, yet the words do not. I find them a concern."

"Sir Henry," Margaret paused, choosing her words carefully. "I wonder, I mean, I know I would be far overstepping my place, but could I perhaps see one old such letter, just to get the feel of it? I certainly wouldn't want you to show me anything I shouldn't see, being just a woman and a civilian and all, but if I knew his ways, perhaps I could help you understand? I shouldn't think a, say, year-old letter would compromise secrecy; things discussed would have already happened and thus be no longer secret?"

"Mrs. Brush," he continued haltingly, "…You do have a good ear for hidden meanings…My secretary knows them all…"

He thought a moment longer. "Wait here."

He rose and left the room only to return a few minutes later with several papers in his hand.

"These are from last fall, all of our correspondence then. Read, and please tell me what you see."

Margaret read carefully, several times referring from one paper to another, pausing to think on occasion. Once she breathed, "I thought so." The

165

general sat quietly, watching her expression. Nearly fifteen minutes passed. She looked up.

"Sir Henry, this is amazing. Your concerns are well grounded..."

"That's a relief, I wondered if I were imagining the whole!" he interrupted.

"No, no. I think it's quite real. Almost every instruction is qualified; 'If you think it best'...'Use your best judgment'...'it may be advisable.' If he thought you were not using your best judgment, why has he not replaced you? He should be assuming that you were. The man is devilish clever. If something goes well, he may say 'I directed Sir Henry to do thus and so.' If it does not, the onus falls to you 'I only made a suggestion, Sir Henry made the decision.' He's setting the stage so that he may succeed, or you must fail. Any one sentence, out of its context, the way Parliament would read it, makes him the wise statesman, and you the damned fool. Excuse my language, sir. These must be infuriating things to receive!"

"There are that," he agreed ruefully. "What am I to do?"

"Well, your responses are quite good, direct and manly. You do report conditions truly, as far as I know. I couldn't fault a thing you wrote. Do you suppose that his is the attitude of the Ministry?"

"I don't know, but I fear it is. My friends are perhaps less effective that I might wish. The Duke of Newcastle is a mild sort of man and is not a force in the government. He often seems more interested in his fields than in his friends."

"And he is your cousin-german?"

"Yes, and my strongest reed. That is a worry, but from here, I can do little. You didn't see it in those letters but I am directed to remain at my post. Germain chooses to make that very clear. I cannot return to London to explain myself. I sent Drummond home to argue my affairs. He tells me that all is met at every turn with 'the King wishes it thus'...or some such. He could make no head against it. Now I fear he has fallen into line with them. His last letter is filled with explanation and excuse as to why they cannot provide me the troops I need." His voice rose, so that even the music stopped for a moment. "They bind me up like some damned pig on a spit and then want me to do grand things!"

166

"He holds you captive here while he persecutes your reputation there." She laid her hand on his arm. "I understand, sir. Let me think on this. You know I'll help you any way I can."

"Thank you. May I call you Margaret? We do seem to be conspirators somehow. Talking with you helps prepare me for my staff meetings, lets me try out thoughts *sub rosa*, so to speak. It's amazing that a woman can have a mind so keen as yours."

"Why, thank you, sir! And yes, you may address me as you please. You honor me by asking. I'm so pleased to be of service, Sir Henry! Know that I have no friends in London, no one there to whom I could disclose our discussions nor would I. Our words shall not leave this continent. I assure you of that."

*****

The courier was an intelligent young fellow, but repetition had bred complacency. He had made the journey from Peekskill to Newark and back dozens of times over the last year and had never been questioned. He would spend tonight at his uncle's near Passaic, then finish tomorrow with a fresh horse. In two days, he would return, exchanging horses again.

He was trotting through his least favorite patch, a high bank on his right and a marsh on his left. It was not that he apprehended danger there, it was just a depressing piece of road, gloomy and often damp. All the rest of the way, he had witnessed the late spring, he had smelled the plowed fields, the lilacs in a farm yard. Everything was new and fresh, everywhere except here. His horse splashed though the shallow puddles in the road and the swamp smelled of decay.

There were five men, redcoats, standing across the road as he rounded the sharp bend. He reined in and wheeled his horse. There were four more red-coated soldiers blocking his retreat.

He could not be taken. Too many would be endangered if he should be questioned, and he'd be hanged anyway. He eased his pistol from the holster, cocking it as he did. He took a deep breath and spurred his horse toward the four. Long odds, but better. He let out a long yell.

He shot one before they could fire. Then man and horse went down. The horse struggled to rise. His mangled shoulder would not support him and he fell, legs flailing in uncomprehending terror.

The officer approached from behind and dispatched the animal with his pistol. He turned to the other body in the road.

"Damn it! I wanted him alive. Search him. We're looking for papers. Strip him naked. You two, go through the equipage. Show me everything you find."

"Harley is dead, sir."

"Regrettable. Bring my horse, we'll have to take him back for burial. This one, throw in the marsh when we're done."

"I don't think he is dead, sir."

"Really?" He grasped the courier's lapels and lifted him a few inches off the ground. He shouted at the face. "Where were you going, you damned rebel? Where did you come from?

The eyes opened groggily. "Rot in Hell," he said. The eyes closed.

The officer dropped him onto the road.

"He might as well be dead. Kill him."

It took the soldiers ten minutes to carefully inspect the clothing and saddle. Even so, they almost missed the dispatches sewn into the lining of his waistcoat.

"Well done," he said, as he skimmed the letters. "For a moment there I wondered if he were an innocent, if there is such thing as an innocent colonial. Form up men. We've gotten what we came for."

*****

John Montraville was slightly dissatisfied as he entered General Clinton's second floor office in City Hall. He had spent half a day studying the letters

168

he had taken from the dead courier, but was no closer to understanding them than when he began.

"Yes, Montraville, what have you found?"

"I don't know, sir. We intercepted a messenger in New Jersey yesterday. As we had suspected, there is communication between the Colonial headquarters and the Hudson, Peekskill or West Point. We captured several pages of correspondence but we can't read it."

"What language is it?"

"It's not the language, that's plain English. It's just too plain. I've brought them for you, sir." He handed them across. "Why would anyone sew a letter to an 'Aunt Betsey' into the lining of his clothes, and risk death to protect it? It just doesn't make sense."

"Have you questioned the man?"

"He was killed in the capture, unfortunately. He made a run at the men, they fired in self defense. He killed one, but I surely wish they had not fired so well. I never thought I'd be cursing that the men knew how to shoot."

"You're right, Montraville, this is nonsensical. Why write a letter to Aunt Betsey and then secret it in the lining? Say, have you explored sympathetic ink?"

"I hadn't thought of that. Shall we try heat? Your candle?"

"No, no. Listen, take this to Andre—he has a fellow who's wonderfully good at this sort of thing."

"What do you suppose this number at the bottom represents? A code key, perhaps? I'll take these to Andre—he might have an idea."

*****

"Damn it!" Kathleen Browning rarely swore, but this called for it as nothing ever had. "Are you sure he is dead? Did you find his body? I must tell his father something."

"No, Ma'am. We found his horse, shot twice, a mercy. There were his clothes scattered about, they must have stripped him, and his waistcoat was torn open."

"So we don't truly know whether they have him or not." She thought for a moment, controlling her urge to blurt something. "Very well, thank you. May I rely on your discretion, both of you? No one must know of his mission or his possible capture. May I?"

The men, known to Sally as Bill and Tom, nodded. After a few words, they left her alone with her thoughts.

Best case, he is dead...Sad, really, he was a good lad...They'll have only the dispatches with no way to read them...They'll probably figure out the sympathetic ink, Andre is no fool...They won't know the contents, but they'll know it was something and from where...

But suppose they do have him? What changes? No one can withstand determined questioning...they'd all be known...what then? Wait, he knows only me—and Richard at headquarters, but that's no danger to him...they'd expect him to receive dispatches...only me...

✱✱✱✱✱

Sir Henry Clinton sat with Margaret, talking quietly as Mary and Fanny worked out a new piece.

"No...that's not right, can we go back to the double bar and go again? I got off again." Fanny sounded annoyed with herself.

"I think it's me. I have all that noodling to do there, and I feel honor-bound to include all the notes. I think I'm late getting through the measure."

"I'll wait for you, ala cadenza"

"They get on well together, don't they, Sir Henry?" said Margaret.

"Yes. I'm glad they do. Mary needed a friend her own age. She was feeling a bit lonely with none but my staff and servants in her life. My position isolates her from most people.

"I want to tell you something, Mrs. Brush. You remember I said I would not loose the Loyalists on the people without a direct order? Well, the damned thing has come. The units are to be collected and put in the field. Until now, I've distributed them among the Regulars by company, for garrison duty and the like."

"Are they to be an independent command, as you feared?"

"Even that idiot George Germain would not say that—although the order is vague on that point."

"Lord George is laying off the responsibility to you—credit to him if what you do works, blame to you if it doesn't."

"Typical of the man."

"What shall you do?"

"They'll get as little as I can give. They can act, but only with my approval. They'll not have power to negotiate anything, not prisoner exchanges, not terms, not anything! I'm the general here, damn it! Apologies, Madam."

"None needed, sir. Thank you for telling me. It is sad and unfair that Lord George throws you into such dilemmas. How stands the Ministry at home?"

"Gasping and wheezing like some old duke who hasn't the decency to lie down and die so his nephew can inherit politely. They still don't understand this war. Still I get no naval support—they're sending out Mariot Arbuthnot, of all people. Met him once, he's seventy if he's a day, not shifted himself in a decade and a fool besides. They didn't know what to do with him, so they foist him onto me! I'll have to get everything I can out of Collier while he's still here."

*****

Heads tuned as Richard Browning entered the office, interrupting a conference.

"Apologies, Your Excellency, important dispatch. From New York."

171

He handed the note across, General Washington read it quickly.

"Verified?"

"Yes sir. Culper Jr. also reports approximately 40 sail of transports are seen loading in New York harbor. It is estimated that they will sail with the dawn tide. More are massing at King's Bridge."

"The destination?"

"I expect Stony Point, sir. Passing by those narrows to get to West Point would leave his train exposed."

"Hamilton," called Washington, "what troops at Stony Point?"

"Company strength, sir."

"They'll not long stand against these 6,000. Orders to burn the works, then get out. They are not to sacrifice themselves. Verplank's Point across the river?"

"About the same, sir."

"Very well. They'll not hold either. The same to them."

Yes, sir."

"Browning, Verplank's is too close to Peekskill, only ten miles. We have people there who must be protected. Take a cavalry company and escort them to Continental Village. If you hurry you can still use Dobb's Ferry. You take my meaning?"

"Yes, sir. Thank you, Excellency. A company is too many, sir. We'd never find enough fresh horses. I'll want to be there by morning. Half that will do."

"Very well. Carry the orders with you to Stony Point and Verplank's. Hamilton, prepare to break camp. A winter in New Jersey is enough. The army moves north."

*****

172

"Well, Andre, could you make anything of my find?"

The two sat, sipping their drinks. The back room of the little shop was as dark as their coffee.

"Yes and no, Montraville. It was sympathetic ink. The letters you could read were worthless, just camouflage. Unfortunately, the revealed writing was just groups of numbers. Always the same series, number, comma, number, comma, number, space. My man says it's a dictionary code—page, line, word. I've seen something similar before. Unfortunately, without the right dictionary, the meaning is as opaque as ever. I've tried all I could procure, without success."

"Where else did you see it?"

"Last year, we caught some messages from a shop we used to operate; the rebels thought it was their secret network, when it was in fact ours. We copied dozens before the place was burned."

"Do you think they discovered the imposture?"

"I suspect so, but it was well done, not a trace."

"What shall we do now?"

"Watch and wait for more, Montraville, watch and wait. They'll make anther mistake. They always do. You say this man was coming from Peekskill?"

"I believe so. No real evidence, but it makes sense, the only thing about this that does."

"I'll cut you orders. Take a troop from Verplank's Point and go to Peekskill. Shouldn't think you'll meet any opposition. Find out who has left town suddenly. If the rebels have an agent there, they'll not risk having such a one captured."

*****

Richard Browning leapt from his horse in front of Kate's house in Peekskill.

"Richard! What are you doing here?"

"At the moment, Kathleen, I'm embracing my wife. Didn't you notice?"

She pushed him away with regret, playfully. "Not quite the question I was asking."

"Clinton comes, with his friends." Their mood changed at once.

"Yes, I know. Edward sends me notice of all that goes to the headquarters. The movement is confirmed? When shall they arrive?"

"Culper Jr. confirms it and they should arrive mid afternoon, we think. We need to get you out of here."

"You came alone?"

"I have a couple with me, a troop is following within the hour. How much must you pack?"

"Sophie!" Kathleen called. When the girl appeared, she continued. "Pack quickly. A week's worth of day dresses and accoutrements. The same for yourself. You have an hour. Get on it. Don't be too particular." She turned to her husband. "Richard, there are others who must also know. I'll give you the names. She made a list quickly. "There are things that I must pack myself. You understand?"

"I haven't seen you for four months, yet you send me away so soon?"

"Well, you ordered me to get packing!"

He stole another kiss before he left.

✱✱✱✱✱

Mary Baddeley hurried into the parlor, waving a paper in her hand.

"A letter from Sir Henry!"

"Wonderful! Has he news?" asked Margaret.

174

"Let me see…He says they have taken a place called Stony Point and another named Verplank's Point…the rascals absconded…four score prisoners…He's staying at Colonel Phillipse house…going to send some troops back to New York…too few here now to properly defend…more troops to punish the Connecticut seacoast…those to be Loyalists, in hopes that will silence them…Oh, I won't read <u>that</u> part," blushing."

"Does he say how many men he is sending to Connecticut?"

"Um…no. He'd not bore me with such unimportant things." She didn't notice Margaret and Fanny exchange a quick look as she read on. "He wants me to join him there. I'm to take the coach up."

"That's nice. It's a lovely house, at least it was. I stopped there once with Madam Schuyler. The Colonel used to keep a wonderful table, and the gardens were magnificent. I wonder how they have survived this war."

Mary finished the letter and looked up. "You two will be all right here, keep the home fires burning and all?"

"Of course we will. Does he give any hints as to how long you'll stay?

"No, I should think at least a week."

"So like a man. No concept of what a woman needs to know! If you find you need anything, just send to us and we'll pack it off to you. And be sure to let us know when you are returning so that we may have Mr. Thompson properly supply us."

"He certainly is the most attentive food monger I have ever met. He must value Sir Henry's custom highly."

"I think that is not the business to which he is so attentive."

It was Fanny's turn to blush.

*****

Margaret sat on the edge of her bed, unable to sleep. The cool June night eased in through the open window.

What was it that John Andre had said the other night? That Sir Henry suspected powerful people in London wanted him to fail? And just evenings before, I had said something about shooting a general. But you didn't have to really shoot him, do you?

But it was so cold Not cruel perhaps, but cold, some would say treacherous It was something Lady Macbeth would do. Will I go mad too? No...am I mad to even think that I am able? How would I feel about myself afte? Was it dishonorable? Not one in a hundred would understand, not one is a thousand would blame her...

Dishonorable or not, this was war. Certainly this would shorten it. But of Sir Henry? His career would surely be over, but isn't it anyway? Neither his estates nor family would be injured Mary would stand by him, she was sure of that. He wasn't a bad man, just the wrong one for this job. He antagonized too many people, too unsure.

What might happen if a different man were sent? But who would come? America was a graveyard of careers. Would she be making the situation worse? I'm being drawn further and further into this war. What was impelling her? Could she be sure that her inner compass still found north?

She felt cold.

But how, exactly. I demanded specifics of Oliver DeLancey, now I must demand them of myself. If you shoot a king, make very sure that he is dead. Lady Macbeth couldn't do this, like Sir Henry, the wrong person for the job.

She searched her reading for a character who might guide her; she at last found one and shuddered. She lay back down, pulled the light sheet to her chin and stared into the blackness toward the ceiling. With the dawn came clarity.

*****

It was another of those hot, sunny, windless summer days for which New York was so well known. Sally came into the little closet off the kitchen where Margaret worked the household accounts.

176

"Mr. Thompson is here, Ma'am."

"Thank you Sally, I'll be along in a moment. You'd better tell Fanny."

"No need, she seems to have found her way out to greet him already."

"Did I never tell the girl not to appear too eager?"

"I don't think she's any more eager than he is."

"In normal times I would welcome the attachment. He's a good man. Just now though, I'm not so sure. Lovers can be dangerously impulsive. We never were, were we?"

"I'll pass on that question."

They both half-smiled, thinking privately, recalling days past. Margaret went into the yard to the pair who were talking quietly, trying not to stand too near while wishing to be nearer still.

"Good afternoon, Mr. Thompson. What have you for us today?"

"I brought your order complete, Mrs. Brush. I brought along some beans, and I have some early peaches, the first I have seen this year. They're eleven shillings the bushel. Shall I put you down for some?"

"I'll ask cook. With Sir Henry away, we'll not need so much this week. Here is your list." She handed across a piece of paper with surprising amounts of space surrounding the provision order. "Any news from New Jersey?"

"Little, I'm afraid." He continued in a voice loud enough that others could hear, 'The Continentals have broken quarters, the word is that they'll move into the highlands around West Point."

"Mr. Thompson, have your man put the things in the root cellar. Fanny, I'll be some time consulting cook about those peaches. Perhaps you and Mr. Thompson would care to wait in the drawing room, out of this hot sun?"

Fanny shot her mother a grateful look as she took his hand and led her young man inside.

177

*****

"Good morning, Your Excellency."

"Good morning, Browning. What have you today?"

"From Odysseus, sir. Clinton will withdraw significant portions of his expedition. Twenty-five hundred will return to garrison around the city, but another two thousand, Loyalists, will be sent for punitive raids along the Connecticut coast, Governor Tryon to command."

"Do we know when?"

"Not precisely, but it will be soon. Clinton needs to act before Admiral Collier is supplanted if he wants transport from the navy. The consensus is that Arbuthnot, once he arrives will be hard to budge."

"We'll send word to Governor Trumbull to alert the militia. I'll have Hamilton send the Connecticut line as well. They'll probably be too late, but we can't have them sitting here, watching an enemy doing nothing while their homes are burned."

"Very good, sir. On another front, Clinton has issued a new proclamation, freeing the slaves of all patriots living outside his lines. They're not even required to join the army. He promises freedom, land and protection to all."

"That sounds desperate to me. Some of our people will be injured, to be sure, but not so many, I hope, as he thinks. They'll have to cross the lines to take advantage. I wonder how he proposes to feed those who will come. You tell me that food and housing are already scarce there."

"Very true, sir."

"Anything else? Did you get Mrs. Browning away safely?"

"Yes, sir. Thank you for your concern. We were just in time. A troop rode into town hours after we left. It was good to see her, if only for a few days. They were asking questions about who had decamped quickly. I wonder if they know of her."

178

"Let's hope not. You know how important her information is to us. The redcoats would love to get their hands on her, if only they should discover who she is. I do envy you your respite; Mrs. Washington is so far away.

"Tell me Browning, was your house in New Haven damaged in Tryon's raids?"

"No, Thank you sir. The fire was confined to the east side of the river, away from the college and my house. All is ashes there. There was looting of course, everywhere. But my man there says we came away pretty well."

*****

"You're angry with me, aren't you, Mrs. Brush." The candles in the wall sconces of the drawing room gave flickering light to the scene.

"I'm just angry, Sir Henry, with all respect. You know my thoughts on raids of no purpose but punishment. I think them a poor policy and bloody cruel besides."

"You remember my orders?"

"Yes sir. But the true effect will be to make the King many more enemies than friends. Many of the Loyalists I know are become neutrals; some of the neutrals are wondering how to leave this city. In the country sentiment is higher than at any time since Lexington. Governor Tryon and his coterie of radicals have no idea of the hornet's nest they have kicked over. The public outcry is immense, even among moderate Tories. It probably will be in London as well. It was barbaric and vindictive of them with three whole towns burned. It's hardly the sort of thing that makes the rebels eager to be loyal subjects again."

"He claims his acts were not prohibited by my instructions."

"Well he might, sir, to protect himself. It's like the five year old looking up at his father, all wide eyed, 'No one told me I shouldn't paint the kitty, so I did.' You can expect the same from Lord George in London. It will be 'General Clinton should have been more clear, it's not the Governor's fault, and it certainly isn't mine.' Trust me, this will settle on you. It's unfair, but it will."

179

"Have I no recourse?"

"Write to your friends in England sir, do it quickly. The first voice will be the loudest. And I do pray that you will be painfully explicit in future commands."

"Mrs. Brush, I must ask. Have these events altered your own attachment to the King?"

"My attachment is unchangeable, Sir Henry."

*****

"Well, Montraville, how did you do in Peekskill?"

"The birds had all flown, regrettably. I have a list, I think it complete, of those who fled. It's a safe wager that our man is among them, but which?"

"May I see it?"

Andre read down the list, thirteen names. "I don't recognize a one of them. That makes sense, when you think on it, it would be someone we don't know, some minor figure beneath our notice. The question is, where does he stand in the order of these spies? Is he the master, or just a minor cog in the works? Are those dispatches you intercepted orders or reports?"

"I think I shall show this to Mrs. Brush. After a lifetime here, she may know these people."

"Mrs. Brush. John, a colonial? Are you sure that is wise?"

"Listen, Montraville, I know there is bad blood between you two. Lord knows I don't know the cause, and don't want to, but there is. Nevertheless, she is an intelligent woman with a wide circle of acquaintance, and her loyalty is unquestionable. A part of this intelligence business, as you shall learn, is the determination to use the people available, not necessarily the people you might choose to invite to tea. Besides, I find her company agreeable."

"There was a time when I did too."

Andre regarded his friend closely. "But no more?"

"Never more."

"Your choice or hers?"

"Mutual, I suppose you could say, although now I wish it were not so absolute."

"The rumors are true, then?" as Andre slipped back into the intelligence analyst's role, interrogating his subject.

"I cannot say, John. It would be unpardonable."

*****

Lieutenant Barlow greeted Margaret as she entered Major Andre's outer office, and showed her directly in.

"Margaret, I asked you to come to my office because I wanted to show you something that I can't carry around with me. I hope you can help me with it."

"You know I will if I can, John."

"It's rather a long story, but the short of it is, I sent a troop to find the names of everyone who had run from Peekskill as we approached. I think someone there is a spy, connected to the city. We had intercepted dispatches from there to Washington. I have the names of suspects, but every one is unknown to me. I wondered if you might identify some?"

"May I see it?" She tried to keep the tremor from her voice. She took the list and stepped to the window, the light was better there. She kept her back to him as she read. She caught her breath.

"There is only one name that I may know. I knew a Mrs. Browning once, during the old war. I lost touch with her some time ago, I don't know if it is she or not. Her husband was teaching at Yale College, ancient languages. A bookish sort of man, but very kind. All the others are strangers to me."

181

"There is a fellow named Browning on Washington's staff, sort of my opposite number."

"It's possible, we all knew Washington. We messed together one winter. The husband had a lieutenant's commission then, Horatio Gates' company. He resigned it after the Monongahela massacre.

"You know," she continued, "if they are the same, and I'm not saying that they are, it makes sense that she would avoid you—if she were hostage, you might affect her husband in his duties. People have betrayed for far less cause."

"Perhaps we should make an effort to snatch her up."

"Oh, I think not, John. Kidnap an innocent wife to compromise her husband? The rebels tried that with me, except that I walked up to them. It was a barbaric way of conducting a war. Surely we are better people than that! Poor policy besides! The outcry would be deafening."

"Wait, opposite number...I've just thought of something. There is a number standing alone at the bottom of each page. Perhaps that number is an address, 'to person number such and so.' We had thought it indicated a different code key altogether. If they are all the same, the problem is simpler."

"But I'm far more interested in the notion that you know Washington. I never knew that. Can you tell me you opinions of him?"

"Well," she hesitated. "The man I knew then was probably a different fellow than the one you now face. He was only in his early twenties then, and we all change over years."

"Nevertheless, tell me."

"He's a large man, quite strong and a good horseman. He has a good head, but not a profound one. He didn't care much about learning in general, though he had some. He read pretty much whatever he could get about whatever task lay ahead. Then, he was learning to be a regimental officer. Before that he had learned to be a surveyor, a farmer, even how to run a distillery. I suspect he has since studied to be a general. His decisions have certainly improved since Long Island. He was chivalrous, but had a fierce temper. He was very aware of his shortcomings and publically modest of his accomplishments though inwardly, he was very jealous of them. He was a very impressive gentleman. Does that help?"

"Yes, everything does."

"Was the messenger any help. Did you question him?"

"Unfortunately, the man got himself killed trying to escape, so we couldn't."

"Just what does such a dispatch like that look like? Were you able to read it?"

"Want to see? We've had good people working on the text, but it's coded beyond belief. Sympathetic ink and all was just the beginning." He reached into a drawer and handed two papers across. She was relieved to see that neither was hers, but recognized Kate's hand.

"When we found them, none of these numbers were visible. They're a kind of code, but we haven't the key. We need to know exactly what dictionary they used as a source, and we don't. I've tried every one I can find."

"John, does it have to be an English dictionary?"

He looked at her, surprised. "No—blast! There are Frenchmen all over that army. I hadn't thought of that! Thank you—you may just have given us the answer."

"I don't want to make your life more difficult, but German and Dutch are common here too."

"Oh, Lord! You said that the Browning you knew taught Latin and Greek? Is the wife a Grecian too?"

"I have no idea. I never heard them use it. Actually, I wouldn't know if they had." Her heart beat faster. "Remember speaking and writing a language are different—my spoken French and German are quite passable, but reading and writing them are very difficult for me. But you're jumping on the name alone as proof positive. I think that's too far without more evidence!"

"It won't be hard to track a college professor. There aren't so many of them. I think I shall snatch up this Mrs. Browning."

183

"But the outcry?"

"I'll risk it—she doesn't look so innocent to me now."

"John, I really think you need to verify just who it is that you're going to seize up before you send men. If this one is innocent, the reaction will be fierce. Already moderates are beginning to desert the King's ship—there have been so many wanton provocations by our troops. How long will it take you to discover whether this Browning is the same I knew?"

"I should think only a day or two—there are surely other professors from Yale in the city, or people who know them."

"Then, what would be gained by precipitate action? We know much could be lost. I have heard that Washington is moving into the Highlands, so this Peekskill person may even be irrelevant by now."

"You really don't want me to do this, do you, Margaret?"

"I don't, John. I have told Sir Henry numerous times, and I tell you now, that you can't win this war without winning the people. Actions such as you propose will surely alienate more than they will intimidate. You'll be driving them into the rebels' arms. My countrymen are too jealous of their freedoms to bow like the squires' tenants. They just won't. They need to be, let us say, wooed."

"We're getting to a place that will do you and I no good, so let us leave this philosophizing behind. I'll stay my hand until I am certain. Satisfied?"

"Thank you." She gave him a peck on the cheek. "I knew I wasn't wrong about you."

"Is that all I get?"

She smiled. "For now."

*****

"Sally, will you show Mr. Thompson to the parlor, please? Fanny is waiting for you there, sir."

He entered eagerly and took her in his arms. She returned the embrace, but then pushed him away and led him to a settee.

"Listen carefully, John!" she whispered fiercely, "This is too important to be put into writing. I don't know how much time we'll have before we may be disturbed. Don't interrupt," as he leaned forward for a kiss. She paused to make sure he was comprehending. "Mama saw Major Andre this morning. A courier from your mother to headquarters was intercepted in New Jersey. He was killed…

"I knew him." He rose and turned his back. "His name was Amos Staughton!" His voice broke as he continued. "He was one of my best friends!"

She went to him, touched his arm softly. "I'm so sorry, Edward," she said gently. "Can you be sure?"

He nodded as he reached for his handkerchief to dry his eyes. "He was the only one Mother trusted with them. I'm embarrassed to have you see me thus."

"Manly grief is becoming, dear one. Edward, I love you. Your pain is mine as well." He turned to face her; she rested her hands on his chest. "There is more at stake here. Listen. They have two dispatches in your mother's hand. They are unable to decipher them, although they have beaten…

The drawing room door opened suddenly as Sir Henry entered.

"Oh, so sorry Fanny, I had no idea you were entertaining." He looked between their red faces, and understood exactly what he had interrupted. "My apologies."

"This is your house, Sir Henry," she said with a laugh. "I believe you are allowed to enter as you wish. May I present Mr. John Thompson, Mr. Thompson, Sir Henry Clinton."

"A pleasure, young man. I just came to fetch something…"

"Over on the mantle, I believe," said Fanny.

"Ah, yes. Thank you my dear." He collected his spectacles and eased himself out. Fanny waited a full minute before pulling Thompson back to the settee.

"He hates to admit that he needs those! Now...they have beaten the sympathetic ink. They are convinced that the code is based on a dictionary. Mama set them on a chase by suggesting that it might not be an English one, but Andre has guessed at your mother's role.

"They also have the names of thirteen people who ran from Peekskill as their army approached. The only name Mama recognized was your mother's. Mama tried to explain it away as her attempt to avoid being kidnapped to compromise your father. She thought she had it contained, but then Andre jumped on the idea that the dispatches might be coded Latin or Greek, which led him back to your father, and by extension, to her. Do you understand what this all means? She is in gravest danger. He plans to arrest her! How quickly can you warn her?"

"I'm meeting my boat crew at three o'clock and the tide turns at five. I can be there by tomorrow morning, if the wind holds. When are they coming for her?

"Mama thinks they will wait at least a day. She convinced Andre to verify that the man on General Washington's staff is the same who was at Yale College."

"Wait, how do we know the dispatches were from Mother?"

"Mama saw them. The number code was plain as day, as was her hand. She also saw the list of names."

"How could she? What if they had caught her?"

"Not to worry. Major Andre kindly showed them, asking for her advice."

"I don't know whether to marvel at her temerity or their foolishness!"

She arched an eyebrow. "Oh? Are you suggesting that asking my Mama's advice is foolish?"

"Of course not! You know I have the highest respect for her," he sputtered, flustered.

"Well, you may marvel at your leisure, right now however, you must kiss me before Sir Henry blunders in again and wonders why you are not. It would be a help if you should mention that you love me too." She closed her eyes.

"Must I?"

She was about to say 'yes' when she felt his lips on hers.

*****

Edward hurried up the path from the river landing to his mother's little house. Peekskill's early risers, mostly servants, were beginning their daily routines, fetching wood and eggs, turning animals to pasture. Smoke rose from the chimneys as breakfast fires were stoked. He could hear the wooden blocks protest as a sloop raised its mainsail out on the river, a sloop bound for Albany.

"Mother!"

"Edward! Why do I always find myself asking my men what they are doing here?"

"You must leave Peekskill now. Andre has tumbled to you. Aunt Margaret has stalled him a day or two, but he is sending men to arrest you."

"How did he find out?"

"He hasn't, not yet. But he will identify Father, who he knows to be with General Washington, with the Yale College quickly enough. He's taken with the idea that you two are communicating in coded Greek."

"I know no more Greek than I do trigonometry! How did he settle on this?"

"He was showing Aunt Margaret the dispatches they captured, the ones from Amos. They killed him. He resisted the capture and they shot him. Andre was explaining the method to her. He believes it is based on a dictionary. She tried to confuse matters by suggesting that it might not be an English one, and his mind leapt to ancient languages. He wanted to come that minute for you; she talked him out of that, but you have little time."

"She's seen them?"

"Yes. They have revealed the hidden ink, but have no clue how to decode. She also saw a list of suspicious names from here. You are honored there as well."

"I suppose, if I am this famous, I might as well repair to West Point. It would be expected, anyway. Edward, I'm sorry about Amos. You all grew up together. You know I was always fond of him." She opened a door. "Sophie!"

An hour later, Edward found his mother sitting on the step of her house, fiddling with a maple leaf.

"The boat is almost loaded, Mother. Have you anything else to add?"

"No," She spoke absently. "Edward, do you know what this poor leaf's problem is?"

"Other than that you picked it?"

"No, I didn't. It dropped in my lap. But why is this one different?" Her son awaited the explanation he knew would be forthcoming. "His problem is that he became an individual once he fell. All those other leaves on the tree are anonymous and so are safe. We don't even know if it fell from this tree or that one. I need a way to become like those leaves, not this one.

"They have our names from their visit. Some will be bystanders caught up in the panic who ran too. Too bad for them, chaff among the wheat. That should delay them because they'll need to investigate us all.

"Do we know why Andre thinks those dispatches came from here?"

"No, but he seems prone to guesswork."

"Then his conclusions will be vulnerable. I wish I had time to ask Meg. She'd probably know. I've been trying to think of a misdirection that doesn't injure anyone."

188

"Give him a Tory."

"I'd prefer to give a clue that leads directly to the middle of Long Island Sound and nowhere else. But come, we should be going. Let me talk to Sophie, then I'll be down."

*****

Montraville was in a sour mood. He had ridden all the way from New York to Ossining yesterday, hidden in the woods until dawn only to ride further and find his quarry had flown. The stupid cow of a maid had even pointed to the boat carrying her to West Point, insolence dripping from her extended finger. Did they truly expect him to believe she was simply going to be with her husband? Somehow she had had word of his coming. There must be a spy somewhere close to headquarters, but who? John Andre had told him that this Mrs. Browning might have been at Fort Cumberland, that he should recognize her. He thought he remembered a small, rather pretty, not commanding person. She might have appeared in a better light were it not for her friend Margaret. Many women paled in that comparison. He smiled. But the remembrance only improved his mood for an instant.

These damned rebels couldn't even concoct a plausible lie! Even when he threatened to burn the place, they stuck to their tale. He ordered his men to search the house, and not to be overly careful about it. He heard the sounds of furniture being broken, and now a window upstairs. He took his satisfaction where he could. An angry crowd was gathering. Probably an urgent message had already been sent to Continental Village. A cavalry troop would be soon on the road. Militia would be raised. It was time to retire, with absolutely nothing found to reward his efforts. He swore vehemently.

*****

"Andre!" Sir Henry Clinton called through the open door connecting their offices in City Hall. "Letter bag from the rebels. Come see what we have." He fished among the letters, pulled out one from Washington, setting it aside.

"That's odd, one for Mrs. Brush. Say, Andre, are you going to see her soon? I'm going out to Long Island this afternoon, shouldn't be back for a day or two. Could you take it to her?" He handed it across.

"My pleasure, sir." He glanced at the address, then looked again in shock. "Sir Henry, this is the same hand as the dispatches we captured in New Jersey last week!" He looked at his commander, confusion showing on his face.

"What! Are you sure?"

"Yes, sir, I never forget a hand. It's kind of a parlor trick of mine. What does this mean?"

"Open it." His voice was cold.

Andre broke the seal and looked quickly for the signature. "It's from Catherine Schuyler, I think General Schuyler's wife. I'll check." He scanned the contents. "Yes, here he's mentioned. Apparently they're friends. Blah, blather, blah." He finished. "It's just a newsy sort of thing that women might write, inquiring about her health, and so forth. I'll check it for codes."

"Do that, Major. In this light, don't make her aware of this until I return."

"Yes, Sir. This does put a different perspective on those dispatches. From this, it appears they may have come from Albany, not Peekskill."

*****

Henry Clinton leaned forward in his chair and ran a hand over his cheek.

"Margaret, I find myself in a difficult position. I must ask you a personal question, which you could rightly refuse to answer, and I wouldn't hold it against you if you did. I feel I should know the nature of your relations with Major Andre. You know I think the world of him but people sometimes talk more than they should at certain times."

The musicians at the other end of the room stopped again at some problem which only performers could understand. The two were having difficulties with this piece. They grumbled amongst themselves as Margaret responded.

190

"Yes, sir. I understand. The Major and I are good friends. Sometimes he takes me to the theater; sometimes he takes pretty young things. Sometimes he desires my company, sometimes theirs. We both derive…certain benefits from our arrangement, but there are no entanglements, nor does either of us want them. Does that answer you satisfactorily?"

"Very well. Now I must ask you a more piercing question, one which I shall require that you answer. This came in the mail bag two days ago. Can you explain it?" He handed across the letter. There had been no attempt to re-seal it.

"This sounds very much like an accusation, Sir Henry and I take offense. May I read before I answer, as I see others already have?"

"Of course. I'm sorry if that came as accusation, Margaret, truly I am. I'm concerned, I'm puzzled. This was written by the same person who sent those codes last week. Why is she writing to you now?"

"Are you certain, Sir Henry?" Kate must have had no time to explain the game—she had clearly written this, but signed it as Catherine Schuyler. The salutation alone had warned her—Kitty would never have begun 'Dear Meg.' What was she expected to do? She could find no clue in the body of the letter.

"Mrs. Schuyler and I are old friends," stalling to gather her thoughts, "We lived together for several years during the old French War, while her husband, General Schuyler, was on campaign. She wrote to me while I was in Boston, and out of our ancient friendship, managed to ameliorate the conditions of my captivity somewhat. I sent her a quick note as I was coming to New York last year. I guess she is still concerned about me. She is a fierce enemy, but a fast friend. I have not written her since I got here. I value her friendship; given her husband's position, I thought it best to remain incommunicado. I have formed many friendships over the years with people from whom I am now separated by politics. We choose to break off communication rather than break off our friendships. Many Loyalists are in this position. I fervently hope that one day we may converse again.

"I suppose she used the official mail as the easiest thing. She must have assumed that I'd be known to someone who saw the pouch."

191

"Civil Wars are a damnable thing, aren't they? I accept your explanation, it is perfectly logical. It means that Mrs. Schuyler is sending secret communications to Washington's headquarters. That also is not to be wondered at, at least not that someone in Schuyler's camp would be. I should warn you that Major Andre will be annoyed. This ruins his grand theory of their provenance, and he was very proud of it."

"This paper feels strange, Sir Henry, like those dispatches. Has Major Andre been testing it for secret codes as well as reading my mail?"

"Yes. He found none."

"I must tell you that I am deeply disturbed that neither of you chose to trust me. You have known me for almost a year, sir. Have I ever done anything to raise questions of my loyalty? I have not! Yet you treat me as a common thief…"

"Margaret, I…"

"Don't you 'Margaret' me, not tonight!" her voice rising. "I will excuse myself before I say too much! Good night, sir!" She stormed out of the room, leaving the three gaping and two of them mystified.

*****

"I tell you, Andre, she knew we were coming! I cannot accept that her leaving was just happenstance. There must be a spy quite close. There must be!"

"Well, Montraville, who did you tell? I certainly told no one."

"Nor did I. I tell you bluntly, Andre; I don't trust Mrs. Brush."

"Come now, John. You're letting your animosity color your thoughts. The fact that she's a colonial who knows just about everyone does not alone make her a spy. Think of all she has lost to the rebels in this war. She'd have no love for them!

"You're focusing too closely upon her. If you're to be my man for catching these spies, you must learn to be more objective. Now, what progress have you on this Culper person? Focus yourself. There lies the greater threat."

"Very well," he snapped gracelessly, "but I shall still be watching her."

"Montraville, you will not! Do you understand? She is a loyal subject of King George III and you will not disturb her. Come, man, think of all the clerks who knew of your orders. It will be some scrub, mark my words."

*****

Driven snow beat against the windows; a good fire warmed them as they sat in the drawing room. The parlor was too chilly for comfort, far too chilly for music-making. Mary stared dreamily at the flames, her mind far away. Fanny worked at cross-stitching.

"There," as she clipped the last threads. "Mary, what do you think?" She held up her work. "Do you like it?"

"Fanny! It's beautiful. You're always so cunning with your needle!"

On the opposite side of the fire, and a world away from the young women, Henry Clinton had been fidgety since supper. He turned in his chair and said, "Margaret, I may depend upon your discretion? Nothing we say will find its way to Major Andre?"

"Absolutely not."

"Good. I want to show you this from Lord George. Arrived yesterday, and I'd like your opinion on it." He handed across a letter. Margaret read slowly.

"So General Cornwallis is to join us again. How do you feel about that, sir? I know things were becoming strained between you when he was here last year."

"He knows his business, but he's a difficult man to work with. He hungers for independent command and sometimes assumes it when it is in fact not his."

"Is he to succeed you?"

"Someday. Lord Cornwallis holds the dormant commission, but Germain refuses to give the order, leaving us both twisting in the wind. He will be hard to contain, once I leave the south."

"Seeking glory and your command?"

"Precisely. Lord George is binding my hands again."

"That he is, Sir Henry. I think it wonderful how you manage under these constraints. I don't see anything here that will affect your Charleston expedition."

"No, thank goodness! It's gotten so that I expect him to undo whatever I have planned every time I break the seal."

"Do you know when you'll be sailing, sir?"

"Within the week. Ordnance is aboard ship, stores commence tomorrow. Loading troops and horses will commence probably Monday, if this weather breaks. You will be alright here while I'm away? I expect it will probably be several months, spring even, before I'm back."

"Surely. We'll keep watch on all. There's the theater, and plenty of dinners and a ball or two. We'll keep quite busy."

"'I'll feel better about being away from Mary, knowing that you and Fanny are here. Thank you again for your help."

"No, thank you, Sir Henry, for allowing us to reside here. You've saved us."

*****

"I find it difficult to believe, Your Excellency, but Odysseus sends a précis of Germain's instructions to Clinton! How could anyone have obtained it is a mystery to me."

"Mrs. Browning believes it genuine, Browning?"

"She does. She told me once that she has an agreement. Neither she nor Odysseus will ever directly lie to the other. Withhold things, perhaps, but never lie. She trusts him implicitly."

194

"Once this war is over, I want to meet this fellow, if he doesn't get himself hanged before! He must be the master burglar."

"Indeed. Anyway, we have learned that Cornwallis is coming again, landing in Carolina. After he and Clinton reduce Charleston he is to have independent command in the south. Clinton will take half the army from New York to join him for the campaign. He's to leave within the week."

"Good, then he has already settled into defensive positions for the winter. This weather is so brutal—it is well that the men are better barracked than last winter. Tis too bad that we have had to disperse the horses, but at least they will be alive when we call them back from Pennsylvania in spring. Browning, get yourself to your wife until after Christmas. Mrs. Washington is coming, you should go."

"Thank you, Your Excellency."

"And Browning—find out more of this Odysseus fellow."

"I will, sir, if my source will divulge anything!"

1780

Snow blasted again at the dining room windows, making the four of them look up from their cordials. It was only mid-January, yet this was already the fourth blizzard of the season. The snow outside lay two feet deep. The drifts climbed the walls daily. Even since John Thompson had arrived in mid-afternoon another nine inches had fallen. Now, the dark windows reflected their own images. Inside, the entrée had been cleared away, the floating island and sherry served. Mary sat at the head, Margaret at the foot of the table, Fanny and John Thompson eyed each other over the centerpiece. Beneath the table, their ankles touched.

"Mr. Thompson, I'm glad you agreed to stay the night! That river would be impassable tonight. It would be folly in day time. You must resign yourself to spending the night with us.

"A pleasant resignation it is, Mrs. Baddeley. No man could object to passing time in such company."

"You flatter us, sir."

"I think I rather understate the case."

Mary nodded at the compliment. "Fanny has shown you to the green room? Is it satisfactory?"

"Oh, more than! I expect I shall be very comfortable." He felt Fanny's slippered foot caress his calf. She smiled slyly across the table.

"Fanny?" Her foot retreated to its proper place. "Why don't you and I get the kitchen staff straight on things while Mary shows Mr. Thompson the parlor? It's more comfortable than here."

"Yes, Mama."

When they were alone, Margaret took her daughter's hands in her own. "Honey, be discrete tonight."

"Are we that obvious?"

"Do you have to ask? You two are so hungry for each other that it frightens me. I'm only that afraid you will do something foolish and jeopardize us all."

✳✳✳✳✳

That same storm battered the windows of John Andre's office in City Hall. A few flakes filtered through the gaps around the sash and a draft had caused him to move him from his desk to a chair beside the fire. John Montraville sat across from him.

"I think you're wrong, Andre. I'm certain there is something in Peekskill that we need to pursue."

"I know you do, Montraville, but I think I'm right and my vote wins. Listen, did you ever hear of William of Occam? No? Well, he's one of those old dead chaps only talked of in university anymore. He posited that when two answers are given to a question we are bound to accept the simpler. Here, the simpler is that Schuyler's people are communicating with Washington's, as well they should. There is no wonder that they would use code.

"Leave this line. Rather than chasing ephemera, I want you to concentrate on the Culper group. There's a target we know exists."

Montraville recognized the implied order. "Yes, sir. But I'll still keep an eye for intelligence going northward from here as well."

✳✳✳✳✳

198

Fanny heard the big hall clock chime midnight. She waited an agonizing few minutes, straining to hear any sound. She rose from her bed; she pressed her ear to the door, listening intently. She opened it a crack, peeking out. She slipped through and quickly padded the few steps to his room, opened the door and stepped inside.

He stood by the mantle, barefoot and shirtless, his breeches unbuckled at the knee. The orange-yellow glow from the coals struggled against the dark night only to be subdued in the far corners of the room. She closed the door silently and walked slowly, with eager trepidation, toward the fire.

✵✵✵✵✵

The whitewashed Ford house in Morristown almost disappeared into the deep drifts surrounding it. The path was visible only as a depression in the snow fields—the fences that should guide the visitor were but small ridges. Richard Browning stopped at the stoop, stamping his boots, shaking the snow that had accumulated on his shoulders in the short walk from his quarters. The warmth struck him as he entered. An aide greeted him inside.

"Mrs. Washington is with him this morning, sir."

"Thank you." He would have to revise his report.

"Good morning, Browning. What have you?

"A brief note from a source, sir, that Odysseus will be silent for a time. His contacts have all gone south with the army."

"Regrettable. Did you find anything about him?"

"No. Absolute silence, for his safety. I'm sure you understand, your Excellency? Only one knows and insists that it remain so."

"Prudent, I suppose, but it does pique the curiosity, does it not?"

"Indeed, sir."

"Colonel Browning," Mrs. Washington interjected, "do you two always speak in riddles, or might a proper noun escape into conversation from time to time? Is it just my presence?"

"I'm sorry, Madam Washington, but we do suffer from an excess of caution. Sometimes it is the best, so no accidental slip may cause a calamity. I certainly intend no offence."

"None taken, Colonel. I'm trying wit this morning to see if it may warm me."

"Wishing you success, Madam. You will share your methods?"

"Methods, yes, warmth, no."

"In any event, with the state of our army it is of small concern. Until Clinton returns, this will be a war for the militia—raiding and stopping raids. We all seek forage more than position or advantage."

*****

Audiences never laughed as they left Othello, Montraville thought. *They were generally silent and thoughtful.* He could hear the occasional snide comments about amateur actors attempting such a play. He ignored them all. He was focused on the young couple leaving. His hand was on the small of her back, guiding her possessively through the crowd. He was walking too closely, imposing himself on her, yet she made no attempt to move away. He knew those signs, he had studied female body language for decades. He knew exactly what it implied. He didn't like it.

"So that was not your vision of Desdemona?"

"No," thoughtfully. She spoke over her shoulder as they passed. "I think she was more complicated than that. She must have been. I mean, the portrayal was consistent and believable and all, but I think there must be more there. Women in love can be foolish, but not simple-minded."

"Unlike men?"

She flashed him a smile. "Men are just confused and confusing creatures who know neither what they want, nor how to get it."

They passed out of earshot. Montraville, since his teens, had been quite sure what men wanted, and in the twenty-odd years since, had become quite good at getting it. That was not going to happen, not with this girl! He glared after the boy. Well, unlike fathers since time forgotten, he <u>was</u> in a position to find out about this jack-a-napes sniffing around his daughter.

They had been introduced once, at Margaret's house, before he had moved in. John something, Thomas, Tompkins, Thompson. That was it, John Thompson, New Jersey somewhere. Merchant. Not much, but enough to start. He knew just the man to run the fellow to earth. Tomorrow.

*****

Enoch Robbins was a non-descript sort of man, of average height, average weight, average appearance, the sort of man who was easily lost in a crowd, his presence never noticed. His only distinguishing feature was the dark eyes which darted constantly from place to place, focusing instantly, capturing an image never forgotten. Had he ever been caught, he would have been hanged as a thief or a swindler. The military government of New York had chosen instead to make use of his talents. He only came to City Hall when he chose and he only chose when he was offered employment.

He sauntered into John Andre's office and seated himself insolently without it being offered.

"Robbins, sit down." Montraville sat behind Andre's desk, the window overlooking the harbor behind him. He did not offer to shake hands. He detested the man and Robbins knew it. "I have a project for you."

"Andre has always hired me. <u>You</u> can get me paid? What assurances?"

"Major Andre is in the south with Sir Henry Clinton. In his absence I am acting in his stead. You'll be paid."

"What do you want?"

"I want a man investigated. I want to know what he had for dinner Tuesday last, I want to know where his grandfather is buried. I want to know where he gets his substance and where he spends it. Any questions?"

"How soon?"

"As soon as you can, damn it! This is important. A life hangs thereby."

201

"How much?"

"£20."

"£20 plus expenses. This may be difficult. I assume he is a fellow of little importance to the world. They're harder to track than a general."

"Don't assume anything. I assure you that it is of utmost importance.

"Very well, £20, plus expenses and I'm in."

"Done. Now, here's what I know of him…"

*****

"A letter from Sir Henry!" Mary hurried into the parlor. "Only two weeks old!"

Margaret looked up from her book. "That's quick time, Mary. What does he say?"

"That the siege is progressing, they have finally gotten the ships over the bar. They have just closed the neck and Charleston is finally encircled. It is only a matter of time now. He says the Loyalist turnout is a disappointment though."

"Any indication of when he may be back?"

"No." Mary had already read it twice, especially certain parts which she chose not to reveal. "I guess early summer. How long can a city hold out?"

*****

"This is nice, John. I so enjoy talking with you when I have no secrets to impart!"

"I always enjoy it. I need no excuse while with you, Miss Brush."

"So formal…" She was interrupted.

They sat in the drawing room, on the settee which had become their rendezvous. Outside, servants were unloading his wagon, carrying supplies to the cellar. Spring was finally coming to New York, and being agonizingly coy about it after the snowiest winter anyone could recall. Ten nor'easters had rolled up the coast, as regular as Atlantic packet ships, each with its own heavy load of snow. Now spring toyed with them, first a warm day, then a chilly one, showing a bit of leg, and then cruelly taking it away again.

"So nothing to report?"

"John, John." She put a hand on his cheek. "This is the time when you tell me that you love me, not the time to ask about the war."

"I shouldn't think a woman of your intelligence and bearing would need constant re-assurance. You know that I do."

"I know you do too, but I still like to hear it. It makes me all warm inside." She glanced from the corners of her eyes. "Warm and compliant."

"I do so like it when you're compliant."

She leaned her head against his arm. "So do I." It was almost a whisper.

He kissed her again.

*****

Margaret stopped by the kitchen door. The slave stood in the yard, hat in hand. He clearly wanted permission to speak.

"Yes, Cato, what is it?"

"Ma'am, I doesn't know if I should say...my mama told me no, she says 'you stay out of white folks bus'ness Cato. That way is nothin' but troubles, that's what she say."

"But you want to say?"

"Yes'm. They was a man yesterd'y, askin' about Mr. Thompson, what brings the food? All 'bout where he lives 'n such. I didn't tell him nothing, ma'am, I swear I didn't! None of us knows anyways."

"Thank you, Cato, you were right to tell me." She worked to keep the concern from her voice. "Now not a word of this to anyone. We don't want your mama mad at you, do we?"

"Yes'm. You been good to Cato, I jus thought I should say."

✳✳✳✳✳

The sun shone in Robbins' eyes as he reported. He didn't like the sunlight. Darkness better suited him. Montraville didn't move to ease his discomfort.

"Consider this an interim report, Montraville. I still have interrogatories outstanding. Thompson has been surprisingly difficult, even for a nobody. I need £10 for expenses. I've had to advance monies to men in rebel-held country."

"For £10, you'd better have something."

"John Thompson, 23, rising food broker from Newark. Supplies markets in the City, even your general's house. Reputed as sound merchant, pays on time, buys well, sells better. Last Tuesday, he had the shepherd's pie at Scotch Johnny's. No known address in the city, although he spends time here. Owns a boat with crew to transport his goods across the river, often uses the Paulus Hook ferry as well. Ambitious. Seems to be chasing some twit in Clinton's family. I've seen her, I commend his taste."

"She's no twit, you idiot! They were at the theater again last night. And remember your place."

So there was a woman at the bottom of this. Montraville wanted to scotch his rival...interesting.

"The thing is, he has little history. He succeeded to the business two years ago, from an uncle, an estate settlement. Arrived in town with no fanfare, possibly from Philadelphia, but no one seems to be certain of it. That's what I'm pursuing now. Give me another week or so."

204

Margaret met them as they came in from the side garden. "Fanny, you and Mr. Thompson go to the drawing room. I'll join you in a few minutes, as soon as I have all settled here. Sally, will you bring the tea box?"

John Thompson was puzzled by this imperative, Fanny appeared anxious. After they were inside, he asked, "What's that about?"

"We have a problem. She'll explain."

"For a minute, I thought I had displeased her. That <u>would</u> frighten me."

"No, it's far worse than that."

Sally burst out laughing as she entered the room to see the two perched on opposing side chairs.

"Look at you two, all so innocent! Do you think I don't know what goes on in here?"

"I have no idea what you're implying, Aunt Sally. We discuss only business."

"Yes indeed."

Margaret entered and began, "John, there was a man here yesterday asking about you. He talked to some of the servants, but avoided Fanny and I. We don't know if he really was probing you, or using your connection as a way to us. We don't know who is asking, but this is the first time suspicion has settled here. Have you noticed anything elsewhere?"

"I haven't, not really, wait, I did notice one of my customers looking at me differently this morning. I didn't think anything of it then, but now I wonder if I should have done." He considered. "Nothing across the river though. What shall we do if it is an official investigation? I'll not have it settle here. Do we need to get you all out of town?"

"No, not yet. We have too much advantage to discard it casually. I think we must commit nothing to writing, but we shouldn't change the appearance of what we do. That would be suspicious in itself. We need to keep the format

205

of our orders and invoices the same, but we absolutely must not use any codes. We must assume they can read sympathetic ink. Everything must be verbal. It mostly has been since winter—we've had nothing to report, thankfully.

"Mr, Thompson, what do you do with our orders once filled?" asked Sally.

"With all my other customers, once in my ledger, I burn them. Yours just go straight in"

"You send our originals to your mother?" asked Margaret.

"Yes. If I don't take them myself, the courier knows to destroy them if threatened, and he has not been."

"Very well, no copies lying around on your end. I have Sally copy your bills, then burn the originals. Sir Henry needs to have them to justify his accounts when he gets back to England, or else we wouldn't bother. So, we think all old messages are safely destroyed?"

She looked from one to the other and received nods from each.

"Can either of you think of anything else? No? Remember, we must be very careful now, until we can determine who is behind this."

"Who might it be, Mama?"

"Andre is out of town. Much as I am loathe to suggest it, it may be Montraville."

"That wouldn't surprise me!" said Sally.

"Is that bad?" asked John.

"We have an unpleasant history. He would be relentless."

✳✳✳✳✳

Montraville swallowed hard as he knocked at the door. Why did this damnable woman always make him nervous? He turned to glance at the street. He could hear a harpsichord through the open windows of the parlor.

Lilacs bloomed somewhere nearby. A slave with impossibly white teeth opened the door. He waited in the hall until Margaret came.

"Good morning, Margaret"

"Morning, John. What may I do for you?"

Get right to the point, man. "I don't like this fellow, Thompson, hanging around Fanny and I want it stopped."

She almost laughed. "It's none of your concern, John. Stay out of this."

"I tell you, he's not who he claims! There is no record that he existed until two years ago! He's some kind of swindler."

"Oh? Who has been swindled?"

"No one yet that I know, but that's not the point. I don't know what his game is, but there is something wrong about him."

"So you have no evidence that he's not who he says, you just can't find evidence that he is? Show me the evidence that proves you're Montraville. On second thought, don't bother. I don't care, and I don't care if you don't like him. You forfeited any parental rights in Quebec. If there's nothing else, I have duties…"

"Damn it, Margaret! I'll not have her associating with such a one! I'm trying to protect her." His voice was rising.

Hers was not. "She neither wants nor needs your protection. Leave this John."
He grabbed her arm and pulled her close, glaring down at her. In a fierce whisper he spat, "You force me, Margaret. In my official capacity, I demand the receipts of his business with this house. Something in there will prove me right."

"What?"

"You heard me, give me the receipts of his business here. My people will find something in them that will surely incriminate him."

"No."

"You refuse a command in the King's name?" his voice rising again.

"Produce a judge's warrant, John."

"I need no warrant! There is treason afoot here. Produce those records, Margaret, do it now!" His voice was becoming louder and more emphatic.

"I refuse in Sir Henry's name," she replied, still calm. "Those are his private records, and I am charged with their care. You'll not see them unless he directs me to show them. He'll be back next week. Shall we ask him then? If I were you, I'd be careful about demanding such a thing from my commanding officer! Clearly you're attempting to incriminate him and not John Thompson!"

"How dare you suggest such a thing! Why don't we just ask Mrs. Baddeley? Perhaps she'll be more reasonable!" He was shouting now.

"Let's not. Even if she directed it, I would still refuse you. My duty is to Sir Henry."

He paused, breathing heavily, trying to kill her with his eyes. She stood impassively. Finally he turned and stamped away. Now he remembered that damned impenetrability of hers that always made him lose his temper.

*****

"You haven't cause to be so short, Montraville. I'm working for you, after all."

"I don't have time to humor you, Robbins, nor much inclination. What do you know?"

"It's a curious thing. I can't find any clue that John Thompson existed more than two years ago. No relatives, not in Philadelphia anyway. No one knows where he came from. He keeps pretty much to himself outside of business, where he has become well known."

"Everyone must come from somewhere."

208

"So I have been told. Looks like your man might be smuggling. His boat goes up the river as often as it comes to the city. Gone for a few days at a time, then returns. Sometimes Thompson is aboard and sometimes not. That should give you reason to run him out of the girl's life."

"Not your business. How big is this boat?"

"Four or five tons, I should say. Ketch rigged."

"So he could carry goods? Does he have passengers?"

"Oh yes, and don't know. They could be concealed from shore."

"Has he a schedule for these trips?"

"No. His only schedule is to come to General Clinton's house each Tuesday. Stays longer than a body would think necessary for a grocery delivery. His men return to the boat and go back to New Jersey while he remains behind for some hours. Takes the ferry back in the evening. I think the girl's mother likes him. Now, I'll bet she was a nice piece when she was young! Still not bad at all, just the one to teach a young man how. She's living there too."

"Leave the mother out of this too, Robbins. Believe me, I know all about her. Concentrate on Thompson."

Montraville didn't see Robbins raise an eyebrow. This might be far more complicated than he had thought. Complication usually meant more money.

"I need £5 for expenses."

"You're a damned thief."

"Among other things, and I'm good at it. That's why you came to me."

"Then exercise some of that vaunted thievery and find me something. All you have so far is supposition and hearsay." He counted out the coins angrily.

*****

Sally poked her head into Margaret's little office. "Mr. Thompson is here, Ma'am, asking for Fanny."

"What—he was here just yesterday!"

"Yes, she asked if you could occupy him for a few minutes."

"You go back and help her—I'll go to him. The drawing room? Come join us when she's ready."

Sally nodded. Margaret closed her ledger, stepped out into the kitchen, locked the door behind her, and pocketed the key.

"Good afternoon, Mr. Thompson!" as she entered. "To what do we owe the honor of seeing you again so soon?"

Thompson peeked to make sure no one was behind her, then stepped very close. He spoke in an anxious whisper.

"My business was burgled yesterday whilst I was here!"

"Are you certain?"

"Yes. I keep certain things, small things that most people wouldn't notice, arranged just so, and last night they were not so."

"Was anything taken?"

"No, not so far as I could tell, and I looked carefully."

Fanny entered, looking as if she always had her hair perfectly coiffed. Sally was with her. The scene was quite different than she had expected. Tension filed the room.

"What's going on? Fanny asked, warily.

"Mr. Thompson was burgled yesterday." Quickly, they added the details.

"Did anyone see anything?" Sally asked.

"My neighbor volunteered that he had seen someone who seemed to be hanging about, but his description could be a thousand people. Just an unremarkable chap."

"That could well be the fellow here the other day. Absolutely nothing about him excited attention!"

"I think we have to assume they were the same. Could you tell exactly what he was after?" said Margaret.

"The bookmark in my ledger was moved, and he had gone through the desk drawers, looking for something. There's nothing of value there."

"So he was looking for your business records. No invoices lying about?"

"No, all burned and the ashes broken up."

"Good. Listen, we must assume that someone is investigating all of us, with malicious intent. No more spying, none of us, not 'til this blows over. John, you must not go to your mother's. I think you should even be very careful about sending a messenger."

"Mama..."

"He must continue to come here, Fanny. John, you must pay court still on my daughter. Can you two stomach that? On the surface, we must not respond to this attack. Perhaps that will draw them out. Sir Henry is due back next week sometime, let's see how that affects things. Agreed?"

＊＊＊＊＊

Montraville sat with his boots on John Andre's desk. He had come to regard it as his own. Robbins had dragged a chair from the fireplace and sat casually, annoyingly casually, across from him.

"Face it, Montraville, this fellow may be an honest man."

Montraville's boots thumped on the floor as he sat up quickly. He slammed his fist on the desk. "Damn it all, man! I don't want to know that he is 'an honest man.' I want to know what game he's at!"

"You pay me to tell you what I find, not just what you want to hear! If you think you can do so much better, pay me the final £10, and I'll be on my way. If you want to hear more, sit like a man and let me finish."

Montraville grunted.

"I'll take that as a 'yes'. I went through his ledgers pretty thoroughly. All looks ordinary. The odd thing is, there are no invoices or bills to be found. He must destroy them as soon as they are entered. Unusual, but most offices are so clogged with useless paper that I don't blame him. Seems to be a business decision, and it's across the board. Every customer, every supplier.

"He is bringing goods down the river from rebel territory, but it's all duty paid when it lands in the city. Don't know who he pays to get the stamps, but he has them. You can't touch him there. You can't touch him anywhere. The rate he's going, he'll be making more than you in three years. In ten, he'll be clearing £1000 per annum. It's no wonder the girl likes him. The 'game he's at' is wooing a pretty girl. You might as well forget this one and find another to chase."

"I will not! There's something rotten about him, there must be. Find out what's in his customers' records."

"You want me to break into a dozen establishments, and a general's house, just so you can score another girl? You're mad. I won't touch Clinton's house, but the others will cost you £20 alone. I don't think I'll find anything. Their records wouldn't incriminate him. Do you want it?"

"Let me think. There must be some way to bring him down. I'll let you know what else I need."

"I need the £10."

✱✱✱✱✱

"I want to thank you for standing fast against Montraville's demands, Margaret. He had no right to make them and you were quite correct to refuse. I can't imagine what he was thinking."

"He has formed an aversion to Mr. Thompson, Sir Henry. He thinks him not a suitable person to be courting Fanny."

"By what right..." He stopped and looked at her. "Oh. I see. There have been rumors, you understand..."

"Quite all right, Sir Henry. I've heard them all. He can't seem to understand that some rights are not granted by birth, but must be earned. He has certainly done nothing to earn them in twenty years."

"Perhaps he only pretends not to, hoping you'll fall into some sort of trap? You do know the man far better than I."

"Not any more, sir. But I know Mary will be happy to have you at home for a time—she really did miss you, you know. Now, hush, they've been working up this piece for you all spring. I gather it's quite difficult. We can continue later."

✲✲✲✲✲

Robbins preferred meeting here, in the back of the coffee house. Proximity to City Hall government made him nervous. The bright June day outside was nowhere in evidence here. He found Montraville in a corner.

"Hiding, Montraville, now that Andre is back and you're kicked out of that fancy office?"

"None of your business, Robbins. "

"What do you want?"

"I think it would be terrible if some accident were to befall this Thompson character."

"I don't murder, Montraville. I expect you know someone else." He rose to leave.

"Wait, I'll pay well!"

"From the King's purse? I doubt it. This project will end poorly Montraville. You haven't the skill or stomach to do the murder or the deception."

213

*****

"You seem distracted this afternoon, Sir Henry. A shilling for your thoughts?" The summer heat had chased them into a secluded side garden, in the shade of a large chestnut tree.

"You are being generous, Margaret. My thoughts are hardly worth so much.'

"You undervalue yourself." From their seats, they could be seen neither from the street or the house. Even the noise of the city was distant.

"Debatable. No, I'm thinking on these damned Frenchmen off Newport. We have reports of eight ships of the line, along with all their frigates and such, and twenty-odd transports. King Louis has sent them an army, after toying with us for three years."

"Do you know who is to command?"

"According to John Andre, the Comte De Rochambeau. Don't know him. They probably haven't landed as yet. Twenty transports speaks of five thousand troops, more or less. I'm less concerned of them than of how Lord Germain will expect me to react. I'm now on the horns of a dilemma. Move this way to capture this and lose that, or capture that and lose this. Of course, I could simply pass and stay where I am. It is not a pleasant position. If only the ministry would give me a fleet!"

"Could you not send a force against each? I mean at the same time? Of course I'm just a woman with no expertise in this."

"If I did, each would be destroyed *en detail*. No, I must keep my army concentrated, and watch for a mistake by either of them. If I could only catch one on the march! Now, that would be interesting indeed."

"But Lord George will not be content with your waiting?"

"Not for as long as it may take. I've come to believe he wants me to fail!"

"Terrible as it is to say, I think you are right. A spectacular defeat that he can lay to you would absolve him of responsibility for any of it. Is that treasonous?

214

"Not legally. It's politics. I expect the next packet will bring demands for action, which he can never admit of being less than successful."

"Of course, he will not order it."

"Of course not. He still purports to believe the Tories of the south will rise, but they haven't. Not significantly at least. The sense I got from them was that they don't believe England can win; they'll not risk their necks for a losing cause. Tories in the north are even more disgusted. They're all desirous of riding off after windmills and getting themselves killed doing it. I'm half inclined to let them go, just to get them out of my hair. I know, I said I wouldn't, and I won't, but Lord, the temptation!"

"Will you be boarding ship soon?"

"I'm not sure I'll be going at all, Margaret. That fool Arbuthnot now refuses a trial of strength with the Frenchman at Newport. Says the approach is too hazardous and the numbers not suitable enough, as if any would be. All he would have to do is deliver the army and then blockade."

"Wouldn't taking the army leave the city vulnerable?"

"It would. Our only chance is a quick strike there, and be back before they know we're gone. Now with the admiral's dithering, we probably shan't be able to do one at all. Washington already has half his army at Peekskill, and could be at Kingsbridge in a day if I go."

"With all the spies about, I suspect he already knows you're loading ship."

"I'm thinking a feint toward Newport, to test his intent. Perhaps he'll follow me across Connecticut to support his new ally. I hope so, because I don't want him behind me. If he doesn't, we unload and protect the city."

"Washington is getting more clever, isn't he?"

"Yes. As you predicted, the man learns. If then I march after either, the other falls on my rear or on New York. If we lose our seaport, my army will starve and so will the ministry. Any success we might have in the field will be negated by that. So, the short answer is, I fully expect that I must sit still and fortify this place, in spite of Germain calling on me to do something dramatic to return public opinion to its former place."

215

"You know he is more concerned with his own skin than yours."

"Indeed."

*****

"Well, Browning," said Washington, after the morning greetings had been exchanged and the coffee poured, "what have you today?"

"From Odysseus, Excellency...

"He's reporting in again? I was afraid we'd lost him."

"He is, sir. Clinton knows of Comte Rochambeau. Odysseus believes Clinton will not divide his forces to attack either him or us, as the residuum would be too vulnerable to attack by the other. He expects Germain will pressure Clinton to do something, but he intends to resist. He would love to catch either of us on the march. Northern tory units still want blood, but he is loathe to release them. Clinton estimates that it would be a suicide mission for them, they are too eager for revenge and too little disciplined to stand, even against our army, which he persists in regarding as a motley bunch of peasants. He thinks the tory units are worse, even by our standards. They do have bright uniforms, though. Clinton is disappointed at the rally of southern tories. He believes they suspect the Crown cannot win in the end and they refuse to back a dead horse. Germain still insists that a great rising against us will happen tomorrow. So great is his belief that he takes no measures to procure it."

"How much of this is certain, and how much is Odysseus' interpretation?"

"Kathleen says that Odysseus is always very clear about the distinction, and fact she passes verbatim, opinion is paraphrased."

"Here's to Germain's delusion. May he persist in it."

"Amen, Excellency."

*****

The soft breeze of a summer evening flowed across the harbor. The ensigns of the anchored ships waved lazily. They had had a good dinner. Sir Henry had ventured the jest that John was now enjoying the very food which he had in fact sold, thus both having and eating his cake. John had refrained from second helpings. Not that anyone took them, there seemed always to be a next course in the offing. They had left the old folks, Margaret and Andre, Sir Henry and Mary, talking in the parlor, rehashing the successful spring campaign against Charleston. Fanny and John were walking near the waterfront, neither really cared where, just walking together.

"I guess we should be heading back, John," with a smile and a sigh. "It's getting late."

"I suppose. I'm enjoying this day too much to want it to end."

"I suppose everyone is. It has been pleasant."

"Tell me about Major Andre and your mother. They seemed very chummy this afternoon."

"They do enjoy each other's company, that's all, in all sorts of ways. It's an affair of convenience."

"I enjoy your company too, in all sorts of ways. Is ours an affair of convenience?"

"Don't you say that, Edward!" she used his true name only when agitated. "Don't you ever say anything like that again! Don't you even think it!"

He had the good sense to retreat. "I'm sorry, my love. It was a feeble attempt at humor."

"It had better have been." She hugged his arm to let him know he was forgiven. They turned into a deserted side street. "Uh-oh. What's this?"

The two men stood, blocking their path, big, unshaven, crude looking, gap-toothed men with knives.

"Get away from him, girlie, our business is with only him."

John pushed her aside, releasing the catch on his sword cane as he did. The sheath fell away, revealing his rapier. Fanny stumbled and fell to the ground, her hand found a loose cobblestone. It was a perfect rock, egg-shaped, heavy, smooth and rounded, the size of an osage orange. It filled her palm, her fingers curled around it.

The assassins had turned their backs to her as John stepped away. They advanced slowly. They had not expected him to be armed.

"That little pig sticker won't do much against two now will it?" sneered the red beard. "Let us finish this quickly. Your girl is safe. If she is hurt, we won't be paid. Come, take this like a man."

"I intend to."

Fanny leapt on the bald red-bearded one. She locked her ankles around his waist, her arm around his throat. She tightened her arm, he struggled for breath. He cursed and spun left and right to dislodge this pest. He reached wildly but could get no purchase. She struck with the rock. She struck again and again. Blood from his scalp splashed across her face. She was choking him. He began to thrash violently to shake her.

She hit him again and he dropped to his knees. She disentangled herself. She swung the rock again with all her strength. She put her back into the blow. She grunted as she struck. The front of her dress felt warm and sticky. She saw a depression in the shining skull. She struck again, just as hard. He pitched forward, face down in the street, motionless.

She turned to see Edward withdraw his sword from the other man's chest. They all stood transfixed as the man looked in surprise at the jets of arterial blood spurting between his fingers. She found herself counting them. At seventeen, his eyes rolled back and he collapsed to the cobblestones.

Their eyes met. "Edward! Are you all right? The blood?"

"Not mine. And you?"

She looked down, her bodice was wet with blood. "Not mine either. It's a shame I shan't be able to wear this again."

218

He came to her, withdrawing a handkerchief from his pocket. "Hold still Boadicea, close your eyes." He carefully wiped away a streak of blood extending from the side of her neck diagonally across the bridge of her nose and into her hair. There were other droplets as well. He dropped the handkerchief on the ground when he was finished. At least her face was cleared.

"Come, let's get home. I doubt these two have any friends, but I don't want to chance it."

There were curious stares as they walked. She had John's jacket thrown over her shoulders, She clutched it closed at the neck. Both still showed blood spatter and there was no way to disguise it.

They met Sally as they entered the house. "Oh my God!" She grabbed Fanny's shoulders and anxiously examined the blood stains. "Fanny, are you hurt?

"No. Aunt Sally. I need you, upstairs."

"You go, I'll get your mother."

She followed John into the parlor, where the mere sight of him ended all conversation. Sally stepped out from behind. "Ma'am, Fanny needs you. Upstairs."

John added. "She's not hurt, Ma'am."

Margaret and Mary hurried up the stairs, leaving John to explain himself.

*****

"Fanny, what happened? You're a bloody mess!"

They helped her out of her dress, Sally fetched a basin while Margaret supervised the cleanup.

"John was wonderful, Mama. These two banditti set upon us as we were walking home. They wanted to kill him. He would have sacrificed himself. Mama, I couldn't allow that! I think I beat a man to death, Mama, but I don't feel badly—is that wrong? Am I mad?"

219

"Is your mother mad? asked Sally.

"Mama, have you?"

"She has, twice."

"But you never told me…"

"I didn't want you to grow up knowing that—it was war time and rules were suspended, as they are now. You'll think about it from time to time, but what you did was necessary. Between you, you two defeated an enemy intent on harming you. A soldier feels no remorse after the battle. There is no wrong in that."

"You need to throw something on as soon as you can, Fanny, the men downstairs will insist on seeing you."

"As soon as my hair dries, Mary. Can you go down and tell them?"

Fanny waited until the door closed behind her. "Mama, they were sent to kill John. They said they were to be paid but would not be if I was harmed. Someone knows about him. What are we to do?"

"They specifically mentioned you?"

"Yes."

Sally's eyes met Margaret's. "She needs to know, Ma'am. I heard him the other day. Others may have as well."

"She needs to know what?" demanded Fanny.

Margaret hesitated, then nodded. "I—we--suspect it may have been Montraville. He is determined to separate you two. He has suspicions about John. He can find no evidence that John Thompson existed until two years ago. He has decided he is some sort of swindler. He has this delusion that he must protect you."

"He's wrong and he has no right!"

"So I told him, but he is hot headed and stubborn. A bad combination."

"Wait-- he has been investigating John?"

"He's been making inquiries; so far, everyone has given John sterling endorsements. I need to get Andre to focus his attention elsewhere. Dig enough and even Sir Henry can be made to look like a thief."

"Mama, I'm frightened. For the first time, I'm frightened."

*****

Fanny came into her mother's room. They were alone and spoke very softly. "Mama, Mr. Thompson gave me message from his mother." She paused, recalling the exact wording. 'Montraville is investigating you-- all of us. He has a man making inquiries, here and in New Jersey and in Peekskill. Be very careful; the man is skilled. His name is Enoch Robbins, a petty thief and swindler. Unremarkable appearance, pleasant but oily manner. Beware.' Do you think he's the one who's been asking around here?"

"It seems likely. Damn him! Why can't he leave us alone to destroy royal governance in peace?"

"Robbins or Montraville?"

"Both."

*****

Montraville sat across the desk from his chief. The September sun streamed through the window into his face. He shielded his eyes, then got up and began to pace slowly.

"John, I've been thinking about Thompson again."

"Montraville, not this again. I thought you had got over that."

"No, this is different. Think on it. We know that we are stymied at almost every move. The Americans seem to know in advance what we are going to do. They have some good people over there, but they can't be that good.

221

Suppose for a moment that Thompson is a spy. He could tell a lot from the grocery orders at Sir Henry's house. A slender order would mean the he was leaving for a time and taking his official family with him. Thompson sits at table sometimes, and can watch and learn, probe with intelligent questions. The man is no fool."

"Does that mean that your opinion of him is improved?"

"That I should like a spy more than a swindler? No, it does not."

"Is Fanny complicit? Is their whole affair just stage dressing, do you think?"

"I doubt it. I think she is genuine in this. She's a girl. I must believe he is using her. And that's another reason for me to dislike him, but not relevant. Of course, if she is involved, so is her mother. The two can never be separated."

"What do you propose?"

"We need to get people into New Jersey. When he comes here he is never alone, unless with Fanny. Those two boatmen of his travel with him everywhere."

"Since that attempt on his life in June, you mean. You should know that Mrs. Brush suspects you had a hand in that."

"It's a shame it was not successful. Then we should not be having this conversation now."

"Think more on this, John. What should we be looking for over there, and how do we find it?"

After Montraville left, Andre sat musing. *Suppose a syllogism:*

Proposition the first, Thompson is a spy.

Proposition the second, Fanny does love Thompson.

Therefore, Fanny must be a spy also? And so Margaret?

His mind sought actively to reject it.

Does he love her? That might be the more crucial question. When did spy catching become dependent on the loves of two children? Old Professor Higgsbottom would have been derisive of my logic. The only meaningful proposition was Thompson's spying. I'd like a simple battle, where a man knew what he should do. Sir Henry will hear nothing of this unless I'm were absolutely certain.

*****

"Margaret, how well do you know Mr. Thompson?" They were walking on a Sunday afternoon. It had become one of their favorite pastimes, now that the summer heat was broken. Walking afforded them their opportunity to talk privately.

"My daughter is in love with him, John. That's all I need to know."

"Do you know anything of his past, his family? When did they meet?"

"You're starting to sound like Montraville, John," she answered warily. "This may become a very long and disappointing evening. Why do you ask?"

"Truly? The Americans are too good at figuring out what we're about. Some suspect there is a spy very close to headquarters, and I wonder if it is he."

"Some, meaning Montraville. Shouldn't you first determine whether such a spy does exist rather than chasing one man?"

"Good point. Thank you. The suspicion was distasteful. I do like the lad. How should I find out?"

"Let him know something false and see if Washington responds. To be meaningful, of course, You would have to act alone. No one else could know, not even Montraville. Say," she stopped and turned to face him, alarm on her face, "have you thought of him? What better blind for a spy than throwing suspicion on another? He fits all the requirements. He knows your plans. He's been in the colonies for over twenty years, so far as I know not even returning home once. At the same time as Thompson, you could give Montraville some different morsel and see what happens. That would save you some time."

"Ugh. I find that thought even more distasteful."

"Me too. I dislike him intensely, but to doubt his loyalty...that's a big step."

"You know you still haven't answered my first question."

"Thompson? His father was one of Mr. Brush's clients," she lied pleasantly. "I think he and Fanny first met as children at his office back before the war. It seems he's been around forever."

*****

The stiff breeze made the boat heel as it tore up the Hudson. He could hear the river slapping against the hull. In only an hour they were halfway up the Palisades, but now the tide was beginning to flood, shortening the chop; spray flew over the weather gunwale.

"Edward, don't look up, but I think we're being followed."

Edward Browning concentrated on the report he was writing, down in the belly of the boat. "Where away?"

"Larboard quarter, holding about a mile distant."

"Keep her steady, Bill. Let me get this done." He finished, rolled the paper tightly and slipped it into an empty wine bottle. He slapped the cork home and set the bottle in its place among others, packed in wood shavings. He moved other cases of wine to cover it. Someone would have to inspect every one of the thirty to find it. He smiled--another case of port for his father. How many he had brought up the river this summer to a man who took water with his meals!

He stood and stretched, unconsciously flexing his knees to remain upright and stationary as sailors do as he surveyed the horizon. He saw the boat, over against the Jersey shore. "The sloop?"

"Yes. She came up on us, then shortened sail. That's what made me notice. Flying no colors."

224

"So we can assume she has the speed advantage, and that she's not on official business. We'll go about our lawful concerns at Dobb's Ferry and let them fret."

"Good enough for me."

*****

"We had a lovely sail up the river," Robbins began. "Fresh breeze and all. He stopped at Dobb's Ferry, delivered cases that appeared to be wine. On to Van Cortland Manor, where he picked up bags of wheat, then home. The only suspicious thing was that that much wine was clearly intended for the Americans. Otherwise, merely a man trading. There must be a hundred such trading with both sides. He had no contact with anyone beyond the dock workers. If he's up to something, he's very deep about it."

"But something could easily have been concealed among the bottles?" asked Andre.

"Of course. You didn't want me to be obvious. That would put him on his guard even if he is innocent. I want some more of this coffee."

"These rebels may have discovered something, refusing to drink tea." Andre signaled the waiter. "What will you do next?"

"The only thing is to follow him again, to see where he goes. If he appears to be following their army, it's at least something. You know how it goes in this business. Lots of little bits added together make a picture. I'll precede him next time; I think he knew we were following. Then I'll go back and inspect his cargo at night."

"Have you men watching Montraville?"

"That's as futile as watching Thompson. He works, he eats, he gambles. No regular woman, goes to Smithson's often. Expensive place. Not many friends, but close. Lives quite high. He could easily pass messages to anyone working in any of the places he frequents, and there are dozens."

"Keep on him."

"The King is paying, correct?"

225

"Yes." Andre slid a purse across the table.

*****

"Now, John Andre, you must tell me what has been bothering you these last weeks." They were walking in the early fall evening. The sun had been hot, but the day was cooling quickly in the lengthening shadows. Margaret had suggested getting out; the parlor was still too warm for comfort. She patted his hand. "Come on now, tell mama what's on your mind."

He stopped and turned to look at her, debating. They began to walk again, slowly. He took a deep breath.

"I feel this war drawing to a close, and here I am stuck with little to show. In the north we are at a stand. Any army that moves will suffer for it. In the south there are chances for glory, but not here. There's nothing so pitiable as an old soldier with nothing to point to."

"You can point to your service to Sir Henry. Surely that's a valuable thing? I know how highly he thinks of you."

"I know that he does, and it's gratifying, but I hanker after something...dramatic, something that people will talk of for a generation. I should not tell you this, I suppose, but I have a project in train that will change the whole course of this northern war, even of the war itself."

"God, John, I pray you be careful. I have seen others on this strangely male quest for renown over my life; many, no, most of them found an early grave instead. Women everywhere would rather a live man at hand than a dead hero."

"Mrs. Brush, are you contemplating violating our pact?

"Indeed not, Major. We both know that such a thing is impossible. But I can be fond of you, can't I? I do enjoy your company. You have many talents which women particularly treasure and I would prefer that you remain alive to demonstrate them. When this war ends you will board a ship and sail into the sunrise. I will remain here. I have no wish to leave my native land and I would not fit into yours."

*****

Enoch Robbins sat at a small pine table in his windowless room, counting. This war was a blessing! Andre was paying him to investigate Montraville. At the same time Montraville was paying him to investigate Clinton's family, who were probably, but unprovably, spying on all three of them. And Clinton sat there oblivious to it all. Then there was that Colonel paying him £5 a month to not inquire any further about the boys in his regiment. Ah, these British! He would be sorry to see it all end. If he played this right, it could be extended forever. A clue here, a word there, they'd all be so busy chasing each other that nothing would be accomplished. All the while, he'd be getting paid these lovely gold coins, and all of it the King's money!

He counted them again. He liked the feel of the heavy coins in his fingers. Did he have enough? Why not? Someone would give him as much more tomorrow. It had been a month since he had. He slid ten coins into his pocket, carefully concealed the rest beneath the floor and set off to Mrs. Smithson's. He wondered if Bess would be available. He smiled. He hoped so.

*****

"How is this secret project of yours coming along, John?" Margaret asked. Making progress?"

"Pretty well, I think. I've been working on it for over a year, and it should come to fruition soon. The other party's demands are great, but reasonable. Sir Henry has agreed to it. There are a few more details to work out. In a few days, I'll go to execute it."

"Must you go yourself? It's a departure from your practice."

"Yes, but I must. This is too important to entrust to anyone else."

"And besides, who so ever carries it off will be remembered for generations?" she said, teasing him. "You be careful, John Andre!"

"I will be. Think on it! Communication with Montreal; New England isolated! The rewards make the risks small!"

227

"But the great chain at West Point? How will you get past it"

"Perhaps I have an excellent blacksmith."

✶✶✶✶✶

"He asked me to marry him, Mama."

"I know. He asked my permission and I could not be more pleased. You know I think the world of him. What did you say?"

"I said yes, but…"

"But?"

"I told him I would marry Edward Browning, but not John Thompson."

"I see." Margaret took a moment to digest this. "How?"

"I'm not sure. We won't be able to do it in the city, at least not for a long time, and we don't want to wait."

"Listen Fanny, my dear, you understand that I'm in full support of the what, but we need to think carefully about the how? And you know I can't leave New York? I'll regret not being at the event, but I do understand your haste. I can live with that, as long as you are happy."

Fanny hugged her mother, her eyes moist.

✶✶✶✶✶

They were all gathered in the drawing room, talking in hushed voices. Sally stood guard at the door.

"Listen, John. We believe there will be an attempt on West Point in the next few days. We don't know who or how. We must get this to General Washington."

"What forces?"

228

"I suspect none. This originated with Major Andre. He's executing it himself, so it will probably be by subterfuge rather than assault."

"A traitor?"

"It fits. I don't know who."

John fell silent for a minute. "This must be terribly difficult for you, Madam," he said with awed respect. "You understand what this could mean?"

"Fully and regrettably. Sometimes life can be unbearably cruel. Listen, John, This is so important that I think we need to send it by two messengers and they must use different routes. It has to get through!"

"Mama, John and I could go. There is that other business…"

"Don't you be too eager, honey. But you do have a point—it would explain both your absences. It's a shame you two decided to run off to marry, though. The details fall to you, John. What is possible?"

"Fanny goes in my boat. I trust my crew. They'll die before she could be taken. I'll go by horse to Peekskill. I think the General is still there. We can both be there by morning."

"John, it will be dangerous for you! What about the guards at Kingsbridge?"

"This is my job, my love. I must, and so must you. You go throw a few necessaries together, I'll advise Bill and Tom. We should leave within the half hour to catch the tide. When you get to the headquarters, tell them you have a message from Odysseus. That will admit you. Remember, 'a message from Odysseus.'"

*****

The sentries at Kingsbridge stood in the hot sun, sweating in their wool uniforms. They saw hundreds of people a day, passing in and out of the city, while they were condemned to stand wishing they were anywhere else. They vented their annoyance any way they could.

"State your business." The man was hot and disagreeable.

229

"Food broker. I have concerns in Eastchester."

Passes had to be examined first by this man and then by that, questions answered again and again. Edward found playing the part of the vexed commercial traveler easy. He had actually passed here before in the course of his business. That he was really anxious to be on his way leant verisimilitude to his terse responses.

"Your pass?"

"Here it is."

The man pretended to read the pass carefully. Edward wondered if he even could.

"Sergeant! This man claims to have business in Eastchester."

He sergeant was no more pleasant.

"Well, Mr. ...Thompson." He suddenly looked more closely at the pass. "What might this business be?"

"I supply produce to markets in the city. I'm to talk to a man about selling his."

"Huh." He studied the pass again and peered at Edward. "Let's see what you have. Turn out your saddlebags." He seemed disappointed that they contained only a spare shirt. "How do you come by a pass with General Clinton's signature?"

"I supply his house. He's really looking for some turnips. Shall I tell him I could get none because I could not pass?"

Anxiety crept into the sergeant's voice. "No. You may pass. You'll need to hurry to get to Eastchester by dark."

"Yes. Thank you, sergeant." And he rode on. The two devoted themselves to harassing the next in line, a man and woman with an empty pushcart. They didn't even notice that he took the wrong road, heading for Peekskill instead of Eastchester. Now the only danger was the roving bands of looters that infested Westchester County at night.

*****

"Bill!" said Tom, pointing.

"What the devil? What's a warship doing way up here?

"Miss Fanny, I'm sorry to trouble you, but I need you to get under that little foredeck. We can't risk having you seen by them. That's it, close against the leeward side. They can't see through planking! Close the curtain."

"As you wish, Bill. For how long?"

"About a half hour-- they're faster than we are. They should overtake and pass. We can still talk quietly."

She could hear the water against the hull, feel the changing heel of the boat as the wind increased. They were starting to pitch into the waves. Right in the bow, she needed to brace herself to avoid being thrown about. Soon she could hear the ship passing, the sound of sails being adjusted, the shouted orders. As she peered through the parted curtains, she could see a shadow pass slowly over them. She felt a wave of fear as a sudden shout made her think she had been seen. Gradually the sounds died away.

"How much longer, Bill?"

"Soon, Miss Fanny. We're even with Spuyten Duyvil. Uncomfortable down there?"

"I'm sorry, yes. Carry on, I'll manage."

"Very good, Miss."

Bill's sense of 'soon' was different than hers, she decided. At last he said. "I think you can come out now, Miss Fanny. They're a half mile beyond us." She sat up rapidly, her hand over her mouth.

"Leeward side, Miss!" said Tom, pointing.

When the heaving stopped, she dipped her hand in the river, washed her face and wiped it with her sleeve. She turned sheepishly toward the two men. "Not very ladylike, I guess I'm not much of a sailor. Sorry."

"Fix your eyes on the shore, Miss Fanny. That will help. As to the other, it happens. I apologize, but it was necessary. It will be dark soon. Perhaps you'll be able to catch some sleep—there's little for you to do, and at night, nothing to see. Just settle yourself against the hull and relax. Watch the stars later; they'll help your stomach too. We'll be to Peekskill before dawn."

* * * * *

Bill led her up the short path from the riverbank to the back door. The smells of breakfast greeted them as he pushed the door open without knocking.

"Morning, Sophie. Is Mrs. Browning about yet?"

"Just, Bill. If you had knocked like a civilized person, she would be waiting for you."

"I have one here who must see her at once. Mister Edward sent her from the city."

"What? You keep a lady waiting in the kitchen? What kind of man are you? You come with me, Miss. I'll show you to Mrs. Browning. Do you take coffee?"

"Today, desperately," said Fanny.

She was shown into the dining room. "A lady to see you, Ma'am, from Mr. Edward.

"Good morning, Aunt Kathleen. How long has it been?"

"Gracious, Fanny Brush! What are you doing here? Is Edward coming?"

"He should be, he came horseback while I used his boat. I need to speak privately," She glanced at Sophie, who knew enough of her mistress' affairs to withdraw.

232

"Mama is quite sure that an attempt will be made on West Point, in the next few days. She has intelligence that Major Andre is the source of this, so she suspects it will be by subterfuge He has been unusually circumspect about it, but has hinted that a significant sum of money is involved, and probably a commission and pension besides. He is to execute it himself, indicating that there is an important person on the other side. We thought this so important that Edward and I came separately with the message, in case one were detained.

"We saw a sloop of war last evening, coming up from New York, and passed it again, at first light anchored off West Haverstraw. This may be happening even sooner than we thought it might."

"I see. Eat something, Fanny. Let me think a minute." After several minutes, during which a Fanny drank a cup of coffee and ate a biscuit, Kathleen said, "The problem is that General Washington is in Hartford. That means the senior officer nearby is General Arnold. Unfortunately, everything you've said points to him as the traitor. We're going to Major Talmadge. He will be able get this into the chain of command. We don't always see things the same way, but I trust him. Sophie!"

The girl popped into the room so quickly, Fanny thought she must have been listening at the door.

"Run to Major Tallmadge, tell him he will shortly have two guests. We'll follow as soon as Fanny is ready. You can finish your coffee, dear, slowly. He'll need time to dress."

After Sophie was on her way, Kathleen continued, "Fanny, during our conversation you will hear of someone named 'Odysseus.' This is a name I have given to the four of you collectively, but I am the only one who knows your identities. The men at headquarters have decided that this Odysseus is a man, and it would be well if they continued to think so, for your safety. Tell your tale as if Odysseus sent you and do not reveal how you know what you do. Do you understand? What you saw in the boat you may say plainly. You know firsthand how a spy can infiltrate even the innermost circles!"

*****

Benjamin Tallmadge had barely dressed when the two descended on his door. All he had to offer was coffee.

233

"Good morning ladies. To what do I owe the honor?"

"Benjamin, we have a problem. This," she said, indicating Fanny, "is my friend...let's call her Penelope. I am well acquainted with her and her family and can give witness to her veracity and acumen. She brings a message from Odysseus..."

"You and your classical jokes, Kathleen." She nodded an acknowledgement. "What has 'Penelope' to say?"

When Fanny had repeated all she had told Kathleen, she added, "I hope you will be able to scotch this treason."

"Damn his eyes! This is most disturbing. Have you any proof of this plot? Any evidence?"

"No, sir, you must accept my word or not. I have no further assurance to offer."

Just then they heard a commotion in the hallway and Edward burst into the room.

"Edward," Fanny hurried to him. "You're safe. I was so worried."

"Benjamin, this is my son, Edward. He brings the same message, I believe. Edward, tell the man what you know."

He told his tale, similar to Fanny's, embellished by an account of his journey, interrupted as it was as he hid from banditti and then by the questions of Colonial sentries who seemed skeptical that his mother truly lay dying in Peekskill.

"You two came separately?"

"Yes, sir. Odysseus deemed the message that important. He felt it was imperative that it get through."

"Very well. I appreciate all that you have done to deliver this, and I do not question either your honesty or sincerity. But you understand, I just can't go around accusing generals without evidence, something I can take to court.

234

His Excellency is due back from Hartford today. I'll send a courier directly. It won't change his arrival much, but he must know.

"In the meantime, we need to get to General Greene with the army at Tappan to have him alert the troops. They don't need to know why."

"I have a boat," said Edward.

"Good—you're all coming with me to explain!"

✳✳✳✳✳

Robbins sat on the end of the dock, pretending to fish. They might have been biting, but he had no luck as he had no hook. He could not be bothered to land a fish while he watched. This might be one of the last good days of the season; high clouds were filling from the west. A cold was coming. He had been watching this sleepy, boring village for two days. Montraville had better pay him well for his time! He wanted to get back to the city, to Mrs. Smithson's. That thought made this damned waiting worth it.

The ketch, the one he'd been waiting for, pulled into the creek. She came to anchor one hundred feet offshore, a quarter mile from where he sat. He watched, as everyone does when a boat enters a harbor. The Brush girl was here! She and the big man climbed down into the dinghy and rowed ashore, to the house he suspected. He saw them walk into the kitchen without knocking.

A few minutes later, Bill came out with another girl--a maid, he guessed. They had just begun to walk along the stream when the maid was called back inside; tryst interrupted. He lowered his head. He could not be seen. Moments later she could be seen hurrying off down the street.

After a half hour, Miss Brush and Mrs. Browning came out and hurried after her.

An hour later, they returned with Thompson and another man he had never seen. Thompson called to Bill. They rowed out to their boat, hoisted sail, pulled up the anchor and left, heading back toward New York.

If ever there was damning evidence, he had just seen it! It took him only another hour of casual questioning to get the name. Edward Browning. The other man was Major Tallmadge! He knew the name. It bothered him that Montraville had been right, but he would pay well for this intelligence. Now he only had to wait until Mrs. Browning returned.

He was impressed that they had maintained the imposture so long.

* * * * *

Progress was agonizingly slow. The coming storm had stilled the winds. The contrary tides had slowed them to only a few miles in the hours since they had sailed. Bill fretted over each little puff of wind, Tom constantly worked the sails to generate some speed. Edward fussed over everything and they were all becoming testy.

"Edward, come sit by me. You must get some sleep. You got none last night."

Edward smiled indulgently at her. "No, I must help. These conditions are the most trying a sailor can face."

Fanny let it ride for fifteen minutes. "Edward, I'm chilly. Could you not sit close with me for a moment, just for warmth?"

He sighed and sat as she cuddled close. Within minutes, the inactivity, the warmth of her body and his own fatigue, all conspired against his resolve. He jerked his nodding head back up. "Scooch down my love, lean your head." She laid her arm across his shoulder and guided his head. He felt her fingertips adjust his forelock, then he slept. Kathleen looked across at her, smiling benevolently.

"Well played, Fanny, I'm very pleased. You're good for him."

"Thank you, Aunt Kathleen. Men can be so stubborn sometimes."

"They can, and at the same time so yielding. So, what plans do you two have?"

"I shouldn't tell you, he should have the chance…"

"I promise I shall act surprised!" with a conspiratorial laugh, "Come, tell me…"

236

*****

The wind increased from a whisper to a zephyr an hour later, just as Bill had predicted. Edward still slept. Kathleen surveyed the river. Ahead the warship with loosed but useless topsails hanged on her anchor ahead of them, toward the middle of the river, tide borne. She could read the name 'Vulture' in gold leaf across her transom.

"Bill, have you a glass aboard?"

"Yes, Ma'am, in the cuddy, to starboard. Tom--fetch it for her."

She first looked at the ship, then swung to find the small boat she had noticed close to the shore. She studied it for a moment as she brought it into focus. Two men were rowing hard toward the ship; their passenger sat in the stern, grim faced. She drew in her breath sharply.

"Benjamin, come look." She pointed. "Look at the passenger and tell me what you see."

Tallmadge studied as closely as she had, then suddenly turned to look at her, his face pale.

"Benedict Arnold?"

"That's who I saw too. Bill, can we intercept that boat?"

"Maybe. Tom, let's bear away a bit. Mind the jib. I want to get between the boat and the ship."

"Bill, have you any firelocks aboard?" asked Tallmadge.

"An old musket and a couple fowling pieces. Not much good unless we can get much closer. Up forward."

The sudden activity woke Edward. He rose regretfully and stretched. He gave Fanny a grateful look. "What's about?"

"You two appear to have been right, Edward. Yonder is Benedict Arnold selling his soul! Bill is trying to cut him off."

237

They heard the sound of a bosun's pipe from the ship, then saw a splash near the stern. The two men in the small boat realized their danger and began to row furiously, the figure in the stern urging them onward.

"He's dropped a second anchor!" said Bill. Slowly, agonizingly slowly, the ship began to pivot between her two anchors as one rode was payed out and the other tightened. Edward was first to recognize the stubby black teeth extending from her side.

"Wear ship, Bill! She's going to fire on us!"

"Up vangs! Jibe-o," called Bill as he pulled the tiller sharply over. They heard the deep sound of a cannon as the side of the ship belched flame and smoke. The shot whistled as it came, black streaks against the blue sky. They could only watch helplessly as they came nearer, and nearer still. Tall columns of water rose close by, where their former course would have carried them. Spray fell all around.

"Someone over there is too damned good at his job!"

They heard a lone cannon from Croton point firing on the ship. The first ball fell well short, the second sprayed the river onto the quarterdeck. The third struck home as the Vulture completed her turn back to return fire.

"That will give them something to think about!" The small boat drew alongside the ship, and Arnold scrambled aboard. *No one, especially landsmen, ever looked dignified on a ship's ladder,* thought Fanny.

"Get close to shore, Bill, and we'll be able to slip past them, out of the field of fire. If we can get to Tappan before him, perhaps the field artillery will be able to knock them about enough to stop this treason!"

*****

Nathaniel Greene's headquarters were in a farmhouse overlooking the Tappan Zee.

"Are you telling me, Tallmadge, that General Arnold has gone over to the enemy?" asked Nathaniel Greene incredulously.

"I am, sir. Early this morning I received intelligence from New York that some plot was afoot against West Point, and just hours ago, I myself witnessed Arnold go aboard a King's ship, under cover of cannon fire. There can be no doubt."

"And this ship is now proceeding down river?"

"Yes. It had just hove into view as we landed, perhaps an hour behind us. Please, sir, if we place some field artillery on the shore, we may be able to impede him. But we must act quickly!"

"Impossible. My closest battery is over an hour away, and not limbered up. It would take four hours for them to reach the shore. Damn it! Is his Excellency aware?"

"I sent a messenger this morning. He'll be here by tomorrow."

"Good work, Tallmadge." He summoned his staff. "We need to assume that the enemy will come up-river and we must reposition ourselves to stop him. If you'll excuse me, Tallmadge, I have work to do."

"General, will you be needing us further? These people are the ones who brought the first warning."

"Oh...my thanks to you all, but I think your service here is complete. Mrs. Browning, Mr. Browning, I see that patriotism runs deep in your family. My regards to your husband, and to you, Miss Brush, my thanks as well."

"General," said Kathleen, "could you direct us to your chaplain? These two have some urgent business, pending too long."

"Mother!" Edward looked between the two women. "I guess I shall have to get used to these womanly schemes from you two!" He was not the least displeased.

"It appears my congratulations are in order as well as my thanks." He summoned an aide. "Take these people to Mr. Miller, with my blessing. Tell me, may I kiss the bride?"

"You may, sir," said a blushing Fanny.

239

*****

Kathleen Browning was subdued for a mother whose son had just married a girl of whom she approved. She and Tallmadge walked behind the couple to the tavern. They were busily engaged in all the foolishness of newlyweds while their elders were deep in conversation. Tallmadge had proposed a toast then made his excuses and left.

"Now, you two, have a good dinner. You have a long night ahead of you." She saw the look they gave each other. "Not that. Affairs of state sadly trump affairs of the heart. I'm not sure that that's right, but it is. Major Tallmadge and I need you to get back to New York tonight. We must know what Clinton is planning in light of Arnold's treachery. Is he coming up the river, with what troops and when? These we must know, and Meg will not know to look for them unless you get word to her. I mean, she'll know of Arnold-- he'll probably have dinner with Sir Henry tonight-- but she must be aware of the consequences. Do you see? I am so sorry, children."

"I...we, understand, Aunt Kathleen," said Fanny.

"Please, call me 'Mother' or something now."

"I needn't try to hide a certain disappointment, Mother Browning." She stumbled over the unfamiliar title. "You wouldn't believe me if I tried, but we do understand."

The couple looked to each other and then to her. "Yes mother. We understand." He looked regretfully at his bride. "Another night?"

"Oh yes!"

"How will you go?"

"We'll take the dinghy—it has a sail. Bill can take you and Major Tallmadge home, then go to Newark and pick up the produce for tomorrow. There's a cove we sometimes use, a mile or so above the city. We can leave the dingy there for Bill to get on his way down. If we leave now, we should be there at twilight."

240

"Have you time to eat? Of course you do, I insist upon it. It is a poor welcome to the family, Fanny, but the best under the circumstances. We shall celebrate properly in time. You two have your whole lives ahead of you."

"Regretfully, Mother, we shan't wait. Let's have a toast while the kitchen throws something together for us to take away."

*****

"Good afternoon Mr…" Kathleen paused to look at the man's calling card, "…Robbins. How may I help you?"

"Actually, Mrs. Browning, I find myself in a position to help you. Quite by accident, I've discovered that certain persons in New York are exchanging information with certain persons here in Peekskill. A particular officer had been very interested in that, and was to pay handsomely, but before I report, I thought I would offer you the opportunity first. This intelligence will be worth so much more to you."

"Mr. Robbins, we are both adults. If you truly expect me to honor anything you say, I will require some names." She moved closer to the mantle, she knew he could see the pistol resting there.

"As you wish. Montraville has offered to pay me £50 for this. Your son was receiving intelligence from Fanny Brush and her mother and passing it to you. Names enough?"

"How shall I know that you haven't already told him?"

"Because I just this morning discovered it. Why would I give it to him at 50 per centum? I can't stand him anyway, the uppity snob! I did happen to tell him of the cove Edward prefers, just as a tease."

"I see." She fought for composure. "And what price your silence?"

"£100 sterling. It's worth far more to you than it will be to Montraville."

"And what guarantee have I that you won't be back in six months for £100 more?"

"That would be unethical of me, just as it would be for me to sell it to both of you. First come, first served. I do have standards."

"I'm sure you do," flatly. "I will need time to gather that much…"

"DON'T you toy with me woman! I know you have access to funds, they're probably behind some loose brick in that fireplace."

"I do, but not that much. If you will accept £80, I can gather that within the hour. More means tomorrow. Your choice."

"Within the hour then."

"One other thing, Mr. Robbins. You will not return to New York. Head up the river to Albany, never to be seen again. I can offer you transportation if you wish."

"With your crew? I'd be safer walking."

"Walking up the Hudson with £80 in your pocket does not strike me as a safe course. Nonetheless, you <u>will</u> go there. I will give you the name of a man to see. If you do not report, various men will be looking for you, and they're quite as good as you at learning things accidently. Any questions?"

"I understand. I'll think about it."

"Very well, come back at five o'clock. Your money will be ready."

✱✱✱✱✱

There were clouds scudding across the full moon as the dinghy flew down the river. A fresh breeze drove them across the black water. Fanny spoke quietly.

"This has been a day we'll never forget! Chasing a traitor in the morning, wed in the afternoon, sneaking into enemy territory at night! You must be exhausted, Edward. I'm glad you got a little sleep this morning."

"As near to beaten as I ever want to be, although I did have a lovely nap."

"I offer my shoulder for your use any time."

242

"As do I mine. Were I not busy with the boat, I'd kiss you right now."

"Were you not busy, I hope you'd do more," she said demurely. "Now, shush."

They dropped the sail once they were close; Edward rowed silently toward the shore, glancing over his shoulder to check his course from time to time. To Fanny it all looked like one dark tree line, but Edward seemed certain.

"We're here." He stopped rowing and the boat nosed into the soft graveled shore.

Edward paused to get his bearings. "There's a path that way in about one hundred yards. It leads to the road. Once there, we can walk boldly into town. It's about a mile. Only a little further, my love," he whispered. They began to walk silently.

"HALT! WHO GOES!" The shout paralyzed them for a heartbeat, then they began to run down the narrow path, single file. The footfalls of running men pursued them, gaining. As they rounded a bend Edward stopped suddenly and pulled her close. He pointed. "There's a thicket that way. Get to the middle of it and lie absolutely still. I'll come for you."

"But Edward…"

"Go Fanny, I'll lead them away. Go!" Then, in a whisper, "I love you."

"And I you." They could hear the footsteps approaching. She darted into the bushes and lay, making sure her boat cloak covered her light dress completely. Beneath the bushes, she could still see Edward running down the path in the moonlight.

The soldiers were nearly even with her when the officer call out, "Thompson! Stand where you are." Then he raised his pistol and fired. She saw Edward stagger. She bit her knuckle to keep from crying out. Edward ran a few more painful steps, then stopped. There were a dozen soldiers close upon him. He turned and stumbled down toward the river, along a small jetty. He dove in the water just as hands reached for him.

The cold water made him gasp involuntarily. He inhaled the river. The pain in his side had been excruciating, but was nothing to the crushing pain now in his chest. In the instant before darkness he knew he had succeeded.

Deprived of buoyant lungs, his lean body sank slowly to the bottom.

The soldiers stood on the jetty, looking down into the dark water for any sign.

"What are you fools waiting for, damn it! The other is getting away! Come on, follow me!"

And then the moonlight caught Montraville's face.

*****

Enoch Robbins was feeling proud of himself. He had just got the money out of the woman, and now he was off to New York to get more from John Montraville. Business was good. Did that silly sow think she could threaten Enoch Robbins? "Nobody threatens me!" he said aloud.

"This isn't a threat, Enoch," said the big man who suddenly grabbed his arm in the darkness. "Neither is this," said the man who grabbed the other arm. First one hit him, and then the other, in rapid succession.

When he awoke it was fully dark. His hands were bound. He felt a noose resting on his shoulders. He had the worst headache he had ever experienced and his stomach was heaving. He could feel the heavy bark of a tree behind his back.

"Good, you're awake. I was getting tired of waiting. Enoch, you're a spy. You're going to die."

"Wait, I have money!"

"Not any more you don't"

He heard a whip crack and a wagon begin to rattle away.

Enoch started to protest, but the sudden tightening of the noose prevented it. He felt himself jerked into the air, a swinging, mad pendulum. He kicked, he

244

writhed, he tried to scream. Bill and Tom each lit a pipe and watched him die.

✳✳✳✳✳

Fanny watched the moon, judging time. For an hour she waited but there was no sound. She rose slowly, drawn to the jetty. She stood at the end, looking down. A single tear escaped. He had wanted her to live, had sacrificed himself so that she might, and *God Damn It!* That is what she was going to do. Montraville would not.

She turned and began to walk home, her face hard, her mind numb.

She could never remember the walk. She remembered turning onto the street and seeing the candles in every window of Sir Henry's house. Through a fog she saw men in uniforms going in and out, some silhouetted in the windows, others clustered on the sidewalk. She brushed past them, entered and went straight to her mother's room and collapsed on the bed.

"Fanny? What's wrong?"

"He's dead, Mama! He's dead and Montraville murdered him!"

Saying it made it become true and she sobbed. Margaret silently hugged her daughter. Fort Cumberland flooded back upon her. There was nothing that could be said.

She held her daughter for a long time; it seemed like hours. After a time, Fanny stopped, exhausted, and began to listen. "Mama, what are all these men doing here?

"Fanny, did you get the message through?"

Margaret watched her daughter collect herself. She took a deep breath and let it out slowly.

Then she told of her day. Margaret was by turns fearful, worried, elated, disappointed, proud, grief stricken and angry. She was unable to form a comforting thought.

Fanny lifted her head. "Why are the men here?"

245

"Ahh—They're planning an offensive up the river, as far as West Point at least. This Arnold fellow—now, he's an oily one, he claims to know the way in. I met him at dinner and dislike him intensely. Sir Henry is not much pleased with the bargain he has made."

Just then a burst of male laughter carried up the stairs.

"What! That voice...Is he here? Is Montraville here?"

"Yes, Fanny, I wanted to spare you that..." She was talking to her daughter's back as she stormed out of the room.

*****

Crowds of soldiers parted before the disheveled girl like the Red Sea before Moses. Montraville stood with a group of junior officers.

"...and then I shot the bloody bugger. He didn't have the decency..."

"YOU BASTARD! YOU ROTTEN FUCKING BASTARD! YOU MURDERED MY HUSBAND!"

Montraville had had experience with angry women. In a way he rather enjoyed it as they futilely beat their little fists on his manly chest. He was unprepared for the first blow, a blow that loosened some teeth. The second was a near miss to his groin. He struck back, a series of body blows that drove her back a step.

"You stupid little colonial slut! Would that I <u>had</u> murdered you in the womb...would that I had killed your mother as well! You're both just army whores, pretending trash, so far above yourselves!

She stood, half facing him, breathing heavily, ready to spring. She had wild hair and wild eyes that blazed hatred like flame from a cannon. There was not a soldier in that room who chose to approach her.

The sound started low in her throat, a sort of growl, rising in pitch and volume, until with a bloodcurdling inchoate cry she launched herself again.

246

Her fist broke his nose, the second blackened an eye. After her third blow he spit out a tooth. This wild fury was outside his experience. He had fought Frenchmen, he had fought Indians, and even Americans, but they always came in trained, predictable ways: this mad woman's berserk assaults had no pattern. He hit her again and again, then a roundhouse right caught the side of her head. She staggered back, her heel caught the edge of the Turkey carpet and she went down hard.

She struggled to rise as he approached to finish. A dozen hands restrained him..."Hold on now...get a grip, man...remember yourself...what the hell are you doing...she's just a girl..."

Margaret knelt beside her. "Fanny?" Mary came to her other side.

She looked up. "Mama?" It was the voice of a child, hurt and afraid.

"Come honey," she said softly, "I think it's time for bed."

They rose slowly and made their way to the doorway. Margaret could hear Montraville shouting hysterically at their backs, "He should have been hanged, not shot, damn his eyes! You all should be hanged! You damned colonials are all lying whores and thieves! You may have deceived this old fool, but you haven't deceived me!"

She turned and shook her head sadly at him. "Poor man."

Sally met them. "Cook is warming some milk."

"Go with her, Sally," said Mary. I'll bring it up when its ready."

Together they got her to her bed, the milk came. The three undressed her and got her into a nightgown. Fanny was now sobbing and beyond consolation. They convinced her to lie down and drew the covers over her. Still she wept.

*****

Montraville was holding a handkerchief to his bleeding nose, still flushed with anger and shame. At that moment he had not a friend in the room. General Clinton approached.

"Is this what you call catching spies Montraville? Are you mad? Shooting a man bringing his bride home? You call yourself a British soldier? Get the shit beaten out of you by a girl? You rain abusive language upon my family in my own house? I shall send for you if I ever wish to see you again. Remove yourself, sir, immediately!"

He turned on his heel and went to knock anxiously at Fanny's door.

Margaret came out to meet him in the hallway.

"Is she going to be all right?"

"I don't know, sir. She's had a truly awful shock. I've never seen her like this. I must get back…"

"Yes, yes, of course. Know that I am with both of you."

"Thank you, Sir Henry." She turned and slipped back into Fanny's room. She sat gently rubbing her daughter's back, then lay down with her, holding her until she slept.

*****

It was mid-morning when Jupiter knocked at Fanny's room. Margaret came to the door.

"So sorry, Ma'am," apologetically. "Captain Montraville is here. He wishes to speak with you."

"That's nice. I'll not receive him."

"Very good, Ma'am." He turned to deliver the message.

"No wait, Jupiter. That's unfair of me. I shouldn't put you in the middle and I don't want him to raise his voice and disturb Miss Fanny. Put him in the drawing room, I'll be down in a few minutes."

She swept into the drawing room, interrupting his pacing. She had a fresh dress but her hair was still loose, hanging to her waist from a ribbon. She almost laughed at his appearance: one blackened eye narrowed to a slit, a distended cheek, a huge plaster across his nose.

248

"You look as I remember you at Quebec." He spoke as if he had a bad cold.

"You look like a damned murderer." The deadly calm of her voice should have warned him.

"Margaret, please don't...I need your help. Will you say a good word for me to Sir Henry..."

"I have no good words for you. Were I a gentleman, I would be asking the name of your second. Your latest unforgivable actions cap a quarter century of pain you have caused me and my family. Now you expect a kind word?"

"But I have nowhere else to turn...," He was begging.

"Wrong. You have nowhere to turn."

"But..."

"Goodbye, Captain." She turned and left the room.

*****

When Margaret got upstairs, Fanny was sitting up in bed, sipping coffee. Her eyes were still red. Bruises were showing everywhere.

"Good morning, sleepy head."

"Morning, Mama. Is that odious fellow back?"

"He wanted me to plead his case. He looks very much the worse for wear. You damaged more than his pride last night."

"Not so much as I wanted to. Are they going to hang him? I really wanted to kill him--I vowed to."

"In a way, you have. His career has taken a fatal blow. Sir Henry will send him back to his regiment and for a while he'll have a dreary existence, supervising the digging of latrines and such. Eventually, Sir Henry will recognize that he needs Montraville back—he has so few other experienced intelligence officers. I'd rather have him in that position than someone I don't know. He'll never enjoy the trust or access he has had though. But I haven't asked how you are today."

"Grieving and sore. I expect him to walk through the door any minute. Do I need to be ashamed of anything besides?"

"Heavens no! You <u>were</u> out of control last night, but everyone will give you pardon, under the circumstances. Sir Henry supports you. He's said so. As to the other, the sun will rise a little brighter each day. It seems a hackneyed thing to say, but it was so for me. That certainty is the only thing I can give. And my love."

"I need that as never before." She smiled wanly. "I thought I understood what you went through, when Lieutenant Soumain was killed, but it's only now that I begin to. What an awful place to be!"

"I think it would be good if we got away from here for a time. We could go up to Albany or even Westminster. You need time and peace and there'll be none of either here."

"I need to tell Aunt Kathleen."

"<u>We</u> need to tell her. Shall I make the arrangements with Sir Henry?"

"I think so. I'm just so tired." She carefully set her cup and saucer on the table and lay back against the pillows.

"I'll need to find someone to escort us through Westchester…"

"Mama, I own a boat." Her voice broke as she said it.

✳✳✳✳✳

The little room Sir Henry used as his personal office was no bigger than the one she herself used off the kitchen. He looked up, clearly distressed, as she entered after knocking.

"Good afternoon, Margaret. Please, sit."

She sat on the edge of the only chair. "You sent for me, sir?"

"How is Fanny? What a terrible shock she's suffered!"

"A bit better today, she's awake and has eaten a little. I think she's still numb."

"That's a relief, that she's eaten. I can't imagine what got into Montraville— disgraceful, that's what it was."

"He used to be such a sane fellow, very able--motivated by self-interest, but sane. Perhaps he's just been here too long. He seemed positively distracted—he was here to see me this morning, to ask me to beg your forgiveness."

"What did you say to him?"

"That nothing could induce me to intercede."

"Revenge?"

"Probably. Not dignified, but satisfying. I'm precluded from dueling."

Sir Henry smiled. "Yes. Well, the asking was more bloody poor judgment on his part. Possibly he has been here too long. This is the damnedest duty station in the empire—excuse my language.

"But the real reason I sent for you--I've just received a most disturbing letter from Washington. The Americans have captured Major Andre, beyond their lines, out of uniform. He was carrying the plans for the West Point fortifications."

"Oh." There was a long pause. Margaret sat silent and pale. "What will they do?" Her voice was small and distant.

"They want to exchange him for General Arnold. Otherwise, they propose to hang him."

There was another long silence as she considered, assailed by guilt. Finally she trusted herself to speak. "But, of course, you can't make such an exchange—the precedent."

251

"I'm relieved you understand. I was dreading this conversation. Why did he have to go there himself! I advised against it."

"So did I. He was suffering that strange delusion of young men, sir: 'glory'."

"I daresay. You knew? I know you two are close."

She fought to recover from the blunder. "I knew something was about, but not what. We're very good friends, sir, just as you two are. I am fond of him but he knows as surely as we what must happen. He is a soldier." She struggled with the words.

"Sir Henry, to get back to Fanny, She needs to be away from here. *So do I*! The bustle and the red coats and all will make her recovery more difficult. I have friends in Albany. I'd like to go there. You understand?"

"Yes, yes, of course. Whatever she needs. I'll be sending the Vulture back up river, under a flag, to collect Mrs. Arnold and bring her off, just as soon as they agree. I can have you delivered at Robinson's house—would you like that?"

"No sir, thank you. As Fanny pointed out, she now owns a boat. It's small enough that it can pass the great chain. We'd like to leave tomorrow, as soon as we talk to the boatman. Could we have a pass, sir?"

"Will you be coming back, Margaret? I especially value your counsel. All these young fellows around here would sell their souls for a colonelcy, and mine too. You don't have any such interests."

"You truly honor me, sir. Truth is, it will depend upon her."

"You'll consider it?"

Just then, Jupiter knocked. "Sorry to intrude, Sir Henry. Mrs. Brush, Mr. Thompson's man is here with the delivery. He's asking for you, Ma'am."

"Thank you Jupiter. I'll be along directly. If you will excuse me, sir? I will consider about the matter."

*****

252

Margaret sat with Bill on the low stone wall that marked the stable yard. "There can be no doubt? They really killed him?" He jumped up. "I'll kill the bastard myself!"

"Sit, Bill. Get a grip. Fanny did a pretty good job on him last night. But, yes. Thompson is dead. She saw the whole thing. He went into the water and never came up."

"How is Miss…Mrs. B…Thompson? What an awful thing to see, and on her wedding day!"

"Careful, Bill. Words can kill us dead as surely as he."

"Sorry, Ma'am. It's hard."

"It is. Listen, we want to go to Peekskill. I need to be the one to tell his mother. Can you take us tomorrow? We can talk more on the boat."

"Of course. Mrs. Thompson is my boss now…what's to become of the work?"

"One of those things we'll talk about tomorrow. Mid morning?"

*****

It was a foul, foul fall day. The blustery wind made them hold the hoods of their boat cloaks. The cold rain soaked them. Bill led them up the little path, into the warmth of the kitchen. Sophie greeted them.

"Bill, don't you ever use the front door? Mrs. Browning! May I be the first to congratulate…" then their faces registered with her.

"Is Mother Browning in? We must see her."

"Of course, follow me, please."

Kathleen rose. "Fanny! What a surprise! Is Edward coming? Meg?"

Margaret went to her friend. "Twice you've had to do this…I never realized how hard it is." She took a breath. "Kate, Edward was killed night before last, as they got to New York."

"No…"

Kathleen sat heavily. Margaret sat beside her and told her, as gently as she could, what had happened. When she finished, Kathleen sat, pale and silent, dabbing tears from her cheeks with her handkerchief.

"Kate, we have been friends for a long time. Deputize me to look after your household for a few days, until you get your feet back beneath you. Please do."

She nodded dumbly. "I'll go talk to Sophie. Fanny, will you stay with her? You two need each other just now." Receiving nods, she rose and left them.

*****

"Good morning, both of you. Hungry?"

Kathleen and Fanny entered the dining room together, both red-eyed and poorly rested.

"Good morning, Meg. I am. Fanny how about you? I usually take some oatmeal with raw sugar and milk."

Sophie appeared miraculously, as she usually did, with one bowl for her mistress, looking expectantly at Fanny. "What will you have, Ma'am?"

"The same, please, Sophie, thank you. And some coffee if you have it ready."

"Very good, Ma'am." She left for the kitchen.

"I'm not sure if I want to be Ma'am'ed yet. It's strange."

"You'll get used to it. Here you are, a respectable war widow, a rather well-off one. Edward's business was quite prosperous. We can go over it later. He kept most of his papers here. But, Meg, what about you? Will you go back to New York?"

"Kate, are you sure you want to get into all this so soon?"

"I need to work. I can only get relief if he did not die in vain. I really need to work. What about you? Fanny told me about Major Andre."

"I'm going to lose a friend--you have each lost far more."

"So Clinton will not make the exchange?"

"No. He cannot, though he really wishes to. Prisoner exchanges have a well defined price structure, rank for rank, or two of these for one of those. This would be all upside down. General Washington would rather a dead Arnold than a dead Andre; Sir Henry would rather a live Andre than a live Arnold. Neither can have what they want. Sir Henry has a brigadier he neither wants nor needs and he doesn't have West Point, which he does. I'm afraid John Andre's fate is cast. "

"Would you like to see him?"

"Yes, but I can't. He would understand the implications of how I might, and that betrayal, no, that's what it is!" she snapped as both started to protest. "The betrayal would wound him more than any pleasure at seeing a friend."

"Meg, you're too hard on yourself."

"Not really. I don't want Sir Henry to ever know either. Both have trusted me, will trust me. My agenda is different and they never realized it, nor will they. I have taken this path; I must finish the journey."

"Mama. You frighten me. You make it sound like a protracted suicide!"

"Maybe—I've done things in this war of which I can never be proud. A series of events I started has put Andre where he is. Every soldier in every war has done horrible things, no doubt. They don't all kill themselves, nor shall I."

"I don't like this new mood of yours, Mama. Think of all the lives you've saved by your actions—surely that is honorable."

"Honor is such a damned fickle thing, not even real."

"Then why is it so important that Sir Henry never know?"

She shrugged. "Cowardice, I guess. I could not bear the opprobrium of people I have come to like. He really is my friend and I have and will systematically betray him, just as I have betrayed Andre. What have I become? What I did started John Andre on his fatal mission!"

"No, Meg. He started the events which led him to his fate. What you did was not cause his capture. That's all on his head."

"And for all, we failed! Arnold is now counted as among the enemy!"

"He should have been for years, apparently. Just it's that now we know it. The enemy does not have West Point, and in that you succeeded wonderfully."

"Why do good men have to die? How many have I led to their deaths?"

"Mama. You're exhausted!"

"I suppose. I'm just so tired."

"Wait, does that mean you'll go back?"

"If you will let me. I told Sir Henry that we were going to Albany, to stay with friends. Fanny, I can't have you come. This will become enormously more dangerous than it has ever been. I won't have you exposed."

Kathleen had been silent in this exchange as the bitterness in her friend's voice increased.

"Meg," Kate said quietly, "I am so, so sorry."

"What?"

"I was so blinded by my own grief that I could not see yours. You must go to him."

"I can't, I told you…"

"You can, you must, and you will. There is no discussion. Bill can have you there and back before supper."

Margaret sat, the objections in her mind colliding with her desires and losing the ground steadily. She sighed. "Thank you."

✳✳✳✳✳

"Here's the money, Mrs. Browning."

"Thank you Bill. You have done me a great service. Would I have been pleased with the means?"

"I think so, Ma'am. He knew the what and the why."

"Good. I want you to keep this, Bill. Split it with Tom. I've never been able to properly reward you two for so many services. Take it as partial payment of a debt ever outstanding."

"No, Ma'am. It's blood money. It should go to Mrs. Browning, the young one."

"That would be blood money. Bill, talk with Sophie before you refuse this sum. She might have a more pragmatical opinion. Women often do."

"Ma'am?"

"Do it, Bill. The both of you come to me when you have decided."

✳✳✳✳✳

The room was quite pleasant, a bedroom in a proper house, unlike the cell she had experienced. Two windows looked out upon the Hudson. Two guards with bayoneted muskets looked into them alternately as they finished their proscribed rounds. John Andre sat at a small writing desk as she entered. He looked up, surprised.

"Margaret, how…?"

"John!" She hurried to him. "Are you well?"

257

"As I can be. I'm a curiosity here, the dead man who won't fall down. I'm sure there is furious betting—will he crack? Won't he? I'm determined to disappoint the former." He glanced at the face peering in the window. "I'm saddened that this room is so public…"

"As am I," Margaret gave him a conspiratorial wink. She glanced around; the bed was the only place. "Come, let's sit. They've given us an hour." And so they sat, touching at shoulder, hip and thigh, each feeling the other's warmth while disappointing the voyeurs with muskets.

"They've given me paper. I'm writing to friends, to Sir Henry, one of my old professors, and one for you." He rose and fetched it, returning to sit as closely as before. "I hereby deliver it."

"May I read?"

"Surely. What have I left to be embarrassed by?"

He waited, blushing, as she read the pages. There were tears in her eyes as she finished. "Thank you, John." She put her hand on his cheek, turned his head and kissed him, gently. "It's very sweet. I shall treasure it."

"I've been sketching, too, just to pass the time."

"May I see?"

He rose again and picked two more papers off the desk. "This is me, watching you, and this one is of you, as I watched."

The first was little more than a pencil sketch, unfinished and rough. The other was carefully finished, a study in light and shadow and texture.

"You've been too kind! I didn't look that good when I was twenty!"

The figure, infinitely calm, looked serenely at the artist. The bare shoulders and loosened hair cascading over one to conceal an unrendered breast made it clear that the subject was unclothed. "It's lovely, John. Isn't amazing how hints can imply so much? Half the people who will never see this would swear that I am shown fully naked!"

258

"You were, as I recall. It looks like you. I'll never forget that moment. I want you to have this, so you can remember too."

"Oh, John! Thank you! I'm so sad that you're caught thus. The world will be a poorer place...." She couldn't finish the thought.

"Sir Henry can do nothing?"

"He's tried and he heartily wishes he could. The price of your freedom is Arnold and he can't make that exchange. He paid £20,000 and a brigadier's commission for him and can't throw him back now. Having met him, both Sir Henry and I think that he got swindled. He is heartsick at this, believe that, you must! Everyone who knows you laments your fate."

"But I arranged it. I was careless and over-confident and I walked into captivity. A proper spy would have escaped without detection. Had I listened to you and Sir Henry, I would not be here now."

"I should have tried harder to dissuade you!"

"Nothing you could have said would have succeeded. The truth is, being a spy is not in my nature. I should not have attempted it. I didn't fully understand what was required to be one. I mistook those fellows for Tories. I wanted so much to be done with the hiding and the sneaking and the tension. I just walked up to them and as much as said 'Good morning, arrest me please!' You'd make a good spy, Margaret, but I don't have the stomach for it."

"I know—that's why I tried..."

"Margaret, you did all a person could. I blame only myself and I absolve you of all guilt. If you require it, I forgive you. Go forward with a clean conscience. I insist.

"Now, what else is happening in the city?"

"Well, a lot, really. Montraville has murdered Mr. Thompson on his wedding night"

"What! How did that happen?"

She told him.

"She really broke his nose?"

"Oh yes, his nose and his pride. He lost a tooth too. I saw him the next day--he was a mess."

"I feel badly for Fanny: she never deserved anything like this. I liked Thompson too. In a way, I suppose this is my fault as well. I was so busy with this Arnold affair that I hadn't been keeping up with whatever Montraville was doing. I should have steered him away, but I hadn't seen him for a week before I left."

And so they continued, sitting close, talking quietly until a knock at the door signaled time. An embarrassed lieutenant had to interrupt their last embrace.

"Be strong John. Do it for yourself. People will remember that."

*****

Margaret sat on the little foredeck of Bill's boat, her shoeless feet were hanging over the side in a most un-ladylike posture. She leaned back against the jib boom as the boat headed northward. The little fingers of a fresh cathartic wind were pulling her hair astray.

Does it count as forgiveness if the forgiver doesn't know what they're forgiving?

She heard Bill calling from the back of the boat. "Ma'am, come down from there. You'll get a soaking if it breezes up!"

She looked back at him, waved and smiled and didn't move.

Spray splashed in her face. *Go forward with a clean conscience. Easy for a condemned man to say. Do I even have one? How could I and do the things I have done? Kate said I was cold-blooded. Me with my beady little eyes and forked tongue! Seducing men into failure and betraying them to their deaths.*

Another, stronger wave wet her.

260

Motive! Crean said it always comes down to motive! Was it a just cause for which she worked? Well, I do know how this war will end. I'm just helping push it along. At least, I'm think I am, and I think that's good.

Another wave, the largest so far, sent a solid sheet of water over her. She laughed. She turned to Bill and waved, and then she laughed again.

After the boat anchored behind Kate's house, she went in through the kitchen, dripping wet, cold and certain.

*****

Sophie and Bill came into the dining room at breakfast.

"Mrs. Browning, Ma'am." Sophie had never been so nervous in her entire life.

"Yes, Sophie?"

"Bill and I have been talking—how did you know?"

"Honestly, Sophie! The whole bloody village knows. You two are the only innocents here."

"Yes, Ma'am. Well, as I said, we've been talking, and we think you're being too generous. Mrs. Browning, Miss Fanny that was, should have this money. We'll accept it only if she will sell us the boat for £50. Bill thinks we can do shipping up and down the river."

"I've no head for figures, Ma'am, but Sophie here does. Together, we think it should float. I can sail, she can cipher."

"Well, Sophie, and you, Bill," said Mrs. Browning, Miss Fanny that was. "I spent yesterday afternoon looking through my husband's records. He paid £17 and 6 for that boat two years ago. Now, it's had some wear since, and you yourself, Bill, told me the mizzen sail wants replacing. I will not accept a farthing more than £16 for it. But wait," as Bill looked about to protest. "It may happen, from time to time, that I may need the services of a reliable boatman. I would hope I may count on you, Bill,?"

"You've but to say the words, Ma'am."

261

A week had passed since the town had found the strange man hanging from the tree, the word 'traitor' painted across his shirt. No one knew who he was or where he had come from. His pockets empty, he had been buried in an unmarked grave and forgotten. Lynchings were more common in the lowlands of Westchester, but not unknown in Peekskill. It was wartime. People found it more exciting to marvel over John Andre's calm at his execution than the death of some unknown traveler. An attorney had been hired to unravel Mr. Thompson's business affairs, to sell everything and collect all owing. Fanny would now have money, most of it in bonds of the Continental Congress. She stood a better chance of being paid than the soldiers did.

The three women sat in Kathleen's parlor. The weather outside had turned nasty again. Leaves were falling, blowing past the windows in the wet northerly wind.

"I'm ready to go back, Kate. I don't want Sir Henry to forget how much he needs me."

"Are you sure? Your mood was as foul as the weather just a few days ago; I couldn't have you go feeling that way."

"Now that fate has become history, I'm ready." She looked to her daughter. "I don't want you to come. I know you're not ready. My loss was nothing compared to yours."

"Fanny! Stay with me! I've never had a daughter. I've discovered that they are delightful creatures to have about. Can I borrow yours, Meg, please?"

Fanny put up a feeble protest, but the matter was as good as settled as soon as it was broached.

"How shall we communicate?"

"Let me think. Read your book a bit..."

Twenty pages later, she said, "All right. Here's what we're going to do. Do you know Moll Smithson?"

262

"Slightly, we've passed pleasantries a few times. We don't really run in the same circles."

"Ah, but many of the men do. She's about to feel the stirrings of faith in her bosom, and, coincidently, so will you. Her brother died recently—syphilis-- and you've just lost your friend Andre. It would not be strange if two similarly affected women met by chance when they go to meditate in St. George's on Tuesdays and Thursdays, about mid-morning."

"But Mother Browning she runs a brothel! Mama can't be seen associating with her!"

"Fanny!" Honestly, you young people have the strangest ideas these days. Where did we fail them, Kate?"

"Have you ever been to a church on a weekday morning, Fanny? Trust me, few will see them and none will care. Truth be told, her story is similar to Meg's. Raised in plenty though she had no claim to privilege, married young, a child, her husband carried off by disease. Left with a small child and with a small competence, she made decisions to survive. She bought a small house and turned it to profit. Then a bigger and then a bigger still. Now she has a dozen girls, for whom she cares like a mother. She employs tutors for their children, seamstresses for their dressing, feeds and houses them, pays them well, and is fiercely protective. Gentlemen prefer her house for its opulence, discretion and safety. That her girls are very skilled is a bonus. Some of them are also skilled at getting men to talk."

"She's one of yours?"

"For several years. Men do talk sometimes. It was through her that the warning came to you this summer."

"I'll thank her when we meet. Now, about the messages…"

"We'll use a code developed by the Culpers. Less cumbersome than the one we used to use. I'll give you a list of names of important people, colonels, government types, and usual events; troop movements, sailings and so forth. Each will have a number assigned. Just write out your message, inserting the number representing the noun or verb you want. Only the common words will be plain. Better, have Sally write them for you…"

263

"No, I don't want Sally to come back either. Fanny needs her more, and if I think it's too dangerous for Fanny, then it's too dangerous for Sally too. I won't have her in this again, I won't! Can she stay with you too, please?"

"You're scaring me again, Meg. If you think it's too dangerous for them, then it must be too dangerous for you. I'm not sending my best friend to her death!"

"It is my choice, Kate. I can risk my own neck--I want to end this war. It's the only way I can vindicate my behavior. I will not risk other necks in my quest."

Kathleen looked searchingly at her friend, trying to understand what lay behind her impassive face. "You know that they won't hang you? Clinton's position could not endure the embarrassment that would bring. You would simply disappear some night."

"Mama, no!"

"I will go, Fanny. I must."

Kate sighed, at last, resigned, "Very well. Give your paper to Moll, she has a means to smuggle it out."

"Will she be able to read mine?"

"No, the numbers will be jumbled in the list she uses. Only I will have both lists."

"I'm not sure that I'm comfortable with you two being so good at this! What deceptions have you been practicing on me?"

"Many and varied, honey. You'll do the same when you're a parent, out of the purest love."

1781

"Damn and blast!" Sir Henry swore across his scone as he read the report.

"What is it, Sir Henry?" asked Margaret, looking up from her own breakfast.

"You remember that I had sent two good follows down to Morristown, to foment discontent among the Continental line. They succeeded, to the extent the Pennsylvania regiments are now disbanded but somehow Washington tumbled to them, and now they're both hanged."

"Sir Henry, that's awful!" said Mary Baddeley. "Can't you find someone to do this spy thing for you? You've so many things on your plate and this is so distasteful."

"I daresay…Margaret, I'm sorry, but I've had to call Montraville back. He's the only one left who knows the lower orders in this town. Why did Andre have to get himself caught!"

"You must do what the war requires, Sir Henry. If you need Montraville, use him. Know, though, that I shall not be in the same room. You would not expect two of your officers in our situation to sit at table together, nor shall I."

"Fair enough. I don't much like him either but he has skills. You accept his presence?"

"He's just the man for everything distasteful or ugly, Sir Henry." Margaret felt her lip curling. "He's good at it. It comes naturally to him."

Henry Clinton looked across at her. "Remind me not to make an enemy of you, Margaret."

✳✳✳✳✳

"Good morning, Mrs. Brush." The woman, in her mid thirties, tall, well and conservatively dressed, sat down in the pew next to her. "I've been watching for ten minutes, to see if you were followed."

"And good morning to you, Mrs. Smithson. I was careful. What with Major Andre dead and Captain Montraville just returned from the regiments, Sir Henry's intelligence apparatus is a shambles. There's always some amateur with a bee in his bonnet though."

"True enough." The two spoke in hushed tones. A thrice folded sheet of paper passed surreptitiously from one's hand to the other's. The other three parishioners scattered through the silent church could not hear them. Outside, a light snow fell from the windless sky. Muffled street sounds barely interrupted their thoughts. They had been meeting this way for a month and the solemnity of the church always made Margaret return home slightly red-eyed.

"I've been thinking, Mrs. Smithson, that it might be beneficial to our cause if Sir Henry's subordinates became dissatisfied and distrustful of him."

"Bad morale is good, quite the opposite of what my establishment generally seeks to engender. How might that happen?"

"I was wondering if some of your girls might plant the seed among your guests. The soil is fertile, and it would spread like wheat blight amongst the officers."

"A gossipy sort of thing?"

"Exactly so. What do you think?"

"Have you one of these seeds?"

"Well, he will not use the Tory regiments as fully as he might. He positively refuses to. One might wonder if he were secretly in sympathy with the rebels and not using every weapon available to defeat them."

Moll Smithson thought for a moment. "You know, Mrs. Brush, I quite like the way your mind works. I have a few girls who would be up to that. It would have to be done very carefully; infect the man without him knowing he had been bitten. The girls must not arouse suspicions. I'd be on the road to poverty and besides the men would stop coming."

"We can't have that!" Margaret laughed. "For either reason."

They stopped as the side door opened and slammed shut. A young man stomped the snow from his boots and took a seat across the center aisle a row ahead of them. He sat with his head bowed, and as they watched his shoulders began to shake.

"I do so hate to see a man in distress," said Moll. "Wife or child, do you think?"

"Possibly both. You have a good heart, Mrs. Smithson."

"Few think so. If that notion got abroad, I'd be finished in this town! My friends call me Molly, Mrs. Brush. May I count you a friend?"

Margaret patted her knee. "Indeed you may, Molly. I am Margaret, and your secret is safe with me. Until Tuesday?" She stood and slowly left the church.

The man watched her without turning his head.

*****

There it was:

281 27 that 568 711 a 398 8 783 of 159

Margaret almost laughed at the brevity of it. She consulted her lists and began to write the words below the numbers. Some she remembered, some she needed to check.

'Wash. desire that Corn. remain a separate command.   Advise of movements.'

She stopped writing. It was clear, even without the names complete and the verbs mangled. She approved, but how? She thought a moment, then burned the message and thought some more.

✱✱✱✱✱

Even Margaret, totally unschooled in music, could tell that the evening was not going well. Sir Henry and Mary had stopped again. He was becoming exasperated with himself. He sat back in his chair, the cello resting near his chin.

"I'm sorry, Mary, I guess I just can't do this now.   I just can't bring concentration to bear. Shall we stop for tonight?"

"Certainly, Sir Henry." She laid her violin on the harpsichord and stood behind him, massaging his shoulders. He leaned his head back against her and closed his eyes. "I'm sorry I dragooned you into playing tonight. I had hoped music might help you relax a little. I take it the letter from Lord Cornwallis was upsetting?"

"To say the least! First he does exactly what I told him not to do, abandon the coastal link, then he detaches troops on whimsical missions and they get themselves whipped *en detail*. Then this fop of his, this Tarleton, gets his ass kicked at Cowpens. Casualties of eighty per centum! I've never even heard of such numbers! To top all, Cornwallis burns all his baggage so he can catch up with Greene, and fails to do even that!"

"Sir   Henry,"   asked   Margaret,   "does   Lord   Cornwallis   still   have communications with the coast? How is he to be supplied?"

"He maintains contact, but tis thin and easily broken, from what I understand. Not that he'll tell me much. He has more correspondence with Germain than he does with me. So much for being in command in North America."

"However does he plan to eat? Isn't it far too early to live off the land? I mean, I've never been so far to the south, but there must be little forage even there in winter! And tents—I remember Virginia as being very wet in winter, wet and muddy. He's picked the very worst time to go adventuring."

268

"That he has, Margaret. And now Washington has sent his own fop, this Lafayette, south to contend with General Arnold in Virginia. Cornwallis will get no aid from him, unless he can punch through Greene to make a junction."

"How many does Lord Cornwallis now have?"

"Under 3,000, by now, I'd guess. The attrition has been terrible down there. He's lost over half, the best half, of his troops already. Does the fool think His friend Germain is going to pull more out of the God damned air! I know how that works. Cornwallis is trying to raise the Loyalist militia and finding it tough going. The people, it seems, are not so eager to fight for King and country as he believed, especially after that King's Mountain debacle last fall."

"I suppose, Sir Henry, that the question is not so much the news, but how you react to it. What choices have you?"

"Very few, I'm afraid. I'll have to send more men to him, but not until he begs. I need to have him admit his need, his failure, before I can give him more. General Phillips is drawing plans for a Virginia expedition, around Portsmouth, to draw Lafayette out, but I'll not allow it just yet. I have half a mind to go myself. Things went well at Charleston, perhaps we can duplicate those successes."

"I think it's wise of you sir, to wait until he asks. Without that there will be no record of his need." She paused for a moment. "Sir Henry, if you will permit me, could I play the devil's advocate for you? I often did it with Mr. Brush when he was preparing a case. He found it useful in anticipating legal arguments. I should imagine a staff meeting is rather the same as a court."

"Let's give it a go. 'I think I should go to help Cornwallis.'"

"But sir, Lord George has been quite clear that Lord Charles is to have free hand in the south. Cornwallis would resent the devil out of your presence and cry foul loudly."

"I suppose you're right, but its damned frustrating to sit here doing little while Cornwallis marches across Virginia like a conqueror!"

269

"But he's not, is he? Isn't he just running about after ephemera and mistaking scorched earth for victory, even while the people are more disaffected than ever?"

"That would be an argument for me to go to him, wouldn't it?"

"Does George Germain mistake it for victory? If he does, then you must not go. It would be seen as a dishonorable attempt to claim the credit. If he doesn't, you shouldn't go as there is no honor to be gained.

"I think," she continued, "that the situation now is quite different than Charleston was. The enemy can move at will, and they are better at that than we, so we will always be chasing and at the disadvantage. Remember you still have Washington camped all around you here, waiting for a chance to steal this city!"

*****

The cold wind bit his face. He stamped his feet for warmth. Owen Montgomery hated this weather. He had hated it when his father had made him milk the cow at dawn before a long day listening to him drone forth the Gospel. He had hated it as a divinity student at Yale College. He had hated it at Valley Forge and he hated it now, standing in an alley across from the whorehouse. He hated that this was as close as he would ever come to this particular one; that these women were so far beyond his means that he could barely afford to fantasize about them. Yet others could and he hated them because of that: the officious, the incompetent, the fortunate few who had no better right. He had suffered more in this damned war then they. His education was gone and so were the three toes lost to frostbite, lost for some foolish revolution that he had come to despise. Barely tolerated by the British army to which he had deserted, he had deserted again to hide in the byways of the city, one of an anonymous horde of malcontents living along the docks.

At least he now had a job. Not glamorous, not even dignified one, but a job. He did not know why the man wanted to know nor did he care. He was to follow the whores to find out what they did and who they met when they were not servicing the mighty officers of this Goddamn army.

Yesterday it had been the blonde one called Abigail. A whole day wasted watching her buy a hat and some damned ribbons. Today it was the brunette named Bess who came out first. A pretty little thing who would probably lead him on a similarly useless hunt for some frippery that any good woman would shun. He shrugged and left the meager shelter of his alley to follow her. At least he was getting paid. There was another house by the river he would visit tonight. A shilling and he would be warm there.

*****

Margaret and Mary Baddely watched as Henry Clinton entered the parlor and sank into his big wing chair. He looked as if he had aged since the morning.

"Sir Henry, What's the matter?" asked Mary.

"Atkinson."

"Colonel Atkinson?" she asked.

"The same. He skirts mutiny. I had ordered him to move to Staten Island a week ago, and now I find he has not stirred an inch! It's open defiance! Worse, I fear he is not alone."

"Have you confronted him?" asked Margaret.

"Not yet" with a sigh. "He's to report in the morning. What am I to do with him?"

"Is he a good officer?"

"Not really, of the 60 or 70 colonels I have, he'd have to be in the bottom half dozen. His regiment is always ill-prepared, ill-clothed and ill-equipped."

"I'm just wondering, Sir, if there is some way this could be turned to your advantage." said Margaret. "What sort of fellow is he?"

"Do you have something in mind?"

"No, not really. Think of this as a battle. The enemy have opened on your front. Can you turn his flank somehow?"

"Again, I ask what is going on in that head of yours. It's usually interesting and I suspect there's more than you've shared thus far."

271

"Well, I don't really know him. I mean, I've met him once or twice, but a man at a dinner is different than the same man in your office. That's really nothing against him, or men either, ladies are the same way. If one is to know a person they have to be observed in the sole company of their own sex. Introduce even one member of the opposite and everything changes. We all seek approval so earnestly that we turn into shameless flirts and fools."

"True enough, but not germane. What am I to do with this one, a fool in any company?"

"Do his peers feel the same about him as you?"

"I expect so but I don't really know."

"I see." She paused. "He has directly questioned your authority and that must be answered or you will lose the whole of the army. You would be within your rights to post him to the most God-forsaken spot in the colonies, hold a court of inquiry, even drop a house on him if you wished. He may expect something like that so he can be a martyr. Perhaps you could do just the opposite—draw him closer to yourself. Firstly you could better watch him, and secondly your other colonels, knowing that it was undeserved, would come to shun him. His regiment must already hate him if he is shorting them on supplies and rations to line his own pocket. Is his second of any worth? "

"He seems steady enough. But wouldn't the others emulate his behavior?"

"I don't think so. You could make it known that this was a consequence of his incompetence, that you no longer trusted him with command. Besides, this drawing closer must give him an unpleasant duty."

"Interesting, let me think on this."

*****

Henry Clinton was chipper when he came to breakfast. "I have my plan, Margaret, and I have you to thank for the meat of it."

"What shall you do?"

"I have acquired a new inspector general, only he doesn't know it yet. Everyone will hate him, all inspectors general are hated. Yet still they must be allowed access everywhere. I shall know exactly what my regimental commanders are doing, because Atkinson is going to tell me. I'll finally know who is writing to London behind my back. If he doesn't tell me there will be a court-martial and I shall preside over it. He'll have no choice."

*****

"Molly! Come quick—he's back!"

Molly Smithson hurried to the front parlor, so ornately furnished that only a man could call it tasteful. Bess was standing near the window, looking through a narrow gap in the heavy curtains. "Where?" She reached to move the curtain for a better view. Bess grabbed her hand.

"Don't. He's watching us. He'll see the curtain move. There! In the alley. He's the one who followed me all day yesterday!" She stepped aside so that Molly could see what she had seen.

"Oh, you're right, he's not one of ours. Wait! Oh, my God! He was in church the other day! I took him for a grieving widower. Go get Chester. I want him to see." She called to other girls, dressed for shopping. "Suzette, Polly, wait a minute before you leave. Come here."

Ten minutes later, the two girls boldly walked out of the house and turned down the street, laughing at some private joke. Owen followed a hundred feet behind, so intent on them that he didn't notice the clean cut, muscled young man following him.

Chester was not pleased. Normally, he stood in the parlor, to politely regulate any clients who enjoyed the ardent spirits too much. They would be gently escorted to the street and advised to return on a different evening. They always did. Molly paid and fed him well for his services and the girls indulged him often enough. Now this fellow was threatening his girls, his world. His impulse was to teach him a thorough lesson, but Molly had been insistent. He was only to follow and report.

Suzette and Polly led them on a seemingly aimless expedition, stopping in a dozen shops, buying very little, changing direction, reversing course, once even walking straight around a block. Owen had dutifully followed and so had Chester.

Two hours later, they returned home. Owen wondered off, his day's work done. Chester followed him to a cheap ordinary where he ate some stew that smelled foul, even from across the street. He followed him to a well-known house of very ill repute by the docks. He came out an hour later looking proud of himself in the streetlamp's glow. Chester followed him to a rooming house as cheap as the ordinary. Satisfied that his quarry was done for the day he went back to Owen's prostitutes. They wanted him to sample their wares; all he wanted was a name. He was the more successful.

✳✳✳✳✳

"That's about it, Molly. He was definitely following Suzette and Polly. I think someone is probably paying him to. He felt flush enough to go to that place for a woman though I can't imagine anyone wanting to be with those cackling hens. His rooms are in a part of town I wouldn't willingly visit after nightfall. You know, there must be a murder or two every day down there. Another would not be noticed."

Molly smiled indulgently. "No, Chester, thank you, but not yet. If he's being paid I need to know by whom. I don't think he's a threat to any one of the girls. He's followed four of us that we know about already."

"Should I follow him again tomorrow?"

"No, not early anyway. First I need you to go to St George's Chapel. I'll give you a message to deliver. I'll need to send some of the girls too. Then follow him. We need to see who this Owen Montgomery meets."

✳✳✳✳✳

"Why, good morning madam! I had no idea you were in New York. You remember me surely, Billy Smithson, from Westminster?"

Margaret was startled when the young man stopped her on her way to the church. She played the game. "Why, yes, Billy! I haven't seen you in how long? Five years? How is your mother doing with her gout?"

274

"Quite well thank you. Say, may I walk with you for a bit?" She nodded and he fell in beside her. Then, *soto voce*, "Molly sends a message." He slipped a paper into her hand. "Read it in church." Margaret looked sharply at him in surprise and alarm.

"We have your back," he said mysteriously. They walked together for half a block, chatting like old friends. Then Billy stopped to enter a tobacconist's shop, leaving her to walk on.

She sat alone and still in the quiet of the church, waiting for her heart to stop beating so violently. When her hands were calm she unfolded Molly's message carefully, to make no sound.

M-----

We have attracted attention. Some of this house have been followed over the last few days. When you leave the church do not go directly home. Turn right and go toward William Street. At the first corner you will see one of the girls walking toward you. If she nods a greeting, know that you are being followed. Continue straight into the next block. There will be an alley on your right. Take it and walk straight through. Turn left. You will see another girl. If she shakes her head so slightly, you have lost your shadow. You can go home. If she too nods, walk the town for two hours, we will take measures to protect you.

M-----

P.S. Wait the usual time before you leave.

She spent the next hour reviewing everything she had done since returning. *Had she slipped somewhere? Had Sir Henry behaved any differently? Had Mary or the staff? Had that devil's advocate thing gone too far? Thank God for Molly, but was she to be trusted? Kate had never been wrong about these things so far. If it was a deception why would she even bother with the message? That was a risk in itself. She could as easily sit back and let Margaret be taken up.*

She waited, all thoughts of John Andre lost. She rose and left the church, trying to walk as she normally did; thinking about it made it suddenly difficult. She turned to the right, and near the corner, a pretty young girl she had never seen gave her a smile of recognition and a nod as she passed.

Owen had left his post beside the church as the woman came out. She was the one, he knew, that he had seen talking to the whore before. She had not appeared, but maybe if he followed this one to ground, he'd learn something worth selling. This was not a bad job, he thought as he turned into the alley, following attractive women around.

Margaret turned left at the end of the alley. A half block later, another pretty girl nodded and smiled. *Now What?* She stepped in to the next shop she saw, a milliner's. For fifteen minutes she fussed over the latest new fashions from London, daring hats that Fanny might wear, but that she could not. She left and walked on slowly. *A bookseller's, perfect!* Another half hour; she bought The Sorrows of Werter. As she left the shop, she saw the man leaning against a tree across the street. *That fellow from the church! He's not very good at this.* She walked on. *I hate tea!* She entered the shop, ordered a cup and opened her book. Through the shop window she could see him, again across the street, staring at the door, waiting for her, daring her to leave. *What was Molly going to do? That Billy had promised protection, but here she was, still being followed. She simply couldn't go home with this lout after her! Was there a back door?* She surveyed the shop; she sipped her tea slowly, pretending to read.

Through the shop window, she saw a dark haired girl walking toward the man. She stumbled; she almost fell but grabbed his arm to steady herself.

*****

Owen saw Bess walking toward him. *God should not allow women to walk that way, it was unfair!* She stumbled, he felt soft womanliness pressed against his arm. She looked up at him, her dark eyes wide.

"Oh! Thank you sir! You've saved me from a nasty fall!"

"Not at all, Miss. I really didn't do…"

"Nonsense." She stroked his scrawny arm. "Had you not been here, I'd be all in a heap on the ground. Thank you again." She moved to take a step, but grimaced and clutched his arm again. "Oh dear! I've turned my ankle! These tall heels can be so treacherous, don't you think? Say, I hate to impose, but could you loan me your arm and walk me to my home? It's not far, really. I'd be so grateful." Those hypnotic eyes gazed up at him. "Truly grateful." She blushed, the eyes flashed away.

Truly grateful! He glanced across the street. *Another day—I can always follow her another day—Montraville won't know.* "It would be my pleasure, miss."

"Yes, it will." She winked. "It's this way."

Still clutching his arm, she led him onward. "This way, it's a shortcut." They turned into an alley.

Owen felt the elation of a man with a beautiful woman on his arm. *She's one Montraville said I'd never get close to! And I won't have to pay!* He looked down at her in surprise as she suddenly dropped his arm and jumped nimbly away. He never heard a sound. The stocking filled with birdshot laid him senseless on the ground.

Bess and Chester stood looking down at Owen.

"God! Thank you, Chester! He stinks!"

"You know I'd never let him near you. Get going, I've got this."

She kissed him firmly. "I owe you one." This time she meant it.

Chester quickly rifled the man's pockets, to mimic a robbery. Six lousy shillings? This fellow was poorly paid indeed. He left the unconscious man where had fallen and took post across the street. Sudden poverty might make this fellow seek his paymaster.

*****

I could learn something from these women! Margaret smiled as she watched the little play from the tea shop. She watched the actress lead the man down the block, saw them turn into an alley, saw Billy Smithson enter it a few steps behind. A moment later she saw Bess leave alone and walk quickly away, without any trace of a limp. Margaret dawdled a bit, stalling. She closed her book, rose and walked back to Sir Henry's.

*****

"Here's the thing, Montraville…"

"It's <u>Captain</u> Montraville to you!"

"Yes. Anyway, I don't know who this other woman is. The whore met her twice last week, but I couldn't leave the church to follow without arousing suspicion." The two sat in John Andre's old office at City Hall. The connecting door to Sir Henry's office was conspicuously closed. A heavy bureau blocked it on the other side. "Smithson always left after she did. Then today she never came. I started to follow this other one, but some damned footpad laid me in the dust and stole my money. That's why I came to you; I need an advance of pay, just to get me through."

"I don't see how your bad luck becomes my problem. Can you describe this woman, Montgomery?"

"Tallish, late thirties, maybe, well dressed, nice looking. Carried herself like a lady. And it's your problem because if I can't eat, I can't make inquiries on your behalf."

"Not more than a few hundred women in this city like that! Keep an eye out for her, but the whorehouse remains the real target. Keep a close watch on the girls. One of them is surely passing intelligence to the enemy."

"I'm hungry."

Montraville angrily counted out some coins. "There, that should keep you in victuals and women until next week. Don't come to this office again. Understood? Only at the coffee house."

*****

Molly's private apartments on the third floor of her house were a surprising contrast with the heavy and dark lower floors. Windows in the rear looked out over an open deck built upon the larger second floor below. The tops of crocuses in heavy wooden planters, a sort of railing around its edge, showed in the windows. The first warm spring breeze played in the gossamer

278

curtains. Bright sunlight flooded the room. It was simply but carefully furnished with good country furniture and good paintings. Molly sat at a writing table; Chester reported standing. He had always liked this room.

"He puked a couple of times Molly, then he went directly to City Hall. I went inside but I couldn't see him in the entry hall. I reckoned he must have had ready access to one of the offices. I waited about a quarter hour—City Hall would be a good place to spend some time on a cold day—all those place seekers would make it warm. He came downstairs, I couldn't tell from which office. Then he went off to his usual routine of bad food and bad women."

"Bad women, Chester?" said Molly quizzically. "Have you become judgmental?"

"You know what I mean, Molly. The ones he uses are nothing like our girls. I'm surprised they don't slit his throat when they're done."

"That's easy. They want him to come back and bring more money. They'll just dose him with syphilis. Do we know who has an office on the second floor?"

"I'll check the offices tomorrow. I know that Clinton does and Andre used to, but I don't know the others."

"School's out, Mama! Can we go to the park? Please?" Ten year old Alice bounded into the room from the deck, followed by a young governess hurrying to keep up.

"You've finished all your sums?" Molly hugged her daughter and looked to the governess for affirmation.

"She has, Ma'am, and quite well too. Only one mistake today."

"Tell me then, what is…seventeen and five more?"

Alice thought quickly. "Twenty two!"

"Good! Well then, my dear, I suppose you may go. Have her back by five o'clock, Emma. Early supper tonight."

"Yes, Ma'am. Alice, go fetch a light coat. It's still chilly for all this sunshine."

The little girl bounded out of the room with the same speed she had entered. Emma gave an embarrassed shrug and went off after her.

Molly turned back to Chester and to business.

"Do we know who is doing Andre's job now?"

"Clinton has called Montraville back from his exile. He did some work in that area before. Maybe him? Do we know what he did to so anger Clinton in the first place?"

"He killed a man he shouldn't have, one connected to Clinton's private family. Montraville comes to see Bess often enough. I'll see what she can find. I don't think you need to keep following this Montgomery any longer Chester. We've run him to his keeper and he might come to recognize you. Now we just have to figure out what to do."

✳✳✳✳✳

"This is really insipid stuff."

"Drink it anyway, Margaret. It's part of your disguise."

"I suppose." The tea shop in Maiden Lane practiced *de facto* segregation. No men ever came here and they would have been glared out had they tried. Men had their exclusive coffee shops, the ladies had their tea. The few women who recognized Molly had raised an eyebrow when she arrived, boldly entering this sanctum of propriety, but everyone was too polite to object.

"So we know that Montraville has suspicions. Molly, you mustn't underestimate him. He's a very sharp fellow, and when he gets a bone in his teeth there's no getting it back. He's also, I've learned, one of the meanest men in New York."

"You're sure of his assignment?"

280

"Absolutely. Not just you, but all of Sir Henry's intelligence efforts. As near as I can tell, he has no subordinate officers. He runs everything himself through a net of civilians and not a reputable one in the lot. Nothing but thieves and cutthroats. Your house is as close as he can get to the leaders."

"I noticed that people were keeping their distance from him last night, afraid that he might trap them in an indiscretion."

"They have reason for caution. I don't think he has many contacts outside of New York, so he is going to spend more effort in catching spies than spying. Tell your girls to be very careful. You're sure he didn't have you followed?"

"As I can be. I sent a girl out half an hour before I left and his dog dutifully followed her. I have my own shadow who is quite capable of dealing with anyone else following me that we haven't yet identified. How about you?"

"I haven't your resources, Molly. I stop and start and stare into shop windows, looking from the corners of my eyes for anyone who is there when any right thinking man would have walked past."

"Margaret, I'm going to assign you a bodyguard when we come to meet. His name is Chester. He's very good. Do you recall Billy Smithson? I'll introduce you when we leave. He's outside now."

"Your own shadow?"

"I can easily recruit another. They don't need to know why."

✱✱✱✱✱

"I must say, Sir Henry, that's a particularly fine jacket you have this evening. Is it new?"

"It is." He escorted Mary and Margaret to their seats. "Just the three of us tonight, a private family affair. I do get so tired of all this state dinner business. But, a toast! To General Phillips and success in the impending campaign! Confusion to the rebels!"

A chorus of 'hear, hear's'. Margaret rose, "And to Sir Henry and further confusion, particularly to General Washington."

Later as they sat in warmth of the drawing room she asked, "Tell me, Sir Henry, How is your new friend Atkinson doing in his duties?"

"Well enough. As planned, no one trusts him, and the colonelcy has discovered that they have few friends among themselves as well. They report to me much more often and more fully than they used to do."

"Excellent!"

"Yes, and tomorrow General Phillips will sail for Virginia to help General Arnold. He'll be taking one of the worst troublemakers with him. Those rebels down there don't seem to appreciate what they're against. He proposes to inform them."

"It must be a little sad for you, Sir Henry, seeing your friend off like this."

"It is, Margaret, but a soldier gets used to it. We need to break the enemy's supply lines to Carolina. Without supplies, I think even Nathaniel Greene will find his army wilting. This Greene is a slippery fellow--the best general I've seen in their camp, better even than Washington. Phillips will have his hands full with him. Whether Arnold is up to it, I'm still not so sure. He's more interested in counting enemy bodies than strategy."

"I suppose he behaves much as a Loyalist might."

"That's it exactly, Margaret! You do have a knack for putting your finger on things. Yet the rebels thought highly of him. I take it that you have reservations?"

"Not so much reasoned ones, Sir Henry. He has the reputation of being an excellent battle commander, but a general should be good at more than that. He does seem avaricious and there is the question of his provenance."

Clinton laughed, "That's quite the most diplomatic way I have ever heard it expressed!"

"You know, said the devil, I've just now thought of an interesting point. We know that a colonel's job is far different from a general's, and that a captain's is little like either. The question is, what is the prince's job? I remember once thumbing through a book of Major Andre's, by that Machiavelli fellow, about the art of war. Ah, you know it? Well, I found there how to dig a

282

latrine, how to deploy a cavalry platoon, even about siege works and such. But nowhere did it mention why anyone might want to do those things. Nothing about why a prince should choose to maintain men at great expense, just for marching and shooting. And from that author I expected it."

"I'm sure expectation is a part of it, sort of the dues to join the king's club. And there is the defense of the realm bit—surely Louis XVI would be in St. James's Palace by now had we not a standing army to dissuade him. If you have an army, it needs exercise to be sharp. You know how garrison duty dulls. So you send off expeditions, just to flex the muscles, so to speak."

 "So," she said teasingly, "the putting down of this rebellion is just so you all can exercise?"

"Blasphemy! I should never say such a thing. Margaret, I must ask, have you any thought of writing your memoire of your time with us?"

"Good God no!" she said with a laugh. "I'm a reader of books, not a writer. I tried it once and it was dreadful! I burned the whole lot of it before anyone could see. I have too much respect for paper mongers to ever try that again. Why?"

"I suppose I'd feel more constrained if I thought you were taking notes to edify our grandchildren, that's all."

"No, Sir Henry. I'll not write a word for either of our grandchildren. It's better to remain a sort of mysterious personage of the past than spew nonsense and embarrass yourself, don't you think?"

*****

She began to code her message:

73 to 41 XXII 726 for 311 XX XXXV LXIII 327

Phillips to sail 22d instant for Portsmouth. 20th,35th,63d regiments.

*****

"Sit down, damn it, Montraville! You're distracting me standing there." John Montraville sat in one of the chairs across from the heavy mahogany desk from his general. "Better. Now listen Captain, I don't like you and you don't like me. Just do your job..." Montraville interrupted him by glancing at the blocked door to his own office. Following his eyes, Clinton continued, "That stays. Now, you were saying..."

"We've made some progress with that spy nest at Mrs. Smithson's. It appears to be one of the girls, but we haven't yet determined how she gets messages out. Tomorrow we'll start to shadow her and everyone she meets. Give me a week or so on that."

"How about what's going on in the Americans' camp?"

"I've sent a couple of men across to enlist but they haven't yet reported anything we couldn't see from here. Since the Arnold affair, it's hard to penetrate the upper levels. They're suspicious. We do know that many of the line regiments are angry over back pay. Washington keeps them in line by hanging a man every few days."

"Listen Montraville, we need better intelligence of the other side. There's more to your job than just catching a prostitute. Set up our own house over there! Send across some of those peddlers that continually pester us! Come on man, use your wits!"

"I've thought about the prostitution thing, Sir, but the problem is that these damned colonials are so church-bound that many will not use them. Others won't because their wives are so close at hand. Besides, they move around a lot."

"I don't want to hear about your problems, Captain, I want to know what the Americans are up to. Your job is to find out. Now, get on it. Wait--on this whore thing... there would be consequences among the civilians. Keep me informed before you do anything overt. "

"Yes sir, but know that I would prefer to tell no one. Secrecy in these matters is paramount..."

"Now you dare suggest that I'm going to warn them? Dismissed!"

*****

284

Outside the summer rain beat heavily against the windows. Clouds hung low over the city. The coffee house was darker and smokier than usual. From their back table, Montraville and Owen Montgomery looked through a gray haze toward the front of the shop, inspecting anyone who entered. A buzz of male conversation surrounded them.

"Very well now, Montgomery, Bess is the one we must watch. Ignore the others..."

"How do we know this? I haven't seen her do anything differently than the rest."

"You don't need to know! Stop interrupting me. I'll give you a few men. We need to follow not only her, but everyone she comes in contact with."

"Even her customers? I for one would like to see what goes on upstairs there. Has it occurred to you that she may just get information from one man and simply give it to the next?"

"Unlikely. It's some anonymous shopkeeper--count on it. There must be some shops she visits more regularly than others. Follow that man and we'll have this thing licked."

"So, how was this Bess? As good as a man might hope?"

"You'll never know." Montraville suppressed a smile.

"Give me a couple of pounds and I'll find out."

"You'd never get past that big lug in the parlor. He'd pitch you to the curb in a heartbeat!"

"I'll risk it."

"Not with my money you won't."

*****

"Well, Cornwallis has finally made a juncture with Arnold's army. He now has a force powerful enough to stand against Lafayette and Wayne. How

285

that man managed to reconstitute the Pennsylvania line in three months is a mystery!" Henry Clinton slumped in his chair.

"Now what shall he do?" asked Mary.

"Regardless of what he should do, what he now does is ask for directions."

"Yes, sir," said Margaret. "Now that he's dug this hole, he will want you to get him out of it. He's cut off from Carolina, has the Continentals to his north and wilderness on his west. The only thing he can do is go east, go back to the shore. You may have to carry him off, and that will require a good harbor."

"Isn't it interesting that now he chooses to correspond with me instead of Germain? Of course, at this distance, it still takes a month for query and reply to make their journeys."

"Sir Henry," as Margaret slipped back into her role, "I should think it wise not to order any particular action. The distance in time is too great. Might you instead adopt Lord George's tactic of suggestion? Suggest an easterly course, suggest that he get to the coast, but leave the details and the responsibility to him."

"Three months ago you were no more pleased with Germain than I am. Are you now defending him?"

"No, sir, he has played you poorly, and you wouldn't be doing Cornwallis any favors either. I don't have to be consistent in my arguments, it's my job to forward them for your consideration. But I do have a better understanding of his position than I did. I think, in this case where you are the power, it is a discreet course. Let Lord Cornwallis assume the blame and you the credit."

"I've half a mind to go there myself again, to bring 10,000 men and end this war down there."

"But sir, you still have the responsibility to hold this city. Were you to take that many to the south, would not Washington then have sufficient advantage to take the city? And how would Lord George react if you superseded Lord Cornwallis after he put him there, in command of the south?"

286

"Let Lord Charles Cornwallis pout. Washington would have to follow us south, I think. His southern army would be lost if he didn't and I don't think the Congress would suffer that well. They couldn't raise another and holding this city is not cheap. They're penniless beggars at the French court as it is now."

"Or, sir, he might keep his northern army intact and take this city. That would mean the end of any Loyalist support and likely end the Ministry as well. Think about it. The reason why it is so difficult to raise the southern Loyalists is that two or three thousand of the best of them are trapped here in New York. So are the best of the northern men. The whole body of the people would be decapitated. There wouldn't be a leader in the hinterlands anywhere, no one to raise a company, let alone a regiment for the King.

"Think even of the body of them. They've been dispossessed and starved, they've suffered for their King. If you were to take a significant army south, they would see themselves as being deserted by him. The army is unpopular enough here as it is. In that event, they would have to face Washington without and a civil rising within."

"I shan't forget the city, Margaret. And now Rochambeau is reported on the move from Newport. He can only be coming this way. Would that I knew what he and Washington were cooking up!"

"Has Montraville given you any hints?"

"No. I'm beginning to wonder if I've the wrong man in the job. He's all about catching imagined spies rather than spying. Right now I'm far more interested in what Mr. Washington is doing than in what he's finding out about us!"

"Sir Henry, could Rochambeau be planning on Long Island? Suddenly turn left and take shipping across the Sound? He could probably roll across a good deal of the island without much resistance. That would interfere with our food supply, and even liberate rebel officers there on parole."

"Possible, but why then would he not have taken ship directly from Newport?"

"Well, he's in friendly country across Connecticut; he wouldn't be if he were to march the length of Long Island. Or perhaps they don't have enough shipping to move the whole army at once? It's just a thought, sir."

*****

Somehow, the weather was always fine on the King's birthday. Crowds gathered outside the ballroom to watch the great folks arrive. Most enjoyed watching the gentlemen arrive trying not to perspire under the weight of their best uniforms while the ladies arrived cool and shimmering in satin. Owen glowered in the crowd, nursing his persistent grudge against those who dressed and ate and lived better than he. It was a lump of hatred he liked to polish. The June evening was warm, the stars shone. Owen Montgomery mingled in the crowd. After a time, even hating the beautiful people began to pale. It was tiring. He was turning to leave when he heard a cheer rolling down the street toward him. General Clinton's open barouche turned the corner, pulled by four fine bays. There he was, sitting alone in the forward facing seat, lazily waving to the cheering crowd as he passed.

As the carriage passed, he could see the two women sitting facing him. His jaw dropped. He began to force his way through the crowd to get a better view. A last he was positive. It <u>was</u> her! The one who met with the prostitute! Oh, would Montraville pay dearly for this!

*****

The summer breeze through the open doors cleared the smoke from the coffee house. The sunlight revealed the worn and tattered furnishings.

"So, Montgomery, what are you so smug about? You're sitting over there grinning like a little boy on his birthday. Spill it, man."

"Not for nothing! This little bit is so good, I want a pound or my lips shall be sealed. Believe me, it's a bargain. It's the answer to every question we've been pursuing all spring and you won't believe it when I tell!"

"You're talking shit. What can you possibly know that might be worth that much?"

"I know the woman the whore has been meeting."

288

"Who!"

"My money."

Montraville slid a guinea across the table. Montgomery seized it and tested the metal in his teeth. Satisfied, he paused to admire it before he began. "I was in the crowd outside the King's birthday ball two nights ago. Who should arrive but General Clinton...."

"Naturally. If that's all, I want my money back."

"Of course it's not all!" he said scornfully. "He was riding in his carriage with his wife and daughter. It's been the wife who's been meeting with the whore!"

Montraville sat back astounded. It was the bit he'd been searching for, and this idiot didn't know the worth of it. Now he had Margaret at last. She'd not wriggle out of this! This fool had confused Margaret for Mary Baddeley, based on their ages! He sat silent, thinking. *No one else can know this until I'm ready*!

After a long pause he spoke. "Listen, Montgomery, I believe you, but you can't go around charging a general's wife without proof! They'll hang <u>you</u> instead. This is over your head. Leave this with me and I'll run her to ground. You must not tell a soul. You understand, not a damned sou!! That would be the death of you." *And it will be*, he thought. *No one can know but me.*

*****

Montraville had learned that he did not sit while reporting to Henry Clinton unless he was invited. He seldom was.

"So, Montraville, you propose to raid Smithsons?"

"Yes sir. I have identified it positively as the hub of this ring. The women there ply their customers with alcohol and favors and get them to reveal whatever they wish. I suppose it has been always so in whorehouses. There's not a decent woman in the place."

"Very well, but do it in the morning, after breakfast. I would prefer that no customers are swept up—some important men resort there."

"Yes, sir. No one is allowed to stay the night. At one o'clock, they ring a great gong and Smithson and her tough make sure every room is vacant. The girls don't stir before noon so the catch should be good."

"What about Smithson?"

"Tomorrow is Tuesday--she goes out early for tea. I'll hit the house while she's absent and the girls will be without a leader. I can get her later after her morning tea."

"So tomorrow, ten o'clock, then?"

"If you wish, sir. One's as good as another."

"I do so wish. Carry on Montraville. Oh, Montraville? This had better not be a fool's errand. If you ruin the best house in the city for nothing, many people will be upset with you."

*****

The boat crew from HMS Vulture found the body floating in the East River. The day the fleet didn't find at least one was memorable. Nothing remarkable, just another piece of low trash, unshaven and cheaply dressed. The throat cut, it was just another piece of flotsam from the underside of the city. The only interesting part was that the corpse had only seven toes. There would be an entry in the ship's log and oblivion.

*****

Breathless, Margaret hurried up the steps to Molly's. She pounded on the door. She could hear stirrings within. She pounded again. The door flew open. The small brunette with startlingly dark eyes, clearly expecting to find some dissolute male, was surprised to see a woman.

"We...I'm sorry, may I help you?"

290

"I bring a message from Molly. The word is 'scatter.' The army is coming to raid this place. You must all run. Run now!"

"But...You're Mrs. Brush, aren't you?" Margaret nodded. "How can you know?"

"General Clinton told me. Now run, damn it woman! There's no time to lose. You must get away. They'll hang every last one of you. Run! I must go find Molly before she leaves the tea shop. They're going to take her up there after they have this place. I must go warn her."

The girl hesitated a moment. "Go! Tell Molly that I will have Alice with me. I'm Bess. We'll meet in the appointed place. Go, save her, she's the best of us!"

She found Molly sitting at a back table of the tea shop. The half dozen women had looked up, surprised at the urgency of her entrance.

"Margaret...what?"

Margaret spoke with hushed intensity. "Chester is waiting in back. I gathered him up as I entered. The army is going to take you up as you leave here. I've already warned your house. You must fly! Quickly, out the back!"

"But...how...Alice! I must get to her!" She rose to leave.

Margaret gripped her arm. "No, Molly. I spoke to Bess. Come, out back where we can talk." She guided her, lead her, to an alley. "Bess told me to tell you that she would have Alice and would meet you where you planned. If you go home, they will arrest you and they will hang you. A dead mother is of little use to Alice. Stop, think. What must you do?"

Molly looked around desperately, trying to collect herself. "I must...my girls...Alice is with Bess...Oh, my God, Emma! She's not one of us...she knows nothing, not even to run..."

"Chester, can you take her? Don't let her out of your sight—she might do something foolish."

"Yes, Ma'am. Molly, come, we must go."

They didn't knock. A burly sergeant put his shoulder to the door and it yielded with a splintering crash. Montraville and a dozen men entered while another dozen surrounded the house. By plan, half ran through the ground floor, while the rest followed him up to the girl's rooms on the second. Doors stood open with clothes thrown about--evidence of hasty flight. They hurried up to the third floor to Molly's apartments. The flimsy door fell to another shoulder.

Bess stood inside, a pistol in her hand. "Get back you bastards! Not another step!"

Montraville stepped forward. "Now Bess, is that any way to greet a friend? Come, let's talk about this. We don't want to hurt anyone, do we?"

As the puzzled girl lowered her guard he punched her in the face.

"Bind her hands!" he called over his shoulder as he passed through the parlor out onto the deck. He saw them there, the child and the young girl, huddled low in a corner. "Come here!"

The girl stepped ahead, "No! You shan't take her!"

Montraville regarded her for an instant. He grabbed her elbows, picked her up and threw her aside. She staggered back, her arms flailing to recover her balance, until her momentum carried her backwards over the low railing. Her scream lasted a second before it ended abruptly.

It was a grotesque sight, two dozen armed men marching a child and a bloodied woman with bound hands. When they stopped, the child took her skirt and gently wiped the blood away from Bess's mouth. There was a trickle of blood trailing from her ear, down the side of her neck. A soldier yanked Alice back to her place.

Montraville took a squad and entered the tea shop. The crowd waited as they searched. The customers, wives of some of the most powerful men in the province, were herded out of the shop at gun point and detained under a tree. They were angry and the growing crowd took their mood and began to murmur. The bystanders began to press the soldiers. They jeered their bravery and denounced their actions. The soldiers were becoming edgy. A sergeant ordered them to fix bayonets to their muskets.

Montraville came out minutes later, followed by the proprietress telling them in un-ladylike terms what she thought of this invasion. They had not found Molly and Montraville was angry. His whole plan had fallen apart. No band of spies, no Molly and worst of all, no Margaret. He had counted on her being there. Only a single whore and a child. There was no way to charge Margaret, not yet. The whore would talk--he'd see to that.

He ordered the crowd to disperse; he drew his sword and marched his prisoners through them to the jail. The riotous, jeering people followed as closely as they dared. Not one of them doubted that the bayonets might be used.

*****

Margaret forced herself to sit in her room. The book she was pretending to read lay face down on the table beside her. The waiting. She fought back the urge to do something, anything. Outwardly she must remain calm and unknowing.

Jupiter knocked quietly at her door. She answered, the useless book displayed in her hand. "Ma'am, there's a young lady, Miss Rathburn, here. She's is asking for you. She seems all worked up, Ma'am."

A girl here? What had happened? Had Molly sent her?

"Jupiter, thank you. Would you wait above stairs for a moment? I'll go to her. Give me a minute with her, then you can come down."

She found the girl standing in the hallway, trying to appear as if she often came here, all the while dabbing her eyes and wringing her kerchief. She recognized her as one of Molly's.

"Oh Ma'am!..."

"Shush, girl." Margaret spoke in a hard whisper. She took her arm and guided her into the bowels of the house and out a side door to the secluded garden. She indicated a seat, one which would conceal this fresh face from both the street and the house. "Sit there. You have taken a frightful risk coming here! Have you any idea of the danger you have placed us both in?"

"I know, Ma'am, but I didn't know what else to do! It's awful, such a day."

"What's awful, my dear?" She softened her tone. The young woman's fear filled the garden. "Tell me all you know."

"He came, Montraville came, with soldiers. He murdered Emma! The sweetest, most inoffensive creature ever God made, and he just killed her! She was just trying to protect Alice and he just picked her up and threw her off the roof like a sack of rags! Then he beat Bess--she was bleeding something fierce--and marched them both off to jail! Are they going to hang Alice too, Ma'am? She's only ten!"

"How can you know this? Miss Rathburn, I'm sorry, I don't even know your name..."

"I'm Abigail, Ma'am. I was hiding in a house behind ours. I could see everything through a back window, but they couldn't see me. They never looked beyond the house. I've been trying to think what to do for hours, and then I thought of you—can you save Alice?"

"Perhaps. How about you—do you have a safe place?"

"I was to go to Hoboken, but by the time I got to the ferry, there were soldiers watching everyone. Now I must find a place to hide, I have some friends..."

"But Hoboken would be far safer..." *I need to get this one out of town. She'll break at the first question!* Just then she heard a cart enter the yard by the barn. *Tuesday! Bill with the kitchen order!* "Wait here, Abigail, stay just where you're sitting; no one can see you in that one spot. I must see to something. I shall return in a few minutes. I may have an answer to your problem."

294

Margaret returned a few minutes later, followed by Bill. "Here she is, Bill. Can you get her to Hoboken?"

Bill looked the girl up and down. "Not dressed like that. She's stick out like a sore thumb at the docks. We'll need to dirty you up a bit, your pardon, miss, and find you something worn out to wear. Yours is a fine dress, but too grand. I know a woman…"

"Here in the city? Abigail needs to escape today."

"We can do it, Ma'am."

"Good. Abigail, you are to go with this man. He has a boat. You must trust him. Do exactly as he says and you will be safe. Fail to do so and we will all be lost. Do you understand?"

* * * * *

The cell stank. It was disgustingly dirty. Alice clung to Bess; they were both terrified, although Bess tried valiantly not to let Alice know. Montraville entered, his face composed. He untied Bess' hands and helped her to a seat at small table. He guided Alice to a corner, returned and sat across from Bess. "I'm sorry about that one at the house, Bess. I didn't mean for her to die."

Bess stared across the table, trying to merge the doubled images. "Come now, Bess, we've had some good times, you and I, haven't we? I don't want to hurt you either so please don't force me to. Just tell me where Moll is, and you can leave. That's a simple thing, isn't it? I know she has been passing secrets to Mrs. Brush, I just need to know how they get them out and Moll can tell me."

Bess shook her head slowly. The blow sent her over backwards to the floor. Her head struck the flat stones violently. He carefully helped her to her seat. "Now, Bess, I wish you hadn't made me do that. I really don't want to hurt you. Now, tell me please, where is Moll? I won't hurt her. Mrs. Brush is the one I want."

Bess shook her head slowly. I don't want to be rough with you, Bess, please tell me." He leaned back in his chair to survey her. "Where is Moll?"

295

Bess shook her head slowly. He knocked her out of the chair. The blow broke her jaw. He picked her up and threw her onto the bed. She lay confused, softly whimpering. His voice, filled with menace, came again. "Where is Moll!"

Bess shook her head slowly. The pain behind her eyes was beyond anything she had ever known.

"I ask again--Bess, where is Moll?" Bess looked at him steadily, but did not answer. He struck her again, but now her mercifully damaged brain could register neither fear nor pain. Her eyes followed his motions without comprehension.

Montraville appeared above her in a haze, lazily waving a knife before her eyes. "Where is Moll?"

Nothing hurt anymore.

"WHERE..." He realized that the eyes were no longer following the blade. He felt for a pulse. Angry and frustrated, he plunged the knife into her heart. Even dead, the eyes looked at him still.

He rose in disgust and turned to the child huddled in the corner. "That's what we do with spies! That's what I'm going to do to your mother!" And he left the cell.

*****

Margaret burst into Sir Henry's office, followed by a frantic aide calling "But you can't just go in Ma'am" behind her. Henry Clinton looked up in surprise.

"Why Margaret, what is happening?"

"Montraville has raided Smithson's, and he's arrested a child, not ten years old. She can't be a traitor or a spy! It's impossible! Give me an order releasing her to me. I'll take that responsibility. Please, Sir Henry, no child should ever see the inside of a jail. It's too horrible!"

"How can you know this?"

296

"A friend of Fanny's saw them, a score of men marching one woman and one child to the jail. The woman had already been beaten bloody. There was an angry crowd. She was so disturbed by it that she came to me. Please, Sir Henry, an order, Please!" The entreaty in her voice was genuine. "I've never asked for anything, but please, sir. That poor little girl. Let me take her from there."

Henry Clinton pulled a sheet of paper close. "This grand raid that he promised would yield a nest of spies has caught but one and a child?" He wrote quickly, signed and blotted it. He held it up, waving to dry. "Here, Margaret. Rescue the child."

"Thank you sir. I swear, she shall be at my charge. Thank you, thank you!" She hurried away to the jail.

*****

Montraville, carrying his uniform coat so that it did not touch his bloody shirt, brushed past Margaret as she entered the jail. She could see the blood. "What have you done?" she called toward his back. He appeared not to have heard and hurried off.

She entered the cell. A glance at the body on the bed and she understood what had happened. The knife still protruded from the chest. Not even a savage would have used her so! Two men were preparing to bundle the body.

"Stop! By order of Sir Henry." She waved the paper toward them. "Nothing in this cell gets touched until the doctor says. Any man who does will see a court-martial. Leave this cell now!"

They were soldiers and they followed orders. Neither could have read the order if she had allowed them to.

Margaret turned to the white faced girl in the corner. "Alice," she said very gently, "My name is Mrs. Brush, and I am a friend of your mother's. Can I take you from this place, please? Will you take my hand?"

The girl stood, wide eyed and motionless. She passively allowed Margaret to take her hand, to lead her away. They stopped at a house two blocks away. Margaret knocked. A servant opened the door.

297

"Mrs. Brush to see Dr. Osborne. It's please, it's an emergency." The doctor appeared quickly; his servants were used to this sort of visit.

"Mrs. Brush! What seems to be the problem?"

"A prisoner has been murdered inside the jail, Doctor. You must go examine the body. The perpetrator must be punished. Please hurry. I ordered the men away, but they may not stay."

"Usually when one prisoner slays another, I just offer my thanks for the trial saved. Is this case so different?"

"Yes, Doctor, very different. This was a young woman and the circumstances of her death would repel any Christian gentleman. Worse, John Montraville, a King's officer, did it inside the jail. His shirt was covered in blood as he left. He did it with malice and he made this child watch. There will be public outcry unless a full investigation is conducted."

Dr. Osborne turned his attention to Alice. "Tell me, my dear, are you all right?"

Alice did not respond. She stared straight ahead. Her skin was deathly pale.

"She hasn't said a word or responded since I found her, Doctor. Some food and sleep might bring her to rights. You can examine her later if you like, but first, to the jail!"

*****

"Mrs. Brush! Wait!"

They had gone scarcely a block from the doctor's when Chester called to her. Margaret waited as he hurried up in the twilight.

"Thank God! You have Alice. Molly is frantic since Bess did not come as they planned." Then as he observed the child more closely, "What is wrong with her?"

"She's had an awful shock. Where is Molly? Safe?"

298

"She's nearby, I'll take you. She can't come to the streets."

He led them down a narrow alley to the rear of a darkened house. Molly had heard them coming and met them at the door.

"Alice!"

The girl ran to her mother and clung desperately. Hugging her daughter, consoling her, Molly looked her gratitude to Margaret.

"We have much to discuss, Molly, but look to Alice first. Is this house safe?"

"Yes, it's one of several that we have. It can't be linked to me."

"Good. See to Alice. Then we'll talk."

$$*****$$

Dr. Osborne looked up as the young man entered the cell. His examination of the body had not taken long, but he took careful notes; these events would certainly lead to a court-martial. He was already preparing his testimony.

"Are you a relative?" asked the doctor.

Chester had thought he was prepared for what he would find.

White faced and red eyed, he could not look away. "She is, was, my sister. May I take her?"

"Yes. I am sorry, young man. It's hard to believe such brutality can exist in the civilized world." He watched as Chester gently closed her eyes and began to tenderly swaddle the body. He moved to help.

"NO! I'll do it!"

"She wasn't your sister, was she, son."

"No, but I must take her to her family. For burial." He looked defiantly at the doctor, daring him to object.

"Can you tell me her name? For my report?"

"Bess Smithson."

*****

A single lamp lit the room, heavily curtained so that no light could escape. Alice, exhausted after the day's ordeal, lay curled on a sofa, her head on her mother's lap. Margaret sat with her. Bess lay in her coffin beside them. It was stuffily hot in the closed room. On hearing of Bess' death, Molly had become coldly silent.

"What will you do now, Molly?" asked Margaret.

"Tomorrow I'm going to bury my little sister." Her voice broke as she said it. "but tonight..." her voice trailed off. "Tonight is for vengeance. After that, I can't stay in New York. Alice and I will go up to the little village in Massachusetts where I grew up. No one from there comes here, and no one from here would ever want to go there."

Chester entered and quietly sat on the only other chair.

"Did you find Montraville, Chester?"

"Just located him at City Hall. I have two men watching. He'd have had to report his attack; Clinton knew of it and would want to know. There will be ripples in the community now that your house is destroyed. Important men will be angry."

Molly was silent for a minute, thinking. "Chester, gather some men and take up Montraville when he leaves. Bring him to me in Winslow's pasture. When you have secured him, send to me here and I'll meet you there. And Chester—I want him alive."

Chester looked his displeasure.

"Alive, Chester. I want him. Break him a little if you will, but he must be aware when I kill him."

"Molly," Margaret spoke, "I would consider it a favor if authorities came to think he had deserted—could that be arranged?"

300

"Another of your seeds, Margaret?"

"Yes. He has come to suspect me and it would be good if he were thoroughly discredited."

"Chester?"

"If I can't kill the man, I surely will kill his reputation. Small comfort."

"Good, now be off with you."

"What will you do, Molly?" asked Margaret.

"I'm going to kill him." She said it very quietly, very coldly, very certainly.

Margaret nodded slowly. "Had I done that twenty years ago, how many good people would be alive still?"

"Do you want to come?"

"I think not. Your grief is fresh and my being there would diminish it. Besides, being there would give him an importance which I refuse. I must be getting to Sir Henry's. We'll not meet again, shall we?"

"No. It has been a pleasure, Margaret."

"And mine as well."

She rose to leave but turned. "Is Molly Smithson really your name?"

Molly just smiled. "Fare well Margaret."

She inclined her head and smiled back. "And you too, Madam."

✳✳✳✳✳

Montraville stood at attention in City Hall. Sir Henry Clinton paced furiously before him, angry and red faced.

"God Damn it Montraville! This is what I get for your grand plan? Two dead women, a near riot among the people, and not a damned spy! Not even any proof that there ever was one! You detained the God damned wife of the God damned provincial attorney general at bayonet's point! And you caught not one yet alive! Not a spy, not an informant, not a document, not even a cut-purse! How can you explain this mess?"

"All is not lost. Sir Henry. We still have the child in jail. We can hang her if the mother does not come forward and give herself up. What better lever could there be, even among that sort of people?"

"She's an innocent child, for God's sake! We're Englishmen, not bloody damned Turkish sultans! Besides, I ordered her released hours ago."

"What! How could you, you old fool?" He felt his cards being stolen away, one by one. His voice became insistent. "This is what happens when you amateurs meddle in these affairs." He continued contemptuously, lecturing a dull student. "The lower orders understand only power! If we become soft with them they assume it unjustly to themselves! What's the death of some damned child to that? They'll breed more.

His voice brightened. "In any case, sir, I know who the leader is, We can still break this up!"

"If you knew that, why didn't you just arrest him instead of all these theatrics," suspiciously.

"It's not a him, it's Margaret Brush!" His voice rose in self-justifying desperation. "She's been spying for the Americans since she returned from Boston. That's why I shot Thompson last year—he was the courier!" His desperation became frantic. "I wanted them all, General, every damned spy in New York!"

"If you knew that it was Thompson you were shooting, why didn't you just take him up? Did you need to inflict such pain on Fanny? She's your own daughter, you bastard! Are you devoid of feeling? Do you have any proof of these outrageous allegations?"

"No, sir," He was now very much deflated and now fearful. "My informant has disappeared, but he saw Margaret in close conversation with Moll

Smithson often! He can swear to that when he is found; I can produce a deposition"

"You mean you can forge one!"

"So what? They're spies! They lie and so can we. I was going to extract a confession from the whore but she must have had poison, she killed herself before I could question her...."

"If she had poison, Montraville, it was on the point of your knife!" Dr. Osborne inserted himself into the room. "Sir Henry, I have examined the victim. Never...never have I seen so brutal a murder. That poor woman was beaten such that her head was cracked. That alone would have killed her, as if that were not sufficient, she was stabbed through the heart! The whole platoon of guards is shaken to their core, they won't speak of what they know happened, of what they were ordered to do!"

"Montraville, what the hell do you have to say?"

"Sir..."

"Shut your mouth, you lying son of a bitch! I'm tired of hearing you! There've been nothing but lies coming from you! You lie to your commanding officer? You're the poorest excuse for a King's officer I've ever seen!" He stomped to the door. "Guard!" The two sentries always stationed at his door entered uncertainly. "Take this man in custody. Take the bastard to the jail and see him locked up!"

"General," Montraville drew himself tall and proud, "I am required only to surrender to a like commissioned officer. By regulation, these two cannot take me."

Henry Clinton stared at him in disbelief.

"You're mad, Montraville—first you lie and try to incriminate Mrs. Brush to save your ass, then you spout legalities to avoid jail?"

"General," said Dr. Osborne, "I hold a dormant major's commission. Would that suffice? I'll be quite happy to take this one. I know just the place for him."

303

"Thank you Doctor. You two—Fix Bayonets!"

The two men looked about uncertainly. It was an order never to be given within doors.

"Do it, men. If this one offers the least resistance, use them."

*****

It was a half mile walk from City Hall to the jail. Dr. Osborne led his little detachment through the streets. They were near the midpoint when six men stepped from the shadows and accosted them.

"Stop, Doctor, please. We will relieve you of your duty. That man is coming with us."

The doctor recognized the voice. "He's certain to hang, young man."

"He's certain not to live so long. We don't want to harm you sir, nor the soldiers, but he _is_ coming with us. There will be no discussion."

The doctor looked uncertain; the soldiers looked frightened. Imminent violence hanged in the man's voice. "I think you will have to mark him as a deserter in the muster rolls. It's a shame he eluded you in the crowd and escaped. There is no dereliction in that."

Dr. Osbourne looked steadily at the hard young face. "Turn about, men, I'll have to report this escape to Sir Henry. Tis a pity he eluded his trial. Be silent and it will not rest on you. Follow me."

"Wait, don't leave me with them!" Montraville screamed, "They're murderers!"

"So are you Montraville. Desertion seems a just sentence to me."

"But I have served the King loyally my whole life! To be branded…"

He fell silent as Chester struck him.

*****

304

Montraville's legs had just begun to function again as they entered the pasture. The lights of the city were well behind them. Chester called softly.

"Molly?"

She stepped from the shadow of an elm tree. The full moon revealed her features clearly. "Here, Chester." Then to the prisoner, "I hear that you have been looking for me, Montraville. Here I am. You murdered my sister."

Montraville stood, weaving slightly. Chester held one arm fast, another man held the other.

"Chester, dump his body where only the rats can find it. I only hope they'll not be sickened by his evil flesh."

The horror of that image struck him. "Please, I didn't know, Moll—I had my duty!"

Molly watched the fear take possession of his features. She pressed the muzzle of her pistol against his chest.

"Moll. Please, I swear! I didn't know! I..."

Anything else he might have said was lost in the sound of her pistol.

*****

Margaret sat quietly in Sir Henry's little office. "He's deserted?"

"Apparently. He managed to elude the men taking him to the jail and hasn't been seen since. After what he's done, I doubt that we ever shall."

"He said I was a spy?"

"He did."

"Sir Henry, I never..."

"I know, Margaret. Calm yourself. He was lying to save himself, the base wretch. He even wanted to hang the child to force the mother to surrender

305

herself. I'm sorry I ever brought him back here. Your judgment, it seems, was once again better than mine.

Where is the child, by the way?"

"Oh. I met the grandmother as I was leaving the Dr. Osborne's and gave her up. I thought she would be better off with family than here with strangers." *Lying is becoming too easy. Will I ever be able to stop?* "Forgive yourself, Sir Henry. I had had more experience with him than you. He had the mien of a gentleman concealing the heart of a blackguard. It is sometimes so hard to know…"

"Yes."

"What could I have ever done to make him hate me so…"

*****

Margaret was walking, pensive, in the summer afternoon, alone. It seemed that everything she did now, she did alone. She missed Fanny, she missed Sally and she missed Molly. Crean and Edward were dead and so was John Andre. So were so many more, including Montraville, but that she didn't mind. He had deserved it. None of the others had. Kate might have been a thousand miles away. Margaret had not heard from an ally in three weeks. What was she supposed to do? She was tired, she admitted, tired of the deceptions she must practice, tired of war and tired of New York. She just wanted to go home. This war had dragged on since the dawn of time; the whole world was tired of it. Britons wanted it ended and Americans wanted it ended. Almost, it was reaching the point where large portions of each didn't care who won anymore.

She sat on a bench looking at the harbor, the warships at anchor, the small boats crossing and re-crossing. A seagull sat on a nearby piling nagging her for a handout. She closed her eyes and sighed. The bench creaked as someone sat on the other end.

"Excuse me, Dearie, you have maybe room on your bench for old Mrs. Williamson of Eastchester?"

She turned to the sound, unsure and incredulous. "Sally?" The eyes, far younger than the voice, smiled at her.

"Now don't you go doin' nothing foolish, Dearie--you'll get Mrs. Williamson all ruffled and this get-up takes time."

Margaret fought off her impulse to hug or to cry. "How did you find me?"

"I followed you from Sir Henry's. You've had a busy summer, Ma'am."

"I have," she said, tiredly.

"I'm sorry, Ma'am," Sally reached over and took her hand. "It's been three weeks. And you've had no one to talk too? I'm so sorry!"

"It hasn't been easy." Margaret wiped away a tear.

Sally looked at her searchingly. "Do you want to come back with me?"

"I can't, Sally, not yet. I really think this campaign will end the war. So, I think, does Sir Henry. Unless Cornwallis gets lucky, he'll be done in a month or two. The British public will not stomach another army lost. A few months and I can come. I want to."

"I can tell. Now, here's what we're going to do. Soon, Sally is going to reappear on your doorstep. You can't do this alone. You'll slip and get yourself killed. You haven't hired on another maid, have you?"

"You know I couldn't. Is that truly Sally in there? You sound different."

"It is, Ma'am. I'm just trying to sound like you. You know this will be best. Go'wan, don't be a pesterin' Mrs. Williamson with questions, Dearie!"

Margaret grinned for the first time in weeks. She rose to leave. She turned back;, she asked, "Everyone in Peekskill?"

"All well. Ma'am, and eager to see you. Go, do your job so that they can."

*****

Sally was smiling as she paused in the doorway of Margaret's room. "Good afternoon, Ma'am."

"Sally!" Margaret rose to greet her. "What did you do, sneak in through the kitchen? I had no idea that you were coming today!"

"I had things to arrange." She regarded her mistress closely. "Now you need to sit--your hair wants my attention." She closed the door as Margaret sat at her dressing table.

"I come with instructions, Ma'am."

"From Kate?"

"Yes. The delay was in getting them sorted out. First, you're no longer to report regularly. Your assignment is too important to be jeopardized by suspicions. If we need to get something out, I am to go to a certain stall at the market. Me, not you. General Washington is concerned about further reinforcements to Virginia, but he is still considering an attack here. You are to try to keep Sir Henry focused on defending New York and to ignore threats to Cornwallis. General Washington needs to know that Sir Henry was going to do the one or the other."

"That sounds so simple." She thought through the import carefully. "The war ends in the south, soon." She said it softly. It sounded so final, almost tragic. She was surprised that the words brought no elation. She turned to look up at Sally. "Can we remember life as it was before?

"It won't be as before, Ma'am. This will finally be a new world."

"You've gotten poetic!"

"Eager, Ma'am. Now turn around and behave so I can get you to dinner on time."

*****

"Do I detect a spring in your step since your girl has returned, Margaret?"

"I shouldn't be surprised if you did, Mary. She fussed over me this afternoon like a mother sending her child to church. I half expected her to spit on her kerchief and wipe my cheek! Having an old familiar around makes life seem easier, don't you think?"

"I do. Do you worry that Fanny will be alright without her?"

"Strangely, no. Sally was with me when Fanny was born, and has spent barely a day apart from her since. She would not have come here if Fanny were still in need. Her very coming gives me reassurance that my baby is well."

"I'm glad of that." Mary sighed, "I miss having my friend about though."

"I feel badly for Sir Henry, not having a friend—since General Phillips died, I don't know of anyone he can just talk to. It's hard not to have a friend at hand."

"Margaret, you're his friend now. You will probably never grasp how much he depends upon you, as a safe sounding board for his thoughts. All the officers around him have their eye on their own careers, not on the task here. Everything they might say is colored by their ambition. I'm not able to help him in that regard; strategy and tactics are beyond my feeble wits. He speaks of your assistance in those matters often."

"I'm glad I can help. I hope you feel no anxieties?"

"Heavens, no! You're my best friend now too! I admit it; at first, I tried to listen, to look for signs, but I was soon satisfied. The ideas of you two leave mine in the dust. Half the time I had no idea what you were even talking about. Without you, I think we would both be adrift."

*****

"This damned French army is the key to the whole thing. I wish I knew where Rochambeau was going to stop."

"Well. Sir Henry, do we know exactly where he is now?"

"We do, Margaret. Today I got word that he had reached Dobb's Ferry. The question is, does he continue his course into New Jersey? And if he does, how far?"

"What choices does he have?"

"Only two really. He can continue into New Jersey, but the only reason would be to chase after Lord Cornwallis. He can stop where he is and prepare for an assault on the city. Washington still wants New York, I'm sure of that. From Dobb's Ferry, the Frenchman can quickly come down into Westchester if I move across Kingsbridge. I suspect he's not worried about any flanking movement to the east. I don't have the fleet here now to carry a sufficient force to say, Norwalk or New Haven, and I'll bet he knows that."

"I'll not take that bet. So with Rochambeau on the Hudson, they can rotate the American army to the southwest. Staten Island, do you think? Put the city under siege?"

"It's certainly possible--a movement to Staten Island, I mean. A siege, no. It wouldn't work. Too much water, too porous a line. And there are too many of us here. We would have to fortify the land side of the Hell's Gate so that ships had a chance of getting through with powder and such. Our food would still come in from Connecticut. Our position would not be good, but tenable, I think.

"We demonstrated the path through Staten Island for them in '77. First there, then a short hop to Long Island, then they have us cut off from the sea and long guns on Brooklyn Heights with half the city in their sights. Life here would be damned uncomfortable."

"Could Rochambeau block Kingsbridge and the path through Westchester? That would stop up our food."

"It would be a hard place to defend, from either side. That's why I haven't gone there myself. Too flat and open."

"He just has to burn the bridge to starve us. But you still think a frontal attack on this city?"

"Perhaps. I've sent the orders to Cornwallis a few days ago to go to Portsmouth and to begin to embark troops for an expedition against Philadelphia. We'll see if the enemy's intelligence is as good as we fear. If it is, I expect Washington will have to dispatch troops from here to counter. Maybe that will make him think twice about Staten Island. If not, we'll know they are blind in our direction and then make my defensive preparations to deter them."

310

"Another bet I'll not take—that they're blinded. This city is the key to the war. You've said it often yourself, Sir Henry. How is the army taking this news from the south? It must be difficult for them, to know it is not going well there."

"There's something about lieutenants, Margaret. To a man they know how to conduct the war better than their general. It has always and will be ever so. By the time they become colonels, half understand, the other half are interested in only their own chance. That will also be ever so. The soldiers go and do what they are told, what they think, if they ever do, is without consequence."

"So the grumbling is within the normal bounds?"

"Perhaps a bit louder, but I can't notice. In the end, it comes still to New York. It must be held and I'll not be lured out, no matter what the people may think."

*****

"Good morning, Browning. The coffee is terrible this morning."

Richard Browning took a careful sip. "That it is, Excellency. But on a happier note, Kathleen has re-established communications with Odysseus. He knows what we need; now he just has to get it."

"Here's hoping. We really need to know how Clinton will respond if we go adventuring into Virginia if the chance comes. It could well decide the war."

"Odysseus reports that Clinton has ordered a feint toward Philadelphia, to discourage us from an attack on Staten Island. Troops went so far as to begin boarding in Virginia before he called it off. That we didn't move indicates to him that we are not getting intelligence from New York."

"We weren't, then. It was just dumb luck. We never knew about it."

*****

"You know, now I'm beginning to wonder if Montraville <u>was</u> the spy—Washington didn't take the bait about Philadelphia. It's the first time he

311

didn't seem to anticipate what we were going to do. I should thank him for saving the Crown the expense of a trial."

"You've heard something from New Jersey, then?"

"That troops are moving all around. Something is up over there but I don't know what. I'm going to send a few more regiments to Staten Island just in case, but generally, I'm going to sit tight and make them come to me. If Rochambeau comes into Westchester to stay, I can recall them double quick. They have been exploring the county, reconnoitering. Rochambeau and Washington themselves have been down to Throgg's Neck, probing."

"The streets are full of that. What from Virginia?"

"Our friend Mi'Lord Cornwallis is heading for Yorktown. I told him to pick a deep water harbor, and that was his choice. As I remember it, not easily defended, but it's not like he has to face the French proper. Against Wayne and Lafayette and their rabble he'll be all right no matter the ground."

"I should think ports in general would be hard to defend. I can't remember one not at the bottom of a bowl with high ground all around. That's the way nature makes them. Boston, Halifax, Louisburg, even the lower town of Quebec, all the same way. When he gets in there he's going to depend on you to get him out."

"That's why I told him to get to the coast, so that the navy could save his bacon if necessary. That, and so that he could be resupplied. As long as he has superior numbers he should be able to hold out indefinitely."

"If he can keep the numbers and if the navy can. It must be hard that so much depends on one man 400 miles away."

"Especially when that man does not bother to read instructions carefully! I showed you my letters—I told him to send men to Philadelphia if--if mind you--he no longer needed them. What does he do but begin to board them and complain of my mistreatment."

"You did Sir Henry, and I thought the orders were quite plain. The man must read with a chip on his shoulder."

"Chip on his shoulder? I haven't heard that one."

312

"When two boys want a fight, they'll put a bit of wood on their shoulder, and each dare the other to knock it off. Rather like nations do so they can satisfy themselves that the other is the aggressor." *Or generals*, she thought.

✶✶✶✶✶

"Here's a small bit, Excellency. Clinton still half expects us to attack him in the city. He will not initiate any attacks from New York, no adventures against us. There will probably be company level raiding but no regimental movements. He will remain on the defensive pending events in Virginia."

"Damn it, man, I need more than that! I need to know positively that he will not follow us to the south. Does Odysseus understand this?"

"I believe he does, Excellency. Perhaps Clinton has not yet made such a decision. Our man can only report a decision after it is made, but his is a most delicate situation. He's giving us the best he has."

"Apologies, Browning. But you see my frustration? After endless talks with General Rochambeau I am coming to think that New York is too hard a nut for us, even now. I do feel we're about to run a raccoon up a tree in Virginia and I want to set another pack of dogs on him to make sure."

"Yes Excellency. Here's another interesting bit—Clinton complains of poor knowledge of what we are doing, especially in New Jersey. He claims to be blinded in that direction."

"How can this be?"

"His networks never recovered from Andre's loss last fall. The next man in the job failed miserably. Clinton thinks he has deserted even though we know he has resigned more absolutely. Now there is no successor named. His intelligence gathering is a shambles."

"May it continue so!"

"Amen."

✶✶✶✶✶

313

"'Resolved that His Majesty's armies shall pursue those of the enemy if they are discovered to be on the march toward Virginia.' Isn't that elegant, Margaret? That is the question I will pose at tomorrow's meeting. Now I just have to figure out my own thoughts."

"It is, Sir Henry. And your answer is?"

"Not sure. Look, they are not fools. We know they will always leave a significant force behind, to maintain the semblance of siege. And so must we, or they will simply walk into the city."

"So there would be four armies involved here, ours marching and ours staying, and the same for them. How formidable would be each?"

"Well, I don't believe Washington would go unless his juncture with the southern army would provide overwhelming force."

"But still he wants New York?"

"Above all, I think."

"Here's another way of looking at it. When do you find out he is moving? If his journey is just begun, you could advance across New Jersey quickly and hit his flank before he could gather his army to make a stand. If on the other hand, he was in, say, Princeton when you discovered his march, you would be chasing his tail, hurrying him on his route. The rebels have demonstrated over and over that they march more quickly than we. They don't have the funds to buy any of the baggage that hampers our armies. In that case, it might be better to take ship and leap over him to arrive in Virginia first."

"Two problems with that. Firstly, there is this damned French fleet sailing around the Atlantic and another in Newport. They'd like nothing more than a troop convoy on the high seas. They could destroy an entire army before it was capable of firing a shot. The other is, if we took ship the enemy would know it. We must depend upon that. Washington could reverse his course and take New York before we knew to turn around. Actually there are three problems. I don't have any warships to escort a convoy. They're all out wandering around the ocean, looking for the damned Frenchman. Without them, it would be madness to embark."

314

"So then, your solution is this: if discovered early in his march, hit him hard in New Jersey. If discovered late, the response is take to shipping, dependent upon the Navy owning the ocean between here and Cape Henry?"

"I guess—it's an unsatisfying answer."

"Sir Henry, I'm sorry, but this thought will make it less so. The only way this could end well is if you could make a successful voyage to Virginia and your combined armies defeat Washington and Rochambeau. However, there are numerous ways it could go astray. If you sailed too soon or with insufficient escort, there is a real chance you could be destroyed at sea. Lord Cornwallis would probably be lost as well. Leave too late or not at all and Lord Cornwallis may be lost, but you still have New York. You have not only to consider what may happen in battle, but also how what happens will be received in London. If Lord Cornwallis were to lose his army, likely the public would blame him and demand peace. If you went to sea too early and lost yours, and also Lord Cornwallis lost his, one can picture King George, like Augustus Caesar, beating his head against a wall, calling, 'Clinton! Give me back my legions!' The blame would fall to you. Any army captured in America is going to stay here until King Louis decides they can go home. The ministry must still consider an invasion across the Channel. Those regiments would be sorely needed to defend the Isle. Opposed to this, remember Admiral Bing."

"Thank you," he replied sarcastically. "You may believe that there will be minutes taken tomorrow, and I shall demand written positions from everyone present."

"They'll school like fish."

"I expect so. At least I wouldn't be the only target when the firing squad is mustered."

"If it is any consolation, remember that it was Lord George who insisted on Cornwallis' operating alone in the south, dividing your command and leaving you too weakened for offensive actions."

"Damned slim rations, that. You know, Margaret, you have done so well at playing the advocate that I now can longer distinguish what you really think in your arguments. I miss that."

315

"I'm sorry! You know I don't mean to cause confusion!" She paused, *Dare I?* She plunged ahead. "I think, Sir Henry, that the government has no clear vision of their desired end to this rebellion. I think that they believe somehow that Americans will return to their previously blissful state of tame subjects if only a few troublemakers could be removed. I think they are sadly mistaken in this. They have no plan of how to achieve their end because they have of no idea of what it is. The Americans, on the other hand, do know what they want. They want independency and will accept no less.

"I think in that sense, their leaders are your strongest ally. They impose discipline on their followers and that allows you to focus your efforts. Suppose, by some chance, you were to capture Washington and the entirety of the Continental Congress. You could hang them to a man. They have committed treason. What then? Would the populace rest quietly? I think not. Every one of those men has sons and daughters and friends who would be only enraged by your actions. Some would take to the forest where they would form alliances with the savages. They would limit England's expansion into the continent more effectively than ever the French did. It would take a hundred regiments to effectively police the frontier. Others of them would disappear into the cities, faceless and anonymous, they would here murder Mr. Attorney General on his way to the theater or there kill Mr. Councilor in his bed chamber. Public buildings would be burnt. They would become skillful at it. It would become a way of life for them and their children would follow them into it. You would never catch all of them. You've called this the worst duty station in the empire—it would become far worse. The beauty of a wasp's nest is that you know where the stingers are. If you bring it to the ground and break it to bits, you have a horde of them coming at you from all directions. My country would become a horrid place."

"You paint a bleak picture. Why then do you aid me so?"

"The key to social order lies with you."

"Yet you are saying that the Crown cannot win this war."

"I don't think the Crown is willing or able to commit enough resources to win."

316

"What should I do?"

"You must defend New York."

"Even if it is futile?"

"Especially because it is futile. England will need a bargaining chip in negotiations and New York is the best one there is. Sir Henry, Americans are not England's enemy, France is."

"Would they not become a French puppet if we were to let them go?"

"No, not for long anyway. They're grateful for French help right now, but that will sour quickly. Beggars are never fond of the hand that feeds them. There are stronger ties to England among them, ties of language, history and kinship. There are still memories of the Old French War alive in all of us, too many animosities. Well handled, America could become a powerful ally against enemies in Europe. If the colonies remain in rebellion, France would continue to supply them even if Comte de Rochambeau is recalled. A few stands of muskets is a small price to pay if the gain is England wasting her strength 3,000 miles from the real campaign.

"This war must be ended. You know your regiments are needed at home more than here. If Cornwallis falls, so too does the government and then you can all go home to face the real foe. It is the wisest strategy. Sacrifice a rook to save the king."

*****

"Your Excellency, we have a rather terse message from Odysseus. 'Clinton shall not pursue.'"

"This is sure?"

"He is certain, or he would not have sent."

"This is the last piece to the puzzle, Browning! Send to General Rochambeau for a meeting! And I must write to General Lafayette. Now it is imperative that Cornwallis stay in Yorktown. He mustn't let that damned raccoon out of that tree!"

"Yes, Your Excellency. I might wish for a more declarative sentence."

"Clinton is reserving to himself the option to fall on our flanks in northern New Jersey if the chance presents. If we can pass there, he will not follow! That's the message! Think on it, man!"

"If I were not so hesitant to use the word 'giddy,' Your Excellency, I might so accuse you."

"And well you might, Browning. This time we have him! I have just word from Admiral DeGrasse. He is going to the Chesapeake with two dozen ships of the line—he may well be there already. We have positive knowledge of DeGrasse and now Barras, who has put to sea from Newport too. The ocean is closed to them, what with two French fleets, each equal to Admiral Graves, out there looking for a fight. If he can chase Admiral Graves away then Cornwallis is done! Done, I tell you Browning!"

✱✱✱✱✱

"Good afternoon, General Arnold, Mrs. Arnold. It is good to see you about again," Margaret lied pleasantly. "I trust your illness is in the past?"

"It is, Mrs. Brush, I'm glad to say. The gout is a terrible thing we inflict upon ourselves!"

"I'm pleased to hear, sir. Come. We're all assembling in the parlor until dinner is called. The others have arrived."

Margaret led them through to the parlor where a rumble of conversation announced the guests, a half dozen senior officers and half that many more women, all enjoying the company and Sir Henry's liquor. Sir Henry himself moved among them, playing the host. Laughter erupted sporadically as someone passed a particularly witty observation.

A nervous aide slipped in, found his chief and passed a folded message. Sir Henry paused to read it.

"God damn it!" The room fell silent as everyone turned to him. "GOD DAMN IT!" again. Henry Clinton usually tried successfully to control his parade ground manner in mixed company but he was utterly failing now.

318

"Gentlemen, and ladies, I have just received word that the armies of Rochambeau and Washington are in Philadelphia!"

A general murmur arose. "How can this be? We had no notice! I saw men near the Kingsbridge this very afternoon! At least the navy..."

"Gentlemen," Sir Henry spoke. "There shall be no dinner this afternoon. Assemble at City Hall in thirty minutes. Mrs. Brush..."

"Yes, Sir Henry. I'll have a cold collation sent over. I expect it shall be a long evening."

*****

Margaret sat still as Sally worked up her hair for dinner. The house was unusually silent.

"This feels very strangely, Sally. I have nothing to do. The war is in Virginia while everyone here just holds their breath, waiting."

"Yes, Ma'am. In the streets it is the same. Speech is muted. Every ship that enters port is scrutinized. Every traveler is quizzed. No one knows anything. The wildest rumors are flying about."

*****

As they spoke, a frigate entered the harbor. A grim faced naval lieutenant was rowed ashore. He made his way quickly to City Hall and was shown directly to Sir Henry Clinton.

"Lieutenant Darcy reporting, sir. Dispatches from Admiral Graves."

"Very well, Darcy, hand them over. Your face tells me that I won't like what I read."

"No, sir."

"Save me some time, man. What's the news?"

Darcy glanced around uncertainly. "Sir?"

319

"Tell it man, these are good people."

Darcy took a breath. "Admiral Graves met Admiral DeGrasse on the 5th, off the Capes, sir. A fleet battle. We were outnumbered, sir, and battered considerably."

"Who holds the capes, lieutenant?"

"The Frenchman, Sir Henry. The Capes and the whole of the Chesapeake. Admiral Graves is making his way here to re-fit."

Sir Henry Clinton could not even swear. "Thank you Darcy. Dismissed." He turned to his staff. "The rest of you, out. I need to think this through."

He sank into his chair and held his face in his hands.

* * * * *

The whole city was still in shock. When the first news of Cornwallis' surrender had filtered through Philadelphia, everyone thought it false. Then gradually, over several days, confirmation had come; acceptance had come even more slowly. Stony-faced people made the motions of living while wondering why. Men met in small groups at the street corners, ladies talked quietly in the drawing rooms. Even the children were cowed, though they knew not by what.

Margaret rose early and sat under the chestnut tree, wondering with herself what she should do. From the corner of her eye, she saw Cato slinking out of the barn, a bag over his shoulder. An aged scullery slave that Margaret took to be his mother hobbled after. They saw her at the same time and froze, terrified. Margaret rose. She motioned them on their way and mouthed "Go!" Cato bowed his thanks and they hurried around the corner of the barn before she could change her mind. Half the slaves had now run, as had some of the servants.

They met at breakfast, Sir Henry, Mary and Margaret. There was little conversation, little to do, nothing to plan. Washington had agreed to a truce. There would be no more active campaigning because there was no reason to.

All now lay with politicians while the military men stared across static lines at each other.

"Sir Henry, I'm sorry, but I want to see Fanny. I want to go home." There, she'd said it.

"As do I, Margaret. As do we. I speak for both of us when I say that you will be missed, and that we understand. This is not a surprise. I shall be forever grateful for your service. You understand that there can be no mention of your role in the dispatches?"

"I do, sir. I would really prefer it that way. My advice seems not to have been of much advantage."

"Oh, don't fault yourself. You have helped make this duty bearable. There was probably no favorable outcome possible given our situation. Now I just sit and wait with nothing to do. I'm now only a caretaker for whoever shall follow me. How long will it be before you leave?"

"I'm not sure. A day or two. Fanny's boatman still works the river; I can get him to take me up to Albany. I'll have to find him. I shall miss you both— and be forever grateful for your kindnesses." She felt tears, genuine ones.

*****

There was a chill in the air. Heavy gray clouds sped from horizon to horizon, driven by the November wind. Margaret felt a little out of her element here on the docks. Ladies seldom came here. Sally seemed perfectly comfortable. She led them, Margaret and the cartman wheeling their possessions, directly to the boat. She hailed Bill from the pier.

"Morning Bill. Ready for us?" He looked up from his work.

"Hey Sal, sure. Wait, let me help you." He offered Margaret a hand and helped her aboard. "Find yourself a spot, Ma'am. Nothing to load but your things."

"Thank you Bill. Sally, here, for the cartman." She passed up a shilling.

Once they were settled, Bill and Tom began the process of warping the boat away from the pier in the westerly wind. Soon sails were hoisted and they were away.

Margaret sat quietly, watching the city grow slowly smaller.

"Are you a little sad to leave, Ma'am?"

"I suppose, Sally. We've been here a long time and it seems even longer. I guess I'll miss the feeling of being privy to secrets, of knowing more than others, yet I won't miss it a bit. Does that make any sense? You know, I really liked Sir Henry. "

"Do you feel any compunction about what you did there?"

"Of course, but I was a soldier without a uniform. What I did I did not do for gain or lust, unlike Iago. Soldiers do what needs to be done, unpleasant or not. So did I."

"Yes, Ma'am. You've carried a terrible burden for a long time. You were good at it, but now you don't have to any longer. Like taking off a winter coat, your arms feel light."

"Yes." She smiled, then turned to look up the river and settled herself more comfortably. "I'll be content to let someone else steer for a while."

*****

The boat anchored behind the little house in Peekskill. Bill rowed them ashore and they walked unannounced to the door. Sophie, surprised, admitted them.

Margaret hugged Kate, she hugged Fanny twice. It was a relief to be surrounded by friends. As she sat in the parlor it seemed as if she had not exhaled in years. Perhaps she had not. Relaxation was a foreign experience.

"Margaret, come. I want to introduce you to an old friend. You must come too, Fanny." They wrapped their shawls close and walked through the town. Kate led them to the largest house, the door guarded by sentries. Seeing blue coats instead of red ones surprised Margaret. Kate nodded and entered unchallenged. A lieutenant snapped to attention as she approached.

322

"Would you announce us please, Morgan?"

"Certainly, Mrs. Browning. The Colonel is with him."

The two men were standing above a table covered in maps as they entered. "Good afternoon Mrs. Browning. And you too, young Mrs. Browning. To what do I owe this pleasure"

"Your Excellency, I want to introduce you to someone, someone you knew many years ago?"

Washington looked at Margaret, puzzled for a moment. "Can it be Mrs. Soumain, from Fort Cumberland?"

"I am, Excellency, or was. It's Mrs. Brush now. You honor me by this audience."

"How are you, Margaret? It is so good to see you again." Richard Browning advanced and kissed her cheek. "Excellency, she is also my daughter-in-law's mother."

"Yes, I see that," said Washington, looking between Fanny and her mother.

"General," said Kate, "you also know her by a different name. May I present Odysseus?"

There were astounded comments from the men. "You! No! But Margaret! Kathleen? But how could you? Fanny, even you've said nothing for a year?"

"For some years I have lived in Sir Henry's house. I was his confidant since Major Andre died."

"Kathleen, this is the secret you've been so jealous of? I can see why. Margaret, you're really Odysseus?"

"I guess I am. I didn't know I had a code name--I feel quite important!

"Wait a minute--Brush--was your husband the late Crean Brush--I remember quite a stir after Boston."

"He was, Your Excellency."

"Is this why you wished her freed from Boston, Mrs. Browning? Had you this in mind then?"

"In some sense I did, sir. However, I never dreamed then that she would be so successful."

Margaret spoke. "If I may, Your Excellency? I have one request."

"If it is within my power. What may I do for you?"

"I desire that neither Sir Henry nor anyone else ever know of my role."

"Margaret," Richard interjected, "You do understand that anonymity, if you assume it, is likely permanent? It is difficult to renounce it without accusations of prevarication. Fanny, this will affect you too."

"I'll abide by whatever Mama says. My role was minor. She gets to decide this."

"I think it best, Richard. I liked Sir Henry, as a man. He was always a gentleman with me and yet I played him false for more than two years. That sits heavily."

Washington looked at her for a moment. "I think I understand. This meeting shall remain in this room. It is the least we can do to repay your service."

Kate had been watching her friend closely during this exchange. "This is your gift to him."

The two examined each other's faces. "I guess. I hadn't thought of it that way."

"And yet you accuse me of being a romantic." They both smiled. Richard Browning hoped his wife would explain later.

"What shall you do now, Mrs. Brush?" asked Washington.

"I want to go to my home, in Westminster."

"How will you be received? The temper of the town?"

"I have no idea, sir; it's been seven years since we were back. I just want to go."

"Browning, it occurs to me that they may face an uncertain welcome in Westminster. You are to escort them there. Take a troop, show your uniforms proudly and make the town know that they has been an asset to our cause and that I believe no greater patriots live. Can you do that?"

"You can spare me, sir? It may take several weeks."

"Begone with you." Then turning back to Margaret, "It is a pity, madam, that the nation can never know of your contributions to independency."

"It is enough for me, Your Excellency, that you know."

He kissed her hand. He turned and left the room, and with him history passed out of her life.

Epilogue

Westminster, Vt, October 1786

The two women stood on a hilltop, looking eastward across the Connecticut River. The gusting wind pressed their skirts against their legs and tossed the treetops. They surveyed the spreading forest, brilliant in its fall colors. The first leaves of autumn floated in the river below. Here and there a neat square had been cut into the forest. Cornshalks stood in some, cattle grazed in others. Smoke rose from a dozen chimneys.

"I see what you mean, Meg. This is indeed a view! Now, where are your birds?"

"Be patient Kate, They'll be along soon enough." They stood in the comfortable silence of old friends, then Margaret pointed toward the northern horizon. "Look!" A black streak wound its way towards them, following the river. As it grew rapidly nearer, they could see the sinuous curves of the formation, responding to invisible wind currents. They came rapidly, silently. As it grew abreast of them, they could see the individual birds, thousands of them. The sound of the wind in their wings grew louder until conversation became difficult. The flock was a pointed cylinder, a hundred yards wide, perhaps a half mile long. In ten minutes it was a streak on the southern horizon.

"Passenger pigeons. Their numbers always amaze me. How many, do you think?"

"Tens of thousands, tens of tens of thousands. I don't know a word for that many. I cannot comprehend such a number."

329

"Grandmama!" They turned to see the child pulling her mother toward them. Once the mother was certain she had been seen, she released her daughter, who came running, leaping, through the tall old grass as well as a toddler could. Margaret scooped her up.

"Kate, may I present Miss Fanny Allen. Fanny, this is my old friend Mrs. Browning. Have you a smile for her?"

Fanny inspected this newcomer solemnly and then shyly hid her face. Her mother joined them and hugged Kate.

"Good afternoon, Mother Browning. It is so good to see you again. You should really come up the river more often—Mama misses her old friends, sometimes. So do I. And Mama, Aunt Sally sent us to fetch you. Cook says dinner will be in an hour and don't be late. I left Col. Browning and Ethan telling each other war stories. There was some little brandy involved. I thought I'd escape before I started to believe them."

"I suppose we should start back, Kate." She took her friend's arm as they began to descend.

"Meg? Do you think we'll ever tell anyone what we did?"

"Probably not." She laughed. "Who would ever believe us?"

Author's Note

I couldn't make this stuff up, not all of it anyway. This tale is based, loosely, on the life of Margaret Schoolcraft. As with most people of her station, little is positively known of her life.

She and her sister were christened in Schoharie, NY, about 30 miles west of Albany, on September 29, 1735. She is believed to have been about two years old at the time, her sister was an infant. Ministers did not come often. The village was then the very edge of English North America.

Margaret's great nephew, Henry Rowe Schoolcraft, claimed that she had been raised in the home of General (then Colonel) John Bradstreet, but this is clearly an error, as Bradstreet did not come to Albany until she was about 20 years old. Margarite Schuyler is known to have taken in strays and so I assigned Margaret to her. Somehow she acquired the social skills to become the consort of Lt. John Montressor, who was a far, far better man than I have made Montraville, even though he did repudiate the pregnant Margaret. Fanny is generally accepted to be his daughter, and until recently, Margaret her mother. She was born, according to Ethan Allen, April 4, 1760.

Montressor did accompany Wolfe to Louisburg and Quebec, so Fanny must have been conceived and born there. Margaret must have followed the army.

This is at least the second novelization of her life, the first being Charlotte Temple, A Tale of Truth, by Susannah Rowson, first published in 1794. Rowson was a cousin of Montressor's, and probably heard a version of the story through the family. It is she who coined the name Montraville; hers is a kinder man than mine. Montressor left the Colonies in 1777 with General Howe. He could not possibly have done some of the things I have invented.

Margaret was married to Crean Brush in the home of General Bradstreet, August 10, 1765. Brush was an Irish born lawyer who came to America following the death of his wife in about 1758. He established a practice in New York and later was member of the New York Provincial Assembly, and a principal author of the acts declaring Ethan Allen an outlaw. Both of them wanted land in Vermont and at that moment, Brush had the upper hand. He also had about 40,000 acres around what would become the city of Burlington.

They did go to Boston during the days following Lexington, Brush did confiscate the goods of Loyalists for the Crown, and probably some for his own use too. He was universally despised by the citizenry. He was captured during the British evacuation and thrown into jail. Margaret did come from New York under flag of truce and she did facilitate his escape, much as I have described it. Some people have speculated that she was the archetype for Beethoven's Leonora. It's possible. Margaret was jailed in his place. Brush did commit suicide in New York. Margaret did return there after her release, and so far as is known, spent the rest of the war there. There has always been speculation of female spies close the command structure in New York. So, I thought, why not?

Margaret died in Westminster in 1805. Fanny did become the second wife of Ethan Allen, their first child is briefly introduced. This child became a Catholic sister, a nurse in Montreal, and a hospital in Burlington is named in her honor.

Careful students of genealogy will notice that I have introduced people into her life, Simeon Soumain, the Browning family and not least, loyal and useful Sally. Conversely, I have left some out: Patrick Wall and Fanny's first husband John Buchanan, as well as their unnamed infant among them.

I may have exaggerated Margaret's beauty, her intelligence and her learning, but not, I think, her courage.

Made in the USA
Middletown, DE
23 July 2015